"How can you be so hot when the air is so cold?"

"Mayhap I am hot for you."

"What a sinful thing to say!" she exclaimed with a gasp.

"'Tis human nature. Even your Adam and Eve felt the same, I warrant."

She needed to change the subject before she did something scandalous, like lick the cleft in his chin. "I asked you why you would help me. You are evading the subject, methinks."

"Perchance I am just a noble fellow."

She made a snorting sound of disbelief.

"Or perchance I have ulterior motives for my offer," he said huskily. "Perchance I want something from you."

The glint in his blue eyes spelled danger to her . . . she just knew it did. Still she blundered on, like a lamb before the wolf. "I have naught to give," she said, just as huskily.

"Oh yea, you do, m'lady." His voice was whisper soft and tempting as sin.

A Tale of
TWO VIKINGS

SANDRA HILL

AVON
An Imprint of HarperCollins*Publishers*

This is a work of fiction. Names, characters, places, and incidents are products of the author's imagination or are used fictitiously and are not to be construed as real. Any resemblance to actual events, locales, organizations, or persons, living or dead, is entirely coincidental.

AVON BOOKS
An Imprint of HarperCollins*Publishers*
10 East 53rd Street
New York, New York 10022-5299

Copyright © 2004, 2011 by Sandra Hill
ISBN 978-0-06-201912-7
www.avonromance.com

First Avon Books paperback printing: April 2011

Avon Trademark Reg. U.S. Pat. Off. and in Other Countries, Marca Registrada, Hecho en U.S.A.
HarperCollins® is a registered trademark of HarperCollins Publishers.

Printed in the U.S.A.

10 9 8 7 6 5 4 3 2 1

This book is dedicated with much love and appreciation to my good friend, Trish Jensen. Not only is she a good writer who helps me make my books better, but she also teaches me so much about friendship and caring and loyalty. And what she doesn't know about romantic humor would fill the head of a pin. A wise person once said that we remember best the friends with whom we have laughed and cried. How true! Thanks, Trish.

Friend I was with the Lord of Spears;
Trusting I was, and kept my faith.
But now the All-Father, God of Battle,
Has turned his face away from me . . .

EGIL'S SAGA *FROM* SONATORREK

A Tale of

TWO VIKINGS

PROLOGUE

*D*ouble the trouble, Viking style . . .

Toste and Vagn Ivarsson did everything together.

They came squalling into this world from the same womb together, bare minutes apart.

They suckled from the breasts of the same wet nurse when their mother died in the birthing.

They were weaned and privy trained at the same time.

They invented their own language—words and body expressions that only they could understand.

They rode their first horses at the age of seven, rode their first maids on Friggs Day of their thirteenth summer, and rode off on longships to go a-Viking as untried fourteen-year-old warriors.

They'd been inseparable till their ninth year when their father, Jarl Ivar Thorsson, who considered twins an unnatural happenstance, came up with the lackwit notion that they would mature best apart. He sent them, kicking and screaming, to opposite reaches of the Norselands for fostering. That lasted a total of three intolerable months afore both were sent home by exasperated Norse chieftains.

Because of their identical appearance, except for a clover-shaped birthmark on Toste's inner thigh, they constantly traded places, to the chagrin of comrades and maids aplenty.

Their father eventually outlawed them from his Vestfold realm on the same day, over the selfsame piddling incident—piddling to them, leastways. Vagn, in a fit of meadhead madness, had referred to their older brother Arne as "Mother's Baby, Father's Maybe," and Toste had piped in with a comment that Arne much resembled a trader called Leif Lousebeard who came into the area on occasion.

They never wed, some said, because they could not bear to be apart from each other. Bolthor the Skald once described them as: Fair of face and form; fierce in the bed furs; even fiercer in battle; quick to wit; loyal to a fault.

In essence, Toste and Vagn were as one.

But, alas and alack, Toste and Vagn, having seen only thirty and one winters, were about to die together.

CHAPTER ONE

❧

*A-marching they did go, a-marching they did go . . .
uh-oh . . .*

Toste Ivarsson slid in the soft earth and almost fell on his arse, to the amusement of the many warriors who surrounded him on their trek through Saxon hell.

"Remind me again why we are trudging about in scratchsome chain *sherts* over padded leather tunics, all that covered with wet fur pelts, carrying heavy shields and swords and battle-axes, during a hailstorm, smack down the middle of enemy lands, like bloody game pigeons?" *Ping, ping, ping*—the icy pellets kept hitting the metal armor and weapons of the soldiers in the *hird*, creating an irksome din—just as irksome, Toste hoped, as the pellets of his grumbles directed in an endless tirade at his equally irksome brother, Vagn. "And the odor! Two hundred men who have not bathed in a fortnight—phew! 'Tis said that women of all nations favor us Viking men because we are so handsome, but mainly because we bathe more often than the average fellow. Well, they would change their tune quick as spit if they got a whiff of this aromatic bunch. I'm thinking of putting a pincher on the nose guard of my helmet to cut out the foul body aromas."

To his frustration, Vagn's response was to whistle. For the love of Thor! Whistling in the midst of this . . . this . . . sure-to-be wasted effort! *The lackwit! No church pillage is worth this time and inconvenience. My toes feel like icicles. By the gods, I would love to be sitting afore a hot hearth, feet propped up, nursing a horn of mulled ale.*

"I was bored," Vagn answered cheerily, even though he was equally laden with battle gear, and led an ancient warhorse named Clod he had won the night before in a game of *hnefatafl*. The destrier, made skittish by the pelting ice, was one of the few horses on the field today. Most of the soldiers preferred to walk the short distance to the monastery . . . which was turning out to be not so short a distance, after all.

It was a rare peaceable time in Britain. King Edgar, being only twenty and one years old and busy fornicating with every female who crossed his path, was heavily under the influence of Dunstan, Archbishop of Canterbury, whom he'd brought back from exile. While Edgar sinned, Dunstan built more monasteries for his king's penance. A good bargain, in Toste's opinion.

Toste reacted to Vagn's remark. "Bored! Why could we not have wrestled a bear, like we did last time you got bored? Why could we not have dug for amber or hunted whales in the Baltics? Why could we not have gone horse buying in the Saracen lands? Why could we not have drunk a tun of mead and slept the ale-head away all winter long? Why could we not have spent a sennight and more in a talented harlot's bed furs?"

"Together?" Vagn asked.

How like him to home in on the last and most irrele-

vant of my suggestions! Toste snorted with disgust. "We have tried it *together* more than once, as you well know, but we were half-brained youthlings then. Now, I much prefer to do my own plowing, thank you very much." He regretted the words the minute they slipped from his mouth.

"Mayhap you are getting old," Vagn commented, as if he were not the same *advanced* age of thirty and one years. "Almost a graybeard you are. For a certainty, I saw a wild hair growing in your ear yestereve when you were retching your guts over the ship's rail into the stormy sea. Up and down, up and down, up and down, our boat followed the path of the roaring waves. Ne'er have I seen a man vomit so much."

"In the midst of that sea-gale, you noticed a single hair in my ear?" Toste arched his frosty brows in disbelief. At the same time, he swiped a forearm across his forehead to wipe away moisture from the melting hail.

"Yea, I did . . . and, come to think on it, there was one in your nose, too. Women do not like such misplaced hairs, you know. Dost want me to pluck it out for you?"

Toste made a coarse observation about "plucking" and jabbed Vagn in the upper arm with an elbow for his deviltry, Toste's hands being full of weapons.

His brother just grinned and danced away.

The hail began to die down and was replaced with sleet, which in turn created a mire of mud underfoot. What a miserable day! If they didn't soon find this monastery, he was going to turn on his heel and head back to the ship, blessed booty be damned!

Then, ignoring Vagn's flummery, he commenced afresh his earlier diatribe. "'Tis all your fault. 'Twas you who convinced me that we should join the Jomsvikings, and look where it has landed us." They were surrounded on all sides by Viking warriors intent on plunder or battle,

or whatever they faced ahead—way too far from the four
longships anchored near shore. "A bloodthirstier lot I
have ne'er met than this mercenary band, including our
chieftain. I swear, Sigvaldi would hew down his mother
if she sneezed the wrong way. And, by the by, you failed
to inform me that no women were permitted at the Jomsviking fortress at Trellenborg. 'Tis a year since we joined
this troop of noble warriors. Nobility is one thing, celibacy is another. Not what I envisioned, I'll tell you that."
It was not the first time Toste had voiced this particular
complaint to his brother.

"Methinks you have lost the adventuresome spirit,
brother. To go a-Viking is a way of life for us Norsemen.
'Tis what men do when the crops are harvested and
high-winter has not yet icebound our longships." Vagn
shrugged as if there were naught more to say on the subject. Norsemen would be Norsemen, was Vagn's simple
philosophy. Toste thought Vagn had finished blathering,
but then he added more of his non-wisdom, "A dollop of
celibacy hones a man's appetite. Makes him a more self-
disciplined fellow."

"Hah! More like a *wallop*—as in overabundance—of
celibacy hones a man's randiness and makes him nigh
beastly when he finally lands betwixt soft thighs. The
monkish life is not for me."

"Me, neither," Vagn admitted. "Shall we go home?" A
dozen hailstones lay in Vagn's as yet unhelmeted, dark
blond hair. Water rivulets ran down his face in muddy
streaks. He looked absolutely ridiculous, and absolutely
endearing, at the same time. Toste loved his brother
more than himself.

Choking back the emotion that clogged his throat, he
asked, "Home? What home? Oh, nay, you surely do not

suggest we hang tail and return to our father's estates in the Norselands? He outlawed us—his own sons."

"He would take us back," Vagn said softly.

"Mayhap, if we would agree to his never-ending demands: Stop being so frivolous. Fight in his army, which is always at war with one minor Norse king or another, or one Saxon thegn or another. Bend knee to our two scurrilous older brothers, who are heirs to the jarldom . . . not that I would want to take on that mantle. Wed a noble wench *of Father's choice*. Make public apology for past misdeeds. Need I remind you of the Helga the Homely incident? Or Ingrid Hairy Chin?"

"Groveling would be required, of a certainty. And much kissing of arse," Vagn pointed out with a wince. Neither of them were ever much good at groveling. "But we are older now, Toste. Being landless knights no longer holds appeal. Perchance settling down with a wife and family would not be the worst thing in the world. Our friend Rurik seems happy enough in that role. And, of a certainty, there is not much attraction anymore in raiding greedy clerics of their gold crucifixes and ruby-encrusted chalices. We have wealth enough, both of us."

His brother's words surprised Toste, mainly because they mirrored his own thinking of late. But that had been the pattern their entire lives. They always thought alike, having the same tastes and dislikes, even feeling each other's pain and joy on occasion.

Toste shifted the halberd—a long-handled spear/ battle-ax—in his right hand to its leather shoulder strap and used his free arm to wrap his brother's shoulder and squeeze tightly. In a voice choked with deep sentiment, he said, "This will be our last battle, then. We will go home to make peace with our father and establish our own families and estates."

"Can our estates border one another?" Vagn asked.

"I would have it no other way."

They smiled warmly at each other, glad to have made a long-overdue decision.

"That reminds me of a saga I have been writing," Bolthor the Skald—also known as Bolthor the World's Worst Skald—said as he huffed up behind them. Bolthor was a giant of a man, still well muscled from fighting, even at forty and more years, but he had lost one eye at the Battle of Brunanburh some twenty years ago. It was a liability for a soldier. Still, he'd insisted on coming with them to join the Jomsvikings. Or more likely, his former leaders, Tykir in the Norselands, and Rurik in the land of the Scots, had sicced him on them, having endured more than enough sorry sagas relating the intimacies and foibles of their lives. Either way, they were stuck with the good-hearted behemoth poet. "The saga could be called 'The Lost Vikings.'"

"Uh, mayhap later," Toste said quickly, noticing a dreamy look passing over Bolthor's face which usually portended a vile poem about to spew forth.

"We are not lost, Bolthor," Vagn pointed out. The fool! Did he not know that it was unwise to encourage the skald in any way? Vagn waved a hand to indicate the vast number of Jomsviking warriors traveling with them. "Surely, we cannot *all* be lost."

"I did not mean the entire *hird* of soldiers was lost. Just you two."

"Oh," Vagn said, still clearly confused.

But then Toste made a mistake as foolish as his brother's. He remarked to Bolthor, "I thought you always started your sagas with 'good' in the introduction. Like

'This is the saga of Tykir the Good.' Or, 'This is the saga of 'Rurik the Greater.'"

"Hmmm. You are right, Toste," Bolthor said, biting his bottom lip with worry. Well, leastways they had time to escape his presence whilst he pondered the dilemma.

Toste and Vagn began to walk faster, but Bolthor yelled at their backs, "Wait! I have the solution." With a groan, Toste and Vagn were forced by politeness to stand and listen. "This is the saga of Toste and Vagn, the *best* Viking twin warriors in all the Norselands."

"That limits our area of greatness, does it not?" Vagn whispered for Toste's ears only. "How many Viking twin warriors do you think there are?"

"I pray thee, Bragi, god of eloquence, to bless me this day," Bolthor continued, his one good eye raised skyward. Then to Toste and Vagn he said, "Methinks a good title would be 'Twin Vikings Who Lost Their Way.'"

"Huh?" Toste and Vagn said at the same time.

"Once were two twins from the Norselands
Who thought they were best at all things.
Running, racing, fighting, swordplay . . .
Flirting, swiving, flirting, swiving . . .
Laughing all the time, changing places,
Till was unclear who was who
And whether there be any point to their lives.
But, by and by, age came upon them finally . . .
A turning in the road men face in middle years.
They began to question the meaning of life,
Which destiny-path to follow,
Whether to replicate themselves by breeding,
Why they were born.
A crossroads in their lives, for a certainty . . .
The question is: Will they choose the safer path,

Or will they jump headfirst into wedlock,
And forevermore question how they landed there?"

Toste and Vagn glanced at each other, stunned speechless. Where did Bolthor come up with this stuff? How did he manage to hit so close to the truth? And most important, where was some other Viking needful of his own personal skald?

"Very good, Bolthor," Vagn said, not wishing to insult him.

"Yea, very good," Toste agreed. *Now go plague someone else with your sagas.*

"Now go plague someone else with your sagas," Vagn said, not nearly as sensitive as Toste. He apparently had no compunction about hurting Bolthor's feelings. But there was no need for worry in that regard, because the insult passed right by Bolthor, who brightened and said, "Yea, methinks Sigvaldi is in need of a good comeuppance . . . I mean, saga. Hey, that can be a new name for a certain type of poem—a comeuppance-saga." Bolthor rushed forward to tell the chieftain his good news.

Toste and Vagn smiled at each other, but not for long.

Up ahead, someone shouted a warning. "Ambush! Ambush! We are surrounded by Saxons!"

Immediately, the two-hundred-man horde of Viking warriors scurried for cover, of which there was almost none in the shallow valley they'd been traversing. Meanwhile, hundreds and hundreds of Saxon soldiers emerged on the small hills surrounding them. Despite their surprise and being vastly outnumbered, the Viking brothers-in-arms soon prepared themselves skillfully for battle with weapons drawn.

Usually, Norsemen preferred the *Svinfylkja*, better known as the "Swine Wedge," a triangular assault formation with the point facing the enemy, or a "shield wall," with a tight mass of warriors surrounding the chieftain. There was no time for those tactics now; Saxons hemmed them in on three sides, including the exitway out of the valley. A blizzard of arrows showered from the bowmen, even as the Saxon foot army advanced toward them.

All around him, Toste heard war cries raised by his enraged comrades. Sometimes just wild whoops, or savage roars of fury. Other times, specific exhortations were called out: "To the Death!" "Luck in Battle!" "Mark Them with Your Spears!"

Toste did not love to fight as some men did, but he would rather be the crow than the carrion, and he had no intention of breaking the raven's fast this day. He raised his broadsword in an arc as a burly Saxon soldier approached him, spear raised with menace. Toste aimed for the "fat line," that section of the body from neck to groin where most vital organs were located. He sliced the man crossways from shoulder to waist before the spear ever left his hand. Wide-eyed with horror, the man, already spewing blood from his mouth, fell in a heap at Toste's feet. "Good aim, brother!" Vagn yelled out to him, while Toste sparred, sword to sword, with another foeman. Next, Toste crouched low and lunged his short sword into a fat Saxon belly. With a grunt of surrender, the Saxon fell, his eyes rolled back into his head, and he died.

For the next half hour, thick fighting ensued, and there was no time to look around. Having the advantage of surprise, the Saxons cleft through the Norse ranks as if through sheaves of wheat. Oh, the Viking soldiers displayed great skill and stamina . . . they were lords of swordplay, to be sure . . . but they could not withstand such a large force. No matter how many of the enemy

Toste slew, no matter how weapon-skillful he was, another Saxon always sprang up behind the ones he slew. It was hopeless, Toste began to realize. The ringing of swords, the screams of the wounded in their death throes, the neighing of frightened horses, the inhuman growls of the berserkers—all of these combined to turn Toste dizzy with terror. The battle was not yet over; even so, the carnage was horrific on both sides.

In his peripheral vision, in the middle of the fray he saw Bolthor, rendered weaponless, lower his head and charge at a menacing Saxon who aimed a crossbow his way. Knocking the bowman to his back like a head-butting goat, Bolthor proceeded to strangle him with his bare hands. After that, Toste saw Bolthor pick up a Saxon broadsword and lop off a man's head as neatly as slicing a sausage. Without skipping a beat, Bolthor then took a young Saxon's face between his massive hands and crushed his skull like a walnut. About them, the stench of sword dew was overpowering.

Shaking his head to clear it of the fuzziness that assailed him momentarily, Toste felt a sudden disturbance. An odd prickling tingled at the back of his neck. *Vagn. Where is Vagn?* Scanning the field, he located Vagn a considerable distance away. They must have become separated some time ago in the melee.

As if in slowed motion, Toste watched helplessly as a Saxon long sword pierced his brother's chain *shert*, passed into his chest, then all the way through his back, directly through his heart. There was blood everywhere—on his face, his body, at his feet a pool of blood.

Toste's eyes connected with Vagn's in that unusual way they had of sensing each other's presence. Vagn screamed out to him, mentally, *TOOOSSSTTTE!* Several quick hand gestures in the silent language he and Vagn had developed said, "Farewell, brother. I have loved thee well." Then Vagn sank to his knees, both hands clutching the sword that his attacker—a huge man with bright red hair and a livid scar running from crown to chin—was attempting to pull out with one booted foot braced on Vagn's shoulder. Once the Saxon removed the sword from Vagn's chest, he stood over him, grinning. With hysterical irrelevance, Toste noticed the bright silver eagle embossed on the villain's shield. Vagn was still alive, but barely. His attacker laughed and left Vagn for dead, obviously wanting him to die a slow death.

A black mist came over Toste, and he went berserk for the first time in his life. Baring his teeth with savage fury, he howled with rage, then fought his way toward his brother. But, alas, though he battled valiantly, hewing down foemen right and left in his path, he had no protection at his back. He knew he was in trouble by the expression of alarm on Vagn's face. When Toste felt the violent impact of a weapon against his skull, he fell to his knees, just as his brother had. But, nay, Vagn was lying on his back now, eyes closed.

Dead! His brother was dead. How would he be able to bear the loss? Toste agonized as unconsciousness overcame him. Then he laughed inwardly as another thought came to him. He would not have to grieve over his brother's death because he was probably dying himself. In truth, the prospect of life without Vagn held no appeal.

Ah, well, he had never wished for a straw death. No Viking wanted to die in his sleep upon the rushes. Still, he would have liked to discuss this happenstance with his brother afore they entered the afterlife.

Will we meet this day in Valhalla? Or even in that Christian heaven? he wondered. *I hope so.*

'Tis said that the Einberiar, the brave warriors killed

in battle, see the flashing swords of the Valkyries just before death. The helmeted maidens ride white horses and escort the dead heroes to Valhalla, Odin's great mead hall in Asgard.

I cannnot wait.

He died with a smile on his face then, envisioning the lovely virgin Valkyries who would soon carry him off. *Imagine Vagn's delight when we meet up in Valhalla with all those untried wenches.*

Yea, death might not be so very bad.

Sometimes girls (even nuns) just wanna have fun . . .

"Bless me, Father, for I have sinned," confessed the young woman kneeling on the hard wooden bench. She shivered as she spoke with foggy breath; it was damp and chilly in the stone chapel of St. Anne's Abbey at the best of times, but in the middle of November in Northumbria the cold was enough to turn one's blood to ice.

A groan emerged from the other side of the confessional screen. "Again?" Father Alaric asked with a deep sigh. "You made your penance just this morn with all the other novices. What sin could you possibly have committed in such a short time . . . in a nunnery, of all places?"

"I blasphemed when I stepped in some droppings from Sister George's goat in the sacristy."

"The sacristy?" Father Alaric sputtered. "Really, those rescued animals of Sister George's are getting beyond bothersome. It's nigh sacrilegious where they show up."

"Wait till you see the five-legged piglet she brought in today. Methinks it sleeps now in the baptismal font."

"What?" Father Alaric shrieked, then seemed to recall his setting. "Back to your confession, child. Which bad word did you use?"

"Christ's toenails," she answered matter-of-factly.

"Christ's toenails," Father Alaric murmured under his breath—whether to repeat her words or utter his own expletive was unclear. "Tsk tsk tsk! Using the Lord's name in vain is unacceptable for a novice with a true vocation."

" 'Tis difficult being good all the time," Esme complained. "Thou shalt not swear." *'Tis hard not to swear when one is living in the midst of a gaggle of fifty lackwit nuns and novices who produce beer to subsist.* "Thou shalt not be greedy." *The person who thought that one up must never have experienced the sparse purse of a convent.* "Thou shalt not be slothful." *Up before dawn, to bed soon after dark, and not a second for dawdling that I've ever seen.* "Thou shalt not harbor unclean thoughts or deeds." *As if I would know an unclean thought if I stepped in it! I haven't seen a man worth salivating over in ten long years.* "Thou shalt not be noisome." *Well, all right, mayhap I do whistle on occasion, or sing unmelodiously, or voice an unsolicited opinion or two.* "Thou shalt not be prideful." *Yea, I take great pride in my sackcloth gown.* "Hah! There are so many *shalt not's,* 'tis tedious keeping track of them all," she concluded to the old priest, who continued to make the tsk-ing noises.

"Lady Esme, I am more and more inclined to believe you are not destined to become a nun."

"I am not *Lady* Esme anymore—just *Sister* Esme."

"Not till you take your final vows, and it appears more and more likely that may never happen," the priest said sternly, then immediately softened his voice and added, "Be reasonable, Lady Esme. You have been here eleven winters . . . since your thirteenth birthday . . . and you have not yet become a bride of Christ. Go home. Be a biddable daughter. Marry. Have children."

"Never!"

"Tsk tsk tsk. Your pride will always be a boulder in your path to holiness."

"Nay, the only boulder in my path is my father. He wants me dead, or buried in a convent."

"Lady Esme! Honor your father and mother; 'tis the first commandment of our Blessed Lord."

"He couldn't have known *my* father when he made that rule. Satan in chain mail, that's what my father is."

She couldn't see clearly through the screen, but Esme would bet her beads that the priest was praying and rolling his eyes heavenward.

"Enough!" Father Alaric said finally. "Go and sin no more, my child. For your penance—"

Esme could guess what that would be: another rosary said on her knees on the stone floor of the second chapel. But, nay, this time Father Alaric had something different in mind for her.

"Go with Mother Wilfreda and several of the good sisters to nearby Stone Valley."

Stone Valley? Why would he send me there? Didn't I hear of a battle taking place there this morn?

"A mission of mercy. If it be God's will, you shall perform a rescue . . . an act of supreme compassion."

"Rescue? Who needs rescuing?" She thought he might mention some injured monk or a Saxon soldier in need of care. Mother Wilfreda was a noted healer, and injured wayfarers often traveled to the abbey for her care. But, nay, Father Alaric had something entirely different, and totally unexpected, in mind.

"A Viking."

Birds of a most unusual feather . . .

Toste lay on the cold ground of a Saxon battlefield waiting for the Valkyries to come take him to Valhalla.

He hoped it would be soon, because his head felt as if a drum were beating inside his brain, about to explode.

With great effort, he lifted his heavy eyelids and gazed upward. What he saw scared him spitless, and he was not a man easily scared. He said something quite embarrassing then, for a Viking: "*Eek!*"

Five black crows stood in a circle about him—very large black crows. In fact, they were the height of humans and they cackled in the Saxon tongue. They must be the ravens of death. In the past, he had seen vultures hovering over battlefields waiting to feast on the mortal carrion, but he'd never seen them up close; nor had he ever imagined them being so big.

"He's awfully big," one of the crows said. "How will we carry him?"

And what is wrong with big?

"Mayhap we could drag him over to our cart."

Birds have carts?

"Are you barmy? The man is half-dead. He would ne'er survive a dragging."

Good thinking. No dragging.

"Each of us could take a limb and lift him. Yea, that's the way."

Take a limb? Oh, bloody hell! They're going to dismember me and gnaw on my bones.

"That would no doubt kill him."

For a certainty.

"He will probably die anyhow."

A little optimism wouldn't hurt, you know.

"He has nice hair. Not quite silver. Not quite gold."

What does the color of my hair matter? Dead is dead.

"Tsk tsk tsk! Who cares what color his hair is! Look at the muscles in his shoulders and arms. He could probably pull a plow for us . . . if he survives."

What? What have the ravens of death to do with plows?

"He's a heathen," still another of the crows whined. "Why should we save a heathen Viking?"

Well, actually, I've been baptized. You could call me a heathen Christian.

Another crow, obviously the head crow, swatted the whining crow about the head. "For shame! God shows His mercy to all men."

God? Uh-oh. Mayhap I'm not going to Valhalla after all.

That thought was reinforced when the crows lifted him unceremoniously off the ground by his arms and legs. Pain shot from his splitting skull through his injured body—*some Saxon bastard must have run a lance through my side, even after I fell from the head blow*—all the way down to his frozen toes, and he surrendered to blissful unconsciousness. With luck, he would not wake up when the crows began to feast on his flesh.

Is well-dangled the same as well-hung? . . .

"Well!" Esme remarked as she gazed down at the fallen Viking, now reclining on a hard pallet in a guest cell at the abbey. A roaring fire at her back provided welcome warmth on this cold day. "Well, well, well!"

"Well, indeed!" concurred a flushed Sister Margaret, who swayed slightly on her feet, tipsy from sampling her own latest batch of mead after their grueling trip back from the battlefield. Margaret was the daughter of a famed Saxon ale maker, and she'd brought his recipe with her to the convent. In truth, if it weren't for the profits earned from the mead enterprise—aptly labeled Margaret's Mead—the abbey would have been forced to close long ago. Esme's knack for growing vegetables in the abbey gardens also helped them subsist.

But that was neither here nor there. More important for the moment was the blond-haired Norseman who lay blessedly unconscious before them . . . naked as a newborn babe. Nay, that was not an accurate description. This man was no child. If he were, they wouldn't be ogling him so. He had no apparent injuries other than a cracked skull, but they'd had to check to make sure. Mother Wilfreda had performed her healing ablutions on the man and left momentarily to get her chest of herbs.

"Well!" added Sister Mary Rose, a worldly nun who prided herself on being sharp as a sword. She used to sell fake relics on the church steps of the Pope's own monastery in Rome and still traded in the toenails of baby Jesus or Virgin Mary eyelashes on occasion when the nunnery floundered in dire straits . . . which was often. "I have seen many a man in my time, and I daresay this one is surely the fairest of them all. And well-endowed, for a certainty."

Esme had no means of comparison other than her two brothers, who were naught to brag about, but she agreed wholeheartedly. That dangly manpart appeared large as far as those things went.

All six of the nuns in the small chamber kept staring at said manpart, except Sister Hildegard, who harbored an ungodly fear of Vikings. She was saying her beads and muttering something about heathen rapers and pillagers.

"I think it moved," observed honey-scented Sister Ursula. She was the resident beekeeper, who supplied the honey for mead and the wax for church candles. Sister

Ursula was slightly dim-sighted, and she squinted at the man's staff. The rest of them could see perfectly well, but they all leaned forward to get a better view anyway. Esme detected no movement, despite a careful scrutiny.

"Whatever you do, don't touch it," Sister Stefana advised.

As if any of them had been contemplating such a loathsome idea!

"I have heard that it bursts forth into huge proportions upon being touched," Sister Hildegard remarked. "With Vikings, it is a call to rape and pillage."

They all looked at Sister Hildegard, wondering if she knew what she spoke of. Her hatred of all things Viking colored everything she said. But 'twas best to take no chances . . . not that any of them contemplated touching such an ugly, wormlike appendage.

It was a wonder the Norseman hadn't died on the battlefield, so severe was his head wound. It was an even greater wonder that he'd survived their clumsy efforts to cart him and another of his comrades back to the abbey on rutted roads. The greatest wonder of all would be if he managed to outlive the fever that racked his body. A fine, fine body, by the by, from beautifully sculpted facial features, including a cleft chin and a full, sensual mouth, to wide shoulders and narrow waist and hips down to narrow, high-arched feet . . . except for the repulsive manpart, of course, which was in no way fine, to Esme's way of thinking. There was an intriguing clover-shaped birthmark on his inner thigh which drew her attention, too.

Mother Wilfreda clapped her hands sharply as she reentered the chamber and immediately threw a linen sheet over the naked body. Then she forced some herb-laden posset through the man's parched lips. When she finished, she turned on the lot of them. "Sisters! Have you naught better to do than stand about gaping at the man? Sister Margaret and Sister Ursula, go down the hall and help Father Alaric with the other Viking we rescued. The one-eyed giant had to be tied to his pallet to keep him from tossing off the hot poultices, and what a job that was. Mary be blessed, the man must weigh as much as a war-horse. Lady Esme, you stay here and watch over the soldier. If he should awaken, or worsen, call for me at once. The rest of you, come with me to the chapel. We will pray for the souls of these two men. The Good Lord placed them in our midst for a reason."

After that, Esme sat vigil over the handsome Viking for an hour and more, wondering why the Good Lord would send a heathen Viking to a ragtag, mostly half-brained congregation of nuns.

What's a Viking to do when a medieval lady says, "Eat me"? . . .

Toste fought desperately to emerge from the ocean of unconsciousness that weighed him down. He felt as if he were drowning in pain . . . mostly in his head, but in his side as well. How could the cool ocean waters turn his skin so blisteringly hot?

His heavy eyelids fluttered half open, and he saw a small, sparsely decorated chamber . . . not the battle-field. A cozy fire burned in the hearth, and the smell of beeswax candles wafted in the air, but he saw no items of luxury. Hmmm. Had he died? Could this meager dwelling be the much-lauded golden hall of Asgard? Nay, he must have survived his injury and been moved to some other site. With great difficulty, he turned his head to the side and noticed a woman sitting on a low stool to the right of his pallet, eyes downcast as she studied some

kind of beads in her lap. She was beautiful . . . nay, beyond beautiful . . . with ebony silk hair held off her face
by a black veil. Her facial features were perfect. She had
a straight nose, not too big, not too small, with a hint of
an upward tilt. Her skin was clear and creamy, like por-
celain he'd seen once in the eastern market towns. Her
lips were rosebud pink . . . full and kiss-some.

*What a thought to be having when I'm half-dead! A
randy corpse. Ha ha ha! Holy Thor, my brain is splintering apart and I make jokes with myself.*

He must have made a grunting sound, for she glanced
up, her grayish-blue eyes wide with concern. "You're
awake," she stated.

Well, hardly.

"I should go get Mother Superior."

He put up a halting hand. "Wait," he squeaked.

All things came together in Toste's mind then, as he
noticed her form, shapeless in a black robe that matched
her black veil. She must be a nun, and those black crows
he'd thought he dreamed back on the battlefield—they
must have been nuns, too. Oddly, he felt a stab of regret
that this beautiful woman had chosen the religious life . . .
and that he was not dead.

He tried several times to speak again—he had so many
questions—but he could not get the words to form in his
confused brain. Finally he gasped out, "Your name?"

"Esme," she whispered.

"Eat me?" he repeated. 'Twas not the first time a woman
had asked that of him, but this woman was a nun, for the
love of Frigg! Ah, well, he supposed even nuns had carnal appetites. Mayhap especially so, if his experience
with the celibate life was any indication. "Mayhap later,"
he offered graciously. At the moment, he doubted whether
he could lift his head, let alone his tongue.

"Huh?" She gawked at him for several long moments before understanding dawned. "Oh, you foul man! Why did we even bother to rescue you?" She looked as if she might punch him, if he weren't already incapacitated.

Rescue? They rescued me? Hmmm. I wonder . . . could it be possible . . . oh, please, Odin or God, I care not which it is . . . please let it be possible . . . "Sister?" he inquired cautiously of the nun who was now wringing her hands with distress, alternately staring at him and the open doorway, probably contemplating escape.

"You may call me Lady . . . Lady *Esme*," she rebuked him haughtily.

Aaah, so that was the reason for her ill-temper. He had misheard her name. He tried to smile, but it was beyond the muscles of his face, which were attached to a scalp that felt as if it were torn in half, which it probably was. Vagn would get a good laugh over his thinking "Eat me" when she'd said "Esme."

And that thought brought him up short.

"M'lady, did the good nuns of this convent rescue more than one Viking this day?"

She nodded slowly.

And gave him hope. *Oh, please, Lord and Odin and every blessed god that might exist, let Vagn be alive. Give me this boon and I will be good the rest of my life.*

"One other," she elaborated.

I will do good deeds only. I will never swear . . . or only occasionally when provoked beyond all patience. I will seduce no virgins . . . unless they beg me. I will rob no more churches. "His name?"

"I know not. He is unconscious, as you have been. He is in another chamber, down the corridor."

Just then he heard a bellow of outrage. He would recognize that voice anywhere. 'Twas Bolthor . . . not his brother Vagn, as he had hoped. His spirits sank . . . not that Bolthor had survived, but that his brother probably had not.

"Were there other Vikings rescued on the battlefield?"

"I think not. You and the giant were the only living men we saw, and Mother Wilfreda made us look, believe you me. Ne'er have I seen so much blood and gore." She must have noticed the horror on his face then, for she paused and asked, "Was there someone in particular you were concerned about?"

He gulped several times before nodding. "My brother," he whispered. Then he did something entirely unexpected. He screamed, pouring all the grief in his pain-ridden body into one single word, "VAAAAAAAAGN!"

With that pathetic wail against the fates, he either succumbed to unconsciousness again, or else he died. He hoped it was the latter, because he honestly and truly yearned to leave behind this life.

CHAPTER TWO

❧

Vagn the Virile Meets Helga the Homely . . .

"Marry my daughter, or you'll wish you were dead," Jarl Gorm Sigurdsson of Briarstead snarled.

"I already wish I were dead," Vagn Ivarsson said matter-of-factly. And if he had to continue this tiresome argument with Gorm much longer, one of them definitely was going to be dead.

The large blood vessel in Gorm's thick neck bulged even more. "If wishes were fishes, Ivarsson, you'd be a bloody whale."

" 'If wishes were fishes,' " Vagn repeated back in a mimicking voice. "What are you? A poet now? I ought to introduce you to my friend Bolthor the Skald."

"I already know Bolthor, and, nay, I am not a poet. I am the angry man who holds your life in his hands." Gorm made a visible effort to control his temper by leaning back in a chair propped against the wall and taking a long swig of ale from a pottery jug. "Be forewarned, though, you slimy cur. If you do not heed me soon, your death will be slow and painful. Methinks a skinning may be in order . . . or a gelding."

"Promises, promises," Vagn taunted bravely . . .

though he hoped he would be able to maintain that bravery if Gorm followed through on his threats. He welcomed death these days, now that his brother was gone, but the slow, painful path of skinning or gelding . . . nay! Bolthor once told a saga about Gorm cutting out the tongue of one of his enemies and eating it raw, but one never knew if Bolthor spun tales of truth or fantasy.

Vagn lay flat on his back, tied to a pallet in an upper bedchamber of Gorm's Northumbrian timber castle, with a guard standing watch outside the door. The room was stifling hot due to a fire blazing in the small hearth. He licked his parched lips, but he'd be damned if he'd beg his vile captor for a drink . . . let alone his life.

It had been more than two sennights since the Battle of Stone Valley, and he'd almost died numerous times. Now that he was starting to recover, he yearned for the peace of death. Who would have thought that the Norns of Fate would save him so many times, just to plop him, not in the hands of a Saxon enemy, but in the hands of one of his own countrymen . . . albeit one living at Briarstead, near Jorvik, the Norse capital of Britain? Whether he called himself jarl or earl, Gorm was Viking to the core, like himself.

"I will not wed with Helga."

"She is no longer homely. And she still has a maidenhead, praise be to Odin!"

If not for his restraints, Vagn would have pulled his own hair in frustration. "Homely or not, virgin or not, she will not be my bride. Nor will any other woman, if that is any consolation. Find someone else. Sweeten her dowry pot enough, and she should have suitors aplenty. In truth, few men choose a bride based on appearances."

"You rejected her once afore . . . on appearances.

Called her Helga the Homely at the Vestfold Althing, you did . . . not to her face, but to plenty of others."

"I did not!"

"Ten years old you were at the time, and Helga only seven, but she has remembered all these years . . . not that she ever mentions it. But I remember, you codsucking weasel."

Oh, bloody hell, could it have been that time when Toste and I were fostered apart? "Twen-twenty years," Vagn sputtered. "You have been harboring a grudge for twenty years over a mere youthling taunt?" *And I do not care what you say, Helga must be homely if she has not wed yet at the ripe old age of twenty and eight. An overaged virgin. Eew!*

"You named her Helga the Homely, and she has suffered mightily for it. Plus, you ne'er showed up for the betrothal ceremony when you were fifteen. I see naught *mere* in that."

"I keep telling you, that was my twin brother, Toste. And he was only a halfling, for the love of Thor!" At the mention of Toste's name, tears welled in Vagn's eyes. He still could not accept the fact of his brother's death. How would he ever go on without his other half? How could he care about Gorm or his threats or some barley-faced maiden lady when his life had lost its anchor?

"If I say you are Toste, then you are Toste," Gorm said with stubborn illogic. "Your father promised you for my daughter when you were a babe, and you will not escape a wedding yet again. Not this time."

"I . . . am . . . not . . . Toste."

"She has no breasts to speak of, and she is skinny as a broom, but you can fatten her up," Gorm continued, as if Vagn hadn't spoken. "Plus, she has a shrewish disposition,

I must admit that to you aforehand, but that is probably due to her being a rejected wench. No doubt her female parts have withered like dried raisins. She is as independent as a man . . . acts as her own textile merchant, she does . . . but a strong Norseman could put her in her place. And she does have all her teeth."

Aaarrgh! Helga had been gone the entire time Vagn had been confined here . . . off on a buying expedition to the Norselands where her maternal grandsire still lived. Gorm had outlived several wives, including Helga's mother and his latest spouse, a Saxon lady. Helga was expected to return this eventide with a shipload of embroidered cloth for her trading stall in Jorvik. *That's all I need—a woman in trade—and not of the bodily kind, either. And what was that about withered female parts? Raisins? Yeech!* "What makes you think she would even want me?"

"Her opinion matters not. I want you for her."

Just then, Vagn noticed an odd expression on Gorm's face. Vagn narrowed his eyes as he studied the old man, suddenly suspicious. "She doesn't know that you've kidnapped me, does she?"

"I didn't kidnap you. I rescued you." Gorm's rheumy old eyes shifted here and there, but never lighted on Vagn.

"Hah!" *Talk about splitting hairs!*

"She'll accept you once she gets accustomed to the idea."

"Hah!" *You don't know women, if you think that.*

"A man has a right to have grandchildren," Gorm said sulkily.

So that's what this is all about. "Thank you for the honor, but find yourself another breeding bull."

"Three wives and Odin only knows how many other wenches I've tupped, and only one living child do I have to show for my efforts . . . and her a split tail, besides. I want grandchildren . . . preferably grandsons."

Vagn had to grin, which caused his dry lips to crack and seep blood. Turned out the mean old bastard was just a mean old pudding heart. That didn't mean Gorm wouldn't skin him, though . . . or geld him.

" 'Tis not funny."

"On the contrary, 'tis very funny. But I'm not going to marry your daughter, even if you have made me smile. Now, pass that jug over here. And untie these ropes afore I piss my *braies*."

"Father!" a female voice shouted from downstairs . . . a female voice that sounded a mite angry. "Father! Where are you? I swear, I am going to whack you over the head with the flat side of a broadsword if the rumors are true." Immediately there was the sound of someone running up the stone steps.

"Uh-oh!" Vagn and Gorm said at the same time.

"There best not be a man in that room with you, tied to a bed, like Rona said there is," she shouted, closer now.

"You allow your daughter to speak to you like that?" Vagn asked Gorm.

"Hah! You obviously have never had a daughter or you would not ask that question. She gainsays me at every turn."

Within seconds a woman stood in the doorway, but she was like no other woman Vagn had ever seen.

Vagn remembered meeting the child Helga, whom his brother had later dubbed "Homely." And she had surely been that, and more. With a big mouth and teeth too big for her small, pale face, she had resembled a horse more than a sweet maid. Plus, her hair had recently been cut and deloused and stood up in spikes about her head. Smitten, she had followed Toste about like a lovesick cow . . . or, more aptly, a pony.

This was a far different Helga than that earlier version.

She stood tall, with masses of typically Norse blond hair spilling out of a knot atop her head. No wimple or head rail for this creature. She wore a gunna of sky-blue-colored wool, with intricate, multicolored embroidery outlining the hem and neckline and wrists, belted at the waist with a gold-link chain. Gorm hadn't lied—she was thin and flat-chested—but other assets made up for those deficits. She was no longer young, but her cheekbones were high, her eyes wide and as brilliant a blue as her garment, and her lips . . . ah, her lips were exceedingly large and carnal; as a child, that big mouth had been a disadvantage; as an adult female, it was beyond seductive. All the components of her being were feminine, but her stance—feet widespread, shoulders thrown back, and the posture of hands on hips—gave an entirely different picture. This was no meek maid, about to do any man's bidding.

Helga would not stand out in a crowded hall because of her beauty, but she would stand out just the same. He didn't know about other men, but Vagn would give her a second look. Mayhap even a third.

"Father! What have you done now? Rona told me you brought a prisoner back from Stone Valley two sennights ago—a Norseman—and that you are holding him against his will. She also told me you have been drinking ale. What if you get those chest pains again? You cannot forever blame it on bad digestion."

"Now, now, daughter! I have everything planned out. You are not to worry. Come closer. There is someone I want you to meet. In truth, you already know him."

Helga gave her full attention to Vagn for the first time. He had never been an exceedingly modest man, but he had not shaved or bathed for at least fifteen days, and his hair had not been cut for a year. Truth to tell, he stank. Bloodstains matted his chest hairs, and smeared much of his body. He doubted he looked much like he, or Toste, had looked twenty years ago. Still, he saw the point when recognition dawned in her big eyes.

"Toste? Toste Ivarsson?"

"Not Toste. Vagn," he corrected her.

Gorm waved a hand airily, persisting in his delusion. " 'Tis Toste. Do not listen to him."

"You have kidnapped Toste Ivarsson?" The woman was as stubborn in her blindness as her father.

"I'm Vagn, I tell you." *Are these people hard of hearing?*

"Not kidnapped, rescued," Gorm said.

"Then why am I tied to this pallet? Why is my body racked with pain? Why does my head ache so? Why am I dying of thirst? Why is my bladder about to explode? I am a prisoner." *Well, all right, Gorm did do everything in his power to save me before making me his prisoner, but that is beside the point.*

"Why . . . is . . . he . . . here?" Helga asked her father through gritted teeth.

Yea, Gorm, tell her why I am here, you gruel-for-brains.

"Dearest Helga, may I present your bridegroom?" Gorm announced cheerily, as if handing her sweetmeats on a platter.

Helga made a most unflattering snort of disgust.

Now, Vagn was not pleased about Gorm's marriage plans, either, but he thought he deserved more than a snort of disgust. *Methinks I may have been insulted here.*

"Have you lost your mind?" Helga asked her father.

"You do not want to wed with me?" Vagn asked with wounded pride. *Lackwit, lackwit, lackwit!*

"Have you lost your mind, too?" Helga asked him.

"Possibly." *Absolutely.*

"I have told you way too many times, Father. I do not intend to wed. Why will you not listen to me?"

" 'Tis unnatural," her father said.

"Do you think 'tis unnatural?" she asked Vagn.

Well, seeing as how I have no intention of marrying, either, 'tis a difficult question to answer.

"Don't bother answering," she said with a sneer. "You men always stick together. You think women should be sheep and follow after the nearest ram. You want us to submit to your greater intellect. Hah! You strut about with that dangly part betwixt your legs and think it makes you superior, when in fact it just makes you look silly."

"I ne'er likened myself to a ram," Vagn remarked with a laugh. "Although I do baaaaaa on occasion." *Did she really say "dangly part"? I do not have a dangly man-part. Mine is quite . . . un-dangly.*

She gave him a glower that pretty much said she'd like to ram him with something. Holy Thunder, the woman did have a mouth on her.

I like it.

In fact, I like her.

Mayhap . . .

Nay.

But what if . . . ?

Nay, nay, nay, I cannot be thinking such nonsense. My injuries must have affected my brain.

What would Toste say to all this?

Vagn thought only a second before deciding that Toste would probably tell him to go with his instincts. "What is her bride price?" he asked Gorm, not that it mattered one whit.

"Two stallions from the Saracen lands, eight ells of silk, five acorn-fed hogs, and fifty hides of land in the Northlands." Helga's dowry appeared fair, in Vagn's estimation, especially for a well-born lady of her advanced years. Still, a smart trader negotiated the best deal . . . not that Vagn was really negotiating. Nor was he a trader. He was just having a bit of fun. He deliberately hesitated, letting Gorm know he wasn't convinced.

"And, of course, Helga will be my heir to Briarstead."

Vagn nodded, still pretending hesitancy. "Yea, but there is the raisin business," he pointed out.

"What raisin business?" Helga wanted to know.

"Don't tell her," Gorm said on a groan, putting his face in his hands.

"Your father said your female parts have no doubt withered into raisins, but that you still have all your teeth. Really, I think you need a bigger bride price, considering that shortcoming. I mean, tupping a raisin requires a bit more incentive, don't you think?" Vagn winked at Helga to indicate that he was teasing.

The woman was apparently without humor, because her upper lip curled back and she growled menacingly, first at him, then at her father. "I have ne'er clouted a wounded man afore, but I am thinking on it now."

"Me?" he asked with exaggerated innocence. "It was just a jest. On my part, leastways."

"Stop talking before I do, in fact, clout an injured man."

"Me?" he asked again with exaggerated innocence. *Someone should put M'Lady Prissy Arse in her place.* He sighed deeply. *Ah, a Viking's work is never done.* "Come closer, Helga—I would check your teeth and your maidenhead. With all due respect to your father's honesty, I will require a personal inspection."

Helga clenched her hands into fists. Her lips quivered with agitation. Mayhap she was about to have a fit.

Good!

"Untie this maggot-head at once and send him on his way," Helga demanded of her father.

"Not till the maggot-head is wedlocked with you," her father insisted, sitting up straight, then standing to glare eyeball to eyeball with his daughter.

Maggot-head? That is a new insult. Hmmm. I like it. Mayhap I will try it sometime. Too bad Toste is not here. He would be a good one to try it on.

"Never!" she said. "You have done outrageous things in your time to bend me to your will, Father, but this time you have gone too far. A raisin! Indeed!"

I rather liked the raisin comparison. Mayhap I will try that one out on someone sometime, too. He noticed her purplish flush then and decided, *Or mayhap not.*

"I was only thinking of you," her father whined, "and I meant no insult."

Whoo! You're getting nowhere with that line of thinking, Gorm. Even I know enough not to try the "I was only thinking of you" argument.

"Withered female parts is not an insult?" Helga's face flamed even more purple than before.

"Be reasonable," her father begged. "Once the mag . . . uh, man . . . is cleaned up and on his feet, he may please your eye."

Yea, I am quite the presentable fellow when I am cleaned up.

"Do you really think I have forsworn marriage all these years because I yearn for a comely man?"

"Well—" her father said.

"Aaarrgh!" Helga said.

"Can I say something?" Vagn interrupted.

"No!" Helga and Gorm both said.

Helga inhaled and exhaled several times for patience. "I will ne'er agree; nor will he," Helga told her father.

"Well, actually . . ." Vagn began. He ever did hate it when people spoke for him as if he were a mute . . . or a lackwit.

Helga and Gorm both turned to peer down at him.

A slow smile cracked Gorm's wrinkled face.

Helga's mouth dropped open and her face turned blood red. She looked as if her head might explode.

To everyone's surprise, especially Vagn's, he was considering taking Helga the Homely to his bed furs.

My WHAT resembles a raisin? . . .

Helga had landed in her worst nightmare.

She put a trembling hand to her forehead and tried to calm herself. Toste Ivarsson, the bane of her life, was in her keep . . . residing in one of her guest bedchambers, and her father, the half-brained idiot, actually thought she would marry the rogue. Even worse, Toste hinted that he might not be unwilling. He was a half-brained idiot, too.

Was it another mockery of his? Like the one he'd leveled at her more than twenty years ago—*Helga the Homely*—the epithet that had turned her seven-year-old life on a horrible course. Even today, after all those years, she occasionally heard men snicker those words behind her back. Some said that a saga had even been written about her.

The worst part was that she had loved Toste, in her own childish way. And he had crushed her. Like a gnat beneath his feet. Or a raisin. Oh, she could kill her well-intentioned father for that coarse description.

As for Toste and his teasing hint that he might marry her . . . well, mayhap it was time to make the miscreant pay for his crime. But wait. Were those bloodstained linen strips wrapped about his bare chest? And was that bruising about his face and shoulders? Had he been injured and left untended? Even worse, had her father done the man injury in his attempts to make the man take her to wife? *Can I be any more humiliated?*

"What happened to you?" she asked suddenly, stepping up to the pallet and sitting on the edge. Even before he answered, she pulled a small knife from her girdle and began slicing off the soiled bandages.

"I was injured in the battle at Stone Valley. A sword wound, front to back, just beneath my ribs. Other injuries as well, but the Saxon sword caused the most damage. The back of my head hurt mightily for a few days, but your father's healer could find no mark on my skull."

Now that she looked closer, she noted his pale complexion and the brackets of pain about his mouth. "When was the last time Efrim changed these dressings?" she asked her father. Efrim was the village healer . . . barely competent, though he tried his best.

Her father shrugged. "Three days ago. Mayhap four. He said that if the fever broke . . . which it did yestermorn . . . Toste's chances of survival were good."

The wounded man seemed amused by the interplay between Helga and her father and only said, "I am not Toste."

"For shame, Father! You know good and well that the man should have been bathed and his wounds cleansed daily." And to Toste she said, "I knew Toste, and you are Toste."

Despite his rope ties, the man was able to lean his head forward and sniff at his armpits. "Phew!" he said. "Why didst you not tell me how malodorous I am, Gorm?" *The fool!* Then he added, to her, "I thought you had not seen Toste for twenty and more years."

"I have seen him . . . you . . . from a distance since then. At the marriage ceremony of King Haakon's youngest daughter two years past, for example." Even filthy and bruised, Toste Ivarsson was a handsome man, with long, dark blond hair and perfectly formed facial features, including an enticing cleft in his chin. Besotted women flocked after him like bees to honey.

"I was there—" he started to say.

She interrupted. "I know. I saw you." *And your buzzing bees.*

"—but I did not see you," he finished.

"You were too busy ogling all the beautiful women at court that day . . . the *non-homely* ones." *Shut your teeth, Helga. You are beginning to sound like a jealous milkmaid.*

He winced at her comment and at her rough handling of the linen strips stuck to his chest wound which she was beginning to peel away. She thought about untying him first, but decided it would be best to keep him restrained till she'd gotten all the stuck bandages off. In truth, sometimes it was less painful to just rip the linen strips off a wound than prolong the pain by a slower process. So that was just what she did. With a jerk of her hand, she pulled hard, and the bloody cloths came away with a good amount of scab and skin, causing new bleeding.

"Jesus, Mary and Joseph! Holy Valhalla! Bloody damn hell!" Vagn roared, arching upward against his ropes. "Are you trying to kill me? Just because I teased you a bit?" He dropped back to the cot and closed his eyes, breathing heavily with pain.

"I did it for your own good," she said and used the linen sheet to dab at some of the oozing blood.

"That's what women always say after they do something feckless," he muttered. His eyes remained closed. The only indication of his pain now was his white-knuckled fists at his sides.

She was about to protest his calling her feckless, but decided to allow him this indulgence, in light of the pain he must be suffering at her hands. "Send for warm water, soap and fresh linen strips," she ordered her father, as if he were a mere servant. The old man turned, about to comply without question.

"Wait," Vagn called out, opening his eyes. They were as blue as the summer sky over a Norse fjord. A foolish maid, which she was not, could drown in their depths. "Untie me first."

"Not till you agree to wed with my daughter."

"Nay!" she said. *If I did not love my father so much, I would hate him for this indignity.*

"I already said mayhap." Vagn did not even glance her way as he spoke, as if she were irrelevant in this discussion.

"Mayhap is not good enough. I know your kind, Ivarsson. The minute I release your bonds, you will run away," Gorm said.

"I am hardly in a condition to do any running," Vagn pointed out, still not looking her way.

"Will the two of you stop talking about me as if my opinion matters naught? I will not wed, and that is the end of it."

"If I cut your ropes, will you agree to stay here for one month and court my daughter?" Gorm asked, tapping his forefinger against his chin.

"Nobody is going to court me," Helga declared vehemently.

"Nobody?" their captive asked her, finally looking her way. "You have no suitors?"

She had been better off when he'd ignored her. He held her gaze, and she felt mesmerized by his attractiveness. She could not turn away.

"None to speak of," her father answered for her. "She scares 'em all off."

Vagn arched his eyebrows at her. "I am not easily scared."

"Oh, spare me from the boasts of a self-important man!" Finally Helga had regained the use of her tongue.

"One month," the Viking agreed, and a grinning Gorm rushed off to find a housemaid and the necessary items she'd demanded. Her father, rarely so compliant, probably rushed off to escape her wrath, which was going to be mighty, once she caught him alone.

She began to examine his injury more closely and while she did, she asked, "Where is your brother? As I recall, you two are rumored to be inseparable."

He did not reply. When she glanced up from her work, she could not help noticing the agony in his eyes. Finally he said in a voice so low she barely heard, "Dead."

She put a hand on his arm. "I am so sorry."

He merely nodded.

There were no words she could offer that would console him, so she returned to the task before her. She'd exposed the wound, and it was grievous, indeed—a deep, seeping slash from nipple to navel.

Vagn glanced down and gasped. "I did not realize it was so bad. I should be dead. Surely the sword missed my heart and other vital organs by a hairsbreadth."

"The gods are watching over you," she opined.

"Or Satan."

Apparently, he was not too happy about the fate the gods had dealt him. She decided to ignore the ungratefulness of his remark and examine him for other injuries. *Blessed Freyja, give me strength.* As lady of the keep, she had often tended the sick, and this man was no different. *Keep telling myself that, and mayhap I will believe it.* She would not feign modesty at this late date. *Here I go.* Flipping the bed coverlet aside, she exposed his nude body to full view . . . to his amusement, she could tell. *Well, well, well!* The fool thought she would be embarrassed to view him as he had been born. *I am too stunned to be embarrassed.*

First things first. Using the small knife she kept in a leather sheath on her belt, she cut away his ropes, then helped him up so that he could go behind the screen and relieve himself. It was an arduous process, because the man could barely stand. When he was done, he sank back down to the bed with a loud sigh of pain and exhaustion.

"You should have let me bring you a chamber pot," she admonished him.

He scowled at her in silent reproval. The half-brain!

Her father came back into the chamber with a housemaid carrying two bowls of water and clean cloths. She immediately began washing Vagn's face and neck and shoulders with a soapy cloth, leaving the wound area for last. He watched her like a hawk as she worked, probably enjoying her embarrassment in dealing with his naked flesh. She tried not to notice the muscles that bunched in his arms and chest. She especially tried not to notice the silkiness of the oddly appealing hairs in his armpits, visible now that he'd stacked his hands behind his neck, watch-watch-watching her.

Once she'd completed her ablutions, including his

long, sinewed legs, his feet and his sinfully flat belly, she frowned, wondering what to do next. Should she hand the cloth to him and demand he wash his genitals himself, thus calling attention to her inability to remain aloof from his nakedness, or should she work on his wound area? Most of all, she tried her best to avoid looking at the manpart standing before her . . . and, yea, it stood upright like a silly flagpole under her scrutiny. *Do not look at it, Helga. Do not look.* "Make it lie down."

He laughed. "How?"

"I do not know how. Just do it." *I am not looking. I am not looking. I am not looking.*

"It just means that he likes you," her father had the audacity to say. She'd noticed the servant leaving, but had forgotten her father remained in the room.

"Well, that is not necessarily true," Vagn confessed. "*It* has a mind of its own. *It* is not always so discriminating."

" 'Tis true, 'tis true, now that you mention it," her father said. "I recall when I was young, the mere sight of a good pair of udders on a wench would light the wick in my candle."

"Coarse, ignorant lackwits, both of you!" she pronounced. Despite her irritation, she dared to lay her hand on the Viking's right thigh and yank it none too gently apart from the other thigh so she could finish her cleansing, but her action caused the manpart to grow even more. Despite his abated fever, his flesh still raged hot to the touch. Was it renewed fever or her touch that caused the heat? Alarming thoughts, both.

Helga jumped back then with horror . . . not because of his outrageous manpart, or his hot skin, or her belated delicacy, but because she'd just realized something. Her eyes bulged with disbelief as she gazed down on his reclining body. "Where's your birthmark?" she asked in a sudden panic.

"How do you know about the birthmark?"

"Hah! You know very well how you talked me into going to the stables at King Haakon's court to show me 'a secret' which turned out to be your nude body and the birthmark. Vile boy!"

"Was that before or after I called you Helga the Homely?"

"Before."

If looks could kill, he would be one dead Viking. With renewed horror, she declared, "You are not Toste."

"He is not Toste," her father concurred.

"That's what I've been trying to tell everyone."

And then his sap began to rise . . .

Vagn was up and about in Gorm's keep . . . but just barely.

Apparently, he had not recovered as much as he'd thought. Two days ago, after Helga had washed his nude body—*and wasn't that an experience to savor!*—and rebound his wounds, Vagn had attempted to leave the pallet, but his knees had given out and pain had shot through his chest, radiating out to all his extremities. It had probably been due to the stress of her endless questioning as to what had happened to Toste, now that she accepted he was not his brother. To his vast indignity, Helga had caught him as he'd begun to crumble in a heap at her feet. He'd learned later that it had taken Helga, her father and the guard outside the door to get him back onto the pallet, where his wounds had reopened and begun bleeding profusely again.

But he was downstairs now, making his way gingerly toward the solar where he heard voices. Gorm was off patrolling his estates, and a housemaid had brought him a morning meal of honey cakes and ale a short time ago. He could not lie on that mattress one moment longer for fear he would have more horrific nightmares, either reliving the battle at Stone Valley or suffering a harsh blow to the head, which had caused his brother's death. Even when he was awake, his head ached and he sometimes saw visions of human crows in black garb gathering about him with squawking voices, about to peck out his entrails. Most of all, he was bored and restless. And, truth to tell, he was randy as a bull whose male-sap had risen.

Besides, he wanted to find Helga and tease her some more. She rose so easily to his taunts about their upcoming wedding. Not that he really planned to wed her. Leastways, he probably didn't. Undoubtedly didn't. Well, all right, he was still considering the possibility, but in the meantime, he would test the waters and see if he could goad Helga into revealing her true feelings.

Thus far, her voiced feelings amounted to "Dolt!" or "Lackwit dolt!"

Vagn chose to interpret that as *I think she likes me.*

He approached the open doorway of the solar and leaned against the doorjamb, not wanting to interrupt what seemed to be a business meeting between Helga and Saleem, an Arab merchant whose trading vessel docked periodically at Jorvik. Saleem was also known as Sly-Boots for his ability to pull off many a shrewd trading deal . . . often to the detriment of his customers. At this moment, though, he didn't appear to be faring so well.

"Five mancuses for these simple fabrics? 'Tis thievery!" Saleem said, fingering one of the ells of finely woven wool spread across a large table. An embroidered diamond design highlighted the jade-green cloth in shades of yellow and red and black.

"This wool is the best in all Britain, and you know it," Helga said, brushing his fingertips away. "Besides that, the exquisite embroidery makes it nigh priceless. But that is neither here nor there. I have changed my mind. I think five mancuses for these three ells is way too cheap. I would need at least six to part with it."

"The fabric is indeed exquisite," Saleem conceded.

"You know, I can always sell this at my own stall in Coppergate." Coppergate was the trading section of the port city.

"It is a deal," Saleem said, "but only if you sell me the white silk over there." There was a bolt of cream white silk set aside on another table. Along its edge was an embroidered pattern of gold thread which enclosed a border of red hearts. Vagn had never seen anything like it afore, and he had been in all the important trading towns of the world, including Birka and Hedeby.

"Nay!" Vagn said, stepping into the room.

Helga's eyes widened with surprise . . . and concern for his health, he could tell.

I am just as surprised as you, m'lady, and just as concerned. What am I thinking? Am I thinking? "I wish to purchase that fabric myself," Vagn shocked himself by saying. *Has some other being taken over my tongue? Why would I want a piece of white cloth?*

"You?" Helga and Saleem said at the same time.

"Yea, I wish it for a bride gift," he announced blithely. "I mean, a possible bride gift." *I mean, what in bloody hell is going on inside my brain?*

"Not that again!" Helga groaned with dismay. "Where would you find so much coin?"

"I had a hide pouch tied round my waist, under my

tunic and armor. The battlefield scavengers never got to it. Besides, I have access to other money, if need be."

She did not seem pleased that he was not a pauper.

"I must have that particular cloth," Saleem whined. "There is an Arab sheik who would give a caliph's ransom for it. His favorite houri has an overfondness for white silk. Five mancuses for that fabric alone." It was a generous amount to pay for such a small swath, and they all recognized that fact.

"I will give you six," Vagn said. *I must be mad.*

Helga's mouth dropped open. Causing a woman's mouth to drop open was always a good thing, in Vagn's opinion. Worth going mad over, he supposed.

"Are you demented?" Saleem wanted to know.

"Perchance," Vagn replied with a shrug. *Exactly my assessment of my mental condition, if you must know. I am beginning to think I might suffer from* Herfjöttr, *the battered-soldier condition that leaves grown men walking about in a daze.*

"Who are you?"

"Vagn Ivarsson."

"I thought you were killed at the Battle of Stone Valley."

Vagn winced. "That was my brother Toste."

"Are you sure?"

"Of course I am sure." *Reasonably sure.*

Saleem shook his head as if to clear it. Then he turned his attention back to Helga, red-faced with frustration. "Seven mancuses, and that is my final offer."

"Ten," Vagn piped in. *Toste, are you laughing at me up in Valhalla? Are all you dead warriors placing wagers over what wooly-witted thing I will do next?*

Helga gasped.

Saleem swore.

Later, after Saleem stormed out of the chamber, carrying only the green wool, Helga shook her head at him and made that tsk-ing sound women love so well. "I am not going to wed with you. So get that idea out of your head."

He made an exaggerated moue of unconcern. Ten mancuses in coin meant naught to him. He had gambled more in one night of dice or *hnefatafl*, which made him think of something else: another gamble—one which he had won. "Where is Clod? Oh, good Thor, how could I have forgotten? Where is Clod?"

"Clod?" Helga said as she folded up some of the loose fabrics lying about. "The only Clod I know of is you, you clod."

"Nay, it is my horse Clod that I refer to. He was with me at the battle. I distinctly recall him standing behind me, neighing frantically, when the sword went through me." *I have become a blithering idiot.*

"Are you referring to that sway-backed horse as old as Odin that followed you here from the battlefield?"

"He is alive?" Vagn asked, no longer feeling like a blithering idiot, just a hopeful idiot.

She nodded, bemused at his concern over a decrepit, useless animal.

Vagn couldn't help himself then. Tears welled in his eyes. He did not know why, but Clod's escape from death seemed to have some meaning to him. Hope, that's what it was. If that old warhorse could survive the battle, there was always hope that . . . well, suffice it to say, there was hope. "Thank you," he choked out in an emotion-thick voice. Then he did the only thing any red-blooded Viking would do in the circumstances. Especially faced with a woman with the most kiss-some mouth this side of an Arab harem.

He kissed Helga the Homely.

And he kissed her good.

Really good.

Helga's knees gave way, and she did not even have the excuse of a battle injury. He caught her as she almost swooned at his feet. He smiled against her mouth and kissed her again. There was one good thing Vagn knew how to do, and that was kiss a woman witless. Actually, there was another good thing Vagn could do equally well, and it also made a woman witless.

"What are you doing to me?" Helga asked when he gave her a moment to breathe.

"Convincing you," he whispered against her mouth.

"To marry you?"

He grinned. "Nay, something else."

He thought she said something that sounded like "Clod," but she probably said that she was "awed." Leastways, that's what he chose to believe, especially since she'd just opened her sinfully large and moist mouth for him.

His knees nearly collapsed . . . again, as they had two days ago. This time it was due to pain of an entirely different sort.

CHAPTER THREE

☙

*T*he abominable Viking . . .

The nun was kneeling on all fours in the dirt, arse up and outlined by her tautened robe, whistling. The whistling was mediocre; the arse was magnificent.

Well, son of a sword! I think I have died and gone to Asgard . . . or is it heaven? Have I sunk so low that I now lust after a nun? Pitiful . . . I have become pitiful. But not in a million years would Toste inform Lady Esme—or Sister Esme—or Eat-me (don't think he had forgotten that erotic misspeak)—of his presence in the abbey gardens . . . not until absolutely necessary. He was enjoying the view too much on this unseasonably warm November day . . . and he didn't mean the scenic village and forests which surrounded the tidy grounds of the religious community. His brother Vagn had always claimed to favor women with big breasts, but Toste ever did appreciate a shapely female arse. *I wonder what she would do if I dropped down behind her, real close, and—*

"Go away, Viking." Apparently, she was aware of his presence, after all, but didn't even bother to turn and look at him, just continued trying to lure a cat out of a low bush by waving a peacock feather about. She'd stopped whistling, though.

"Pssssss," said the cat, who backed up further inside the bush.

"Here, cat. Here, cat," she said, waving the feather in front of the bush.

It was a futile effort. The cat would come out when it wanted to. Still, the two of them—cat and woman—engaged in a hissing-cajoling battle.

"Why do you want the cat?"

"I don't want the filthy animal, but mice dared to enter the scullery today. Mother Wilfreda needs a mouser. Go away."

Never one to be bullied by a lady, Toste stood still, of course. While he waited for her to give up the game, he scanned the abbey holdings. He'd come to know the spartan buildings and their inhabitants well these past two sennights. The well-kept grounds bespoke neatness and efficiency, and would no doubt be lovely in the spring and summer. In the distance, he could see the wattle-and-daub, thatched huts of the villagers. Many hectares of plowland lay fallow for the winter but would spring forth with wheat and oats in just a few months. Sheep grazed. Cows lowed. Dozens of conical beehives, their occupants in hibernation for the winter, resembled squat soldiers watching over the religious flocks.

He inhaled deeply. The scent of winter filled the air, but also the heady aroma of Margaret's Mead, made from the vast amounts of honey gathered by Sister Ursula, the resident beekeeper. A group of the nuns were off now in one of the nearby outbuildings, brewing up a new batch of mead to be sold to area merchants, as well as imbibed in the convent. Apparently, the sisters' vows of abstinence did not include the wicked brew. They sang joyfully as they worked . . . some of their exuberance no doubt due to the ale-joy . . . a song about Sanctus something-or-other. A welcome change, to his mind, from the usual vocal fare.

Toste had spent far too much time in the bed rushes, healing. He swore to Bolthor yestermorn that time passed so slowly in this nunnery that he counted the hours by the drips of his candle. And listening to choirs practice their religious music did not help at all. If he heard "Kyrie Eleison" chanted one more time, he was going to pull his nose hairs out, one at a time, or give these dimwitted females some reason to chant, "Have mercy."

Furthermore, who knew the church bells had to ring so many times each day? For matins and compline and vespers and this appointed prayer time or that designated prayer purpose. Betimes he felt as if he had a gong inside his sore head, with its own personal tolling bell. They even prayed over Sister Stefana's sluggish bowel, for the love of Frigg.

The giggling novices who made excuses to peek in his doorway about fifty times a day were just as annoying. Then there was Sister Hildegard, who had an ungodly fear of Vikings and kept shrieking every time she saw him, "The Vikings are coming, the Vikings are coming." Hah! He had news for her. The Viking was already here.

Sister Stefana of the sluggish bowel was another story altogether. The short, apple-cheeked lady had the peculiar habit of disrobing at odd moments and dancing naked in the halls. To say that Wilfreda, the mother superior and resident healer, was embarrassed by such behavior would be a vast understatement. Everyone ignored Sister Stefana till she invariably regained her senses. They pretended the demented nun wasn't naked or doing anything un-nunlike. 'Twas a bit like ignoring a longship in a mud puddle.

The most outrageous happenstance of his convalescence had been Father Alaric daring to suggest that he might want to confess his sins.

"What makes you think I am a sinner?" Toste had asked.

"Well, I just thought . . . um, being a Norseman and all that entails . . . raping and pillaging and whatnot . . . and being well-traveled . . . and being a heathen . . . well, uh . . ."

"Who says I am a heathen? I worship both the Norse and Christian gods. Like many Norsemen, I have covered my back by being baptized. I am Christian when I want to be."

"I am not certain that kind of Christianity counts toward heaven. Leastways, if you are even half Christian, 'tis a good idea to go to confession on occasion."

"The best part of repentance, in my opinion, is the sinning," he'd quipped.

"St. Augustine said the same thing," the priest had admitted.

I hope he doesn't expect to turn me into a saint. "Did you have some particular sin in mind for me?" It was an indication of Toste's boredom that he'd even carried on such a conversation with a priest as old as that biblical Moses.

"Fornication," Father Alaric had replied without hesitation.

"Ah, that. Yea, I might have done that once . . . or twice." *Or several hundred times.* "But not lately."

"Then, too, there are abominations," the holy man had added. The flush on his round jowls had crept up to his tonsured scalp.

Huh? "What are abominations?" Toste had wanted to know.

Blustering for the right words, the priest had sputtered out something scandalous about men and animals and body orifices.

Toste was not easily shocked when it came to sex, but his jaw had dropped open then. Really, clerics accused Vikings of the most outlandish things. "You can wipe that sin . . . that abomination . . . from my slate," he'd finally managed to say.

But now Toste was venturing outdoors . . . no doubt to save his sanity, or what was left of it. His head wound had been severe, but he should have recovered long before this. Oddly, the pains in his chest and back hurt him more than the head blow. Well, not so odd. It was the type of shared pain he'd always experienced with his twin brother, and he'd seen for himself on the battlefield that Vagn had been speared in just those places by a Saxon sword. But how could his twin's pain linger on, even after death?

Enough dwelling on such morbid thoughts. Toste had more important things to dwell on now . . . like a beautiful woman on all fours with an upraised arse. *I've never made love with a nun afore. Leastways, I don't think I have. I wonder what it would be like. Vagn would say they are all the same in the dark. Then he would laugh and suggest something so coarse even I would blush. Aaarrgh! By thunder, I've got to stop thinking about Vagn.*

He sank down to his knees next to Sister Esme and said, "What are you doing? Can I help? I am a great cat catcher." Actually, he'd never caught a cat in his life. Or tried. At the same time as he dropped to his knees, he clutched at the left side of his abdomen, just below his rib cage.

"What? What is amiss?" she asked, sitting back on her legs.

"Nothing. It's just that imaginary pain again."

"Imaginary?"

"My twin brother. We could always . . . well, sort of sense things about each other . . . even when we were far apart."

"This is *really* far apart if you're feeling his pain now."

Well, well, well! A nun who can make a jest. He punched her playfully in the arm. "Sarcasm ill suits you, m'lady."

She stared for a long moment at the spot he had punched as if wondering whether to punch him back. That would be a sight to behold: a nun who made jests *and* engaged in physical violence. To his disappointment, she chose to do nothing but continue blathering. "I guess it's hard for me to imagine being as close to a family member as that. My mother died long ago, but I have a father and two brothers, and the only thing I sense about them is that they'd like to see me dead." He could tell that she immediately regretted revealing so much about herself.

"Surely you jest."

Sister Esme really was a lovely woman. Even in the drab brown gunna she wore, her figure appeared full and womanly. Her black hair had been combed behind her small shell ears and covered with a matching drab brown veil. No wimple. The skin on her face was as clear as new cream, her mouth a rose-colored wonder. She licked her seemingly dry lips.

Lick your lips again, m'lady nun, and I might just make bold with you right here in the vegetable patch. Of a sudden, Toste recalled that it had been a year and more since he had lain with a woman, thanks to his Jomsviking experience. He must be randy indeed to be salivating over a nun.

"If that were only so!" she said on a sigh.

Oh, good gods, had he spoken aloud of his randiness? But, nay, he shook his head to clear it and realized that the nun referred to his remark that she must be jesting about her father and brothers wanting her dead.

"Explain yourself, m'lady."

"Nay. I've already said too much."

"You cannot tell a man that your life is in peril and then shut your teeth."

"I can and I will."

He shrugged. "There are no secrets in this nunnery. Women like to blab. All I have to do is ask. Someone will tell me your story."

She sliced him with a look that pretty much said he was as bothersome as a gnat.

Undaunted, he scowled right back at her.

"All right, I will tell you. Then leave be," she said testily. "It is four months till my twenty-fifth birthday, at which time my mother's dower lands at Evergreen will revert to me. My father is getting desperate."

Toste figured the wench exaggerated her peril. Women tended to do that. "I have heard of the Lord of Blackthorne, and he is already land-wealthy."

She made a whooshy sound of exasperation at his persistence in butting into her affairs, but nevertheless disclosed, "Yea, he is, but a father with two sons never has too much. Plus, he is a greedy man." She put her hands on her hips and bowed her back, stretching, no doubt to remove the kinks from all the bending she'd been doing.

A part of Toste's body stretched, too. His favorite part. "Have you no love at all for your father or brothers?" he inquired as coolly as a man with a growing arousal could inquire. He would have crossed his legs if he were not still kneeling.

"Hah! I have no use for any man, truth be told. Belch and boast, belch and boast, belch and boast, that's all they are good for."

Toste stifled a smile. *The lady has a sense of humor. How . . . well, refreshing!* A wicked tongue, breasts, a nice arse, *and* a sense of humor. The nun was looking better and better.

She *was* making a jest, wasn't she? "Has your father made actual threats?"

"For a certainty, he has . . . both by word and deed."

Toste peered at her a little closer . . . a comely woman, even with her drab garb. "What mean you?"

"I mean that he has been threatening me for years, and that lately there have been numerous near-accidents involving myself that cannot be explained."

He frowned in disbelief. "Such as?"

"Severe stomach cramps that the healer claims to have been due to poison. A push down dark stone steps at night. A snake in my bed. Little things like that." She narrowed her eyes at him. "Why are you asking all these questions? Even worse, why am I bothering to answer?"

"Because I am bored. Because you cannot resist my charms, despite being a nun." Toste still could not accept a family that would do such things to a mere woman, without provocation. There were evil men in the world, though. He'd met a few. "What will you do?"

"About resisting you?"

"Nay, you saucy nun," he said with a laugh. "About your father."

She shrugged and pushed a strand of hair off her face with a dirty hand. Now she had a smudge of dirt on her cheekbone that made her appear ten years younger . . .

not like the subject of some bloody intrigue. "I will survive, one way or another, as I always have. Or mayhap I will take my vows in the end. It is not such a bad life."

"Vows? You have not yet taken vows?" Little bells went off in Toste's head, and not the churchly kind that had been plaguing him of late. *Ting-a-ling, ting-a-ling, ting-a-ling!* these bells said, *Not a nun! Not a nun! Not a nun!*

She shook her head. "I haven't taken the final vows after ten and more years within these walls. If I do, Evergreen will go to my father. Some say I am the oldest living novice in all Britain." Her rosebud mouth drooped dolefully as she spoke.

Toste's lips twitched with mirth.

"'Tis not funny."

"Yea, 'tis." He rubbed a palm over his mouth to wipe away signs of his amusement, probably to no avail. "Are you a virgin?" he asked suddenly.

"Of course," she replied, then added, "Your question passes the bounds of decency. It is none of your business."

"I was just thinking—"

"Some men shouldn't think. It strains their brains."

"Tsk tsk tsk!" Someone needed to teach this nun-wench her proper place: beneath a man. Mayhap later he would undertake the job. "What I was saying before you rudely interrupted was that you should be more worried about being the oldest virgin in all Britain, not the oldest novice." *There! I got my jab in.*

She swatted him on the face with the peacock feather. He pretended great pain.

"I have noticed that you are an over-jestful man. Do you think everything in life is worthy of jest? Must you laugh at everything?"

"Life is hard, m'lady. Sometimes you must laugh, lest you break down and cry. That I will not do."

Just then, a five-legged piglet ran by, being chased by Sister George, the resident animal rescuer at the nunnery. The pig's gait was lopsided, like a *drukkinn* Viking after a long voyage. The nun's gait was equally lopsided, but only because she was attempting to lift her gunna to her knees with one hand as she ran and hold on to her flying veil with the other hand.

"Oink-oink!"

"Here, piggy, here, piggy!"

"Oink-oink!"

"Here, piggy, here, piggy!"

The pig probably thought he was destined to become a ham and was not about to stop. The nun was equally determined. They disappeared into an empty cow byre beyond the honey shed.

"This is one . . . um, unusual nunnery," Toste commented with a shake of his head.

"Yea, 'tis," Lady Esme agreed. "Unusual but wonderful, in its own way."

Toste wasn't so sure about that.

"But we were talking about life's hardship and the need to laugh betimes." Her face softened. "You miss your brother, don't you?"

"Desperately," he admitted. To his shame, he felt tears mist his eyes. *When did I turn weepish? Next I will be sobbing.* Once he was able to speak over the lump in his throat, he elaborated, "In truth, I am disoriented. My life seems totally off balance. I am like a ship that lists to one side, unable to go forward or backward, just in circles."

"Time heals, I have been told."

He shrugged. "Mayhap."

Just then, Bolthor limped up, aided by a long wooden staff. His thigh had been cut to the bone in the battle, and he had a deep gash in his neck where a Saxon had tried to slice his gullet but missed, thank the gods. Bolthor stared at him through his one good eye and asked, "What are you two doing down on your knees in the dirt? Praying?"

Toste looked at Esme, and she looked at him. Then they both burst out laughing. She had a lovely, dulcet-toned laugh.

"Nay, just talking," Toste said, rising gingerly to his feet, then extending a hand to Esme to help her up. She glanced at her dirty hand, then at his clean one, then seemed to dismiss the consequences and placed her palm in his. His much larger, callused hand engulfed her smaller one. To Toste's shock, he felt the contact of her skin on his in the most erotic fashion, like ripples of pleasure extending out from their briefly joined hands to all his extremities . . . and one special extremity in particular. Esme, who came only to his shoulder, was equally affected—he could tell by her heightened color and the trembling of her hand, still encased in his. She jerked her hand away as if burned, and made a great show of brushing dirt from her gunna.

Toste was well satisfied with his work this day. If he could rattle a nun's composure, then he had not lost his knack. Or an *almost-nun*, he reminded himself.

"What have you been doing?" Toste inquired of Bolthor, who did not appear to be in a good mood . . . though it was ofttimes hard to tell. He was a giant of a man, a berserker, with a black patch over one eye, and scars from numerous battles covering most of his skin. Even when he smiled, he appeared to be scowling.

"Nice of you to ask!" Bolthor snarled. "These nuns

think I am a horse . . . not a warhorse, mind you, just a plain old farm horse." He took on a decidedly feminine tone and mimicked the nuns: " 'Bolthor, can you lift that wagon so we can fix the wheel? Bolthor, the bull won't come into the barn. Bolthor, that barrel of honey is too heavy for me to carry and you are so big and strong. Bolthor, could you do me a little favor . . . nay, 'tis not cleaning the garderobe today, just dig a little moat for me.' " He cocked his head at Toste, seeking sympathy, then remarked, "Hah! There is no such thing as a little moat."

"What would you rather be doing?" Esme asked Bolthor.

"Creating sagas. I am a skald."

"Really?"

Bolthor nodded vigorously. "Wouldst thou like to hear my latest?"

"Nay, nay, nay. Not right now," Toste said. *I think I am going to throw up.*

"Of course," Esme said, just to annoy him, he would wager.

Toste groaned.

Bolthor made that harrumphing sound he usually did before spouting his poems. Then the dream-expression came over his battle-scarred face. Too late to stop him now. "I call this one 'The Warrior and the Nun.' "

"Huh?" Esme said.

"Uh-oh!" Toste said.

*"Once was a maid so fair
But for beauty she had no care.
She had no use for men,
For sex she had no yen.
So she entered a nunnery
And swore she would never marry.*

But along came a man like no other.
He was a Viking who gave no quarter.
What wench can resist
Being kissed
By a bedsport enthusiast?
Soon the maid will have yearnings she had not
    ought
To discover the famed Viking S-Spot.
And now instead of wearing a hair shert over her
    breast
She swoons over one man's hairy chest."

Esme was inhaling and exhaling rapidly like a puff fish, too stunned to speak. That was the usual reaction of people upon hearing one of Bolthor's horrid sagas for the first time.

"Is he implying that I have sinful inclinations toward you?" Lady Esme asked him in a horrified undertone.

Toste grinned. "I hope so."

"Oaf!" she said, referring to him, not Bolthor.

"He called me a bedsport enthusiast. I'm the one who should be insulted."

"What did you think of my saga?" Bolthor asked Esme.

"It was fine," Toste said before Esme could say something offensive, like "Oaf!" Bolthor meant well, and he was a good friend, and Toste would not want to hurt his feelings unnecessarily.

Bolthor smiled widely. "I was not sure about using 'hairy chest' instead of 'manly chest.' Betimes we poets are faced with these difficult word choices," Bolthor explained.

"I think 'hairy' was an excellent choice," Esme said, obviously having found her voice. She looked at Toste and muttered, "*Hairy* oaf!"

But Toste could have kissed her for her sensitivity toward the gentle giant. Actually, he could kiss her for any reason.

"Next methinks I might try 'The Oldest Virgin in All Britain,'" Bolthor told her. He must have overheard the tail end of their conversation.

Esme just gurgled.

At that moment, Bolthor's eyes went wide. "What in the name of Odin is that?" His grin had evaporated as his attention was snagged on something off in the distance behind Toste and Esme. At first, Toste thought the verse mood might be coming on him again, but before he could voice a protest at that prospect, Bolthor tossed his staff aside, lunged forward and knocked them both to the ground. In that instant, as he and Esme lay on their backs with Bolthor's immense weight pressing down on them, they heard a whizzing sound pass over them.

"What was that?" Toste exclaimed, shoving Bolthor off him.

"An arrow," Bolthor said, already standing and gazing off into the distance where not a soul was visible. "I saw a bowman take aim at us from that stand of trees over there. He is gone now."

Thinking quickly, Toste picked up Esme by the waist and tossed her unceremoniously into the overhang of the bush. The cat screeched indignantly at the intrusion and darted out the back end of the bush, running away.

"Stay put!" he ordered Esme.

Fortunately, she burrowed farther inside the foliage and said not one word.

Toste and Bolthor rushed off to investigate, their pace slowed by Bolthor's crippled gait and Toste's throbbing head. By the time they reached the trees, the villain . . .

or villains . . . were gone. They walked back slowly, discussing the happenstance. Attacked in a nunnery, of all things!

When they returned to the garden, Toste helped Esme out of the bush. She appeared shaken, but lifted her chin bravely as she whisked evergreen needles off her robe. Her veil was half on, half off. She threw it to the ground, where it nestled next to the discarded peacock feather.

"Dost think it was some Saxon warrior come to finish us off?" Toste asked Bolthor, even as he watched Esme compose herself.

"The arrow was meant for me," Esme said matter-of-factly.

"What?" he and Bolthor both exclaimed.

"I saw one of my father's men lurking about earlier today. I should have suspected he would try something like this." Her words were brave, but her ashen face and trembling hands betrayed her fear.

Toste quickly explained to Bolthor what Esme had told him about her father's desperation to gain her lands . . . by her religious vocation or by her death.

" 'Tis outrageous that a man would do such to his own blood," Bolthor said, squeezing one of Esme's hands in his.

"Do you want your dower lands? I mean, do you *really* want them? Enough to fight for them?" Toste asked Esme, a little irritated to see his friend comforting the lady.

Her face brightened. In fact, her eyes almost seemed to glow with a blue fire. "Yea, I want what belongs to me. With a passion."

Passion sounded good to Toste.

"I would give anything to get what is mine."

Oh, lady, you should not promise such to a man. "Anything" prompts way too many images.

He paused for several moments before announcing, "Then I will help you, m'lady. I will be your champion."

That certainly got the lady's attention. Her jaw dropped down practically to her chest, which he was beginning to notice had a decided prominence that even nunly garb could not hide. Observing the direction of his stare, she folded her arms over her breasts. "Thank you for your offer, but I have my own plan."

"We will both be your champions," Bolthor added. "We will be Lady Esme's knights."

"Nay! Definitely not!" she said. "I am in enough of a stew without adding two misguided Vikings to the broth."

Misguided? Who's misguided? "Mayhap you could write a saga about it," Toste suggested to Bolthor sarcastically.

"No sagas about my family dispute! Definitely not!" Lady Esme glared most charmingly at the two of them.

"Good idea, Toste," said Bolthor, who was unable to recognize sarcasm even when it smacked him in the face. Really, couldn't the thick-headed Bolthor see that he wanted to be the one and only champion for the lady?

"Is anybody listening to me? I told you I can handle this myself," Lady Esme screeched. "Violence is not the answer here, even though my father does not hesitate to follow that path. I must use my head and outwit my father. 'Tis the only way."

"You are not to worry, m'lady. Violence is the one thing we understand. We are Vikings," Toste said, as if that said it all.

Lady Esme muttered a very vivid expletive, which caused two sets of male eyebrows to rise in surprise. Almost immediately, she grumbled, "To confession again."

Yeah, right! . . .

As Lady Esme walked away, unaware of the seductive,

totally unpious sway of her hips, Bolthor commented to Toste, "Nice arse."

And Toste replied, "I hadn't noticed."

But then he kissed her . . .

"I have mixed feelings about the two Vikings," Esme told Mother Wilfreda.

The abbess raised her eyebrows in question as the two of them sipped small mugs of mead before retiring for the night. They sat before one of the two giant fireplaces in the great hall of the abbey. The pedestal tables had been removed following the evening meal, and now the various nuns sat about, mending threadbare habits, weaving at small looms, praying their beads, or in the case of those at the other hearth, listening raptly to Bolthor as he spun tales about famous Vikings performing extraordinary feats, like Ragnor Hairy-Breeks and Eric Blood-axe. The other Viking, Toste, sat listening as well, with his long legs propped on the hearth rail, but every so often he glanced toward Esme and gave her a disconcerting scrutiny, which invariably caused her to glance away, flustered.

"You've already told me that the Norsemen have offered to help you. What bothers you?" Mother Wilfreda asked, putting aside a lace altar cloth which she was attempting to repair along the edges.

"I want naught to do with them or any other of the male sex. What have men done for me but make my life miserable?"

"Oh, child, not all men are alike. Remember, our beloved Christ was a man. It is un-Christian of you to speak so."

Esme grinned. "Does that mean I will have to go to confession again?"

Mother Superior nodded. Then she grinned, too. "How many times did you go to confession today?"

"Just twice. It was a good day."

The elderly abbess shook her head at the hopelessness of trying to turn Esme into a holy nun. "Back to our discussion and why you distrust all men, including these Vikings."

"You have been my only family for a long time . . . and a good and faithful sister to my mother. But even when Mother was still alive, my brothers tormented me to the point of crying, and my father was more likely to swat me than hug me." Actually, she could not recall one single instance of affection from the Lord of Blackthorne. "I have survived thus far on my own, with your help. With a little extra effort, I might be able to make it to my twenty-fifth birthday."

"And attain freedom and independence from your father?"

Esme nodded. "*Might* is the key word, of course. I do not doubt that I could hide from my father and his men for another four months. You and I have discussed several possibilities. But the problem will be getting into King Edgar's court. I must present my petition for the return of the dower lands which my father has been holding for me. Father will be watching every road to Winchester, where Edgar is expected to keep Easter, three days past my twenty-fifth birthday. What nags me lately is whether I can leave my fate to chance."

"Not chance, child. God. You must pray for His help."

"I don't discount the power of prayer, Mother, but God helps those who help themselves."

"Or those who are not so prideful that they cannot ask others to help them," the abbess offered. "Like two strong Viking nobles with the ability to garner a *hird* of soldiers?"

"Precisely," Esme said.

"Then what is stopping you?"

"I do not know. These two Vikings are not at all like any men I've met afore. Not my father and brothers, who care only for their own welfare, or the few men, including priests, that I've met over the years here at the convent. Oh, do not glower at me so, Mother. I know that Father Alaric is not bad, but he is the exception. Toste and Bolthor are bloodthirsty warriors . . . well, leastways, they are warriors for hire, Jomsvikings."

"But that could mean they are good fighters for the right cause."

"Hmmmm." Did she dare trust them? What would she have to give up in order to hire them and a troop of their followers? Control, for one thing. Esme did not like the idea of putting her future in the hands of others. Somehow, deep down inside, Esme suspected that she would have to relinquish more than control of her life path . . . especially to the one Viking, Toste.

And that prospect worried Esme the most. She was attracted to the man. Unbelievably, after years of cloistered virtue, suddenly her stomach fluttered whenever this man came near. Not that she would ever let him know of his effect on her. Hah! He already thought too much of himself.

He was more than pleasing to the eye . . . tall and well-built and clean, now that he was recovering from his injuries, with a shaven, well-sculpted face and an enticing cleft chin, dancing blue eyes and long, dark blond hair, which he vainly braided on the sides with amber beads. *Not that I noticed all that much.* When he grinned at her, which he did much too often, she felt her insides melt a tiny bit.

But the thing that drew her to him most was the affection he could not hide for his dead brother and for that horrid poet, Bolthor. How could she not be drawn to a man who loved his brother so, and who showed such loyalty to his friend, even praising his awful sagas?

Mother Wilfreda chuckled suddenly.

"What?"

"The wistful expression on your face betrays you, dear."

"I don't know what you mean," Esme said, but of course she did.

"There is naught wrong with woman-feelings for a man . . . as long as there is no bedding afore the wedding."

Esme felt her face heat with embarrassment. "I have no woman-feelings for any man."

"I may have been a nun these forty-some years, but I know this for certain. God meant for men and women to enjoy each other. There is good lust and there is bad lust."

"Good lust, eh? I like the sound of that," Toste said, coming up behind them, then sliding onto the bench next to Esme . . . way too close.

Esme sidled her bottom along the bench, away from him.

He followed after her.

Mother Wilfreda just made a clucking sound at their antics, then rose and said her good eventides to them both. She would be going off to her cell, along with several of the other nuns, but many of the nuns and novices would set up pallets before the hearths to take advantage of the heat. Most of the bedchambers were cold in wintertime, the only heat provided by numerous woolen blankets; wood for the fireplaces was an expensive commodity.

"She is a good woman," Toste said, motioning his head toward the departing nun. Mother Wilfreda was speaking to her flock of young novices, who were yawning and placing no objections to an early bedtime. After all, they would have to rise before dawn to begin a new day.

"Yea, she is. I do not know what I would have done without her these many years. She is blood kin . . . but more than that. She has been like a true mother to me."

"I'm impressed with this abbey. It is pretty nigh self-sufficient, especially with the mead sales."

"Yea, it is bare bones here, but we get by."

"Especially with Sister Mary Rose selling the occasional relic." He waggled his eyebrows at her for emphasis.

"There is naught wrong with relics."

"Hah! She tried to interest me in one of the Virgin Mary's eyelashes today. Christ's mother must have had eyelashes like the tails of a peacock when you consider how many of them have been found over the years. But this is nothing new. When I was in the Rus lands one time, a merchant tried to sell me twelve shriveled-up things which he claimed were the manparts of the twelve Apostles."

"Are you teasing me?"

"A little."

"Well, don't."

"Why?"

"Because I will have to go to confession again."

He tilted his head in question. *"Again?"*

"Yea, I had to go early today for saying that bad word to you and Bolthor. Then again later when I was dusting the altar of the church sacristy and knocked over St. Stephen's shin bone. Broke it into two pieces, I did. It flew through the air like a spear. *Swish!*"

"And that sin would be?"

"Taking improper care of sacred objects."

" 'Tis sinful to be clumsy?"

"Apparently."

"Father Alaric wanted me to make a confession," Toste told her.

"For what?"

"Abominations." He winked at her.

Her mouth dropped open

He laughed out loud and chucked her playfully under the chin, thus closing her gaping mouth.

"Do not do that. It is not proper."

"What is not proper?"

"Touching me . . . a holy nun."

"Oh, nay, do not play that game with me. You are no more a nun than I am a monk. Once I learned that you had not taken your final vows, I began to view you in an entirely different light."

"What do you mean?" She tried to sound prim and uninterested, which she was not.

"It means that I intend to do everything in my power to seduce you to my bed furs."

She gasped. "*You* are an abomination."

"A tempting one, I trust."

"See, I will have to go to confession now."

"Did I miss something? What sin did *you* commit? I am the one who made the sinful suggestion."

"Yea, but you put impure thoughts in my mind."

"It is a sin to think impure things?"

"Yea, 'tis. We are taught to avoid the near occasions of sin. And impure thoughts are definitely in that category."

"Really, you Christians go too far. How can you condemn a person for thinking something?" He paused several moments, then added, "I rather like the idea of you having impure thoughts about me, though. Gives me hope."

"Stop hoping. That is as far as it will go."

"Do not be too sure of that, m'lady. We Vikings have persuasive powers."

That was what she was afraid of.

"Have you thought about the offer Bolthor and I made to you this morn?"

"Not really," she lied. "I have my own plan."

"And that would be?"

"There are places I can go where my father would be unable to find me for the next four months."

"And then?"

How perceptive of the man to home right in on the crux of her problem! "Then I will figure out a way to approach King Edgar himself."

He arched his brows at her. "You are aware of Edgar's penchant for swiving everything in sight with a set of breasts, are you not? In fact, I heard he entered a nunnery one day not too long past and raped a fair-faced novice without any remorse at all. And he killed the husband of one woman just because she caught his fancy."

"All right, I realize it's not a perfect plan, but I have been evading my father and his schemes for ten years now."

"Wouldst like to hear my idea?"

She should say nay, she really should. "Yea."

"There is one last thing I must do, once I am healed enough to travel . . . I hope within a sennight. I must find Vagn's killer and remove him from this earth."

"You are going to murder someone? That is your plan?"

"It will not be murder. It will be well-deserved revenge."

"How will you find him? Do you know his name?"

He shook his head. "I do not know his name, but I saw him clearly that day. His face is branded on my brain, not to mention the eagle emblem of his master. I will find him, do not doubt that, m'lady."

Her shoulders slumped with resignation. There was no arguing with men when issues of pride and fighting were involved. "What has any of this to do with me?"

"I have friends in Northumbria. Lord Eirik of Ravenshire, for one. Bolthor and I will go there and amass a troop of soldiers, using Eirik's estate as our base of operation for finding Vagn's killer. You could come with us. Whilst there, you would be under the protection of Eirik's shield, which is formidable."

"I couldn't intrude on strangers that way."

"Because of the bond of friendship he shares with me, Eirik and his wife Eadyth would not turn you away. Then, and I think this is the best course, envoys could be sent to King Edgar asking for the release of your dower lands. You would not have to be present yourself."

"Hmmmm. That is a wise remedy and worth pondering." Still, she hesitated. From across the hall, she noticed Mother Wilfreda motioning to her that it was time to retire for the night. She stood, and Toste stood as well. He walked along with her to the corridor. "Why would you do this for me? I am nothing to you. I get the impression you are accustomed to traveling unencumbered," she said, as they walked toward the stairs leading to the upper story where the bedchambers were located. She held a wall torch in one hand to light the way. Already the air was freezing cold, now that they'd left the warmth of the great hall. She shivered.

Taking the fur mantle off his shoulders, he placed it over her, locking it in place with a brooch in the shape of writhing wolves. "Oh, nay, 'tis not necessary."

But he just smiled softly and moved closer so that her

back was to the stone wall. She no longer felt the chill of the air. His body heat wrapped her in a warm cocoon.

Oh, he is so attractive . . . for a man. Big in stature. Well-muscled, yet lean at the same time. Even his hair is pretty. And clean . . . do not forget clean, Esme. And that cleft in his chin . . . whew! I wonder how he shaves it. I should not be noticing all these things about him. I am practically a nun. But, Blessed Lord, the man exudes heat like a wicked hearth. Is this how the moth feels afore the flickering flame? "How can you be so hot when the air is so cold?" she blurted out.

"Mayhap I am hot for you."

"What a sinful thing to say!" she exclaimed with a gasp.

" 'Tis human nature. Even your Adam and Eve felt the same, I warrant."

She needed to change the subject before she did something scandalous, like lick the cleft in his chin. "I asked you why you would help me. You are evading the subject, methinks."

"Perchance I am just a noble fellow."

She made a snorting sound of disbelief.

He shrugged and ran a fingertip along the edge of her jaw, from ear to chin, then grazing over her parted lips. "Perchance 'tis just a whim."

That gentle caress stimulated a flood of liquid fire betwixt her legs and a burning at the tips of her peaked breasts. *What is he doing to me? Why am I reacting this way?*

"Or perchance I have ulterior motives for my offer," he said huskily. "Perchance I want something from you."

The glint in his blue eyes spelled danger to her . . . she just knew it did. Still she blundered on, like a lamb before the wolf. "I have naught to give," she said, just as huskily.

"Oh, yea, you do, m'lady." His voice was whisper soft and as tempting as sin.

He leaned forward then, his lips brushing lightly across hers. She heard a soft moan, and was not sure if it came from her or him. She wanted more. God help her, she wanted more. Sensing her acquiescence, the rogue kissed her again, but this time he *really* kissed her. Deep and wet and demanding. When she parted her lips, his tongue slipped inside her mouth, and her knees gave way. But wait, there were other things going on. A tongue kiss . . . she had heard of such, and had always imagined that she would be repulsed. She wasn't. He did not end the kiss. Instead, he put both hands on her hips and lifted her off the floor so that his manhood was aligned with her female place. She began to throb *there* in the most delicious manner.

He wanted her . . . in the way that men wanted women. And she suspected that she desired him, too. Who knew? Who knew?

When he finally drew away from her slightly, he smiled. "I never kissed a nun afore."

"I never kissed a Viking afore."

"A first for each of us, then." He waggled his eyebrows at her as if to convey that there was much more to come. "So, what say you to my offer, m'lady?"

"Which offer?" Her brain was so befuddled by his closeness and the kiss and the ache in her breasts and low down in her belly that she couldn't think clearly. "You make me breathless," she confessed, then immediately bit her bottom lip at her blunder. 'Twas not good to let a man know your weaknesses.

"Breathless is good," he said. His own breath was hot against her mouth.

Of course he would think breathless was good. He

was a man. But she was a woman beneath the nunly garb and 'twas best to guard her vulnerable points. She tried to shove him away. He let her slide down his body to her feet, slowly, slowly, slowly, but would not release her.

"Will it be yea or nay?" he insisted on knowing.

"I do not know. Honestly." She inhaled and exhaled several times, then said, "The only thing I know for certain is that I will have to go to confession again."

"Good," the Viking said, and kissed her again.

CHAPTER FOUR

⊗

*B*ack from the dead, part two . . .
  Would he live or would he die?

Only the gods knew now.

Helga stoked up the fire in the hearth of Vagn's bed-chamber to ward off the winter chill. It had snowed the night before, and through the arrow slit windows, she heard the wind howl eerily outside. Once satisfied that the flames were strong enough, she turned back to her patient. A short time ago, she'd forced a small amount of an herb posset through his lips. Now, with gentle care, she replaced the cloth on Vagn's burning forehead with a cool one and sat down on a chair next to his bed, resuming the vigil she'd been keeping the past two days.

Vagn had suffered a relapse immediately following their outrageous kiss in her solar . . . outrageous because the kiss had caused her bones to melt and her usually strong self-control to disappear like dandelion fluff on the wind. Not that the kiss had been the cause of his decline. Leastways, she hoped not. She would not want to add that to her wordfame as Helga the Homely. Helga the Kiss-Killer, or something equally objectionable. Nay, Vagn had just risen from his sickbed too soon. And his wounds had been grievous, after all.

She'd almost lost him three times when his fever had

raged so high he'd become delirious. Where she'd gotten the idea that he was hers to lose, she had no idea, but for some unfathomable reason she felt a personal interest in his recovery.

Always, in the throes of his delirium these two long days and nights, he called out for his brother Toste. She suspected that his longing for his brother had contributed to his relapse as much as his moving about too soon.

"How is he doing today?" her father asked. He came into the chamber and lowered his massive body into an armed chair on the other side of the pallet. He wore heavy furs over his tunic and *braies* to ward off the cold of the castle corridors.

"I think he's a little better."

"Is it my fault?" For all his blundering ways, Gorm was a good man. He fought like a warrior when called upon, but he cared intensely for those under his shield.

"Of course not. You probably saved his life, bringing him here from the battlefield. And I don't think your restraints did him any harm."

Gorm nodded his acceptance of her words.

"In truth, most men would have died long ago from such grave wounds. He is strong, I will give him that, and, though he claims to welcome death, he is fighting mightily for life."

"I just wanted to find a good husband for you, a strong man to take over my holdings. I will not live forever, Helga. Who will care for you when I am gone?" Her father's lips quivered with emotion.

"Oh, Father, you have never understood. I can care for myself."

"Alone," he said as if that were the worst thing that could happen to her.

"Toste . . . Toste . . ." Vagn moaned the familiar refrain.

Gorm shook his head from side to side. "Ne'er have I heard of brothers so close as those two seemed to be. 'Tis hard for me to understand why he cannot get over his brother's passing. 'Tis not like a beloved wife or child he has lost. Death is a way of life for us men of the North."

Helga shrugged. "They were twins. I daresay there is something mystical about twins . . . something the rest of us cannot understand. I always wished I had brothers or sisters."

Her father sighed deeply. "I always wanted brothers or sisters for you, too."

She had to smile at the old man's lack of subtlety. "Don't think you can guilt me into marriage and giving you babes to coddle." *If I could, I would, Father. Just to make you happy, if naught else.*

"It would be a good match. You and Vagn. Admit that much."

"Don't push me, Father." But in her mind, she kept remembering the kiss. *How can I be indifferent to a man who kisses like that? How can I not at least wonder about the possibilities when the rogue has such an effect on me?* "How is his horse doing? I swear, when Vagn is not muttering his brother's name, he is calling out for Clod. And what a name for a warhorse!"

Her father smiled, exposing his yellowed teeth. "I checked on his horse a bit ago. The starveling beast is not as old and decrepit as first appeared. Just malnourished and mistreated."

"By Vagn?" That surprised her.

Her father shook his head. "Nay. Methinks the animal was not long in his possession."

"I won him in a bet," a croaky voice said.

She and her father jerked with surprise and looked

down on Vagn, whose eyes were wide open. The fever must have broken. Praise the gods!

"Gambling! That figures," Helga remarked prissily, when what she felt was elation that the man just might recover, after all. In fact, tears of relief welled in her eyes. She removed the damp cloth from his forehead, which was still warm but no longer fiery hot.

"Are you weeping for me?" he asked weakly, licking his dry lips.

He lives! Oh, thank the heavens, he lives! "Nay, I weep out of frustration for all the trouble you have caused me."

"Daughter!" her father reprimanded her, but she could tell that he shared her joy that Vagn had wakened finally.

She quickly brought a cup of water to his bedside and held it to his lips. He drank thirstily. When done, he fell back on the pillow and said, "You cannot fool me, wench. You are smitten with me."

"Oh, really? And how wouldst you know that?" She was straightening his bed linens as she spoke, pretending an outrage she did not feel. *I must mask my feelings better, or this rogue will have me drooling over him like a besotted girl.*

"Don't you remember, sweetling?" he chided her softly.

Helga's heart wrenched, at the endearment. No man had ever called her such. "Remember what?" *Surely such a small happenstance as a kiss does not stick in his mind.*

"Our kiss," he replied matter-of-factly.

It did. "I forgot," she lied. *I will remember it always.*

"You kissed?" her father chortled. "Loki's lips! There is hope yet."

Now he has done it. My father will be planning the wedding feast.

"You are mine now," Vagn murmured even as he drifted back to sleep . . . a normal sleep, not the sickbed fever. "Not Toste's. Not any other man's. Mine."

He does not mean it. He must be under the influence of his fever. Brain fuzzy. Still, her heart sang at his words. In that instant, Helga the Homely became Helga the Hopeful. And that was a dangerous thing for her.

"Come closer," said the (Viking) wolf to the lamb . . .

A sennight later, Vagn was in the stable grooming his horse.

"What a good fellow you are, Clod! I no longer see your ribs, and your coat is nigh glossy with good health. Mayhap we both are survivors. What think you of that?"

Clod's answer was to reach back and lip him on the shoulder. A horse kiss.

"Are you ready for a long trip, boy?"

Clod neighed his response, which Vagn chose to believe was positive. After all, neigh and yea sounded much alike.

"That's good. I'm thinking one more week and we should both be in good enough shape."

"Are you talking to yourself?" Helga asked, coming into the barn and shutting the door after her to keep out the cold. She herself was warm in a full-length russet wool cape with a red fox lining. "Father asked me to find you. He is perched afore the fire in the great hall wanting to finish the game of chess you started yestereve."

Vagn did not look at her directly, but he was very much aware of her presence. He was in an odd mood—lustsome, actually, now that his body was regaining its normal vigor—and if Helga knew what was good for her, she would pick up her skirts and run for her life.

"I was talking to my horse," he said, continuing to

run the brush from back to flanks, then over again. "We are planning a journey." *Is that lavender I smell? Uhhhmmm. Come close, Helga, and let me see if it is your clothing or your skin that emits that scent. Just a little closer.*

He saw an expression of alarm flash across her face at the news of his impending departure; she immediately masked it. A good sign. She tried to fight her female urgings, but she was tempted by him. Vagn could tell these kinds of things about women. *Beware, m'lady, this Viking has been celibate for a year. You play with fire coming into my lair.*

"Where are you going?"

Blah, blah, blah! More chit-chat. Ask me why I have turned away from you. Ask me what I hide beneath my braies. "To Vestfold. To my father's estates." *But first, I have a few things to take care of here. Like you. And those luscious lips that beg for attention. Lick them one more time, m'lady. Go ahead. See how far you can push a Viking on the mend.*

She tilted her head to the side, confused. "I thought you had no love for your sire. I thought you mentioned being outlawed."

He nodded. *All right, let's get this somber discussion out of the way and move on to things of an unsomber nature.* "All that is true, but one of the last things Toste and I discussed afore his . . . afore the battle . . . was returning home to make peace with my father."

"So, you will do this in honor of your brother?"

Well, that is like a dose of cold water on my randiness. Why must women ask so many questions? Vagn sighed deeply, no longer in such a lustsome mood. "Nay! I will do it to *find* my brother. If he is alive, he will make his way there."

She gasped. "Oh, Vagn, you cannot go on believing that Toste survived. 'Tis impossible. Father said you were the only living Viking he saw that day, and you had been left for dead."

Do not dash my hopes so easily, m'lady. Do not. "My horse survived," he insisted stubbornly.

"And because this beast made it through the battle, you believe Toste did, too?" She looked at him as if he'd lost his mind.

Vagn decided to change the course of this way-too-personal discussion. "Do not call Clod a beast. It hurts his pride. See how he hangs his head." Actually, Clod was munching on some oats at his feet.

She smiled at his teasing and made a little curtsy of apology to his horse. Perhaps to him, as well.

He liked her smile. He liked the mouth that formed the smile. He liked what he could do with that smiling mouth . . . if she would just stop talking. "It is not just Clod that gives me hope," he said, somber again. "It's a feeling I have that Toste is not dead."

"The headaches?"

"That and much more. Toste and I have this connection, like an invisible thread. Each of us can sense when the other is happy or sad or in trouble." He shrugged, then laughed. "This morning I got a thickening of a sudden, and all I had been doing was shaving off my face hairs."

"A thickening?" she asked, frowning.

Holy Thor! The lady is twenty and eight years old, and she does not know what a thickening is. He waved a hand toward his nether region, which was hardening even more just at the mention of itself. *Well, that should clearly show her where my thoughts dwell.*

"Oh," she said, face flaming. Then she raised her chin

haughtily and said, "Surely you two did not share the same . . . uh, bed pleasures . . . from a distance."

He grinned. "We ne'er did in the past, but as sure as snow is cold I felt it this time. My brother is with a woman and enjoying himself. I would bet my life on it."

"Seems to me that men get . . . those things . . . without much provocation, like a belch or a sneeze."

He grinned. "There is no similarity between a thickening and a belch or a sneeze, believe you me."

She waved a hand as if to dismiss the disagreeable subject.

It wasn't disagreeable to him.

"It would be foolish to make the trip now. As you know, the winter freeze hits the Norselands much earlier than here. Even if you could find a ship to travel the stormy seas and ice-covered fjords at this time of year, it would be highly dangerous. Would it not be best to wait till spring?"

Vagn put aside his brush and gave her his full attention. In fact, he began to advance toward her.

He saw the moment that Helga realized she was alone with him in the barn, dark except for two wall torches attached to the horse stall. She backed up till her shoulders hit the wall with a thud.

"And what would I do with myself here all that time? Twiddle my thumbs?"

She glanced down at his one thumb in panic, as if the appendage were a wicked instrument of erotic torture.

Hmmm. It could be.

He stood so close to her he could smell the cold air on her skin and the wet fur of her cloak.

"Play chess?" she offered.

"For three months?" He arched his eyebrows at the ludicrous idea.

"I'm sure Father could use your help in training his troops, or running the estates."

Vagn braced his arms on the wall on either side of her head, trapping her. His eyes homed in on her mouth.

Her eyes darted right and left, as if seeking some means of escape.

Too late, my lamb. Too late. "You know what that would lead to, don't you? He would be grooming me for son-by-marriage."

"I had not thought of that."

"Do you know, Helga, it has been a year and more since I have lain with a woman?"

"What has that to do with me?" she asked in a near shriek, as he gave in to temptation and nuzzled his face into the curve of her neck.

He relished the softness of her flesh and the silkiness of her blond hair. And, yea, it was lavender he had smelled. Did she bathe in lavender-scented water? Intriguing picture, that.

"Everything," he said and took a small nibble at her earlobe. Then another. And another. He licked, too. What a delicacy! Better than any sweetmeat in a royal harem.

"Don't," she protested.

"Don't what?"

"Play with me. You are bored and seeking a dalliance to pass the time. I will not be used so."

What a perceptive maid! Play is exactly what I have in mind. "You would enjoy it."

"I doubt it, but that is neither here nor there. Do not dishonor me this way, Vagn."

Talk, talk, talk, talk, talk! Why do women feel the need to discuss everything to death? "Why is it dishonorable for a man and woman to pleasure each other?"

"Highborn men and women do not tumble in the hay without a marriage commitment."

They do where I come from. "Do you want such a commitment from me?"

"Nay!" The hands she placed on his chest to shove him away trembled, but he did not budge.

"Besides, do not be too sure about what highborn men and women do in private. You might be surprised."

"I do not care one way or another. I care about myself, and I will not allow you to play your games with me. Do not misread me, Vagn. You have the ability to turn me mindless with your touches and kisses, no doubt due to years of womanizing—"

"No doubt." His voice was droll with amusement, but what he thought was *I make her mindless with my touches and kisses? Very, very interesting!*

"—but that does not mean I am willing."

"You would be willing, believe you me."

"Spare me your boasts, braggart."

"Helga, Helga, Helga. There are two things I do exceedingly well. They both begin with the eff-sound. One of them is fighting. Do not force me to tell you what the other is."

"Crude lout!"

"Open your mouth for me, sweetling. Just so, with the tip of your tongue peeking out."

Her response was to bite her bottom lip with determination, just as he'd expected.

"I hate being vulnerable," she admitted then.

"Must you always be in control?"

"Yea, finally you understand."

"You are wrong, m'lady. I do not understand."

"You are vulnerable, too, Vagn. Do not frown at me. 'Tis true. You are unsettled by your near-death and the loss of your brother. You are looking for some stable, though temporary, lodestone to latch on to. Well, it will not be me. Someday you will come to your senses again. Then where would I be?"

"You think too much." *And talk too much.*

"You think too little. I am a challenge to you. Nothing more."

"Mayhap." *Probably.*

"Find some wench to relieve yourself with. There are willing maids aplenty about my father's keep."

"I do not want them," he said, leaning in close so that she could feel his breath when he said, "I . . . want . . . you."

She moaned. "I am not to your liking. I am not buxom or beautiful."

Your lips alone are enough to turn my legs to water. "You are beautiful to me."

"Liar. You called me homely."

"That was my brother."

"I suspect you and Toste have often traded places over the years. I suspect you called me Helga the Homely on as many occasions as he did."

He ducked his head sheepishly. "I apologize, Helga, for any hurt we may have caused you." *He meant it, too.*

"I do not want your apologies," she said, stamping her foot over his. Still he did not budge. "And I certainly do not want your self-serving lies."

Liar? Did the woman just call me a liar? Oh, the injustice of that remark cuts deep. "Helga, look at me." He adjusted his stance so that his elbows rested on either side of her head, not his palms, thus bringing him in closer. She was tall, only a few inches shorter than he, so her gaze was nigh level with his. "The desire you see on my face is genuine. You appeal to me." *If you only knew how much, you would run for your life, sweet virgin.*

He saw the disbelief on her face.

"Your mouth is exquisite, do you know that? The most kiss-some I have ever seen." *The things that mouth could do!*

"Wretch!"

"Your hair is like spun gold." *I would like to see it spread out on my bed furs.*

"Wretch!"

"I am dying to see your breasts." *And your navel and your hips and your buttocks and your woman's fleece.*

"Wretch! Now you have gone too far. You know good and well that I have no breasts to speak of." She swatted at his immovable chest.

"Aaah, but your nipples are big."

"How would you know that?" she asked with consternation.

"I know these kinds of things." *And well I should, with all the years I've been practicing wenching.*

"Useless knowledge. The kind of thing a philanderer like you would consider important."

"Do not judge me, Helga. You do not know me that well." *Even if you are right.*

"You are right about that, but I do not want to know you better."

"Aha! Now we get to the crux of the matter. You are afraid that you might like me." He laughed as he spoke, then hooked a heel behind her knees, twisted her body with expertise and followed her falling body down to the straw at their feet.

"Get off me, you oaf." She squirmed and flailed, but he just settled himself more comfortably atop her slim body.

"Have you ever made love on fox furs, Helga?" he murmured as he brushed off the fur-lined hood of her cloak and kissed a path along her jaw.

That gave her pause. Her body went stiff as she realized the position she was in.

His body went stiff, too. Leastways, one particular part did. "Just relax, sweetling."

"Are you mad?"

"Mayhap. Just let me have a little fun with you, Helga. I will not do anything serious." *Said the wolf to the lamb.*

"I will not be your plaything."

"Then let me be *your* plaything."

Before she had a chance to say him nay, he reached inside her cloak and cupped her left breast, whisking his thumb back and forth over the cloth-covered nipple. Her breast was indeed small, but the nipple was invitingly large, as he'd speculated, and it was growing larger under his ministration.

Her eyes went wide with wonder. No longer flailing or shoving him away, she just gaped at him.

"Do you like that, Helga?" he asked, kneading her small breast and pulling on the nipple.

Her only response was a groan and a toss of her head to the side, eyes squeezed shut.

He took that as permission to give equal attention to the other breast. Within moments, she was panting with woman-joy. Females with small breasts were more sensitive there than big-busted women. Leastways, that had been his experience. He couldn't wait to take her in his mouth. He made a bet with himself that he would make her reach her peak someday just by fondling and suckling her breasts.

But first things first.

He spread her cloak and then her thighs. Carefully he adjusted his hips so that his throbbing manpart rested against the groove of her womanhood, separated only by his *braies* and her gown. He hoped she throbbed, too. If she did not now, she would soon. That, he promised himself.

"Helga, look at me." Her face was still turned aside, eyes shut tight.

"I cannot. I am so ashamed."

"Of what? Being a woman? Look at me, please."

She did, and he saw that her eyes were wet with unshed tears. "I must be a wanton."

"Silly goose," he said and gently laid his lips over hers. He moved slowly at first, wanting her to become accustomed to him. Women were skittish. Like horses. Especially Helga, who would not appreciate the association, he was sure. That was the last thing she needed to hear. "Helga the Homely" had been objectionable; "Helga the Horse" would be intolerable. So he forgot the horse association and concentrated on worshiping her lips. Holding her face in his hands, he nibbled. He smoothed. He licked. He caressed. Just the friction of his mouth over her so desirable lips was pure ecstasy. He'd meant to please her, but he'd ended pleasing himself.

"You taste like honey . . . and cloves," he said.

"You taste like horse," she said.

He laughed. *It's not the first time I've been told that.*

But she didn't seem to be objecting to his horsiness, so he chose not to take offense.

"Open, Helga," he murmured against her wet lips.

She did—in her innocence, far wider than was necessary. He inserted his tongue and began a slow in-and-out rhythm that simulated the sex act. A most excellent pupil, she quickly learned the lesson and did the same to him. He thought he just might swoon, so intense was his arousal.

And speaking of arousals!

She was undulating her hips against him in a rhythm as old as time. He assumed it was instinct and not experience that caused her to move so enticingly. He pulled back slightly and stared down at her.

Her lips were kiss-swollen and wet. Her eyes were glazed over with passion.

"Are you a virgin?" he asked her of a sudden. *Of course she is a virgin. Her father said she was.*

"Yea, I am," she answered, too dazed to be offended by his question. At first. He saw the moment when she realized just what he'd been asking. Anger suffused her already flushed face. Then she asked him, "Are you a virgin?"

"Nay, but I feel as if this is all new with you."

"Hah!" she said and rolled away from under him, standing clumsily. Apparently his question had been a bucket of cold water on her ardor. His, on the other hand, was still rock hard and ready. "I do not know what trick you played with your lewd fingers to turn me into a harlot, but it will not happen again."

He leaned back on his elbows in the straw. "Methinks your father was wrong about you."

He could tell she did not want to ask, but she did anyway. "What was my father wrong about?"

"Your female parts are not withered into raisins. They are plump and juicy and wet. I would bet my life on it."

She inhaled sharply and tried her best not to react to his teasing. "Are you ever serious?"

"On occasion."

"Speaking of serious, you told me that you would not do anything *serious* to me in the straw. You lied."

He shook his head. "Nay, you are wrong to malign me so. What I did . . . what *we* did was not serious. When I get into the *serious* business of lovemaking, you will know it. And I will see just how juicy and unwithered you are there." He glanced pointedly at the juncture of her thighs.

"You are by far the crudest, coarsest, crassest man I have ever met. They ought to call you Vagn the Vulgar." She was towering over him, hands on hips.

"Now that you mention name-calling, I think I have come up with a new name for you, Helga," he said as he watched her attempt, futilely, to brush all the straw out of her cloak. She even had straw in her blond hair, but he would not tell her that. "Don't you want to know what it is?"

"Nay, I do not. It's probably something crude, like Helga the Harlot."

He made a clucking sound of disapproval with his tongue. "Helga the Magnificent."

"I hope you do not consider that a compliment."

"Of course it is a compliment."

Helga turned on her heel then and stormed out of the stable, but not before telling him exactly what he could do with his compliments. She must have learned that midden-talk in the rough business sector of Jorvik.

Vagn just smiled, well pleased with the events of this evening. Mayhap he would stay at Gorm's estate these three months after all. Mayhap he had just discovered something interesting to while away the time.

But a nagging voice in the back of his head kept asking whether Helga had been right. Was he bored and just using her to pass the time? Was his anguish over Toste distorting his view of Helga and his whole thus-far-pointless life? Was he being fair in seducing Helga when he was unsure of his intentions?

All these were unfamiliar questions for Vagn. And therein lay the problem. In the past, he and Toste had done what they'd wanted, when they'd wanted, consequences be damned. Was he finally, at the ripe old age of thirty and one, growing up?

How to outwit a lackwit . . .

A large wood fire blazed in three of the massive central hearths in Gorm's great hall, providing welcome warmth to the two hundred and more servants and retainers who gathered there following the evening meal. Before one of those fires, Gorm and Vagn dueled over the board game *hnefatafl*, at which they were equally matched. Around them, soldiers diced and conversed, usually on subjects of war or women. Servants bustled about removing the remnants of the meal—primarily roast acorn-fed pig with manchet bread—and dismantling the trestle tables, which would be replaced with box-bed sleeping arrangements around the perimeter of the room.

Helga had disappeared soon after dining. Avoiding him, no doubt. He could understand that. He was a soldier who knew how to stalk his prey. Poor prey! Even when he attempted to curb his baser appetites, he seemed unable to keep Helga out of his mind. His hunger for her grew by the minute—pathetic in its intensity.

"Helga was with you in the stable for a long time this afternoon," Gorm said of a sudden.

Vagn's hunger died a quick death. Had his pathetic mind-wanderings been so apparent? "What? You have spies watching over me now?"

"I have always had spies watching over you. But that

is neither here nor there. Have you made any progress with my daughter?"

Vagn had been sipping at a horn of ale and started to choke. *Progress? Does he mean what I think he means by that word?* "What a question for a father to ask! Do you encourage men to seduce your daughter?"

"Not any man. Just you."

A trap has been set for me here. Be careful, Vagn; be very careful. "Well, I am not going to discuss any love-play there may or may not have been with your daughter. So forget that."

"I did not ask for specifics, just a general progress report."

"Nay!"

Gorm smirked, as if Vagn had given him some significant answer. They continued to play, moving their ivory pieces about the carved oak board.

I wonder how soon I can slip away without offending this wily old bear. "Why me, for the love of Frigg?" he asked Gorm.

"The time is right. I am not well, Vagn . . . oh, do not misread my words, I am not about to fly off to Valhalla anytime soon. But I grow old and my heart hurts on occasion and, well, I feel a need to put my life in order . . . to tie up all the loose ends, to make sure Briarstead continues in good hands."

"One of those loose ends being Helga?"

Gorm nodded.

I wonder how Helga would feel about being called a loose end. Hah! I already know the answer to that. About as much as she liked being called Helga the Homely. Or Helga the Magnificent.

"I indulge Helga overmuch. Always have. But methinks she likes you, and that gives me hope."

"I am not so sure about that." He told Gorm the coarse expression Helga had used with him that afternoon.

Gorm chuckled, not at all disturbed by his daughter's less-than-maidenly language. "That is my Helga," he boasted.

"I do not love her, Gorm." For some reason, it saddened Vagn to say that, but it was the truth.

Gorm waved a hand in front of him and said, "Pfff! Respect her. Treat her properly. That is enough for me. If love comes later, that is good and well, but it is not a necessary ingredient for a noble match."

"Would you force her into marriage?" *Why am I indulging in this ridiculous conversation? It has naught to do with me. Really.*

"Never! I want to secure her future, but not by forcing her into wedlock. But if a good man were to convince her . . ." Gorm deliberately let his words trail off.

"I need time to think on this. I will not be rushed." What he really thought, though, was that he'd better be careful with his seduction tactics. He might go too far and find himself leg-locked in a trap of his own making—or, to be more precise, cock-locked. But then, he had escaped such locks afore.

A maid named Greta walked up and refilled their horns of ale from a pottery pitcher. Then she handed Vagn a linen packet. "Here are the megrim powders you asked me to get from the village healer."

"Still having the head pains, eh?" Gorm asked.

Vagn nodded. "They come and they go, but betimes they are so bad I can barely see."

The maid dawdled about, wiping the table with a damp cloth.

"Thank you, Greta," he said, handing her a silver piece for her efforts.

Still she did not leave.

Greta was about eighteen years old with blond braids, large breasts and nicely rounded hips. She kept slanting her eyes at him through half-lowered eyelids. She was a tempting morsel, and Vagn knew she would join him in the bed furs if he wished. He liked looking at her, but, for some reason, as randy as he had been earlier, he did not wish to bed her.

Just then, Vagn noticed Helga a short distance away, speaking to one of the Briarstead embroiderers. Helga glanced at him, then at Greta, then back at him. He could tell what she thought by her heightened color and the sneer on her luscious lips. When next she looked his way, he winked at her. Their gazes held for a long second, and he knew that she was remembering their meeting in the stable. Then Helga huffed out of the great hall.

When Vagn turned back to the game board, he realized that Gorm had taken in the short interchange between him and Helga. He knew because Gorm was laughing heartily. Only when Gorm had stopped laughing and wiped tears of mirth from his eyes did a beaming Gorm tell him, "Take all the time you want, son."

Give me a peck, baby. Eew, is that worm I smell on your breath? . . .

That night, Vagn dreamed about his brother Toste. Or mayhap it would best be described as a nightmare.

Wherever Toste was, he was surrounded by black crows—the biggest black crows Vagn had ever seen. Some of the crows were singing, of all things. Bells rang. He saw a human shin bone split in half and fly through the air. The smell of honey and beeswax permeated his senses. And the back of his head throbbed as if it might explode.

Then Vagn saw the most extraordinary thing. Toste kissed one of the crows, and it felt good. Damn good.

Vagn slept restlessly all night and awakened in a sad mood. If the ravens of death surrounded his brother, then he must truly have passed over to the other world. But what did the crow-kiss mean?

CHAPTER FIVE

♧

L ike sands through the hourglass...
   Time was of utmost importance to Esme, but, unfortunately, her time ran out the next afternoon.

Without any advance warning, her father and her two brothers arrived at the abbey, armed to the teeth. Obviously, they hadn't come to discuss her health or well-being.

To her relief, Toste was off somewhere practicing his swordsmanship, and Bolthor had gone to a neighboring village to purchase horses for them. Her father hated Norsemen with a vengeance and would kill the two Vikings for no other reason than the color of their hair, if the whim overcame him, which it ofttimes did. So it was best that they stay out of sight. She'd already sent Sister Mary Rose to warn them.

Esme waited with Mother Wilfreda in her solar for her father to come to them. As soon as she'd heard of her father's arrival, Esme had gone to her room and donned a clean brown robe and matching veil over a white wimple. Large wooden prayer beads hung from her rope belt. She looked as much like a devoted novice as she could manage on such short notice. And how pathetic it was that, at four and twenty years of age, she still behaved like a girl trying to meet her sire's expectations.

Her strategy the past ten years had been a good one—as far as it went. Avoid and delay. Oh, it might sound cowardly and meek, but women must needs fight with the only tools they had. Mother Wilfreda had taught her every aspect of running an abbey, which was not so different from running an estate. If she only survived long enough to take over her mother's estate.

Well, her father's unannounced visit might very well place a cog in the wheels of that plan. Leastways, he would try his best to do so.

Father Alaric had volunteered to greet the visitors out in the courtyard. Now, the sound of Lord Blackthorne's booming voice grew closer and closer, mean and menacing.

"Where is she? Hiding, no doubt. And well she should. I have had more than enough of her willfulness. I thought by now you would have beaten some sense into the misbegotten maid," her father said.

"Nay, Lord Blackthorne, she is not hiding. She awaits you in the solar with our good abbess. And be-be-beating? You expected us to whip Esme?"

"*Good*, abbess? Hah! The only good thing about that dried-up crone is she's so old she's bound to die soon."

Esme gasped and looked at her aunt, who just shook her head at her father's coarse tongue and blatant lack of affection for his dead wife's sister. It didn't even bear mentioning that her father and Wilfreda were about the same age, neither yet ailing.

"Relax, child. Do not show your fear," Mother Wilfreda advised as she sat on a high stool before a table, grinding medicinal herbs with a mortar and pestle. A sweet aroma wafted through the air—cloves and something else, possibly chamomile. "Pick up your mending. Do something with your hands so he won't notice their trembling."

No sooner did Esme take a torn surplice in hand than the wooden door swung open and banged against the timber wall, almost breaking off the leather hinges. For a certainty, there would be dent marks in the wood.

"There you are, girl," her father said, giving her a once-over which could be summed up in the sneer on his thin lips. Her father tended to call her "girl" overmuch, probably to put her in her place. There were no happy greetings after an absence of a year, no hugs of welcome. All to be expected. At forty and eight years, with only a sprinkling of gray in his black hair, her father could still be considered a handsome man, if not for the lines of cruelty that bracketed his eyes and mouth. He was a big man, and today he wore fine leather, calf-high boots, a chain *shert* with an attached coif over a wool tunic and *braies*, with sword and long knife scabbarded at his belt, all covered by a sweeping fur-lined wool cloak with a gilded brooch fastener. Similarly attired were her two brothers. Dressed for a fight, they were.

With me?

"Lady Esme." Her brother Cedric greeted her with eyes as cold as her father's. *At least he did not call me "girl."* His quick scrutiny took in her drab attire and dismissed her as beneath his contempt.

"Sister," her other brother Edward said, with an emphasis on the word that said loud and clear he felt no bond with her, despite their shared blood.

Esme nodded her acknowledgment of their salutations, such as they were. *The hostility is so thick in this chamber I could cut it with a knife. And so serious they all are. I feel like sticking my tongue out at the three of them. Well, that is mature, Esme. No wonder my father calls me "girl."*

"I hear you are betrothed, Edward." She tried to make

conversation—a futile effort when faced with the three brooding men, who would rather be anywhere in wintertime but a remote nunnery.

"Yea, and what is it to you, sister?"

Well, that was certainly pleasant.

Mother Wilfreda made a tsk-ing sound of disgust. "Have you taught your sons such ill decorum, John?" the nun inquired of Esme's father.

Good for you, Mother. Stick out your tongue, too. That would show them. Bloody boors! Oops, I guess I will have to go to confession again for saying "bloody." Oh, well, it was worth it, even if I didn't say it aloud.

"Behave thyself," her father said to Edward, clouting him on the side of the head with one of his calfhide gauntlets.

Ouch! Note to myself: Stay out of clouting distance from Father.

Edward winced and backed away, scowling at Esme, as if it were her fault he had such poor manners.

Well, that was certainly pleasant, too.

"How is Elsbeth?" she asked Cedric. *As if I care!* Cedric was the oldest of her brothers at thirty. Elsbeth was his wife of at least ten years. Most times, Elsbeth had her nose so high in the air she could scarce see in front of herself.

"Big with child," he replied grudgingly, casting a surreptitious glance at their father. No doubt he feared a slap with the same gauntlet if he spoke to her with disrespect. "She should be dropping the babe any day now."

Blessed Mary, those two breed like rabbits. "Your seventh, as I recall."

"Yea, and all girls," he spat out as if girls were on a par with slugs. *How like our father he is!*

"Go, holy man, get us some of that mead this abbey is

famous for," her father ordered the priest, as if he were a menial servant. Then he sank down into an armchair far too close to Esme. Her brothers stood on either side of the open doorway since there were no other chairs in the room.

Oh, good Lord, he's sitting down. That must mean he plans to stay for a while. Should I discuss the weather? Or ask about his health? Nay, best to shut my teeth and wait till he tells me the purpose of this visit.

The priest scurried off, no doubt thankful to be out of the nobleman's presence. Esme would scurry off, too, if given the chance. She doubted Father Alaric would return. He would probably go to the chapel and pray. A good idea. St. Jude, patron saint of hopeless causes—that's who would get her pleas if she had the chance.

Just then, through the open doorway could be heard a cacophony of animal and human sounds. "Oink-oink. Ruff-ruff. Come here, you thievin' animals." Almost immediately, they saw the five-legged pig shoot down the corridor, past the open doorway, with a string of sausages dangling from its mouth, followed closely by a dog the size of a pony, drool hanging from its mouth, and those two followed by Sister George. Who knew the piglet could trot so fast? The oinks and barks and shrieks could be heard for a long time after the trio passed. Eventually, the noise faded to silence.

Her father's and brothers' jaws dropped practically to their chests. In the end, her father muttered, "I always knew this abbey was strange. I did not realize how strange."

If you only knew! Pray Sister Stefana doesn't have a nude dancing epiphany about now.

"Not so strange. Have you no animals at Blackthorne?" Mother Wilfreda asked with a chuckle.

"Not a freakish five-legged pig!" he said, giving his head a shake of disbelief at what he'd just witnessed. "Who keeps a pig indoors?"

"There's probably pig shit all over this place," Edward added with a sniff of disgust.

Well, sometimes. And dog, and goat, and horse, and cat, and duck, and whatever animals Sister George has rescued this week.

"Someone ought to give them all a good sharp kick in the arse, including the nun." That was Cedric's contribution.

Nice fellow, Cedric. Kicking a nun.

Her father turned his attention back to Mother Wilfreda and said, "Take your seeds and stinksome powders elsewhere, Freda. I wish to speak with my daughter in private."

Uh-oh.

"Anything you wish to say to Esme can be said in my presence," her aunt insisted.

Bless you, Mother. Bless you.

"You always were a bothersome bitch," her father said lazily, his eyes piercing the nun with hatred. "No wonder you could never find a man to spread your legs."

"That's enough!" Esme said, standing suddenly and letting the surplice float out of her hands down to the floor. Esme had defied her father's wishes over the years, but she'd never taken a stand openly. It was well past time that she did so, even if it meant suffering the consequences. She could not allow her father to take out his frustration with her by attacking those who protected her. "You will not speak to my aunt in that manner. You will treat her with the respect which her holy office inspires." *Are you there, St. Jude? I might be needing you in a moment or two.*

Mother Wilfreda darted a look of surprise her way. No wonder. Esme had suddenly developed a spine. About time!

Both of her brothers took a step forward menacingly, low growls coming through their gritted teeth, but their father raised a halting hand.

"Have you gone mad, girl?"

Undoubtedly. "Nay. In fact, I've never been more sane. I am sick to here of your ranting and raving," she said, slicing a hand across her throat. *Oh, God, some strange being has taken over my tongue.* "It is always about what you want. You. You. You. Well, listen good, Father. You cannot bend me to your will. Not in the past. Not now. Not ever." *Well, I must say I am impressed with myself. Very good, Esme. And I'm still alive.*

Her father clapped sarcastically to show his disdain for her "performance."

She held on to the back of the chair, white-knuckled, then inhaled and exhaled to catch her breath. Being brave took more energy than she would have thought. She hoped her legs didn't collapse.

"This is your fault, Freda," her father said, addressing her aunt. "You have been nurturing this hostility in my daughter, just as you did with my wife all those years ago."

"Anything my sister Anne did was of her own doing, John," her aunt said with a calmness that would do a saint proud.

"I doubt that. Where did Anne get the idea to pass her dower lands on to a daughter, if not from you?"

"Mayhap from you, John," Mother Wilfreda answered, again without rancor. She continued to grind her herbs as she spoke, as if a visit by three armed men, a sudden display of independence by a novice nun, and the growing anger of a Saxon nobleman were everyday occurrences at the abbey.

"M-m-me?" her father sputtered.

"Yea. If you and your sons had not treated Esme so cruelly, Anne never would have insisted on passing Evergreen to her daughter. You forced her to take every precaution the law allows."

"Esme never lacked for anything."

How about love? Esme thought.

"How about love?" her aunt asked, as if reading her mind.

"Love? Pffff! She could have been wed to any one of a dozen *thegns* over these ten years, and she scoffed at every one of them."

"Men of your choosing," Esme interjected. She was tired of everyone speaking over her as if she were a child, as if her opinion were of no importance. "Puppets who would do your will. Decrepit old men on their deathbeds, who would pass my mother's lands on to you. Weak young milksops who tripped over themselves to do the great Lord Blackthorne's bidding. All men who would ensure, in the end, that my lands would become your lands." *By the saints, I must have a death wish.*

"That is neither here nor there. Since when do daughters get to choose their mates? 'Tis a father's role, and always has been."

"Well, this daughter says nay." *Did I say that? Really? I am beginning to be really impressed with myself. Of course, I may be dead soon, but impressive.*

"What would you do with Evergreen, even if I were barmy enough to allow you to receive it? You are a woman. What know you of handling a landed estate, small as that one is?"

"I know more than you could ever imagine," Esme said. "What do you think I have been doing these past ten years? I have learned the ways of handling an estate, everything from planning meals to ordering supplies, directing weavers, planting farmlands, working with the village cotters." She threw her hands out in an all-encompassing manner. "Everything."

Her father snorted his opinion. "What a wooly-witted half-brain! How will you protect those lands? Where is your *hird* of soldiers to patrol the borders and keep enemies from invading? Ah, let me guess. You will hire a troop of nun-warriors to shield you from invasion. Ha ha ha." He looked to one son, then the other, so they could join in the jest. Soon the three were laughing uproariously at her and the image of nun-warriors.

Esme felt heat infuse her face. Her father was right. This was her one weakness, one which she would have to address after she inherited. There were still some of her maternal grandparents' retainers at Evergreen, but they were few and mostly old. She needed hard fighting men, but she could only hire troops after she gained money, and she could only gain money after she regained her mother's lands. Her father certainly hadn't been saving all the revenues for her these ten years.

"Go pack your bags, girl. You are coming home to-day."

"I am not!" *St. Jude made me say it. Or was it the devil? Either way, my father is not going to like my obstinacy.*

Her father stood and advanced toward her. Once he towered over her, he said, "You will . . . even if I have to carry you out over my shoulder. Your charade of being a novice is over. You will obey me."

"Why would you take me home . . . as if I have any

home, other than this nunnery? Will you murder me on the way, or after we arrive at Blackthorne?"

"Murder will not be necessary, wench," he drawled. "Your wedding will take place as soon as the banns can be read. Two sennights at most."

The fine hairs stood out on the back of Esme's neck. "Oh? And who is the lucky bridegroom?" *I can just imagine.*

"Oswald of Lincolnshire."

I cannot imagine what you are thinking. Oswald? Esme tilted her head in confusion. "He is already wed, with several children."

"Not that Oswald," her father said, lifting his chin defiantly.

"I don't under . . . oh, nay, you cannot mean the grandsire. Oswald the Elder?" *Finally my father has pushed the limits of cruelty.*

"The very same. You are fortunate, girl. He is a lord in his own right."

"He is older than you," she said, disbelief ringing in her voice. "And last I heard, he had a disease in his manparts." Inside, Esme felt like weeping. If she had ever hoped her father might entertain affection for her, that hope was gone now. "You are a beast."

Her father shrugged.

"How could you, John?" Mother Wilfreda said. "Tsk tsk tsk! Even for you, that is low."

"Mind your own business, hag," he told the nun without even glancing her way.

"Either pack a bag or come as you are," her father said to Esme, grabbing her forearm in a pinching grip.

She shrugged out of his grasp and yelled, "Unhand me, you demon! I would rather be dead than wed to that sick old man."

Her father swung his hand and slapped her hard across the face, clutching on to her forearm again. "'Tis time you learned to obey your betters."

The blow was so hard, Esme saw stars. She staggered backward and almost fell to the floor. Her father's grasp on her arm held her up.

"You wretch!" Mother Wilfreda said and rose abruptly to her feet, knocking over her stool and scattering seeds and powders all over the table.

Cedric stepped in front of the nun and blocked her passage so that she could not come to Esme's assistance.

Edward, meanwhile, came toward her and grabbed her other forearm. Together, her father and Edward began to drag her across the room and out the doorway. As they headed down the corridor, she noticed a confused Father Alaric walking across the great hall carrying a tray with three wooden goblets of mead. Along the wide corridor that led to the massive double front doors, two dozen nuns and novices peered out of doorways, all of them wide-eyed with fear, some of them weeping. The overly tall Sister Mary Rose held a small skull in her shaking hands, probably St. John the Baptist; she had several of those. She must have been working on her supply of relics when the "visitors" arrived. But wait. Sister Mary Rose had been sent to warn Toste and Bolthor to stay away. Had she returned already, or never gone out?

"Bloody hell! Who are they?" her father asked, coming to an abrupt halt.

Edward and Cedric said foul words under their breaths.

At first, Esme thought it must be the nuns that had prompted their expletives. But when she raised her head, she saw a wondrous sight.

"The Vikings are coming! The Vikings are coming!" Sister Hildegard shrieked suddenly.

"Thank God!" Esme murmured.

Standing in the open doorway that led out to the courtyard were Toste and Bolthor. Each leaned casually against an opposite door jamb, ankles crossed.

Toste's right hand held a broadsword. He was testing its sharp edge with the thumb of his left hand. Back and forth his thumb flicked as if strumming an instrument . . . a lethal instrument. His posture bespoke nonchalance; his gesture bespoke just the opposite, especially when his eyes lit on Esme's cheek, which probably showed the imprint of her father's hand.

In Bolthor's right hand was a mighty battle-ax as tall as he was, and Bolthor was a giant. Its spear point touched the floor, its double-edged ax blade caressed his cheek. His expression was relaxed, but his one good eye displayed outrage as well.

"You heard me, wench. Who are they?" her father asked again and increased the pressure on her forearm till she thought he might break the bone.

Esme was tearful, but no longer fearful, when she answered honestly, "They are my champions, my friends."

Never make a Viking mad . . .

A blazing fury ripped through Toste.

He saw the livid finger welts on Esme's pale cheek. No small slap had that been. Nay, a man of considerable size had put his full weight behind that blow. Her father, no doubt. And the viselike grip the same culprit had on her arm now would leave bruises, for sure. The one brother let loose his grip on her other arm and stepped to the side, still flanking his father's right side while the

other brother flanked the left. It was a strategic move
designed to shield their father and cage in their sister at
the same time.

Oh, you fellows are in such trouble.

Many people, prodded on by biased clerics, liked to
think Vikings were ruthless rapers and pillagers . . . that
greed and bloodthirst ruled their kinder impulses. 'Twas
not so. In fact, afore many a battle, Norse chieftains ofttimes called out, "Spare the women and children."

So Lord Blackthorne's abuse of his daughter sat ill
with Toste and Bolthor, who had been informed a short
time ago of his arrival by a huffing and puffing Sister
Mary Rose.

But a good warrior knew to control his temper. Rage
diminished a man's skills. Timing was all. *Becalm thyself, Toste. Becalm thyself.*

Once the three men and Esme got closer, Toste yelled
out toward the courtyard, "Bjorn and Sveinn, have you
posted guards about the abbey borders? You have? Good.
And close at hand?" He nodded as if someone had answered him.

"The archers are poised on the roof, as well," Bolthor
told him, his voice loud enough for everyone to hear.

It was a ruse, of course. But Lord Blackthorne did not
know that. Leastways, not yet. Or leastways, Toste hoped
not.

"Sister Esme," he said with a nod, putting emphasis
on her nunly title, even though he knew it did not fit her
actual state. He did not want her father to think there
was anything between them. Not that there *was* anything between them. Yet.

Her eyes met his. She blinked several times then, as if
to convey some hidden message. He'd played this game
many times with his brother over the years, and he

"read" her well. She told him she was unharmed and cautioned him to be careful.

"Who are these . . . people?" her father asked her, still maintaining his iron grip on her arm.

"Father, let me intro—"

But Toste put up a halting hand and spoke in her stead. "Mayhap I am a wayfarer just passing by. Mayhap I am a friend to Mother Wilfreda. Mayhap I am here contemplating the religious life for myself or one of my kin." Toste paused, then added, "Or mayhap I am your worst enemy."

Bet on the latter, villain.

Lord Blackthorne's lips curled back, and he actually growled. His two sons put hands to the hilts of their swords.

"I repeat, who are you?" Blackthorne asked through gritted teeth.

Toste looked pointedly at the hand which still held his daughter. "I am Toste Ivarsson, and this is Bolthor the Skald, and if you do not release that nun this instant, I will cut off your hand."

Esme's eyes went wide at his words.

What? You thought I was a pacifist Viking?

The fool did not release his hold on his daughter, who tried to intercede, "Toste is just teasing. Ha ha ha. What a jester he is!"

Do not be naive, m'lady. I would slice your father through in a trice and think naught of it.

Her father looked askance at her. "Toste? You call the heathen by name? By the rood, girl, if you have given your virginity to a bloody Viking, I will take a birch rod to your back till there is no skin left."

Keep it up, Blackthorne. You are tempting my sword.

"Oh, well, I think I would have something to say about

that," Toste said, stepping forth and forcibly pulling
Esme out of her father's grip and to his side, where he
tucked her under his left arm. The sword in his right
hand remained poised at the ready. Bolthor had moved
closer to the men as well, and he held his halberd in
the battle position. "For your information, Lord Blackthorne, though I question your paternal rights at this
point, I have not lain with your daughter."

*I will, though. You can be sure of that. She will owe
me much at the end of this day, and I do not mean coin.*

"How dare you intervene between a father and his
daughter?"

"I dare." *And I want to.*

"King Edgar will have something to say about this
matter, I daresay."

*Blah, blah, blah. Let's end the talking and start fight-
ing. My stomach is growling with hunger and my tongue
thirsts for a big horn of Margaret's Mead.* Toste shrugged.
"Edgar is not my king."

Her father's brows narrowed with suspicion. "Has she
hired you and a troop of Vikings to man the parapets at
Evergreen? If so, you should know that the girl has no
coin. A pauper nun, she is, and not even that."

*Why does he keep calling her "girl"? Ah, I see, prob-
ably to belittle her and make her feel subservient. Voltar
the Vicious used to do that with his young wife, Olga
Quiet-Tongue.* "Oh? Really? Tsk tsk, *Lady* Esme, you
did not inform me of that fact." Esme was looking at him
as if he'd gone mad. He had. Mad with rage. Mad with
the injustice of his twin's death. Mad with the injustice
of Esme's ill-treatment. Mad with the blood-lust rising
in him, along with another kind of lust. Mad, mad, mad!
He turned his attention back to Lord Blackthorne. "Mayhap your good king would be interested in knowing

what happened to Evergreen's revenues these past ten years." He blinked his eyes innocently at the thieving nobleman.

"You . . . you . . ." Blackthorne sputtered.

"Well, it has been pleasant chatting with you, Lord Blackthorne, and you two knaves, too, but Bolthor and I were about to have a cup of mulled mead. It is damned cold out there. Do not slam the doors on your way out." With that, Toste took Esme by the hand and began to walk toward the great hall. He did not mind putting his back to the three blackguards, because he knew Bolthor was watching out for him.

"Thank you," she whispered, now that they were out of her father's hearing.

"Do not thank me yet, m'lady." He stared straight ahead as he spoke, still leading her by the hand. "Your bill will be paid in good time."

"My father already told you I have no coin, but I will be able to pay you eventually . . . if you are willing to forgo immediate payment. I am more than aware that you put your life on the line for me today."

"I have no interest in coin. Wealth aplenty do I already have. But you will pay. You will pay."

She frowned. "How?" She gasped then as understanding hit her. "You would not demand such. Surely you would not."

"I would, and I will."

"You have not seen the last of me," Lord Blackthorne yelled.

Toste had not realized that Lord Blackthorne still lingered inside the abbey. "Yea, yea, yea," he called back over his shoulder. Cowards always threw out threats when they thought they were outside the range of sword or arrow.

"And the banns for your wedding will be called, whether you like it or not, girl." This threat was addressed to Esme, of course. Neither of them turned to look at her father, but pretended they did not hear.

"You are getting married?" Toste asked Esme.

"Over my dead body."

"Good. I never lie with married women." *Or dead ones, for that matter.*

She gasped again. "Your constant jests are . . . disarming."

Hah! I will show you disarming when you are flat on your back, legs spread, with a smile on your face that only a Viking could put there.

"I'll be back afore you can blink, Viking," her father shouted.

"Holy Thor, is he still here? The man never gives up."

"Nay, he does not. I know that better than any," Esme said with a sigh.

"And with me will be a large troop of soldiers." Toste turned his head slightly so he could look back. Yea, her bullheaded father still stood at the open doorway with his two sons, all of them red-faced with frustration and anger.

"He means it," Esme said.

"I do not doubt that, but we will be long gone."

"We?"

"You, me and Bolthor."

He could see hope war with distrust on her too-open face. "Where are we going?"

"Methinks 'tis time for a cart delivery of mead barrels to the trading vessels in Jorvik." He and Bolthor had already discussed a preliminary plan, but the details were yet to be worked out.

"My father and brothers will recognize us."

Women! They must know all the details. They must argue every point. Why can they not just let men, with their greater intellect, handle things? "Not if we are in disguise."

"Disguise? What kind of disguise?"

Be quiet, m'lady, or I am going to abandon you here to your father. He decided to give her one last explanation, and that would be that. "Well, there is no disguising you. You will have to hide in one of the barrels, but Bolthor and I . . . hmmm . . . our best disguise would probably be as . . ."

"What?"

"Nuns."

Big butts are timeless . . .

"My bottom is too big." Esme's voice was muffled, coming as it was from the inside of a barrel. Besides that, her brain was starting to feel fuzzy from the mead fumes still lingering in the oak staves.

"Try to lie straighter so that your buttocks go flat," Mother Wilfreda advised.

"My buttocks never go flat," Esme said. "Standing, bending, sitting, lying down—'tis all the same. My bottom is too big."

It was barely past dawn on the morning after her father's visit. Ravenshire, the estate owned by Toste and Bolthor's friend Eirik, lay a considerable distance away. It would take a full day and mayhap more of hard riding in this cart, with unknown dangers in between, most especially her father's troops. They must needs start soon.

But first, Esme had to fit inside a barrel, which was proving impossible. A barrel had been laid on its side in the back of a market cart. It was the biggest mead barrel they had, and still Esme couldn't fit her whole body inside. First, she'd tried to back in, feet first, but when she'd gotten as far as her hips and buttocks, she'd had to crawl back out. Now, she was headfirst in the barrel, with her buttocks sticking out, and Sister Margaret and Mother Wilfreda shoving, to no avail.

"I do not think your arse is too big," she heard Toste say.

Esme went stiff with embarrassment and stopped trying to squirm herself into the barrel. *Oh, for the love of Mary, the Viking is here and he's looking at my bottom.*

"I agree," Bolthor said. "A wench cannot have too big an arse, to my way of thinking. Gives a man something to hold on to."

Sister Mary Rose giggled and Mother Wilfreda said in a droll tone of voice, "Nice disguises!"

"Methinks it would make a good poem," Bolthor continued. "Viking Men and Their Love of Ample Arses."

"Don't you dare," Esme said as shrilly as she could, still half in and half out of the barrel. "And someone get me out of here."

Toste grabbed her by the waist and pulled her hard so that the back of her shoulders hit his chest, and the two of them almost fell to the ground. Fortunately, his greater weight held them upright, with her legs dangling off the ground. Unfortunately, once they were upright, she found herself still wrapped in his embrace from behind, and the rogue wasn't letting go. In fact, the very bottom she had been bemoaning minutes ago was pressed against a part of him that was rather big, too.

That was when she looked up at Bolthor, who was making a throat-clearing noise as he prepared to recite his newest saga. He wore a huge brown nun's robe with a wimple and veil covering his head. His black eye patch was gone and his dead eye stared straight ahead in a most unsettling fashion. A crucifix hung from a thick chain onto his massive chest, and wooden prayer beads dangled from his rope belt. He'd shaved his face closely and displayed not one single whisker. He was the biggest, homeliest nun Esme had ever seen. And that's not all. His face and hands were covered with "sores," thanks no doubt to some creative use of dough and dyes.

"Did you fall in a patch of poison berries?" she asked.

"Leprosy," Toste answered for his friend. He spoke from behind her, against her ear. " 'Tis a convenient thing that we travel to Jorvik to deliver a batch of Margaret's Mead. We can deliver yon leper nun to the boat traveling from there to Lepros Island. Two jobs, one trip."

Before she could express her surprise at the lackwit scheme, Bolthor started, "This is the saga 'Viking Men and Their Love of Ample Arses.' "

"Uh, Sister Bolthora, I don't think we have time for this," Toste said, against Esme's ear once again. His hands were still at her waist.

She felt his breath on the inner whorls of her ear. Who knew mere breath could feel so stimulating there! It was only an ear, after all. But 'twas best to confine her surprise to safer topics. "Sister Bolthora?"

"We call her Sister Thora for short," Toste said with a chuckle . . . a chuckle that tickled her ear some more. Actually, tickle was too tame a word for what was happening. There appeared to be some connection between her ear and her breasts and that private place between her thighs.

Bolthor ignored them all and started reciting, with a forefinger pressed to his chin thoughtfully.

"What is it 'bout men
and their favoring arses,

especially ones
that jiggle on lasses?
Oh, 'tis not new,
this love of curves
that mark the female
and men unnerves.
Why, truth to tell,
some say Adam said to Eve
in the Garden of Eden,
'Great arse!' Leastways, that's what I believe.
So, 'tis not strange
that Viking men,
who are experts in female bodily appreciation,
would home in on this greatest of the gods'
    creation:
the female arse."

Mother Wilfreda and Sister Mary Rose actually laughed, and Father Alaric, too. He must have come up behind them.

Toste chuckled. "Well said, Bolthor! You have surpassed yourself. Truly, that is the best saga you have ever created. Will you repeat it for us at Ravenshire?"

Esme shoved herself out of Toste's embrace, about to berate him for suggesting such a thing. But the words never got past her tongue, so astounded was she by the sight she beheld when she turned around.

Toste was dressed as a nun, too. And what a nun!

Like Bolthor, he wore the traditional nun's garb—brown robe and matching veil over white wimple, crucifix on chain, prayer beads hanging from rope belt—and he'd shaved closely. But that was where the similarity ended. Not a single blond hair was exposed on his head, and he'd darkened his eyebrows, with charred wood, no doubt. Although he was tall and had wider shoulders than the average woman, Toste's face was beautiful. Really beautiful. He had nicely sculpted cheek and jaw bones, smoky blue eyes, and full lips. And not a sign of leprosy, either.

"What think you of Sister Tostina?" Bolthor asked, slapping his thigh with mirth.

Esme arched her eyebrows. "Sister *Tostina*?"

"Yea, but you may call me Tina," Toste said, a smile tugging at his lips.

"This is never going to work." Esme groaned with dismay. "First, I can't fit into a barrel. And now, you two look like . . . like . . . I do not know what."

"I have noticed that many nuns display masculine traits, if that is what bothers you, m'lady." Bolthor patted her arm with comfort. "No offense intended," he added for the benefit of Mother Wilfreda and Sister Margaret.

"No insult taken," her aunt said with a laugh. "In truth, many clerics have feminine traits, as well."

Father Alaric puffed out his chest as if to show he was not one of *those*.

"Enough about all that. We must get started on our journey," Toste told Esme.

"But I can't fit," she said, practically in tears.

"Never mind, we'll find another way. Sister Margaret is going with us. It won't be convincing otherwise, that three nuns, two of them unfamiliar ones, are transporting her brew into the city."

Esme tilted her head, confused. "And where will I be in this religious troop?"

"On the floor of the wagon, under our feet, covered by a large lap robe."

"Whaaaat?"

"Come see. It could work." He walked her over to the

large open wagon. The bench seat had been lowered so that Toste and Bolthor's height would not be so apparent, and a cloth sack of oats sat in the middle—Sister Margaret's perch, Esme presumed.

Esme peered into the seating area and shook her head doubtfully. "I don't see how I could fit under the bench, or how I could stay in that position for an extensive length of time."

"We'll stop often, and, besides, you won't be on the floor precisely." He grinned mischievously as he spoke.

"Enough foolishness, Toste. My father means to kill you and me and possibly all of us. I will do anything to make this work."

"Good. Do not stand in a place of danger and wait for miracles, that is my philosophy," he said, slapping her on the back with far too much enthusiasm. And she soon learned why.

As they drove out of the abbey courtyard, Esme knelt on the floor of the wagon, facing Toste, between his spread legs under his robe, with her face resting on his lap. It was the most humiliating day of her life.

But worse was yet to come.

CHAPTER SIX

B *eware of women with plans . . .*

It was probably the worst plan Helga had ever concocted.

Or the most clever.

Either way, Helga would have to scrap every inhibition she'd ever held, scrap her morals, scrap her pride and probably scrap her intelligence, or what she had left of it. But it would be worth it, wouldn't it, if the end result was a child . . . a precious little being to satisfy her father's dream of a grandchild?

Oh, she wasn't in any way contemplating marriage, as her father kept insisting and Vagn kept pretending he might accept. Hah! As if she would ever wed under the best of circumstances, giving up her hard-earned independence, and certainly never to a man who *might* be talked into accepting her. She was better than that.

All she needed was a man to bed her once and plant his seed in her, then ride off into the horizon. It sounded simple to her. Wasn't that what every man wanted anyway? Swive a woman to his heart's content, with no obligations?

And what better man than Vagn, who, truth to tell, knew how to kiss a woman boneless. If he could turn her breathless with his mouth parts—lips, tongue, teeth—what might he be able to do with his *other* part? Helga knew instinctively that making love with that rogue would not be a hardship.

But in order to accomplish her plan, Helga suspected that she would have to make the first move . . . be the seductress. Mother of Thor! How was she going to seduce a born seducer, without being too apparent? Of course she could wait for him to continue making advances toward her, at his convenience, but then he would feel guilty when she became pregnant, and he would feel obligated to marry her, or else her father would force him to wed her with a sword at his neck . . . none of which she wanted. It was essential that she be the instigator, the one to control the outcome.

First steps first. She needed help in becoming an enticing siren. *Helga the Homely becomes Helga the Temptress? Yeech! The thought boggles even my mind.* And what better person to give her advice than Rona the Nimble-Fingered, so-called because of her embroidery skills, but she was also known as Rona Roundheels, for obvious reasons.

Helga approached Rona in the downstairs solar where all the weaving and embroidering took place now that the weaving shed had become too cold. There were a dozen women and girls working, but luckily Rona sat off to the side under a wide bladder window which let in some light.

"Rona, I need your advice," Helga said right off.

"Oh?" Rona arched her brows in question, even as she continued working on the varicolored threads which embodied the peacock-feather border of a jade-green man's cloak. Her work was excellent—the best of all Helga's seamstresses. "About that new cloth you brought back from the Norselands? I already told you it is not the usual quality . . . too coarsely woven. The sheep that produced that wool must have been starvelings."

Helga shook her head. "Nay, 'tis not cloth I need advice on. 'Tis a personal matter."

Rona stilled her needle and gazed at Helga directly, no doubt noticing her flushed cheeks and the way she twisted the end of her chain-link belt back and forth between her nervous fingers.

"I need advice on how to seduce a man to my bed furs." No hemming and hawing for Helga. Get right to the point.

Rona smiled. "'Tis my experience that all a woman has to do is blink at a man and he is ready and willing."

"Mayhap for you. That hasn't been my experience." Perchance it was Helga's standoffish demeanor, or her Helga the Homely name-fame, or a mere unattractiveness to the opposite sex, but in all her twenty-eight years she couldn't recall any man actively pursuing her . . . except Vagn, and he just teased her. Rona, on the other hand, at twenty and two, had been attracting men like bees to a flower for the past ten years, and all she'd had to do was look pretty or wag her petals a bit. But it wasn't just her dark exotic beauty—Rona came from the Eastlands, born of an Arab father and an Irish slave mother. Rona carried an aura of sensuality about her, like an erotic cloud.

"Is there one man in particular you want to attract?" Rona asked. "Never mind. 'Tis the blond god from the battlefield, is it not?"

Helga nodded reluctantly.

"But there is no need to seduce him, mistress. The man's eyes follow you where'er you go. He wants you. For the love of Frigg, his staff is at half-mast already, I would wager."

"Nay, you do not understand. I want to be in control. I want to seduce him. I want to be the one to begin . . . and end . . . this affair."

"A woman after my own heart," Rona said with a tinkling laugh.

"Can you help me?"

"For a certainty. There are some tricks to this game of bedsport which I have learned over the years. Five, to be precise."

"Five? There are five specific actual tricks?"

"Five in general. Then under each of those there are many, many variations to the tricks."

"Are you serious?" Helga asked.

Rona nodded. "Are *you* serious?"

Helga hesitated, but then nodded back.

"You should listen to Rona," Bera the Buxom interjected. "Rona helped me woo Bolli the Blacksmith, and he was already pledged to another."

Woo? I am going to woo Vagn? Oh, sweet Valkyries!

"My husband Ragnor has been walking about with a silly grin on his face ever since Rona told me about the flexing of the woman-muscle," Sigrud added, rolling her eyes mischievously.

Woman-muscle? What woman-muscle? Do I have a woman-muscle?

"I still don't have the nerve to try sex on horseback with my man, as you suggested, Rona. But I will. I promise." It was Eve speaking now . . . a young maid newly come to Briarstead, who was wed to Sleipnir the Stable Master. If anyone could ride double on a horse, it was Sleipnir.

I can barely stay on a horse in the best of circumstances. I cannot imagine being astride a man who is astride a horse. All that bouncing . . . and . . . and stuff.

The three women gazed at her then in silence, waiting for her response to their butting in to what was obviously a private, but very interesting, conversation.

"Go on, Rona, tell us of these amazing five rules of seduction," Helga said, half teasing. "But remember, all of you, this is a private talk, not to be spoken of outside this circle."

They all nodded, pulling their stools and chairs closer, all the while continuing their embroidery work.

"First is the Madonna/Harlot Principle," Rona proclaimed.

"I beg your pardon?"

"Men like a woman who appears all prim and chaste in public, but wild as a seasoned concubine in the bed furs . . . just for him."

"Ragnor especially likes for me to wear a gunna with a full-length, open-sided over-apron, with my hair braided into a coronet atop my head," Sigrud confided with pink cheeks, "but no undergarments at all underneath."

Talk about more than I wanted to know!

The others hooted with laughter.

"Makes for easy coupling in the halls, or the scullery, or behind the cow byre," Bera offered, also blushing, "especially if your man is wearing no undergarments, either."

Definitely too much information!

"Or under the trestle tables in the great hall," Eve added timidly.

I can't believe what I am hearing. Do women really do all those things? Just to please a man? "Oh, good gods!"

"If you have trouble with that one, the easiest of them all, then you might as well give up right now." Rona pursed her lips and wagged a finger in Helga's face.

Helga stiffened her body with determination. "Nay. I

can handle it." *Or die of humiliation trying.* "What's next?"

"Next you must cultivate and refine your own individual sexual personality."

"I don't have a sexual personality. In fact, I don't know what a sexual personality is."

"A woman doesn't have to be comely to have men lust after her. That is what Rona is trying to say." It was Bera the Buxom speaking now. "Look at me. I am a perfect example. Oh, my breasts are an asset, but other than that, I am a little too fat. My buttocks even jiggle when I walk."

"But jiggling is good," Sigrud told Bera.

Bera shrugged. "Let's face it. I am not a comely lass, and no longer in the first blush of youth, either. Still, I ne'er had trouble attracting men, and I got my Bolli, didn't I?"

"It's all in a woman's own image of herself," Rona said.

"Huh?" Helga said.

"To be provocative, a woman must feel provocative," Rona explained.

"Huh?" Helga said again.

"Listen, there are things you can do to make yourself physically more attractive. Plump up those breasts with a little sheep fleece, add a few curves to your hips and buttocks—your waist is already tiny enough. And you can sway when you walk—or slither, as I like to describe it. Thrust your pelvis forward a bit when you walk. Like this."

Oh, my God! She looks like a ship's masthead entering a room. Do men really like that? "I have been flat-chested all my life, and I have no intention of fluffing up my bosom at this late date. Everyone would know they were false."

"Those were just suggestions, mistress. Mostly it's what's going on inside your head," Rona proclaimed, tapping her own noggin for emphasis. "Try this afore you come down to dinner this evening. Picture a fantasy scene. Very detailed. Two naked bodies. Hot kisses. Wicked touches. Your nipples getting harder and harder. Aching. And your woman folds weeping with arousal."

Not in a million years could I picture that! And if my woman folds ever wept, I did not know it. "And this will accomplish what?"

"It will change the way you present yourself. Your body will move differently. Your lips will part. Your eyes will glaze over."

"He will think I'm having a fit."

"Not if you do it right."

"I'm going to try it," Eve announced of a sudden. "In truth, I am feeling a bit tingly all over, even at the thought of it."

All right, admit it, Helga. You feel a little tingle. Mayhap you are not entirely hopeless.

"Me, too," Bera and Sigrud said.

"Let's all try it," Eve suggested.

Hell and Valhalla! We are all going to look like a bunch of moony-eyed maids, tipsy from ale or a blow to the head. Barmy as barn bats. Helga threw her arms in the air. "I don't think I can do this."

Rona shrugged. "Methinks you are not ready to be a temptress, m'lady. Best you sit back and wait for things to happen. Let the man . . . Vagn . . . control this love-play."

"Never!" Helga exclaimed. She was a fighter and stubborn as a horny bull . . . that's what everyone said of her. How else had she managed to succeed as a merchant in a man's world? She could not give up so easily. She just couldn't. "What next?" she asked Rona.

"The actual steps to sexual expertise. There are probably hundreds, but I will mention just a few of the tamer ones."

Yea, tame would be good for me. "Like?"

"Learn to caress yourself."

Oh, oh, oh! I don't believe she just said that. And if that is tame, I am in way over my head. "By myself or in company with a man?" she asked, afraid to hear the answer.

Everyone laughed.

"Both ways. If you learn your own body, you will know how to use it."

"I remember the time you told me to lock my bedchamber door, take off all my garments and sit on the floor with my legs spread and a polished brass facing my woman-place," Eve said. "Whoo! The things I learned about myself that day."

Never, never, never had Helga looked at herself *there*. And she was not about to start now. Talk about wicked! *Next they will call me Helga the Sinner.*

"Caressing oneself in private is fine," Rona went on, "but it is even better in front of your man. Men love to watch a naked woman bring herself to fulfillment."

Fulfillment? Helga wasn't even going to ask what Rona meant by that.

"And whilst we're on the subject of self-fondling, let me suggest that you practice flexing your sex muscles."

"That's the trick I told you about earlier," Sigrud said.

Helga's eyes almost bugged out. "What in bloody hell are sex muscles?"

"Those are the muscles inside your female parts." Rona pointed to the area between her legs. "Try putting a candle in there, just as you have a finger, and keep gripping and ungripping, over and over, the way you will eventually grip the man's staff."

"Firstly, I have never inserted a finger there."

"Really? You do not know what you are missing, lass," Bera said, with Sigrud, Eve and Rona nodding their agreement.

Helga's eyes probably bugged out again. "Secondly, I am not putting a candle *there*." She thought a second, then asked, "Do women really do that?"

"They do," all four women chirped.

"Lit or unlit?" Helga asked.

Four jaws dropped open.

"Just teasing," Helga said.

When Helga had first approached Rona for advice, she had never expected to receive such precise, intimate suggestions. She would die if Vagn heard about the candle bit, or self-caressing, or any of it, for that matter. "Need I remind all of you to keep this to yourselves?" she demanded, staring at each of them in turn.

They made motions across their closed lips, indicating their pledges of silence.

"The best part of sex is that period before actual tupping," Rona continued.

There's more? By thunder, I thought she was done. This is way too complicated for me. Who knew?

"I like to call it foresport . . . the period leading up to bedsport. 'Tis that time when the man and woman tease each other mercilessly . . . touching, kissing, nipping, tickling, whispering lewd words, licking. By the time the swiving actually begins, you should have your man as wild as a caged animal, hot with desire for you. And likewise, the woman wild for the man."

"That's enough for me!" Helga said, standing. "Methinks too much information could be a passion killer."

"Tsk tsk tsk!" the four women said at her disdain for the sex principles.

"Oh, do not misread me, Rona. I appreciate all your advice, which I am sure is superior, but I need time to digest it all before implementing *my* plan."

"One step at a time," Rona agreed.

As she walked away, Helga tried to tell herself that it was all nonsense, but how could she explain away her aching breasts and the woman-dew gathering between her legs? Truth to tell, she'd become aroused just thinking about seducing Vagn in all the ways Rona had suggested. There must be some merit in what Rona and the other women counseled.

But did she have the nerve to try it herself?

"Come see my web," said the spider to the fly . . .

By the time Vagn followed a dozen of Gorm's men-at-arms into the great hall for dinner that night, he was physically and mentally exhausted. By design. If he was too tired to think, he could not dwell on his brother's death and how little he had left in this world.

Gorm had called for him and several dozen of his *hird* of guardsmen to ride out with him that morning, circling the far reaches of his estate. They'd patrolled against intruders; after all, Gorm was a Viking residing in the midst of Saxon lands. But they'd also gathered up stray lambs, some of which had the dimwittedness to get themselves stuck in thorn bushes and mud holes. They'd even repaired a few fences that confined a small herd of beef cattle. And, in the end, the bowmen had shot three wild deer, which were now roasting on spits.

Once they'd arrived back at the Briarstead keep, filthy and weary beyond belief, they'd immediately filed into Gorm's bathhouse, which had been built over a natural hot spring. Now, at least they were clean.

In the old days, he and Toste would have relished a

day like this. Good, hard work provided satisfaction to a man. But Vagn felt nothing. *Nothing.*

He had no desire to go a-Viking come spring.

He had no desire to amass more wealth.

He had no desire to soldier in battle.

He had no desire to rekindle old friendships.

He had no desire to gain a wife and children.

In truth, he had no desire, at all.

Well, that isn't quite true. I have a wee bit of desire, low down in my belly, he told himself, chuckling aloud even as his eyes scanned the great hall and lit on the object of his desire.

Then he looked again.

Bloody hell, why is Helga gazing at me like that?

She sat at the high table with her father. Nothing unusual in that. She wore a scarlet gunna, embroidered with gold thread, and her long blond hair lay loose about her shoulders . . . a bit unusual attire for an everyday dinner, but not extraordinary. After all, Helga dealt in fine fabrics. It was the expression on her face that caused the fine hairs to rise all over his body, even those short hairs betwixt his legs . . . *especially* those short hairs. Even as he watched her—probably with his tongue hanging out and drool dripping to his chin—she darted her little tongue out and made a wide, slow lap of her parted, sinfully delicious lips. Her eyes were glazed and her nostrils flared with what appeared to be passion, though he must be mistaken about that. Helga the No-Longer-Homely stared at him as if he were a sweet confection and she a starving glutton.

His cock came immediately to attention, not that it took much to get a rise there, and heat licked out from his core to every extremity. He made his way toward her, but not before he heard Ragnor beside him exclaim,

"Holy Thor, why is Sigrud looking at me like that?" And behind him, Bolli the Blacksmith said, "Why is Bera looking at me like that?" And even farther back, Sleipnir the Stable Master concurred, "Why is Eve looking at me like that?"

They all had silly grins on their faces. Vagn wiped a hand across his mouth to make sure he wasn't grinning, as well.

"Gorm, Helga," he said, nodding to the two of them as he sat down at the high table and reached for the horn of ale that a housemaid poured for him. He drank it down thirstily and held out his horn for a refill.

" 'Twas a good day's work today, Vagn," Gorm said, speaking around Helga, who sat between them.

"Yea," he agreed, and the two of them discussed the day's events and what was planned for the morrow, but the whole time Vagn was acutely aware of Helga at his side. Was that rose scent he smelled on her skin and hair today? Or the usual lavender? And, yea, she *was* regarding him in the most peculiar manner.

Finally, when Gorm turned to address a high-ranking soldier on his other side, Vagn gave his full attention to Helga. "Do that again," he whispered huskily.

"What?" Her eyes darted here and there. She was obviously not comfortable with this game she played.

"Lick your lips. Slowly."

She groaned softly, low in her throat. Then she lifted her chin with some sort of resolve. "I'm not wearing any undergarments," she announced of a sudden.

He choked on his ale. When he regained his composure, he replied, "Neither am I," and accompanied his words with a waggle of his eyebrows.

"Are you teasing me?" she asked.

"Mayhap. Are you teasing me?"

She did not answer. Instead, she did that lip-lapping thing with her tongue again.

A certain part of his body liked that a lot. He smiled. He could not help himself. "Thank you."

She tilted her head to the side. "Why?"

"I find it difficult to smile these days. You made me smile."

"So I am a joke to you. Another jest—just like the one your brother made." She started to rise from her seat, and tears welled in her eyes.

Putting a hand to her forearm, he forced her back down. "Do not be so testy, wench. 'Twas a compliment, not an insult."

She sank back to her seat and let out a long sigh of nervousness.

Something strange was going on here, he thought.

He took a strand of her golden hair between his thumb and forefinger, testing its silkiness.

Under normal circumstances, Helga would have slapped his hand away. Instead, she seemed to steel herself for his touch.

Deciding to test the waters, he let his hand drop lower and caress her arm. Just the backs of his fingers, from shoulder to elbow to wrist. She shivered, as if it were bare flesh he touched, not the fabric of her gown. And it was a good shiver, too . . . not one of revulsion.

"So you are not wearing undergarments," he said, softly enough so her father would not overhear, though Gorm was still talking animatedly to someone on his other side.

"I lied."

"Really? 'Tis a shame. I like imagining you with nothing underneath."

"Why?"

"*Why?* Are you so naive that you do not know the effect a naked woman has on a man?" He glanced pointedly down at his groin.

She blushed but said nothing.

Just as he had thought . . . something strange was going on with Helga. He downed the remainder of ale in his horn, set it down, then rested his chin in his palm, his elbow braced on the table, and scrutinized her closely. "To be more precise, Helga, you have set my manpart to humming."

"Hu . . . humming?" she sputtered.

"Yea—not quite a throb, but certainly not lying still. Humming."

"That is so crude."

He shrugged. "Sex is crude."

"I wouldn't know."

"Would you like me to show you?"

"Nay!" she exclaimed. Then immediately amended it to, "I am not sure."

Whoa! That was a big, big step for this formerly aloof woman . . . the one whose father had described as having female parts like a dried-up raisin. An outrageous idea came to him unbidden. "Are you trying to seduce me, Helga?"

"And if I am?"

Not the answer he'd expected! "Then I'm confused. I would flip you on your back and have my way with you in a trice, and you well know it. Why the sudden turnabout?"

Helga's face was flaming red. She stood and glared down at him. "Never mind, you coarse-tongued lout. I've changed my mind." With that, she stormed off, hips swaying, presumably bare buttocks getting an airing from under her swishing gunna.

"You can't play games with me, Helga, and end it so abruptly," he growled at her departing back.

"The game is over, Viking," she replied without breaking stride and without turning back to look at him. Within seconds, she was out of sight.

"Not bloody likely," Vagn said to no one in particular. There was one thing women just did not understand about men. You could not plant a sexual idea in a man's head and expect it to melt away. This game Helga had started would be played out to the end, Vagn vowed. By his rules, not hers.

He couldn't wait.

Never play with fire . . . or a hot Viking . . .

Later that night, Helga was relaxing in the warm bubbling waters of the bathhouse, berating herself silently for her sad attempt at seduction.

There were certain times of day set aside for males and females to use the steam baths. This was the time for females of the household, although Helga was the only one there now, everyone else having the good sense to go to their bed furs on this cold night.

Just then, the outside door opened and in walked what was definitely not a female. It was Vagn.

"What are you doing here?" she practically shrieked, sinking lower in the water. The room was dim, lit only by a few wall torches. Still, she was naked, for Asgard's sake!

"Come to take a bath," he said, already beginning to disrobe. He undid his belt and tugged his tunic over his head.

"You already took a bath," she pointed out.

"A man can never be too clean," he said, then winked at her.

That wink did odd things to her breasts and woman-place. She could swear she actually tingled.

But Helga was no fool. She knew exactly what the rogue was about. He was putting her at a disadvantage in this game of seduction she had started. She'd known from the beginning that he was a much more experienced player, but she hadn't expected to be outwitted so early. Well, the game was not yet over.

He'd pulled his hair back off his face with a leather thong. His chest was bare by now, and he sank down onto a stone bench to remove his half-boots.

"Stop! Stop right there!"

He stopped.

"You are not getting in this bath with me, naked."

"I'm not?"

"Nay. 'Tis not proper. Besides, men are not supposed to be in the bathhouse this time of night."

"Is that a rule?"

"It is."

He smiled. "Guess what I think of rules."

Helga rolled her eyes at the hopelessness of arguing with the dolthead. Besides that, she'd lost the power of speech once he'd peeled off his *braies* and loincloth.

She should look away.

She really should.

But she didn't.

To give the man credit, he didn't feign false modesty. Nor did he preen. He stood, hands on hips, and let her look her fill. He was a beautiful man, no doubt about it, from his finely sculpted face with its cleft chin to his wide shoulders, narrow waist and hips, and long, sinewed legs. Even his narrow feet were good-looking. And of course there was that part in between which was impressive indeed, as far as those things went.

"Dost like to look at me, m'lady? Nay, you do not have to answer. I see that you do. Know this, I would enjoy viewing your nude body even more. Wouldst like to give me that pleasure?"

Not in a million years! Oh, what was wrong with her? This was the perfect opportunity to launch her plan. All she had to do was stand. *All? Hah! It is everything . . . exposing my skinny body to a man. Can I stand the scrutiny . . . and probably rejection? Yea, I should stand. Go ahead, Helga, close your eyes and stand.*

But she hesitated too long, and Vagn walked into the circular pool and sat down opposite her on one of the lower steps so that water lapped at him up to his waist. He spread his arms out along the edge with his legs extended under the water. The pool was large enough for two full-grown men to stretch across it, so she was in no danger of his touching her from there. For some reason, that did not comfort her. He could look, which he did . . . hotly. And he could talk, which he proceeded to do . . . hotly.

"I want you, Helga," he said without warning.

"For what?" *Dumb, dumb, dumb. Even I know what he meant by that.*

He smiled, slow and easy. Words were not necessary.

"Wanting is not the same as getting." *Has my tongue lost its connection to my brain?*

"For most men mayhap. But, me"—he rolled his shoulders—"I usually get what I want."

"With women, you mean." His arrogance knew no bounds. To her chagrin, she found it oddly appealing.

"With women," he agreed. "You started this game, Helga. Oh, do not try to deny that fact. What I want to know is, what are you about?"

"What? Only men can play at the game of seduction?" *That's the way, Helga. Show a little self-confidence.*

Remember Rona's advice. To be provocative, a woman must feel provocative.

"You misread me, m'lady. Some women are born seductresses."

"And I am not?" Oh, this was too much. So much for being provocative! Apparently, Helga the Homely would always be lacking in womanly ways. She started to rise with indignation, then sat back when she remembered that she was naked.

Just that little glimpse of her nudity and his eyes went wide with interest. He parted his lips and licked them slowly as if she—*Helga the Homely*—had tempted him.

"Oh, Helga, you tempt me without even trying. You do not need artificial wiles to draw me to your bed furs. Just ask. 'Tis enough."

Whoo! She gave a little mental exclamation of victory. *This could be fun.* That bothersome tingling started in her body again. And, despite herself, she wondered if a certain part of him was humming. "I do not believe you, but thank you for saying so," she said politely. *Good gods! Did I just thank a man for lusting after me?*

"Do not get me wrong, dearling, I liked your teasing in the great hall earlier tonight."

"Teasing?" she choked out. *Dearling?*

He nodded his head. "Yea. The business about not wearing undergarments. I liked the mind-picture that gave me. A lot."

She did, too, truth to tell.

"I just don't understand why. You could barely abide me afore. Why this sudden turnaround?"

She should tell him, but did she have the nerve? Would he understand her desire to give her beloved father a grandchild? Would he be offended that it wasn't his masculine good looks that tempted her . . . or not entirely?

"Do you wish to make love with me, sweetling?"

"Do you have to be so blunt?" *And do you have to call me by those enticing endearments? I am trying to think here.*

"'Tis like a giant wall looming betwixt us . . . whatever it is you hide from me . . . the mysterious reason for your pursuit. I would like to knock the wall down and proceed from there. No secrets. No games. So I repeat. Do you wish to make love with me?"

"Mayhap."

"*Mayhap?*" he practically shouted. "What kind of answer is that?"

"I want a child," she blurted out, and could have bit her tongue. *Too soon. It is too soon for him to know that.*

"What?" he exclaimed softly, then more loudly, "*What?*"

Well, now I've done it. I must tell all now. Let us hope he is a man who values honesty. "I am twenty and eight years old, Vagn. So long on the shelf I no doubt have cobwebs coming from my ears. I do not regret never marrying, but I have decided to have a child . . . to please my father . . . and for myself, of course."

His eyes narrowed and his jaw went rigid with anger. "A marriage trap . . . that's what this is all about. I have been in this situation afore, but I thought better of you, Helga. I really did. You and your father in cahoots!"

"You dimwitted oaf! I do not want to wed with you. And my father knows naught of this."

"You just said you wanted a babe." His mouth dropped open and his eyes went wide as understanding dawned. "You want a child outside of marriage? An illegitimate child?"

She felt herself blush, but he could not see it in this

lighting. Lifting her chin defiantly, she said, "There are worse things in life."

"You would be shamed."

"I care not."

"Your father would kill me."

"He would not know . . . till you are long gone . . . and even then I would not have to name you."

"You have this all worked out in your mind, don't you?"

She did not like the hostility in his voice, but she nodded.

"What kind of man do you think I am, that I would abandon my own child?"

"I . . . I did not think you would care."

"What kind of man do you think I am?" he repeated.

"Oh, please! Spare me all these offended sensibilities, Vagn. Surely you have bedded women afore . . . *many women* . . . without a care for any child you left behind. I would not be surprised if you had dozens of children."

"Dozens?" A grim smile cracked his face. "I am not aware of one single child I have begotten. There are precautions men can take to prevent childbirth . . . not foolproof, to be sure, but I have been careful. If any babe has been born of my loins, I would have recognized that child immediately and taken him or her under my shield."

He stood abruptly and stepped out of the pool. She could see by the condition of his manpart that he was no longer "humming" for her.

As he began to pull on his garments, she told him, "Vagn, I'm sorry if I insulted you. I did not think—"

"That is right," he snapped. "You did not think." He'd already pulled on his loincloth and *braies* and was reaching for his tunic.

"Let me make it up to you."

He paused and looked at her. The hurt in his eyes tore at her heart, and she deeply regretted that she had put it there. "How?"

She stood, naked as the day she was born, and held out her arms to him.

Vagn said nothing, just stared at her with continuing anger. But there was a part of him humming again.

Still, he left.

CHAPTER SEVEN

※

A moveable feast . . .
    "Stop moving."
    "I'm not moving."
    "Something's moving."
    Toste laughed. And that part of him where Esme's face was pressed moved some more. "Just whistle some more," he suggested.
    "I only whistle when I'm nervous."
    "You're not nervous now?"
    "I'm furious, not nervous."
    "Now, now, Esme. Just relax."
    I am going to kill the lout. I swear I am. "That's it! I'm getting up."
    Toste pressed his hands down on his lap, forcing her to remain between his legs under his nunly robe. "Not yet. Your father's guardsmen aren't out of sight yet. And this last bunch looked at us with a little more suspicion than the others."
    "What's not to be suspicious about? Two giant, troll-like nuns, one of whom has leprosy, and a giggling little nun betwixt them who appears to have drunk too much of her own mead . . . sounds suspicious to me."
    "Uh . . . would you mind not speaking quite in that

direction?" Toste said in a suffocated voice. "I can feel your lips moving *there*."

"And I take offense, m'lady, at your description of me as a troll," Bolthor said, but she could hear the mirth in his voice.

"And I am not drunk," Sister Margaret said. "Not in the least." A loud hiccough belied her words.

They'd all been sipping the mead to keep them warm on this second day of their cold, uncomfortable journey . . . especially uncomfortable for Esme, who'd had to duck under Toste's robes every time a Blackthorne soldier approached. The fur blanket spread across all three of their laps in the seat of the wagon drew the attention of all who stopped them, and the guardsmen were quick to flip it up, fully expecting to find the errant daughter hiding there.

"If anyone should be offended, 'tis me," Toste said. "That last soldier—the one with the missing front tooth—was eyeing me like a tasty morsel. And me a nun, at that."

"You are not a nun," Esme pointed out from under his robe.

"Well, he didn't know that."

"We nuns get accosted all the time," Sister Margaret remarked. "Doesn't matter if we're young or old, comely or homely as a hog. Men seem to think we are wild for their bodies from being confined in a convent so long. They expect great things in the bedsport from nuns."

Everyone was too stunned to speak at first by Sister Margaret's forthrightness.

"Really?" Bolthor commented finally. He was probably composing a saga in his head about nuns and their wicked appeal.

"There's only one nun I've ever been attracted to," Toste confessed.

And Esme knew by his twitching member which one he referred to.

"But how about those Saxon soldiers back near Jorvik?" Bolthor said with a hoot of laughter. "I thought they would fall all over themselves trying to get away from a leper."

"And one of them said you were giving him the evil eye," Sister Margaret added gleefully. "Little did they know you look at everyone that way."

Esme wondered if Bolthor was offended by Sister Margaret mentioning his damaged eye, but, nay, he quickly replied, "Mayhap I should leave off my eye patch all the time. The evil eye could be a weapon as sharp as my battle-ax, Head Splitter."

"Methinks you are all enjoying this far too much," Esme grumbled.

"Hmmm. I should create a poem to celebrate this adventure," Bolthor said.

Everyone was too tired and cold to protest. Besides, nothing ever seemed to stop the skald once he started.

"This is the saga of 'Toste's Great Adventure.'"

"Great," Esme heard Toste say, but she wasn't sure if it was a question or an observation.

"Once lived a Viking named Toste,
His life was no longer carefree.
Alas, death took his beloved brother,
And no happiness in Toste could stir.
But then he met a nun,
Who was not really a nun.
She was comely of face,
And her body had grace.

Plus, she could whistle
In a way most shrill
But could provide a thrill
If she did it against a man's . . . uh, windmill,
Which was exactly where her face was planted
When hiding from her father as she fled.
On the other hand, she should not whistle,
Because then Toste's manpart would not stand
*   still.*
But, leastways, on this great journey
Everyone was full of glee.
And is that not the best thing about Vikings—
That they can laugh at themselves?
Well, one of the best things."

"Bolthor, if I hear you even once repeat that particular saga at Ravenshire, I will make you wish you were a real leper, living in a leper colony far, far away from my menacing presence," Toste said.

There was a short silence. Then a wounded voice inquired, "Dost not like my sagas, Toste?"

"I like your sagas in general," Toste lied. Esme didn't have to see his face to know it was a lie. "But I do not like that one in particular. It makes me out a pathetic, whining kind of man."

"So?" Bolthor said. Then, "Ouch! Why did you clout me on the head? You almost knocked Sister Margaret's head rail off."

Which prompted Sister Margaret to say, "I liked your saga, Bolthor. Do you think you could write a short one that I could use in the selling of my mead in the Jorvik markets?"

"Hmmm. Mayhap." Within seconds, Bolthor was saying:

*"Margaret's Mead is a wonderful brew,
Sweet as honey, through and through."*

Sister Margaret repeated the poem several times to commit it to memory and promised to have her agent in the Coppergate markets of Jorvik use it as a selling ploy. Bolthor practically sputtered with pride.

"Toste, I have to get up now," Esme said. "I'm getting a cramp in my back."

"Not just yet," he cautioned. "We've already entered Ravenshire lands and should be at the keep within the hour. We must be especially careful for a little longer. Keep in mind that Eirik, the lord of Ravenshire, is half Saxon, half Viking, while his wife, Eadyth, is full-blooded Saxon. Many of their guests are Saxons. We do not want word to get out of your whereabouts till we are ready to face your father again."

"St. Bridget's breath! I am weary to death of all this chaos. I yearn for peace and quiet. Sad, isn't it, that a woman of my age wants only a peaceful life? Is it possible this madness will finally be over soon?"

"Well, you will be out of danger for a while, till after the yule season is past, but peace is the last thing you will find at Ravenshire. And as for chaos—well, I suspect chaos reigns there."

"What mean you?" Esme asked.

"Have you never been in a Viking household over the yule season?"

"Nay," she answered hesitantly, though she could not imagine anything out of the ordinary in the well-ordered Ravenshire keep. Both its lord and lady were renowned for their hospitality and well-run affairs.

"Sweetling, you may never be the same," Toste promised, with a pat on her head which pressed her closer to his twitching manpart.

That is for sure.

Let the good times begin . . .

"Swive me silly, you luscious Viking, you. Awk!"

Four heads in the upper solar of Ravenshire turned to look at the caged bird in the corner. Then three of those heads turned toward Tykir Thorksson.

By the bones of St. Boniface! Will my brother ever grow up? Eirik Thorksson, the lord of Ravenshire, wondered. He couldn't help smiling, even as he shook his head ruefully. "Have you been teaching Abdul perverted sayings again?"

"What's perverted about swiving? And everyone knows we Vikings are luscious," Tykir answered with a grin.

God, I have missed my brother and his warped sense of humor. With all the bad news lately, a bit of mirth is more than welcome.

"Isn't that so, Alinor? You think I'm luscious, don't you?" Tykir asked his wife, who had the good sense to ignore him. Tykir and Alinor had come from the Norselands to spend the yule season at Ravenshire this year, along with their four children, who were off somewhere being entertained by Eirik's seventeen-year-old twins, Sarah and Sigrud.

"Of course, Eirik is only half Viking; so, he is only half luscious," Tykir continued, ducking away when Eirik tried to swat him with an open palm.

"Show me yer legs, Al-i-nor. Awk, awk."

"Tykir!" Alinor exclaimed with a laugh.

"Kiss my arse and call it pretty. Awk, awk."

"Hey, I didn't teach the lousy bird that one," Tykir protested.

"Eirik did." It was Eadyth speaking now, Eirik's lady-wife. "And don't call my pet lousy. He has no lice. And remember, Tykir, you are the one who gave me Abdul as a bride-gift at my wedding."

"Who would have thought it would have lived this long?" Tykir said.

"Dumb lackwit Viking!" the bird said.

They all laughed then, but were soon cut short.

"M'lady . . . Eirik . . . you have got to come see this," Wilfrid, the seneschal of Ravenshire, urged breathlessly as he rushed into the room. It was late afternoon, and Eirik had thought his friend and comrade would be in the great hall enjoying a cup of mulled ale by now. "A cart just pulled into the courtyard."

Eirik did not immediately rise. He'd spent the entire day working on battle exercises with his men in the bitter cold, then helping to dig a dung cart out of a snowbank, followed by a bath, and, frankly, his forty-nine-year-old body couldn't take much more. He was very content indeed to sit before the hearth fire with his feet propped up and a cup of mead in his hands, listening to his brother's nonsense. Eirik was getting too old to keep going at this rate, but he had no sons to take over for him, other than his adopted son John who had work enough on his own estate at Hawk's Lair. And none of his four daughters seemed about to bring any new male blood into the family.

"A cart?" Eadyth inquired indifferently. She did not rise, either. At forty and three, she was still a beautiful woman, even though her silver-blond hair was mostly silver these days. "'Tis probably those new candle molds and pottery jugs I ordered from Jorvik." Eadyth was a successful beekeeper and merchant, renowned for her time-keeping wax candles, honey and mead. Not for the first time, or the hundredth, in the past eighteen years, Eirik told himself how fortunate he was to have her.

"The . . . the cart," Wilfrid stammered. "It's filled with barmy folks."

"Uh-oh! Big trouble coming!" Abdul squawked.

Eirik and Eadyth immediately looked at Tykir and Alinor. They were equally ensconced in comfortable chairs before the fire, awaiting the bell announcing the evening meal. Their two-year-old son Selik slept soundly on Tykir's lap. Tykir was forty-seven, and his bones probably ached as much as Eirik's after their grueling day of work, though he would never admit to such weakness.

"What? Why are you looking at us?" Tykir said with mock offense. "Every time something goes awry you think I had something to do with it."

"You usually do," Eirik responded.

"Shhh," Alinor cautioned. "Do not wake the child."

"Uh-oh! Big trouble coming!" Abdul repeated.

"Did you order more gifts to be delivered here?" Eirik narrowed his eyes menacingly at his brother. Tykir was ever up to some deviltry or overindulgence. "Do you not think you are overdoing the Viking gift-giving custom?"

Tykir told his brother to do something vulgar, the whole while grinning at him. "Didn't you like the leather boots with bells on them that I ordered for you from the Eastlands?"

"They are red, Tykir. *Red*. And I do not much relish jingling when I walk."

"Really? Alinor has a garment that jingles, and I like it a lot."

Alinor made a tsk-ing sound with her tongue.

"You could always wear the jingling boots and naught else. Eadyth would like that, I wager."

His wife, the traitorous wench, said, "Hmmmm," and winked at him.

"On the other hand, I did like the amber navel ornament you sent for Eadyth," Eirik said, waggling his eyebrows at Tykir. His brother was a far-famed merchant in the Baltic amber trade.

"Will you two never stop teasing each other?" Alinor shook her head ruefully at the two brothers.

It always amazed Eirik that Tykir had chosen Alinor for his wife. With her bright orange hair and rust-colored freckles dotting her entire body . . . well, she was not the beauty he would have expected his womanizing brother to pick. But Alinor had turned out to be the perfect foil to Tykir's personality. And Tykir considered her the most beauteous woman in the world, which was the important thing, of course.

"They're like two small boylings," Eadyth agreed.

"Milords, ladies, I must insist," Wilfrid interrupted with a pained expression. "The cart. It contains three nuns, and two of them are most unusual . . . big as oak trees they are, and one of them a leper."

"Uh-oh! Big trouble coming!" Abdul repeated.

"Would someone kill that bird?" Alinor said.

"Bowlegged harpy!" Abdul opined.

"A le-leper," Eadyth faltered, ignoring the interchange with the bird.

"But that's not all," Wilfrid went on. "Eirik, the two big ones told me to give you, personally, a message. 'Sister Tostina and Sister Bolthora have arrived.' That's what they said."

"Huh?" Eirik, Tykir, Eadyth and Alinor all exclaimed at once.

"Uh-oh! Big trouble coming!"

"I have a wonderful recipe for parrot stew," Alinor said sweetly.

"Bowlegged harpy!"

Then of a sudden an idea seemed to come to Alinor, She gasped and put a hand to her mouth. "Bolthora . . . could it be Bolthor?"

Eirik's heart went out to Alinor, and his brother, too, for that matter. They still had trouble accepting the death of their longtime friend, Bolthor the Skald.

"And Tostina . . . could it be Toste?" Eadyth asked, also with a gasp.

Eirik recalled how hard they'd all been hit by the news of the Battle of Stone Valley. So many of their Norse comrades had fallen that day, but most especially they'd grieved for Bolthor and the twins, Toste and Vagn.

"Bolthor, Toste and Vagn all died at Stone Valley," Eirik pointed out softly. "We have discussed that battle at length since Tykir arrived. We all miss our fallen friends. What a cruel jest someone plays on us." He reached over and squeezed his brother's forearm. There were tears in Tykir's light brown eyes.

"But what if it's not a jest?" Alinor said, tapping her chin thoughtfully.

"Tostina and Bolthora . . . that is too much of a co-incidence," Tykir said, already handing his sleeping child to a flustered Wilfrid to hold.

Within seconds, all four of them were rushing out of the solar, down the staircase, across the great hall and out onto the courtyard steps. They came to a screeching halt at the shocking sight they beheld.

In the middle of the cart seat was Sister Margaret from St. Anne's Abbey. Nothing unusual about that. Sister Margaret and Eadyth had often conferred over the years about the best methods for making mead. In fact, a friendly rivalry of sorts existed between them over who made the best mead in all Northumbria.

But Sister Margaret was the only normal member of the frozen tableau they beheld. The first to jump down from the cart was the leper nun. God's teeth! What a big nun she was! And, yeech! The nun's face was covered with oozing sores.

Or were they sores?

Eirik had suffered a lifelong weakness in his eyes which made it difficult to see things up close. Mayhap they were not sores at all. In fact . . .

With a wide smile, the big nun looked at them directly, or as directly as she could with her one blind eye, then tore off her veil and wimple. It *was* Bolthor.

"Thank the gods!" exclaimed Tykir, who was already down the stone steps and hugging his old friend, who had jumped off the wagon and lifted Sister Margaret to the ground. Then Tykir lifted the giant and twirled him about with exhilaration.

"Put him down, you fool," Alinor chastised her husband. "I want to hug him, too." Tears were flowing freely down Alinor's freckled face as she reached up and touched Bolthor's leprous face adoringly. "I am *soooo* happy to see you, good friend."

"Likewise," Bolthor said and gave her a loud, smacking kiss on her cheek.

Eirik and Eadyth welcomed Bolthor with equal enthusiasm.

Then they all turned their eyes to the cart, where a grinning Sister Tostina beamed at them.

"Good Lord! You are the best-looking nun I have ever seen," Alinor said.

Sister Tostina winked at her, then whipped off his veil and wimple. It was Toste, of course.

"I hope you have no Saxon nobles about, other than yourself," Toste said to Eirik. "Otherwise, this two-day disguise of ours may be for naught."

Eirik shook his head. "None but us here . . . for now."

Tykir reached up to help Toste get down, but he waved his hand away. "First, I would like you to meet Sister Esme."

"Huh?" they all said. It was becoming a common refrain this day.

Toste lifted the bottom half of his robe with a flourish and out crawled a woman . . . a nun, actually, who had been kneeling between his thighs. A beautiful nun with head rail askew and face flushed with humiliation stood and moved to the right so she was not directly in front of Toste, who stood, as well.

"Oh, now you have gone too far, Toste," Alinor said. "You have done some outrageous things in the past, but tupping a nun . . . in public?"

"This is as bad as the time he tried to seduce the caliph's daughter atop a camel," Tykir said, but it was obvious from the gleam in his eye he was not offended . . . either by the camel seduction or the nun tupping.

"What do you suppose she was doing under his robes?" Eirik asked Eadyth, and she smacked him on the arm.

"There is tupping, and then there is *tupping*," Tykir answered for her.

It was Tykir's turn to get smacked . . . by his own wife.

Sister Esme looked up at Toste. She looked at all of them standing in the courtyard with Bolthor. Then she looked at Toste again and said, "If you even blink at me in the future, let alone speak, I am going to cut off your manpart with a dull knife."

The men in the courtyard winced.

But the ladies gave little cheers of encouragement. The women of the family ever did encourage independence of spirit in their females.

"Welcome to Ravenshire," Eadyth said, stepping forth.

"Thank you," Sister Esme said, jumping down off the cart after brushing off Toste's offer of help. "I am Lady Esme of Evergreen. Please get me away from this oaf afore I kill him."

"Hey, I am your champion. I am the one who saved you from your father. I am the brave knight who wore this ignominious disguise *for you*," Toste yelled to her back.

Lady Esme said a very vulgar thing then—not at all the kind of thing a nun should be saying. But of course the ladies clapped and the men grinned, including Toste.

Eirik decided then and there that this was going to be a very interesting yule season at Ravenshire.

Everything's turning up roses. Thank God! . . .

Esme half reclined in a large brass tub afore a roaring fire in her small guest bedchamber at Ravenshire. The air was sweet-scented, as would be her body, from the dried rose petals which covered the surface of the hot water. The perfect cure for her aching bones and cramped muscles.

Why then was Esme bawling her eyes out, with loud, hiccoughing sobs? For twenty and four years—almost twenty-five—she had learned to control her emotions. Even when beaten by her father . . . even when threatened with death . . . even when faced with the prospect of a dotty old husband . . . Esme had held her tears in check. Now she could not stem the flood.

It was relief, pure and simple. For the first time in many, many years, she felt safe. Oh, the danger still existed. Her father could petition the king, who would undoubtedly hand her over, if he could find her. But for now, for this short period, she basked in the luxury of tranquillity.

A short rap on the closed door interrupted her tears.

"Come in," she called out to Eadyth, who was no doubt returning with the maid and more pails of hot water. What a gracious hostess Eadyth had been so far, treating her as a welcome guest and not the intruder she was.

The door dosed softly.

Still half reclining with her neck resting on the curled edge of the tub, she said, "Just put the pails next to the tub. I'll ladle the water in myself as needed. And thank you once again, Eadyth."

She heard a stool being pulled close to the tub and a male voice say, "I may wear a gown on occasion, but I'm not Eadyth."

It was Toste, of course. The arrogant, crude, presumptuous Viking rogue.

"Go away, you odious oaf," she said, her eyes flying open as she sank lower in the tub.

"You've been crying." The tone of his voice was so doleful you would think her tears hurt him.

"I got soap in my eyes," she lied.

"I have to talk to you," he said, bracing both elbows on his knees and his chin in his two hands.

"You can talk to me later. And stop looking like that."

"How?"

"Like you are trying to see through the water."

"Well, I am. What kind of Viking would I be if I did not enjoy the sight of a naked woman?"

"Aaarrgh!"

"You are not to worry, Esme. I can't see anything . . . yet. Mayhap in a while, when the petals start to droop, your hidden assets will no longer be hidden."

She closed her eyes and counted to ten silently. When she opened them, he continued to stare at her. "Are you still here?"

"I am."

"Speak your mind and begone," she said through gritted teeth.

"I have been speaking with Eirik and Tykir about your situation. They agree with our plan, as far as it goes, but there is one happenstance we had not counted on."

Esme immediately grew alert and sat up as straight as she could without uncovering any "hidden assets."

"The Witan is meeting next week. The king's council of close advisers, of which Eirik is a member, is holding a regular session in Winchester."

All the fine hairs on her body, wet as they were, stood at attention. "My father is a member of the Witan, too."

"I know," Toste said, his usually teasing expression somber now . . . somber in a way that frightened her. "It is my belief and that of Eirik and Tykir, as well, that your father will bring up your situation at that time. Whether he knows of your whereabouts by then or not, he will petition the king for either your guardianship or your marriage to Lord Rotting-Cock." Esme had made the mistake of telling Toste of her father's latest marriage plans for her.

She should have cringed at his vulgarity, but she was becoming accustomed to his earthy language. "Either way spells doom for me and any future I might have at Evergreen," she mused dolefully.

"Not necessarily. Eirik will be our ears and when the moment is right, mayhap our advocate. For now, you must bide your time, and know that you are safe here at Ravenshire."

"For now," she said.

"For now," he agreed. "One more thing. Alinor has chided me up one side and down the other for my treatment of you. She says I embarrassed a lady of good breeding and that I must humble myself afore you with contrition."

Esme had to smile. "Was that an apology?"

"Yea, 'twas. Do you accept it?"

"I do accept, and despite your crude treatment of me, I must offer my thanks for rescuing me. If you had not removed me from the abbey, I would be in my father's hands by now."

He nodded his acceptance of her thanks, then added, seemingly as an afterthought, "Just how thankful are you?" He was gazing pointedly at the cluster of rose petals surrounding her hidden breasts.

"Not that thankful," she said with a laugh as he got up and prepared to leave the chamber.

She thought she heard him say, just before the door closed after him, "Being a champion is not all it used to be." He was probably talking to his dead brother, Vagn, which was his practice of late.

If Toste only knew how much she appreciated her champion, he would not give up so easily. Lucky for her he was a dimwitted Viking.

You want her to do WHAT? . . .

After dinner that evening, Toste sat in a cozy semi-circle in the upper solar of Ravenshire before the hearth, chatting softly with those around him. In the corner was a foul-mouthed squawking bird, which somehow contributed to the homeyness of the scene. His latest favorite expression, taught to him by Tykir, no doubt, was, "Ye gotta love a Viking!"

No one wanted to retire yet. There was still so much catching up to do, and a lingering relief that at least two Viking soldiers had survived the Battle of Stone Valley. Tykir kept grinning and Alinor kept touching Toste and Bolthor, as if to make sure they really were alive.

With Toste were Eirik, Eadyth, Tykir, Alinor, Bolthor, Eirik's two oldest daughters, Emma, who was twenty-four, and Larise, the widow of a Jorvik merchant at twenty-six. And, of course, Esme, who sat beside Toste, giving him a totally new view of who she really was.

I lusted after her as a nun. Now I lust after her as a lady. What next? If Vagn were here, he would say 'tis past time I got my ashes hauled.

Attired in a sapphire-blue gown edged with silver braid borrowed from Eadyth, she looked like the lady of high station she was.

Esme was apparently larger in the chest area than Eadyth. *Every time she moves my eyeballs practically bounce out of my head. If past experience proves true, I would guess that her breasts would fit perfectly in my big hands. Aaarrgh! Stop gaping, Toste, lest you embarrass yourself.* Toste wasn't sure if it was himself or Vagn talking in his head.

Her long hair, black as a raven's wing, was held back off her face with a twisted silver circlet and hung down to her waist.

Of course, that just made Toste think of other times and places where her hair might lie loose. *Like on my bed furs.*

Her thick-fringed eyes matched her gown, snapping with blue fire whenever she glanced his way. She might claim to have forgiven him, but her eyes and stiff demeanor told a different story.

I ever did like a battle, m'lady. Do not challenge me with your haughty looks, or you might just find out what a Viking soldier can do with his . . . weapons.

Well, that was certainly mature, Vagn said in his head.

When did I ever aim for maturity? he answered his brother. *You are supposed to be having a rousing good time up in Valhalla. Swive a few Valkyries for me, brother. And go away. People are starting to think I am demented. I am starting to think I am demented.*

"Who are you talking to, Toste?" Eirik asked.

"Barmy as a bat," Abdul opined.

That is for sure. "No one," he replied.

The men sat with legs outstretched and ankles crossed, sipping at cups of Margaret's and Eadyth's mead; Sister Margaret had gone to her bed long ago since she planned to rise early and return to the convent under armed guard. The ladies propped their feet on little wooden footstools known as Widow Makers.

"I still cannot believe that Vagn is gone," Eadyth said, bringing up the subject he had hoped to avoid. But he should have known these good friends would want to discuss his dead brother.

I can't believe I'm dead, either, Vagn said/thought. Or was it himself thinking that thought? *Aaarrgh!* He nodded, unable to speak.

"I cannot imagine how hard this must be for you, Toste. You two were inseparable," Eirik said.

Not just a brother. My best friend. A feeling of tightness crushed his chest like a vise. His heart pounded madly.

"Ivan, King Haakon's third cousin, passed by here two sennights ago," Eadyth told him. "He saw Vagn fall with a most grievous sword wound to the chest."

The abdomen, actually. Toste put a hand to said spot reflexively. He still felt sharp pains there on occasion. And itching betimes, too, like a scar healing.

Phew, tell me about it. Vagn made a loud exhaling sigh inside his brain. *There was so much blood, it turned my stomach. I would have been scared witless if I hadn't been dying.*

"Why are you grimacing like that?" Eadyth inquired with concern.

He waved a hand dismissively, overcome by the picture Vagn painted of himself. Toste thought he really was going barmy, and it was getting worse by the hour.

Alinor got up and walked around the semicircle, then gave him a hug from behind. "You loved him dearly, Toste, and my heart goes out to you for your pain." She kissed his cheek, then went back to her seat, tears swimming in her green eyes.

Tears welled in Toste's eyes, too. Holy Thor! Would he ever get past this pathetic yearning for a brother who'd gone to a better life.

Who says it's a better life? After swiving your first fifty or so virgins, Valhalla gets old fast. And all that ale drinking and shield pounding!

"I remember the time you two kept changing places to court that young lady in Miklegard . . . you know, the one with the veils. Finally her father came after you both with a longsword." Leave it to Tykir to lighten the mood.

Esme made a tsk-ing sound of disapproval at his side. At the same time, she squeezed his forearm in understanding. He could forgive her much for that small gesture.

"He still talks to his brother on occasion," Esme disclosed.

Is she reading my mind now? May the gods forbid! Mayhap I should think something particularly lascivious and see if she blushes. Or mayhap I should just go take a nap for ten or twenty hours and try to get my mind in order. In any case, forget about the forgiving Esme business. Why did women always have to blather everything?

"Really?" Tykir asked. "And does he talk back?"

You bet.

"Sometimes," Esme answered for him with a twinkle in her blue eyes. Obviously, she was getting back at him for past misdeeds, like making her kiss his manpart for hours on end . . . well, practically kiss it.

Now, there is a fantasy to play out in my mind. Forget about Vagn and Valkyries. Forget about blood-gushing wounds. How about Esme kissing my manpart? But not in a cart. Nay, this should be on a bed with me naked, arms stacked behind my neck and her . . . well, she could be naked, or . . . wait, wait, wait . . . she could be wearing her nun habit, and—

"Why are you smiling?" Esme wanted to know.

You do not want to know, my lady. To the others, he said, "It's freakish, I know, this talking with Vagn, but I still see him in my head and hear him talking, like I used to do when he was alive. And I share his physical pains, too."

"And his thickenings," Esme offered impudently, to everyone's shock and delight . . . though not his—delight, that is.

You are getting as bold as a Viking, my Saxon lady. Too much bad company. I could think of a better use for that tongue of yours.

"Thickening is their word—Toste's and Vagn's—for—"

"Esme!" he exclaimed. "They know what a thickening is."

"Oh," she said and blushed prettily.

"Mayhap you would like to elaborate on this," Eirik advised.

"Huh?"

"The *mental* thickening business," Eirik reminded him.

"Huh?" *I am beginning to sound like a blithering idiot.* "Dost really want me to explain that?"

"Mayhap later," Eadyth suggested, "when young daughters are not about."

"Oh, Mother!" Larise and Emma said at the same time.

Much laughter followed. Then Bolthor asked him, "Wouldst mind if I tell a saga about you and Vagn?" Bolthor never asked for permission, and everyone knew that. It was a telling moment that he asked now, and Toste did not know what to say. He truly wanted to put discussion of his brother behind him, but he did not want to hurt his good friend, either. Finally he nodded with a deep sigh.

"Hear one and all, this is the death-poem, 'Ode to Twin Brothers, May Their Ties Last Through Eternity.'"

"Very good title," Alinor said. Alinor always did have a big mouth and little sense where Bolthor was concerned.

"Methinks the gods were smiling
the day they sent two babes squalling
from one womb, one mother, one birthing.
Some said they were really one person,
two sides of the same coin.
So how does one survive
when oneself is no longer alive?

Some say the one left behind
must see the departed
in the warm sunshine overhead,
watching a bird flying straight ahead,
a birthing of a horse well-bred,
the welcome of one's own homestead.
But with that I disagree,
in the case of these twins so carefree.
Toste, my friend, I ask you this;
What would Vagn most likely miss?
This is where you will find his spirit
if through this world he does still flit:
the wink of a winsome maid,
a good jest ofttimes-played,
the sway of a shapely female bottom,
a good battle fairly won,
the adventure of a-Viking,
then coming home,
the male pride in a rock-hard staff,
the ecstasy of sexual coupling,
the love of man for woman,
the birth of one's own babe.
At these times, I believe, Vagn will be
there, and you will know:
Even in death, you are still one."

A stunned silence followed, and not the usual stunned silence that followed Bolthor's sagas. For once, Bolthor had composed a truly touching poem.

"Thank you," Toste said finally. "Mayhap you could help me memorize that one so I can pull it to mind when my spirits are low."

You would have thought he'd handed Bolthor a chest of gold, so much did he beam with pleasure.

"Would you mind if I change the subject?" Alinor asked.

"Do horses piss?" Toste muttered under his breath.

Esme elbowed him and muttered, "Coarse lout!"

"We must needs talk about Esme," Alinor said.

"Hah! Your turn," he whispered in an undertone.

She shot him another of her blue fire glares before sitting up straighter, the creamy complexion of her face pinkening with a blush.

I would like to say some other things that would bring a blush to your fair face, Esme. Wicked things. Tempting things.

"I'm sure you are already aware of the plans being made for you regarding the Witan and a troop of retainers that Toste is putting together," Alinor began.

Esme cast him a questioning look at the mention of retainers.

Oops, I forgot to mention that. I forgot to tell you lots of things, faced with your naked body and bobbing breasts in a tub of rose petals. Bolthor ought to create a saga about that! I can just imagine what it would be. "Ode to Bobbing Breasts" or something equally outrageous.

I am still waiting for the "Ode to Eat-Me," Vagn said in Toste's head, which caused him to choke on his mead. He had to give his brother credit; he had a quick wit for a dead man.

"What Alinor is trying to say," Eadyth said, "is that we have been talking about this situation, and—"

"Uh-oh!" Tykir said, rolling his eyes. "The women have been talking."

"Now, Tykir, do not be so quick to judge. I, for one, value the female viewpoint," Eirik said, batting his eyes in a cowlike fashion at his wife.

"You traitor!" Tykir laughed.

Toste missed this kind of brotherly teasing. He missed so much about Vagn, but especially the teasing, he realized now.

Bloody hell! I tease you enough in your head. You want more than that?

"What I started to say, Esme, was that, yea, you should try the Witan, and you should amass a troop for Evergreen, and do everything in your power through diplomatic means, but there may be one thing extra you should keep in mind as a back-up plan," Alinor said.

Blah, blah, blah. Women loved to blah, blah, blah. Why do they not leave man's work to men?

"And that would be?" Esme asked hesitantly.

"Marriage," Alinor and Eadyth announced at the same time.

Whoo-ee, you weren't expecting that, were you, big brother?

Esme rose indignantly. "I have not spent ten and more years in a convent, avoiding marriage, just to give in now."

"Nay, nay, nay!" Toste stood, as well. "Are you two demented? What would marriage solve for Esme?" For some odd reason, the prospect of Esme being married filled him with horror.

A bit of dog in the manger, don't you think?

"Shut up!"

"Who are you telling to shut up?" Esme asked with even more indignation.

He must have spoken aloud. *By thunder, my brain is splintering apart.*

"Sit down, you two," Alinor said, waving a hand toward them. "Give us a chance to explain."

They both sat, hesitantly.

"Esme, we are not saying that you *must* wed. We are saying you should consider it," Eadyth elaborated. "And it would be different from what you have been offered in the past by your father. This would be your choice."

You are not picking some lecherous lout for a husband, I am warning you right now, Esme. Not even a non-lecherous lout. Toste put his fingertips to his mouth just to make sure he wasn't speaking his thoughts again.

"You could pick a man who would be as much a puppet under your control as your father's choices would be under his," Alinor said.

Oh, that is just wonderful. Encourage her to get a milksop for her lifemate. Do this, do that. Hell!

"You could make a list of all the qualities you want in a husband—a good leader to work for you with the king and his court, a good fighter to work for you against the king and his court, a good farmer or man familiar with the land to turn Evergreen prosperous again, a good principled man." Alinor was on a real roll, or so she thought.

"A good lover," Tykir interjected with a wink at his wife.

"That, too," Alinor said.

Toste closed his eyes and swore he saw balls of fire. *Esme is definitely not picking a good lover for a husband. Not while I am around.*

"Do not discard the idea out of hand," Eadyth advised Esme.

Do discard the idea out of hand, Esme.

"Think about it," Eadyth concluded.

"I must admit, you ladies make some good points," Eirik said.

I . . . do . . . not . . . think . . . so.

Eadyth beamed at her husband.

"Well, it is not going to happen," Toste said firmly,

standing once again. "Do not listen to them, Esme. You will not wed, and that is that. I forbid it."

Everyone, including Esme, went wide-eyed at his vehement words.

Uh-oh! Perchance I went a bit too far.

Like ten hectares too far? Tact, my brother . . . where is the tact I taught you so well?

"What right have you to forbid me anything?" Esme said, standing to glare up at him.

"I have the right because . . . because I choose to have the right," he argued nose to nose with her in utter illogic.

Toste could swear he heard laughter in his head.

Bolthor murmured something about green-eyed monsters, whatever that meant, and everyone else in the room nodded with odd little smirks on their faces. He did not care. They were speaking of marrying Esme off, and he could not allow it. He had lost one person he loved and—

Toste stopped himself short.

Now we are getting somewhere.

It could not be.

Wouldst like to wager on that?

It was impossible.

Dumber than a Danish door hinge!

"Dumb dolt! Awk! Awk!" said Abdul.

Grabbing Esme's hand and ignoring the snickers behind him, he began to pull her out into the corridor. "I must needs speak to you in private," he choked out.

"And I have a few things to say to you, as well," she stormed.

This is your chance, big brother. Don't blow it.

CHAPTER EIGHT

&

What did Adam do when offered the apple? . . .

Helga was driving Vagn barmy. Full-blown, pulling-at-the-hair, humming-at-the-groin barmy.

How could she do this to him? Tell him she wanted to couple with him . . . plant that idea in his lustsome brain . . . then add the piddling little detail that it wasn't really him she wanted but his seed. The insult of her offer! The sheer offensive insult of her expectation that he would just flit off like a carefree bird and leave a child of his loins behind, like a molting feather.

Not bloody likely!

If it had not been snowing for three straight days, making visibility impossible and the temperature nigh freezing, he would have hightailed it out of Briarstead on his trusty horse Clod the night Helga first made her offensive offer. But he'd stayed . . . *may the gods and all the fallen warriors up in Asgard stop laughing!* . . . and she'd been torturing him ever since. The deliberately seductive sway of her hips as she slithered by. Licking those big, luscious lips of hers when she knew he was watching. Lowering her lashes and giving him sideways glances in a most inviting way. Always leaving him wondering whether she wore undergarments or not. Once she even winked at him . . . the willful witch.

Aaarrgh!

Gorm had asked him yestereve if he was suffering another headache from his dead brother. What he'd wanted to answer was, "Nay, a cock ache." What he'd actually said was, "Yea, just a twinge."

Gorm's retainers had taken to making a wide path when he headed their way because of his foul temper. He'd heard one man ask another, "What bug crawled up his arse?" He'd wanted to say, "Helga," but of course he didn't.

And some of Helga's ladies . . . her embroiderers . . . had taken to snickering when he approached. He had no idea why, and was fairly certain he didn't want to know.

So now Vagn stomped off toward his bedchamber with a jug of ale in hand. It was barely past dark, but he planned on drinking himself into a stupor. He hoped he didn't have more dreams tonight. Wherever his brother was—dead or alive—he was hot on the tail of a black-haired beauty. Vagn was starting to feel perverted, in-truding on his brother's sexual escapades . . . enjoying them, in fact.

But then, the other alternative was dreaming about Helga . . . mostly about her attacking him in the most incredible fantasies. Tying him to a bed to have her way with him. Licking him head to toe to gain his assent. Dancing for him, naked. Wetting those hot-as-sin lips of hers. He didn't know if these dreams fell into the area of perversions, but, frankly, he didn't bloody well care.

Pathetic, that's what he'd become. He had reverted back to an untried youthling who got his thrills from damp dreams, not real bedsport.

After stoking the fire, he removed his clothing and crawled onto his bed with only a fur pelt over his lower half. He was about to reach for the pottery jug on the floor when he heard a short rap on the closed door. He had only imbibed two long swallows of ale so far—not nearly enough to withstand another of Gorm's marriage proposals. Last time, he'd offered him a toll bridge in the border lands as an added enticement. Before that, it had been a Nubian slave girl from an Eastern harem, yet to be bought. That on top of being named Lord of Briarstead, a chestful of gold coins, three horses and one longboat. *Gorm is relentless. I wonder, what this latest offer will be. Nay, I do not wonder, because I do not care.*

"Go away, Gorm."

The door opened anyway. It wasn't Gorm. It was Helga, which was even worse. Ominously, he heard the door lock click behind her.

"Go away," he said more forcefully, and turned on his side away from her, facing the fire. *I am not going to think about her standing here in my bedchamber. I am not going to think about her offer to come to my bed furs. I am not going to let my cock do my thinking. I am resolved—she means naught to me. So there, you wily wench!*

Silence reigned, but only for a moment before she said in a shaky voice, "How do you feel about self-caressing?"

All of Vagn's good intentions floated away with those few words. He turned back over and sat up. Stacking his hands behind his head, he observed her standing by the door, nervous as a virgin before a ritual sacrifice.

That is not a comparison I should be making.

Her face was flushed with color, but that was all he could see, because her body was covered entirely by a blue cloak which she clutched together with both hands at her waist. But wait, there was another body part exposed. Her bare feet. Her oddly erotic bare feet.

Could she be naked underneath?

At first, he could not breathe, let alone speak. When he got himself reasonably under control, he remarked as casually as he could, "Self-caressing, Helga? Me or you?"

He had expected to shock her with his question. Instead, she seemed to ponder his words. "Well, Rona says—"

"Rona? Who is Rona?" he interrupted in an almost shrill tone. *Helga is discussing self-caressing with me. Have I entered another world—a strange otherworld of demented people? Is this a jest? Toste, are you responsible for this? Did you plant the idea in her half-brain head, from wherever you are?*

Her eyes seemed to light up with pleasure that he did not know this Rona person. "That is neither here nor there, but Rona says men like to caress themselves betimes—"

"Only if there is no other option available."

"Quit interrupting me. 'Tis hard enough to get this out without your teasing," she snapped, then seemed to catch herself. After all, a female should not be snappish when she was engaged in the business of seducing a man to get his man-seed. "What I was trying to say is, Rona claims that men caress themselves betimes, but what they really like is to watch a woman caress herself." She said all in one whoosh of breath, as if she had to get it all out afore she lost her nerve.

Now, to say that this particular assertion got his attention would be the understatement of all time . . . like saying Viking men were somewhat virile. Every hair on his body waved in the wind. His nipples ached, and they almost never ached. His tongue thickened. His staff was thickening, too. And humming, for a certainty. In fact, it was singing "Alleluias." Surely Loki the jester god was engaging in his pranks again, because no mortal being could ever come up with such a notion to tempt an already lustsome man.

Vagn had no intention of getting Helga with child and walking away. The best way to avoid that happenstance was to keep his manpart as far distant from her woman folds as possible, like in another country. So, what did he say? "Mayhap I would need a demonstration to decide . . . whether I would like to watch you self-caress or not." *Liar, liar, liar! Lackwit, lackwit, lackwit! I am a blithering idiot.* Meanwhile, said manpart was making a tent of his bed fur.

"All right," she said.

All right? What does she mean, "All right?" She cannot mean to . . .

Uh-oh!

She unclapsed one of her hands.

She does.

Helga bit her bottom lip nervously, then spread her cloak wide and let it drop to the floor. Tears of embarrassment glistened in her blue eyes . . . an indication of how difficult this disrobing was for her. She probably still suffered from the Helga the Homely misname she'd been given so long ago.

And it *was* a misname, because the woman who stood before him now in all her naked glory presented a picture beauteous beyond belief—to Vagn, leastways. He suspected that some men—*blind dolts*—might find her too tall and skinny and big-mouthed. She was taller than average for a woman and very slender, with small, almost nonexistent breasts and exceedingly long legs. Instead of being put off by her less-than-generous endowments, he found her slimness appealing. Her hair was pale gold hanging down to her hips. Her mouth, one of her greatest assets, was wide and wet from her darting tongue. Her eyes stared at him, direct with question.

"Helga, you are beautiful," he said finally.

"I am not," she replied. She might not like his compliments, but her breasts did. The nipples hardened and stood out like pink sentinels.

He should tell her to put her cloak back on and run fast from his bedchamber, but she had already begun the self-caressing, and he could not have stopped her now even if he wanted to, which he did not.

She traced her lips with the tips of her fingers. The fingertips of the other hand made a trail from her chin down her neck over her shoulder and down one arm.

"Helga, have you ever touched yourself before?" he choked out.

She shook her head slowly from side to side. "Am I doing it incorrectly?"

"How in the name of Thor would I know?"

She frowned. "You have ne'er played this game afore?"

"Never." And that was the gods' own truth.

His answer seemed to please her. With a secretive little smile, she ran the palms of both hands down her sides, over her waist and hips to her thighs, then back up to lift her small breasts from underneath.

He heard a small groaning noise and realized it came from himself. "Did Rona tell you to do that?"

"Nay, I thought of it myself."

"Smart girl!"

She smiled again, shyly, and used both thumbs and forefingers to tease her nipples, which were large considering the size of her breasts. The whole time she gazed at him, gauging his reaction, which was formidable, if she only knew.

"I really don't know what to do," she confessed and let her hands drop to her sides. She was panting lightly at her own self-arousal, but probably was unaware of what she had done to herself.

"You are doing fine so far," he said. "Just imagine as you touch yourself that it is me touching you."

"I already am."

His manpart jerked. *Oh, Helga, you divulge too much. I will use that information against you in some way, I guarantee it.* "Come closer so I can see better," he suggested.

She stepped to the side of the bed so that she stood between him and the hearth. Her body was backlit by the fire, which still blazed warmly, painting her with hues of red and gold.

"Spread your legs."

She did.

"Wider."

She did, but he could tell she was uncomfortable standing thus.

Who cares! I like it. "Look down at your woman fleece, Helga. The curls glisten like gold. Are you wet there?" Her eyes shot upward to meet his with shock. "Touch yourself and see."

"I am. Odin's breath, I have wet myself," she wailed once she touched herself there lightly.

He almost laughed aloud at her innocence. "Nay, sweetling, 'tis woman dew. Your body readies itself for my . . . I mean, a man's entrance."

"Oh." He could tell that news fascinated her, and she touched herself there more thoroughly, then gasped when she must have discovered that particular spot where a woman's pleasure was centered. She jerked her hand away as if burned.

Vagn hadn't had so much fun in ages and ages, and he wasn't about to let it end so soon. "More, Helga—go back to that small bud and stroke it like you would the petals of a flower. Gently. As if your fingertip is the wing of a butterfly."

To his utter amazement, Helga, who could be the most obstinate woman in other circumstances, chose to heed his demands now. But then, she was a woman with a mission.

She stroked herself with one hand down below, and twirled a nipple with the fingers of the other hand. Vagn was so aroused, his blood roared and his cock pulsed. If he was not careful, he would come to peak beneath the bed furs, alone.

Suddenly Helga stopped and looked at him directly. "Are you going to make love with me, Vagn?"

It was the hardest thing Vagn ever did, but after a long pause, he said, "Nay, but I can bring us both pleasure without actually completing the act."

She tilted her head to the side. He wasn't sure if it was because she was trying to understand how that could happen or if she was contemplating his offer. In the end, she commented, "What would be the point of that?"

"Pleasure."

"But no babe?"

"No babe."

She sighed deeply, then walked to the door, where she picked up her cloak and wrapped herself tightly in its folds. Before she left, she turned and told him, "I won't stop trying."

He smiled grimly—how else could he smile but grimly, when his body was tuned like an overstrung harp?—and countered, "And I will look forward to those efforts . . . with a passion."

Once she was gone, a voice in Vagn's head said, *Dumb, dumb, dumb!*

Turning the screws . . .

It was two more days before Helga had the nerve to try her skills at seduction again.

The ice storm that had hit Northumbria was deemed the greatest in a century. Lucky for her. She was fairly certain that Vagn would have run from Briarstead like a scared rabbit if the roads had been clear. Not that he hadn't enjoyed her first attempt at temptation, she was sure. He'd enjoyed himself, no doubt about it.

Now, on to step two of her seduction plan.

"Exactly what is step two?" she asked Rona. It was late afternoon, and they stood in the salon folding and inventorying ells of embroidered cloth to be sold at market this spring. She and Rona were the only ones there due to the poor light caused by the continuing winter storms.

"The Pull-Back," Rona said without hesitation.

Helga stopped working and stared at Rona with amazement. "I hope this one isn't as scandalous as the first one. I don't think my heart could take it."

Rona flashed her a dimpled grin. "Admit it, m'lady. You enjoyed yourself."

Helga pursed her lips and pretended offense, but only for a moment. "I did. Hell and Valhalla! I made myself so hot, I fair went up in flames. So, what is this Pull-Back?"

"Now that you've got his attention, pretend to change your mind. Well, not change your mind so much as change your direction."

"I'm afraid to ask what you mean by that."

"Show interest in some other man."

"What man?"

"I don't know. Any man."

Just then, Finn Finehair walked by their open doorway, never even bothering to look in. Helga looked at Rona and Rona looked at Helga. Then they both smiled. Finn, second in command of Gorm's *hird* of soldiers, was called Finehair because of his impeccably groomed black hair and forked beard and trim mustache. A vainer man there never was. Some said he spent an hour a day just trimming his facial hairs. Others claimed he did the same for his chest hairs, but Helga could hardly credit that. At one time, her father had tried to interest her in Finn as a potential mate, to no avail. The man had the fighting arm of Thor, but the brains of a wood louse

"Mayhap I could imply to Vagn that Finn is called 'fine' for other reasons—reasons not visible at first glance," Helga said.

Rona laughed and clapped her on the shoulder. "Methinks you have a knack for sex games."

Oh, my gods!

Let the games begin . . .

Vagn was in the guardroom honing his sword with a whet stone when Helga came sashaying in. And, yea, "sashaying" was the best way to describe the deliberate, sultry sway of her hips.

It had been two days since the "event" in his bedchamber, and he had not forgotten one single bit of it. His male member remembered even more, apparently, because it was always half-hard these days.

Never in all his misbegotten days had a woman approached him with such an outrageous exercise in blood-boiling, bone-melting temptation. And he'd bloody well liked it. Helga, in all her innocence, was a born seductress. If she only knew!

That was why he'd kept his distance these two long days, and would continue to do so. Like right now.

"Go away, Helga. I am not interested," he lied as she got closer to him. He continued to rasp the whet stone along the blade of his sword as if he were not even aware of her presence. Hah!

She stopped directly in front of him. "You thought I was looking for you? Foolish man!"

Did she just call me foolish? I think I'll use her tongue to hone my sword.

"Ha ha ha."

Is she laughing at me?

"I have given up on my efforts with you, Vagn. So you can relax and stop hiding from me."

Who are you attempting to fool? Me or yourself?

"Actually, I have come searching for Finn. Oh, I see him over there."

What? WHAT? Vagn's eyes shot up.

But Helga was already sashaying off to the other side of the guardroom, where Finn was practicing swordplay with another soldier. Finn was a good enough soldier, Vagn thought, but he spent way too much time on personal grooming. A coxcomb, through and through. The only man Vagn had ever met who was more full of himself than Finn was his old comrade, Rurik the Vain. Not only did Finn trim his facial hairs to excess, but he wore his *braies* so tight that his manparts stood out like two big apples holding up a snake. Probably padding. Helga was too smart a lady to be interested in such a foppish man. She wouldn't give him a second glance. With a resolute shake of his head, Vagn concluded, *She wouldn't want Finn's seed.*

Even so, he narrowed his eyes and watched helplessly as Helga called out to Finn, who stopped his swordplay and leaned down to listen to what she was saying. Before he did so, though, Finn reached down and adjusted the sack of apples at his groin, and Helga the Porridge-Brain watched him do so with interest.

She would *want Finn's seed!*

Vagn couldn't hear from this distance, but he saw Finn smile and at one point throw his head back with laughter.

Is she serious? Or just playing more games?

She placed a hand on Finn's wide chest and giggled. She actually giggled.

Vagn saw red. He literally saw a haze of red afore his blazing eyeballs. *Has she really given up on her quest for my seed? And is she now about to glean seed elsewhere?*

He should not care. What business was it of his? Let her make a fool of herself.

But what if Finn agreed?

I do not care.

Finn would not.

I do not care.

Finn might.

I do not care.

So, what did the uncaring Vagn do? He dropped his sword to the floor with a roar of outrage, stomped over to Helga, who was batting her eyelashes at Finn in the most ridiculous fashion, grabbed her by the upper arm and practically dragged her from the room, proclaiming idiotically, "There is something I must show you."

Hoisted on his own lusty staff . . .

They had gone all the way back to the scullery behind the kitchens before Vagn stopped dragging her. The man had clearly lost his mind.

"Have you lost your mind?" she asked as he backed her up against the wall.

"It would appear so."

Thor's teeth, but he is unusually somber. What ails him? As if I didn't know. "Why is that tic ticking in your chin?"

"Because I am so angry I might just explode if I don't tick."

Good answer! "What did you want to show me?"

"This." He lifted her by the waist so her feet dangled off the floor and proceeded to kiss her hungrily. No questioning first kiss was this. It was hard and demanding and wet. And it went on forever. He put her down, his hands roved everywhere—her breasts, her hips, her buttocks, the backs of her thighs. This was a man of experience who had been pushed too far.

"You should stop," she said halfheartedly.

He just laughed and kissed her some more.

About then, she realized that he'd reached up her gown, his palms bracing the globes of her bare nether cheeks, and his two middle fingers delving into her woman-folds from behind.

"Aaaaaaaaah," she whimpered, too aroused to be embarrassed by the wetness he encountered there.

"Aaaaaaaaah is right," he answered with a groan when she undulated her hips against him and belatedly realized that she was riding the ridge of his hardened shaft. "Do it again," he rasped out.

She did. Several times.

Which caused his eyes to roll back in his head and his teeth to grit.

"Did I do that right?"

He choked on his own laughter. "Wrap your legs around my waist, sweetling."

"Huh?"

"Just do it."

When she'd complied, he kept one hand wrapped around her waist to hold her in position. The other hand snaked underneath her, and before she had a chance to protest, he was strumming her gently in one particular place that caused the most unusual sensations to shoot out to all the important parts of her body. "I think mayhap you should stop now," she said hesitantly.

"Helga, I don't think I could stop now if I wanted to. Just relax and let me show you something special."

She put her hands on his shoulders then and allowed him to touch her most private places, thus building the odd pressure. It was torture and it was pleasure at the same time. She was losing control and yet she, a person who cherished control of her life above all else, made no effort to stop him. When the pressure got so great and she felt herself begin to spasm inside her woman-place, she arched her neck and began to keen out her pleasure.

That was when Vagn began to buck against her, his hardened staff riding the channel of her womanhood. Back and forth. Hard and fast. In the end, he slammed himself against her and she exploded into ecstasy.

For a long time, she just rested her head in the crook of his neck and panted for breath. He was panting, too. Finally, when he pulled his head back to look at her, she asked, "Will I get pregnant from this?"

"Helga! We didn't do anything. You made me come in my *braies* like a boyling." He let her slide to her feet then, and she indeed saw the dampness at the groin of his breeches.

Helga felt oddly pleased at that evidence of his losing control, just as she had. "It felt like *something.*"

"It was definitely something . . . just not *the* thing that

would get you with child. Believe me, there is much more
to lovemaking than this." He was brushing strands of hair
off her face as he spoke. A soft lover's gesture, which he
probably did without thinking.

"Really? I can't wait."

"Nay, you misread me, Helga. There will be no more
than this." He stepped back from her as if suddenly aware
of what he'd just done . . . of the danger he'd placed himself in.

"We shall see," she said and sashayed off the way Rona
had taught her, which was a real feat because her legs
were as weak as melted butter and her woman-place was
seeping moisture.

She thought she heard Vagn say behind her, "Gods
help me!"

*When one clueless man confronts another clueless
man . . .*

Vagn confronted Finn the next day in the bathhouse.

He was bare-arsed naked, as was Finn, but men did not
care about such things. However, Finn was doing something rather outlandish, even for a Viking.

"What in the name of Odin are you doing?"

"Combing my manhairs," Finn answered, not bothering to look up. He was indeed running a small comb
through the short curls that surrounded his balls and
cock . . . occasionally moving his staff from side to side
to survey the effect, even pulling out a pair of shears and
snipping the stray hairs.

"Why?"

"Because women like it."

"They do?" Vagn pulled himself up short before he
contemplated getting himself such a comb, and broached

the subject he'd come to discuss with Finn. "Stay away from Helga."

"Huh?" Dumb as dung, Finn was, in Vagn's opinion. He had to be to be combing his cock.

"You heard me. Stay away from Helga."

"Why? Does she belong to you?"

Vagn felt his face fill with heat, and not from the hot springs. "Nay. But I am looking out for her."

"Isn't that a bit mean-spirited?" Finn inquired with a sly glint in his eye. Mayhap he was not so dumb after all. "You don't want her, but you don't want anyone else to have her, either."

"My reasons matter not. Just stay away from Helga."

"Or?"

"I'll lop off your head."

Finn laughed, showing off way too many perfect teeth. "What makes you think she'd want me anyway? Her father tried to arrange a match betwixt us five years past, and Helga rejected me."

"Really?" Now, that was interesting news. Helga must be playing her seduction game again . . . trying to pretend interest in Finn to make Vagn jealous. Not that he was jealous.

"On the other hand, she may have changed her mind about me. Five years can make an old maid less picky." Finn waggled his eyebrows at Vagn, enjoying his discomfort far too much.

"Helga is not an old maid," Vagn surprised himself by saying. "She is a woman who is alone by choice." *Oh, gods, stop my blathering tongue afore it runs away on me.*

"Hmmmm." Finn resumed his combing and snipping.

Vagn decided it was a useless cause trying to converse with Finn. He turned and was about to don his dry clothes and leave the bathhouse when Finn called out to him. "Have no worry, Vagn. Helga is not to my taste anyhow. I ne'er did relish cold women in my bed furs."

Hah! If Finn and the other men in this keep only knew! Helga was hot as sin. The question was: *How can I avoid the flame? I ever was a man attracted by a good sinner.*

A hard nut to crack . . . but beware of flying shell . . .

"Ooooh, Vagn, could you please help me?"

Uh-oh! Vagn had been walking by the storage room, heading toward the great hall and the midday repast, when Helga called out to him. Once again, she'd caught him unawares. "Help you with what?" His voice sounded more churlish than he'd intended, but, by thunder, the woman had him walking on hot coals these days, so leery was he of being in her presence. But he prided himself on being a hard nut to crack in the games women played with men. He'd never lost yet.

"I can't reach the candles on the top shelf." She was standing at the bottom of a ladder which was braced against a set of built-in wooden shelves that went all the way to the ceiling. Well, that appeared a reasonable request. No harm in lending a hand. So he climbed the ladder for her all the way to the top, not even becoming alarmed at the way she gaped at his buttocks in his tautened *braies.* He did have a good arse. "Which ones do you want? There are many different sizes." They were all the same length but of different widths. He held three out to her.

She pointed to the narrowest and said, "I suspect that one is too small." Then she pointed to the second largest and said, "That one might be all right . . . but, nay, I think I will try the big one. What do you think?"

Big one? "Uh, Helga, exactly what do you want this candle for?"

"Practice."

Don't ask, Vagn. Do . . . not . . . ask. "Practice?"

"Yea. Rona says I should practice tupping with a candle." She looked pointedly at his groin, which was indeed blooming into a *big* candle, and said, "Which one do you think is the right size?"

So shocked was Vagn that he lost his hold on the ladder. His foot slipped. And he toppled to the floor, flat on his back, staring up at a smirking Helga.

"Are you all right?" she asked sweetly.

"Nay, I am not all right," he grumbled, getting to his feet.

She took the big candle which he still clutched in his hand and sashayed away, saucy as you please, having accomplished another of her goals in this seduction game of hers.

Vagn planned to wring this Rona person's neck, but first he was going to wring Helga's neck.

What to do during the winter doldrums? . . .

The betting was fast and furious at Briarstead in the early weeks of December. Would there be a yule wedding or not?

It was the most outlandish situation Vagn had ever found himself in. And there had been more than a few.

On first hearing of the wagers, Vagn vowed, "It will be a hot day in Niflheim afore I wed . . . and certainly not when forced to the bridal tent."

Helga, equally indignant over the wagering, vowed, "I will melt all my embroidery needles and take up cooking, a job I abhor, afore I will wed, and certainly not to a loathsome lout like Vagn. Though I wouldn't mind . . . well, never mind."

Gorm couldn't stop grinning.

If it didn't stop snowing soon, Vagn was going to attach ice skates to Clod's hooves and find a way to escape Briarstead.

But first . . .

CHAPTER NINE

❦

L *ady with a mind of her own . . .*
      "The stables? Why are you taking me to the stables?" Esme asked Toste as he dragged her the short distance from the keep, slamming the barn door behind him. It was bitterly cold outside but warm in the barn from the heat of fifty or so horses.

He did not answer her at first, just scowled and continued to pull her along beside him down the center aisle between two long rows of horse stalls. The Viking was driving her half barmy with his changes of mood.

But, really, she was changing moods by the minute as well. In one instant she was kneeling-down thankful for his help getting her out of St. Anne's Abbey and into a safe haven. *Although I will never in this lifetime forgive him for his manner of rescue. The next time my teeth are that close to a man's most precious part, he is going to find half of it gone. Yeech! What a picture!*

In the next instant she was brain-boiling mad at his teasing antics and overbearing male arrogance. *Why do men always think they know what is best for women? And if this lout thinks he can wink and grin at me and I will do his every bidding, well, he needs to have his brain rearranged . . . with a mallet. Although he does have a nice wink and grin.*

Then, in a third instant she felt overpowering sympathy for him that he had lost a brother he loved so much. *I have never loved another person so much in all my life and certainly never had such affection thrown my way. I envy him this love. I really do.*

In a fourth and most alarming instant, she found herself being attracted to the knave. His person was exquisite, from his endearing cleft chin to his well-muscled form. But it was more than that.

Will I ever forget that kiss in the convent hallway?
Will there ever be a repeat?
I should not care.
But I do care.

Esme was a strong person, much stronger than people gave her credit for. When she wanted something as much as she wanted her home at Evergreen, she would stop at nothing—*nothing*—to attain that goal. Hadn't she spent eleven years in a nunnery to prove that point? Hadn't she fought off her father's marriage and death threats? But it was time to go on the offensive, and if it meant stomping over a roguish Viking to get what she wanted, then so be it. Toste might think he could force her to his will, but he was sorely mistaken. Sad to say, she could be as ruthless as her father if pushed to the wall.

"The stables are the only place where a person can get any privacy here," Toste finally responded in a grumbling tone, still dragging her along. "There are people everywhere at Ravenshire, mostly busybodies who have naught better to do than interfere in other people's affairs."

"They do it out of affection," she argued.

"Hah! You have no idea how Alinor and Eadyth meddled in the life of our friend Rurik till he settled down with Maire in the Scottish highlands. He should have left her hanging in a cage from her ramparts, if you ask me."

"A . . . a cage?" she sputtered. That was one of the few things her father hadn't tried with her, probably because he'd hadn't heard of such.

"Once, Alinor even pretended to grow a tail to scare Rurik into believing she was a witch."

Esme would have loved to see that.

"Eirik and Tykir are just as bad. Especially Tykir. A more jestsome man there never was! Ask Tykir sometime how he kidnapped Alinor because she put a curse on King Anlaf's male staff, causing it to make a right turn."

Esme's eyes went wide. Then she fought back a smile. She would have liked to see that, too. She was beginning to realize how stale and boring her life had been thus far. By necessity, of course. Still . . . "I like them . . . all of your friends."

"I like them, too. In small doses."

"I especially like Alinor and Eadyth. They are exactly the type of independent woman I want to be when I regain Evergreen."

"There is independence and there is *independence*. Eadyth is an accomplished merchant, but she organizes everything. No doubt she even organizes the bedsport with her husband, though he does not seem to complain in that regard. And Alinor, hah! Alinor may very well be a noted weaver of fine cloth, and she breeds prize sheep with exceptional wool, but I would not want to live with the witch. By thunder, her blathering would drive a sane man mad."

Esme was amazed at Toste's longwindedness with regard to his friends. He usually didn't divulge so much personal information. "Her husband, Tykir, does not seem to mind."

Toste shrugged. "He is besotted, for a certainty, even after all these years of wedlock."

There was something endearing about both brothers teasing and openly showing love for their wives, and vice versa. She'd never witnessed such before—not that she would want it for herself. Such caring would weaken her, and that she could not allow, not if she hoped to win the fight before her. Even so, she asked, "What have you against wedlock?"

"'Tis fine for some men. Not me. Though I admit there are a few examples of good marriages, my father and brothers more than prove it is a sad state, to be entered into for family profit. And I have seen marriage used more often as a political ploy than a source of happiness. More trouble than it is worth."

Sadly, he had a point there. "Do you not want children?"

"Not particularly. Do you?"

"I have not thought much about children. I have concentrated so much these past years on avoiding my father's scurrilous marriage plots that the prospect of my body increasing from such ventures seemed intolerable."

They had walked all the way to the end of the aisle. Now they stopped near an empty chamber, and he leaned against the wall. He still held her hand, fingers entwined, and she did not have the vigor to protest. Or the desire, truth to tell. In the back of her mind, still unformed ideas swirled . . . how best to use this man for her purposes.

"You do not favor a child of the loins of Lord Rotting-Cock?" Toste asked with a soft smile.

There he goes, teasing me again. I swear, his smile must be magical. It makes me tingle in the oddest places. And tingling is definitely a weakness I cannot allow. Blessed St. Beatrice, next I will be swooning. "The thought of making a child with Oswald of Lincolnshire turns my stomach."

"Actually, that is why I have brought you out here," he said hesitantly.

"To discuss children?"

"To discuss marriage." The expression of surprise on her face must have scared him, because he immediately amended his statement. "Not to me."

She laughed.

His face was flushed with embarrassment over his misleading phrasing. God forbid that he should offer marriage to some unwitting maid, especially an over-aged almost-nun like Esme. "Do not heed Alinor and Eadyth's plot to coax you into marriage," he elaborated. "Outward appearances can be deceptive. Eadyth and Alinor mean well, but they can be devious and relentless when they get a bit between their teeth."

Why would he care? Could he be jealous? Nay, he has no interest in me that way. Even so, he is speaking in circles. "Why are you stuttering like a dolthead? Speak your mind."

He took a deep breath, then said, "You must make me a promise that you will not succumb to their matchmaking efforts whilst I am gone."

Must? Since when *must* she do anything he decreed? Then his other words sank in. "*Gone?* Where are you going?" Her voice was shrill with distress. During this brief time at Ravenshire, she had felt at peace. Now Toste was going to pull away her anchor? When had he become so important to her well-being? She was the one who would steer the rudder of her life course, but she refused to let him jump ship. If it would not have been too obvious, she would have stamped her foot.

"I must needs depart on the morrow. I will take Sister Margaret to Jorvik with me where she will sell her mead, then travel back to the abbey with a priest from the minster.

I will stay in the city, alone, and try to get information on Vagn's murderer. I have some contacts there who should be able to help me."

"Take me with you." She was as surprised by her request as Toste. *Too obvious, Esme. Try to be more subtle.*

"What? Nay! I'm going alone. Even Bolthor will stay at Ravenshire. I must travel alone."

"You won't come back." *Why should you? You have no ties here. Nay, I will not let you escape so easily, Viking. I still have use for you.*

"Yea, I will. I have no place else to go, for now. Once I have avenged my brother, I will return." He spoke to her in a patronizing manner, as if she were a child in distress. The only thing missing was the pat on the head. *Bungling oaf!*

"Not if you're dead. 'Tis a fool's errand. Your brother would not want you to put your life in peril for him. Revenge will not bring him back," she nigh screamed at him.

"Stop it, Esme. Stop it right now. You have no idea what my brother would or would not want. It is a Viking's way. It is a man's way."

"It is a lackwit's way!"

"Mayhap, but it is what I must do."

She punched him in the chest and pretended to sob.

He was immovable in more ways than one.

"See what you have done. You have made me cry, and I never cry. Loathsome lout. Slimy cur. Bloody bastard. Odious oaf." She was pounding his chest now to the beat of her epithets.

He wrapped his arms around her and trapped her flailing hands against his body. Against her ear, he said, "Leave off, dearling. Leave off."

Dearling? He called me dearling. Whoa, that is defi-

nitely a woman-weakening tactic. I like it way too much. I cannot let the rogue distract me with sweet talk. "You are going to abandon me. I should have known better than to trust a man."

"I am not abandoning you. There will be plenty of men here at Ravenshire to protect you whilst I'm gone."

"Can you guarantee that you will come back?"

"Of course not."

"See? You are abandoning me."

"Because I might die?"

"I might just kill you myself if you keep this up. Mayhap Alinor and Eadyth are right. I should choose a husband myself and be done with it. At least that way I would have some control over my own life." *Let us see how you like that possibility, Northman. Let us see how you accept a woman taking fate in her own hands. Let us see how you like a woman disagreeing with your "superior" intellect.*

He went stiff, even though he still held her arms imprisoned. "That, you will not do."

Just as I thought. A typical man who thinks women are the weaker sex, unable to control their own destinies. "You have no say in what I do, especially since you are *abandoning* me." Esme was not wise in the ways of men and women, but one thing she did know: Guilt was one of women's best tools when dealing with men . . . especially clueless ones. Eve had probably guilted Adam into biting the apple, way back at the beginning of time.

"Must you always be at cross-wills with me? Can you not accept that sometimes I might know what is best for you?" he said.

Ooooh, wrong thing for you to say in my present mood, my lord Know-It-All Viking. Be careful, or you may trip over that runaway tongue of yours. "Nay, I do not accept orders easily. That is why I had to go to confession so many times back at the abbey. But you are not to worry anymore. Release me. Begone. Go fly off to Jorvik or the Norselands or hell, for all I care. I am off to find me a husband." Esme had no inclination to accept Alinor and Eadyth's plan for finding her a husband, but if it annoyed Toste, then she would damn well let him think otherwise. She was discovering there was great fun in needling the bothersome boor. "Yea, methinks I will pick a homely man, one who is not so full of his own conceit, like someone I know. Strong in body, of course, but not so pretty in face. Definitely not a Viking. A Saxon would be best; they do not jest so much."

"Do you refer to me? Because if you do, forget it. I am not in the running."

You have no idea how much I would like to wipe that smirk from your face. "Methinks you don't have a clue what you want anymore, Toste. Methinks you are clueless."

"Clueless? Did you call *me* clueless. I ought to lop off your head . . . or your tongue, at least. And telling me that you will be on the hunt for a husband. I . . . do . . . not . . . think . . . so. I know who is clueless here, and it is not me." Toste practically frothed at the mouth with indignation.

Good. "Blah, blah, blah," she said. "Just like a man. Always blathering their man-nonsense."

His eyes almost rolled back in his head with frustration. "Odin's breath! You dare much, wench, pushing me too far. Be careful when you put your head in the mouth of a wolf. You will get more than you wagered for."

"Oh, please. You are more like a lamb than a wolf." *Mayhap I am being a bit foolhardy, but the man asks for it. He really does.*

"Aaarrgh!" he said.

Another typical male reaction.

"'Twould seem there is only one way to shut your teeth. I will show you how much of a lamb I am."

If he hits me, I am going to hit him back. Lot of good it would do, but I will, anyhow. She braced herself.

With one smooth move, Toste picked her up, tossed her onto the clean straw in the empty stall and came down on top of her.

All right, no hitting. What then? Esme wasn't sure why she'd provoked the Viking so much. Anger, for a certainty, that he ordered her about like a wooly-witted milkmaid. Retaliation for his heavy-handed tactics. Fear that he planned to leave her. Envy that Eadyth and Alinor obviously got something wonderful from their men. And stubborn determination that, before he left, she would get one more taste of the man to satisfy the hunger he'd kindled with just one kiss. Oooh, that last item just slipped in and stunned Esme with its implications. Definitely a weakening of control, if she let it go too far.

"You torture me, m'lady, and I am not a man accustomed to being tortured," he whispered against her ear, then blew softly into the whorls.

She barely fathomed his words, so wonderful did his breath feel in her ear. She girded herself against his temptation and said, "Don't go tomorrow. Stay here with me . . . for a while."

"I have to go sometime. Tomorrow is as good a time as ever. How long would you want me to stay?" The whole time he spoke, he was nibbling little kisses from her ear to her chin and back again.

Delicious was the only way to describe the sensation of his cool lips on her hot skin. "Tykir and Eirik will go to the Witan for me. I trust them to do that. If the Witan denies my petition, I expect my father will demand my immediate deliverance into his hands. Tykir and Eirik could then petition for the return of my mother's lands to me before I am turned over to my father's custody. I'm certain that the Witan would not act on the petition at that session . . . probably they'd wait another month. That would give me till February, only one month from my twenty-fifth birthday. Can't you wait till then?"

"Two months? That's all?" he asked sarcastically, raising his head. He had gone back to kissing and blowing in her ear. He gave his attention to her surcoat now, parting it with his left hand and using his right hand to begin unlacing the neckline of her gunna.

She should stop him. She would, in a moment, once she'd said all she had to say. "Nay, that is not all," she said with a gasp as the backs of his fingers grazed the bare skin of her upper chest. "I would want you to form a *hird* of soldiers for me . . . a hundred should suffice, for a start. Mercenaries would be the best choice, I think. While we are waiting for the Witan's decision, we could establish ourselves at Evergreen."

He had stopped peeling back the neckline of her gunna and was gaping at her. "Why would I do all that? Especially, why would I set aside my own goal— avenging my brother's death—to participate in such a foolhardy plan?"

"I would make it worth your while."

"Oh, really? How?" He made a pointed sweep of her body with his cool eyes.

Surely he didn't think she was offering *that*. "I would make you castellan of Evergreen. Once I regain my funds, I will pay you handsomely."

"I would think so!" he said. Then, after a moment of pondering, "It matters that much to you?"

"It matters desperately to me. I would do anything to outwit my father and regain what is rightfully mine."

"*Anything?*" He arched his brows at her.

"Do not tease me, Toste. I am not worth that much."

"I beg to differ. I have wealth aplenty. I am jaded enough to find appeal in bedding a nun. You would wear your nun outfit, wouldn't you?" He grinned down at her.

He couldn't be serious. It was another jest on his part. Surely it was. But she had to ask. "You will do all that I ask in return for just one coupling?"

"Nay, nay, nay!" he said with a laugh. "I did not say that. It would have to be more than one *coupling.*" He appeared to find much humor in that word. "I would expect you to share my bed furs for the entire time I work for you, or till I grow bored. All without the legal bonds of matrimony, of course."

Of course? Ooooh, the insufferable, overblown lout. I should slap his face and walk away. Right now. This instant. But wait, Esme—mayhap it would be worth the sacrifice if you could regain Evergreen. And be honest with yourself, it might not be such a great sacrifice. You could close your eyes and plan your next day's work schedules whilst it is happening. "So, is it a deal, then?"

"*What?*" The shock on Toste's face that she would acquiesce so easily was priceless. "Nay, it is not a deal. Not yet. I mean, holy bloody hell, dost know what you are offering?"

"I do, and it would be worth the sacrifice if the end result means my return to Evergreen."

"Sacrifice? You consider making love with me a sacrifice?"

The consternation on his face was equally priceless. Really, men and their overemphasis on their bedsport reputations! As if women cared about such things!

But 'twas best to be diplomatic when her future was at stake. "Mayhap sacrifice was too strong a word. But you must agree, men get much more out of the event than women do."

"Oh, I do not know about that. Some men have the expertise to give as good as they get in the *event*."

She almost rolled her eyes but caught herself just in time.

"In fact, I would be a fool to agree to anything without getting a taste aforehand."

"A taste? Speak plainly, Viking. Dost expect me to give up my virginity on the mere hope that you will make a deal with me?"

"Nay, not your virginity. Just a foretaste of the main . . . uh, meal." She could swear his lips twitched with suppressed mirth.

"Just a foretaste," she agreed.

And he did grin then, as if he'd won some battle. *Men!*

"Hmmm. First off, methinks I would have to see your breasts."

"Bare?" she squeaked out.

"Bare."

What a lot of fuss men made over breasts! She'd experienced it firsthand with her father and brothers, who'd practically drooled whenever a big-bosomed maid would pass by. She'd had no doubt, even at that young age, that the maid would soon be spreading her thighs for one of them. Or all of them.

Toste still lay atop her, braced on his extended arms, and he did not seem inclined to move. So she shimmied off her surcoat and ruched the top of her gunna down to her waist, all in a half-reclining position. Then she lay back down and closed her eyes. After a long silence during which nothing happened, she cracked her eyelids open . . . and wished she hadn't.

Toste was staring down at her breasts like a beggar at a feast. Now, Esme was not buxom like the females her father and brothers admired, but her breasts were full and high and apparently pleasing to the eye, if Toste's reaction was any indication.

Braced on one arm, he pushed one breast, then the other, up from underneath. Then he touched both nipples in turn with a forefinger, just the tips, then the sides, then the pink areola, then back to the tips again.

"Jesus, Mary and Joseph!" she exclaimed. Who knew a slight touch there could cause such exquisite pleasure?

"Praying now, are you, Sister Esme?" Toste chuckled.

"I'd better be. This is surely confession material."

He laughed outright. "Because you bared your breasts for me?"

"Nay. Because your touch pleased me so much. I did not know . . . suffice it to say, I did not know."

"Ah, Esme, it gives me pleasure to give you pleasure."

"Does it?" she asked.

He rolled his hips off of her and lay on his side, his left elbow in the hay with a hand supporting his face. His eyes still feasted hungrily on her bosom where the traitorous nipples stood out like pink pebbles. Leaning down, he took one nipple between his lips, then licked it and the surrounding area, then suckled deep and hard. She fisted her hands and arched her back, fighting the overwhelming bolts of ecstasy that shot from her breasts through her body, down to her fingertips and toes, and especially to her private woman-place. She embarrassed herself in the end by letting out little whoof-whoof-whoofs of exhaled breath.

Toste's response to that was a tight-lipped smile and equal ministration to her other breast. By the time he finished, her face felt hot as Hades, and she was aching in some very private parts.

"Did you like that, Esme?" he asked in a husky voice.

"Double confessions. Perchance triple," she answered. "Are you done?"

"Not nearly." He leaned down again, but this time toward her face. Kisses, that was what he had in mind now? Well, he'd kissed her once before, and, though pleasant, the pressing of lips upon lips had been nothing to alarm her.

He soon disabused her of that notion.

At first, he barely touched her mouth . . . just brushed his lips back and forth across hers, as if testing for a proper fit. When he found the arrangement that suited him, he grew more aggressive. His teeth nipped, his lips coaxed, then demanded something from her. When she realized that he wanted her to part for him, he slipped his tongue inside and began what had to be a simulation of the sex act itself. In and out, his tongue stroked her, so slowly she wanted to scream for him to hasten his pace, but what she did was whimper . . . which seemed to be the proper prod for him, because he moved faster now. She wanted to participate more fully in this awful/wonderful exercise, but she didn't know how. So she put her hands on his shoulders in encouragement and opened her mouth more fully to his assault.

He groaned then—a pure masculine sound of sexual torture—which gave her an absurd feeling of gratification. For a certainty, she would be getting a big penance for these sins. And it must be a sin to feel so good.

Finally, when he drew his head back to stare at her, he panted. She probably did, too, though she tried her best to hide his effect on her. His lips were wet and kiss-swollen, his eyes misted with passion.

So this is how lust feels.

"Yea, 'tis."

"Oh, good Lord! Did I speak aloud?"

"You did," he said, chucking her under the chin.

"Now are we done?" she asked, putting a hand up to his hand which held her cheek with tenderness. It was difficult not to feel tender toward a person who made her feel so good. In fact, her body still tingled . . . all over.

"Nay, we are not."

"But . . . but you promised . . . just a foretaste."

"Taste being the key word."

"I don't understand."

"Remember the first time we met, and I was on a sick-bed at the abbey, I asked what your name was, and you said Esme, but I thought you said . . ." He let his words trail off deliberately so she would get his meaning.

She finished for him, hesitantly, "Eat me . . . that is what you said. I still don't understand."

"You will, Esme. You will."

With that, he flipped the hem of her gown up to her waist, exposing her nakedness, and in one fluid move spread her legs and knelt between her thighs.

"Toste! Nay! Oh, this is scandalous, even for you. Eek, what are you doing?" He pushed her feet up so that her heels touched her buttocks, then shoved her knees wide apart. She was fully exposed to his scrutiny *there*, and scrutinize he did. "This is not what I agreed to. A foretaste, that was all. This is definitely not a foretaste." She spewed forth some words then that would definitely earn her a fortnight on her knees in penance.

Toste just chuckled.

She tried to sit up and push him away, but he held her

down firmly with one hand pressed against her belly. The other hand was already examining her woman-fleece.

Then he touched her.

And she was wet.

Could anything in the world be more humiliating than this?

Could anything in the world be more bliss-inspiring?

She had not known she had such a spot there, but Toste had known. That was clear by the way he played that particular piece of flesh. Just when she was becoming accustomed to that play-torture, he inserted a finger inside her. Just one. But her eyes went wide and met his in question.

"Am I hurting you?" he asked.

She shook her head slowly from side to side. In truth, she could not speak. Her inner muscles spoke for her, though, by clenching and unclenching around his finger, which was moving in and out of her. Then he stopped. The brute stopped.

Esme could swear that every fine hair on her body was as stiff as a bristle. Her breasts ached for more of his suckling. And her nether parts had become one long continuous throb. If she were not in this condition, she never would have allowed what he did next. Leastways, that was what she told herself.

Still on his knees, he reached under her and lifted her by the buttocks so that her hips were raised off the ground. Then he showed her—*God's bones and Mary's breath, he showed her*—just what he'd meant by fore-taste and what he'd meant when he'd misspoken her name. With his tongue and his teeth and his lips, he teased her woman folds till they were engorged and she was one keening wail, for what she did not know. Every part of her body, but especially her breasts and woman-place, reached and reached and reached for something beyond reach.

Then it came. Crashing over her, under her, through her. Such sheer, glorious pleasure as her body had never known. She must have swooned for several seconds—and Esme never swooned—because when she regained her senses, she lay spread-eagled and exposed before the still fully clothed Toste. The only thing that saved her from total and utter shame was the fact that he was clearly aroused and fighting his own lustsome urges.

"You were beautiful, Esme," he said huskily.

"Thank you." What else could she say at a time like this? "Now are you done?"

He laughed. "Yea, I am. For now."

"So, you will stay and help me regain Evergreen."

"Nay, Esme, I will not. I must needs leave on the morrow, but I will do all in my power to help you when I return."

She jerked into a sitting position and tugged at her gown so that her breasts and lower region were at least partially covered. "You never intended to stay, did you?"

"Now, Esme, you are being unreasonable." He sat up and watched helplessly as she adjusted herself more fully. Once, he reached out a hand to pick some straw from her hair and she slapped him away.

"Unreasonable?" she shrieked. "I'll tell you what is unreasonable. You thinking that I would allow you to do all those . . . things to me without the possibility of your staying. You tricked me."

"You enjoyed those *things*," he said accusingly.

"Yea, I did," she admitted, standing clumsily and brushing off her gown as best she could. "But it will never happen again. Never."

"Yea, it will. When I return, we will finish what we started here tonight," he argued. Then: "Where are you going?"

"Off to find Eadyth and Alinor and tell them to start their parade of prospective bridegrooms," Esme said without turning. She would not want him to see the tears brimming in her eyes.

"I will be back," he threw out to her backside.

Hah! I've got news for you, Viking. You are not leaving. Not tonight. Not tomorrow. Not for a good long while. Not if I can help it. "You will pay for this, Toste. You will pay."

Esme went off, not to find the ladies of Ravenshire, but to put her own plan into motion. Two could play at this game. Toste Ivarsson was soon going to find that he'd met his match.

The lull before the you-know-what . . .

By the time Toste reentered the keep, Esme was out of sight and almost everybody had gone to bed, except Eirik, Tykir and Bolthor, who still sat before the low fire in the solar. They took one look at Toste, then a quick second look and burst out laughing.

"Look, look, look! Ha ha ha!" Abdul squawked.

"Someone ought to make parrot porridge out of that dumb bird," Toste said.

"You're not the first person to suggest that," Eirik commented.

Bolthor immediately began spewing forth one of his poems, "This Is the Tale of Toste the Torn."

"Toste was a man torn
As ever was a Viking born.
Did he want her?

Did he not?
Should he swive her,
Should he not?
In the end, the maid would take
Things into her own hands,
So Toste would no longer be torn."

"You have straw on your crotch," Eirik pointed out.

"And your lips are red and puffy. Did someone punch you?" Tykir asked with false innocence.

"Methinks I detect a lump in his *braies*. So he might still be a bit tormented . . . and torn," Bolthor concluded.

They were all grinning at him as they sipped their horns of mead. Vikings—and half Vikings, for that matter, as Eirik was—ever did enjoy teasing each other, and Toste did not mind all that much.

Still, he soon changed the subject. "I must needs leave on the morrow at first light with Sister Margaret."

"I will go with you," Bolthor offered, not for the first time.

"Nay. This I will do myself." He'd already explained the details of his plan to the men. "I will be back as soon as possible—by Christmas, I hope. No need for any of you to get up so early in the morn."

"Dressed as a nun?" Tykir asked, a gleam in his merry eyes.

"Yea, dressed as a nun . . . at first. Till after I deliver Sister Margaret to the minster."

"And you will leave Lady Esme here with us?" Eirik inquired.

Toste nodded.

He thought he heard Eirik mutter, "Lackwit!" but he probably said something like, "Holy shit!" 'Twas a favorite expression of Eirik's he'd learned long ago from his barmy half-sister Rain, a healer, who claimed to come from the future.

"By thunder, Toste, do you know how much your brother would have enjoyed this masquerade of yours?" Tykir said.

"I do," he said and fought back tears.

Eirik handed him a horn of mead and said, "To Vagn!" They all raised their horns then and said, "To Vagn!"

It was a fitting good-bye, Toste thought.

I can't believe I'm doing this . . .

Esme worked furiously to complete her plan.

It was the most daring thing she'd ever tried. But desperation prompted daring. That was what she told herself.

Having a few coins she'd garnered over the years, she managed to bribe a retired cook from Ravenshire to help her. Bertha, a slovenly, greedy-eyed crone of more than sixty years, still lived on the estate in her own thatched hut and helped out in the kitchens on occasion.

"Did you prepare the empty woodcutter's hut, as I instructed?"

"Yea, I did, mistress, and I got ye a fire goin', too. It's colder'n hell on a Sunday outside, it is." She scratched her armpits as she spoke, then broke wind loudly.

Esme restrained herself from wincing or clouting the foul woman. She needed her, having had no time to find a better accomplice.

"And you promise not to tell anyone about this?"

"Are ye barmy, mistress? I'd be kicked out of Ravenshire on me arse if anyone found out."

"All right. Now go to Toste and give him my message."

After Bertha left, Esme picked up a bundle she'd prepared, put on a cloak and made her way toward the woodcutter's hut, which she hoped was far enough away from the keep that no one would suspect what was going on.

"Dear God," she prayed, "please help me, and I will say a paternoster every day for the rest of my life."

She thought she heard a voice in her head, presumably God's, say, "You are on your own."

So be it.

Even tricksters get tricked betimes . . .

"The lady Esme wishes ye to attend her out at the woodcutter's hut."

"Huh?" Toste said. He was alone in the solar and nodding off to sleep, having drunk many more horns of mead than he should have. "Why does she want me? And why at the woodcutter's hut? And how in Thor's name would I know where that is?"

The old slattern blinked at him in what was supposed to be a sexual way, he supposed. "I be thinkin' that a virile Viking like you would know what she wants."

"Huh?" he said again.

"Are ye comin' or not? It's past my bedtime, and Lars is waitin' fer me in the furs. Expectin' a second swive, I 'spect."

He couldn't imagine anyone wanting even a first swive with her. "Yea, I am coming," he said. He was too intrigued by the possibility—remote as it was—that Esme wanted something more from him. After all, her last words to him had been, "You will pay." But it was understandable, really. He had always had a way with women. She wanted him, pure and simple. It was the only explanation.

He couldn't wait.

* * *

Caught in the spider's web . . .

Toste made his way clumsily down the path, lit only by the torch the old crone carried before him. He shouldn't have drunk so much mead, especially on the eve of a journey.

If he'd known the woodcutter's hut was this far from the keep, he never would have come. Well, actually, he would have. His curiosity had always been stronger than his good sense.

When they finally arrived and he saw light seeping through the shuttered window openings and smoke coming through a hole in the roof, he breathed a sigh of relief. It wasn't one of Tykir's jokes, as he'd begun to suspect.

The slattern opened the door for him, shoved him inside, then slammed the door after him. He could swear he heard a lock click into place, but he was probably mistaken.

The single room was dark, except for the hearth fire. When he accustomed himself to the dim light, he saw Esme, and he relaxed with a grin.

She wore a gossamer-thin bed rail. Backlit by the fire, the outline of her nude body underneath the rail could be seen as clear as day.

He stepped forward and began to reach for her.

She danced away. "Nay, Toste. Do not be so anxious. Take off your clothing first."

Take off my clothing? Whoa! We are moving a bit fast here, aren't we, my lady? But Toste was not dumb enough to speak those words of caution. "I thought you were angry with me," he said even as he began to disrobe.

"I am, but I find that other emotions inside me are even stronger." She put a palm against her stomach as if to indicate where those stronger emotions were located.

His cock, which had already raised its head with interest at the vision of Esme in the see-through garment, now came to full attention. He'd treated her badly earlier tonight, when he'd implied that if she would do such and such he would not leave. Mayhap he would be able to make it up to her now.

When he was fully naked and she gawked at him as if a trifle frightened—as well she should be—she said something that entirely destroyed the impression of naivete. "Toste . . . uhm . . . would you mind if I tied you to the bed?"

Not only was he shocked but his precious manpart was shocked, too. Why else would blue veins be standing out on it as if it were going to explode? "Why?" he asked her, once he pulled his gaping jaw off the floor. *That has to be the dumbest thing I have ever said.*

"Because I am rather shy . . . and this is my first time . . . and, well, I would feel better if I could explore your body first . . . and . . . oh, I suppose it was a bad idea."

"Nay, nay, I didn't say that. But you don't have to restrain me to explore my body, dearling." *I wonder if I am in a drunken stupor and imagining all this.*

"Oh, you say that now, but if I touch you in the wrong way—or the right way—you might be tempted to . . . never mind."

Tempted? I am so tempted, lady, that my thickening is about to explode. "Nay, we will do it your way," he said quickly afore she changed her mind. He made his way toward the pallet in the corner and was disconcerted, but only for a moment, to see soft cloth strips hanging from each of the four bedposts. She had been prepared for his yielding. Ah, well, he would make her yield much more by morning. He lay down and submitted each of his limbs for her to tie, which she did with surprisingly strong and secure knots.

Then she stepped back from the pallet and said, "Do not be angry, Toste."

"Why should I be angry?" Understanding came to him of a sudden. A trick! He had been tricked. He fought mightily against his restraints, to no avail. "Can I assume there will be no tupping tonight?"

She nodded.

"Do not do this, Esme. You have no idea what the consequences will be. I have killed men for much less."

"You forced me to it. Agree to my plan, give your word of honor, and I will release you right now."

He told her to do something vulgar to herself.

She winced but did not back down. When he continued to glower at her, she walked closer, tied a thin strip across his mouth to prevent his yelling, and pulled a fur pelt up over his body against the chill which was sure to fill the hut in the coming hours.

"I will check on you in the morning," she said after covering herself with a cloak and slipping her feet into leather shoes. To her credit, her expression was filled with sadness. Then she left. Just like that. She left.

Silence filled the hut, and Toste shook his mead-fuzzy head. He could not believe what had just happened. A part of him admired Esme for her daring in pulling off such a trick. But a bigger part of him was blood-boiling angry.

Toste started to laugh behind his gag and couldn't stop. Not even when tears rolled from his eyes. Esme had won this battle, but she'd best beware. This war was far from over.

CHAPTER TEN

❦

Brother, where art thou? . . .

Vagn was dreaming. He knew he must be dreaming. And yet the picture behind his eyelids was so vivid.

He was lying on a bed. Correction: His brother Toste was lying on a bed. And he was spread-eagled, bare-arse naked, tied to the bed posts.

Is someone trying to make my brother wed, just as Gorm restrained me in hopes of a forced marriage to his daughter Helga?

Do people wed in the Other World?

He would be worried about Toste and whatever torture was about to be inflicted on him, except that his brother was laughing uproariously at his predicament. And Vagn saw a woman's form in the shadows. *Was there ever a man's predicament in which a woman wasn't involved?* It was the same black-haired witch he'd seen before, the one who turned his brother hard with lust.

It was all so confusing. First he'd seen images of his brother being picked at by black crows. Then he'd thought his brother kissed a nun. Now he seemed to be involved in bondage, and laughing about it. What could it mean? One thing was for sure: Valhalla, or heaven, for that matter, was not all it was cracked up to be . . . . if that was indeed where Toste resided now.

Where art thou, brother?
How can you speak to me from the Other Side?
Is there a reason you keep calling to me?
Dost need my help?

When Vagn awakened, he found his face wet with tears.

Well, he thought grimly as he dressed for the day ahead and noticed through the arrow slit window that it was snowing again, *much as I would like to help you, brother, I have my own torture to take care of.*

Since when do Vikings sit back twiddling their thumbs, and other body parts, whilst others take the offensive?

Since when do Viking men allow their women to rule the roost?

Since when do Viking men let their women do more outrageous things than they do?

Enough!

Today was the day Vagn Ivarsson was going to show Helga the Temptress that her tempting days were over.

Cosmo, where art thou? . . .

Helga was running out of ideas.

In fact, she was running, period. She'd seen the glint in Vagn's eyes this morning when he was breaking fast with her father's guardsmen and it said, loud and clear: *Helga, you'd best run for your life. There is one mad Viking out for your tail.*

Even Helga recognized that the candle incident went beyond what was proper into the realm of the scandalous. Perchance even the perverted. How would she know? She'd never even heard of perversions till a few days ago.

"Greetings, Helga," a male voice said.

She almost jumped out of her skin. She was sorting embroidery threads in the rear of her sewing solar, out of view from the door . . . or so she had thought. But fortunately, it wasn't Vagn. It was Finn Finehair.

"Greetings, Finn," she replied as he came closer. His mustache was looking particularly fine today and he'd forked his beard. What was the occasion?

Uh-oh! He was gazing at her the way Vagn did on occasion. With hunger.

At first, he just leered down at her, twirling one side of his mustache with his fingertips. Did he have any idea how ridiculous he looked? Apparently not.

"Wouldst like to sit next to me tonight at dinner?" he asked, still leering.

"Why?"

"I have been . . . uh, noticing you of late."

"Why?"

"Do not be coy, m'lady," he said, tweaking her chin. Nobody ever tweaked her chin, but she was too surprised to react before he went on, "I have been getting your hidden messages."

"What hidden messages?"

"Oh, the sway of your hips. The licking of your lips. Your jutting bosom."

Helga could understand how he might have misunderstood the signals she had been sending to Vagn.

"Besides, Vagn said—"

She dropped the threads she'd been sorting. "Vagn said *what*?"

"Well, he didn't precisely say you were hot for me, but the way he worried over your attentions to me, 'twas obvious . . . *you know.*"

"Nay, I do not know. What precisely did Vagn tell you?" *I will kill the lout. I swear I will.*

" 'Stay away from Helga'—that is what he said."

"Vagn said that to you." An odd thrill rippled through Helga. Mayhap the lout did care for her, after all.

"Yea, and I figure that he would not admonish me so if he didn't suspect you are attracted to me. Many women are, Helga; so do not blush. As to Vagn, he obviously envies me my fine beard, and you know what they say about men with mustaches, don't you?"

The waggle of his eyebrows, which appeared to be plucked into a perfect arch, should have told her that further questions could be perilous. But did she listen to her intuition? Nay. "What do they say about men with mustaches?"

"They are better able to please ladies in the bedsport." Now he was twirling the other end of his mustache.

She frowned, unable to picture how a mustache would figure in the coupling in any woman-pleasing way.

Finn must have interpreted her frown of confusion as permission to elaborate. "More friction when the man's mouth is engaged down below."

Helga gasped. She'd never heard anything so outrageous in all her life. Could it be true?

Finn preened as if he'd informed her of some great personal talent. Mayhap it was.

"Methinks that Vagn envies my finesse. After all, I have a fine mustache and he does not. It's all in the bristles, you know, and the wax."

This is more information than I want or need. How did this conversation go so far afield . . . like into the midden?

She decided to let him down gently and tell him she was not really interested in him. But just then, Vagn came storming in.

"I thought I told you to stay away from Helga," he shouted at Finn, fists raised.

"Try and make me," Finn countered, raising his fists, too.

She jumped between the two just in time.

Vagn and Finn were of the same height and build, but to her way of thinking, Vagn was a much more handsome man. Today he wore dark brown *braies* tucked into low boots and a leather tunic belted at the waist. His long blond hair was tied back off his face—a face with high cheekbones, strong jaw and cleft chin. Eyes as clear as a summer sky glared at her icily. This was a man who needed no mustache to enhance his masculinity. He was man enough without adornments.

But handsome didn't matter in her present situation. The man was interfering in her life.

"Who are you to make decisions concerning my life, Vagn? 'Tis none of your affair whom I associate with." She did not stop to consider the irony of the fact that she'd planned to get rid of Finn herself and was now defending her association with him.

"Hah! You made it my affair when you concocted that scandalous proposal."

"What scandalous proposal?" Finn wanted to know.

"Yea, what scandalous proposal?" her father wanted to know. She hadn't realized her father had entered the solar on the heels of Vagn. Her father had probably been drawn by the raised voices . . . as had a dozen housecarls who were gaping at the spectacle.

She would have groaned if there were time, but she had to act quickly before Vagn did something rash, like tell her father she'd asked for his seed.

"I offered to make Vagn a cloak of bright red wool to

match his eyes on a *drukkinn* night, embroidered along the edges with pink tongues. He considered the garment a scandal. Ha ha ha!"

Tongues? Vagn mouthed at her, then gave her a cold look, obviously trying to decide whether to embarrass her in front of one and all by telling the truth. "Notice that I am not amused, m'lady," he said finally. Fortunately, though, his anger seemed to have dissolved.

Finn left the solar chuckling, and her father remarked to Vagn, "You do not think a tongue cloak is mirth-some?"

"Nay, I much prefer a cloak embroidered with . . . oh, let us say, candles," he answered to the bewilderment of all who remained.

Except Helga.

Who discovered she was suddenly left alone in the solar with Vagn.

And he was not smiling at all.

Let's make a deal . . .

"Sit down, Helga. We are going to talk."

Her eyes darted right and left, as if she were considering a run for freedom. When she realized that he blocked any escape route and there was no one left in the room to help her, she sighed in surrender and perched herself atop a high stool. She made sure that a table separated them, though it would offer little protection if he chose to attack. But that would come later. For now, he sat on a high stool on his side of the table, tented his fingers before his mouth and pondered the troublesome wench.

How anyone could have called her homely was beyond him. Today Helga wore a plain blue gunna with a gold braid belt, covered by a sleeveless surcoat of a darker blue. Her golden blond hair was braided intricately into one thick braid that hung down to her waist.

Her blue eyes were wide with embarrassment she tried to hide with fluttering brown lashes. Her lips, large and luscious, parted as if in invitation. If Helga only knew the power of those lips!

"I'm not afraid of you," she said of a sudden.

"You should be."

She raised her chin defiantly.

"I am a man full-grown, not a youthling whose strings you can pull like a puppeteer. For days you have been teasing me like a dockside tart. I have allowed you to think you can manipulate me, just to see how far you would go, and truth to tell, you shocked the spit out of me. No more games."

"I did not play any games."

He raised a halting hand. "Please! Helga the Gamester could be your new name."

"Well, you forced me to use underhanded tactics when you would not agree outright."

He laughed. The woman never gave up. "That is the most backhanded apology I have e'er heard."

"I was not apologizing."

"You should."

She inhaled deeply, which caused him to look at her chest area . . . and wonder irrelevantly if her nipples were large underneath her clothes.

She saw the direction of his gaze and folded her arms over her chest.

Little good that did when his lustsome imagination was involved.

"Are you a gambler, Helga?"

"Huh?"

"You heard me. This sex-dance you have been playing with me is like a game of chance. 'Tis time to even the odds. Are you willing to play?"

"Nay!" she said without thinking. Then immediately amended, "It depends on the final prize, and whether the rules are fair."

"You want a babe."

"You do not."

"I want your body."

He saw her eyes light up and her lips part at that disclosure. He guessed that *now* her nipples were engorged or he was not the man he knew himself to be.

"But I am willing to give my body only if a babe will result. You have told me that is out of the question."

"I'm thinking of another alternative."

"The game of chance you mentioned."

Quick-thinking lady! He had to admire that. "The very same," he agreed. "There are ways for a man to prevent conception, Helga. Ways known all the way back to the beginning of time. 'Tis known as spilling one's seed upon the ground."

Her face flushed as she comprehended his meaning. "And why would I agree to that?"

"Because it is not a certain method."

"Are you asking me to make love with you on the mere chance that I might conceive?"

He shrugged. "Even under the best of circumstances, conception seems to be in the hands of the gods. I know men and women who have been swiving their entire lives and never had children, whilst with others the quickening happens after only one poke."

"My father would have a fit to know that some rogue was defiling his daughter under his very roof." *On the other hand, if it fit his purposes in creating a grand-babe, he probably wouldn't mind that much.*

"*Defiling?* You make sex sound dirty. Well, actually, good lovemaking can be dirty . . . in a nice-dirty way."

His lips twitched with mirth but only for a second. He was not in the mood for laughter just yet.

He could tell that she had no idea what he meant by "nice-dirty," but she wasn't about to ask. Good. In his present mood, he would probably tell her in very precise detail.

"Your father would not have to know . . . if we were discreet. 'Tis not my intent to shame you, Helga. In fact, I would insist that no one know of our arrangement or our doings, including your carnal mentor, the ill-famed Rona, or that peacock Finn."

Her lips twitched with mirth then, too, at his accurate description of Finn.

Vagn gave her a level somber gaze. He was taking this all very seriously, and he wanted her to know that.

"It all seems so secretive . . . as if it were dishonorable."

"I prefer the word 'private' to 'secretive.' "

"I understand how the game would work if I do not conceive, but suppose your seed did manage to find my womb. What then?"

His own face flushed now. "I would not abandon my son."

"And if it were a daughter?"

"I would not abandon my daughter, either."

"Explain yourself."

"I would wed you."

She threw her hands in the air with exasperation. "Then I gain naught. If I were willing to wed to gain a child, I would have done so long ago."

He would like naught more than to reach across the table and shake the willful wench. Why must she always be at cross purposes with him? Why could she not be biddable for once? He counted to ten silently, then offered, "A compromise, then."

She tilted her head in question.

"If I should get you with child, I would offer for you. If you refuse, then you must let me acknowledge my child and be a part of the babe's life."

"You ask much."

"Nay, Helga, you are the one who asks much."

"Why would you be willing to make this compromise?"

"Because I want you so bad my teeth hurt and my loins ache. I have never wanted a woman as much as I want you." *And because my cock is so hard it hurts and must soon find a sheath. And because you are driving me eye-rolling barmy. And because I keep picturing candles. And because I want to see for myself if you have turned into a raisin down there.*

He could tell that his words pleased her. Good thing he'd kept his coarser thoughts to himself. "Besides," he said with a grin, "Toste wants me to."

She grinned back at him. "Been talking to your dead brother again, have you?"

"Yea. All the time." He reached across the table and took one of her hands in his. Just that gesture gave him a thrill, so besotted was he. When he laced the fingers of her hand in one of his and their wrists pressed against each other, he had to close his eyes against the intense emotion he felt. He could not imagine the outcome of this strange pact they were making, but it felt right. "Will I come to you tonight, or will you come to me?" he asked in a voice raw with need.

"I will come to you."

And so their fate was sealed.

When a man loves a woman . . .

Vagn had told Helga that he was a full-grown man who was too old for games, but he felt like a youthling now. And games were beginning to hold way too much appeal. Sex games, that is.

He swept the stale rushes from his bedchamber and replaced them with new fragrant ones. He put clean linens on the mattress and shook out the bed furs. An extra candle burned on a low table. A warm fire burned in the small hearth. All this he did himself, wanting to please Helga with these intimate courtesies.

As for himself, he bathed, shaved off his facial hairs and braided war braids on either side of his face. A man needed his hair off his face when leaning over a woman. Then he donned clean garments.

He looked down at his hands as he waited for her and saw that they trembled. The sight pulled him up short.

Was the trembling from excessive arousal? After all, it had been almost a year since he'd lain with a woman, thanks to his and Toste's forced celibacy as Jomsvikings.

Or was he suddenly nervous about his talents in the bedsport? That could not be. He'd been making love for fifteen and more years, and his expertise had never failed him.

Then it must be Helga who turned him into a jittery halfling. Scary prospect, that. No woman had ever had such an effect on him. It made him feel vulnerable and lacking in his usual self-confidence. Like a needy milksop, for the love of Frigg! Good thing his old friend Bolthor the Skald was no longer in this world. He would compose a horrible poem about Vagn's present dilemma . . . something like "When Viking Men Lose Their Swagger."

It was unacceptable, he decided, slamming his cup of ale down on the table and causing the candle flame to flicker. *I am Vagn Ivarsson. I do not humble myself for anyone. Not even a woman for whom my lust is high.*

He undid his belt and jerked his tunic over his head, tossing it to the floor and no doubt mussing his hair in the process. He did not care. He was angry with himself. Next he sat down on the bed and pulled off his half-boots and short hose, pitching them across the chamber to land hither and yon. He was about to shimmy out of his *braies* when he heard her soft knock on the door. He stopped in mid-shimmy, unsure whether to take them off or not. But Helga took that decision out of his hands by entering without waiting for his response to her knock. He yanked the breeches back up.

Before she even looked at him, she turned and made sure the door was locked so they would not be disturbed. Smart thinking. At least someone in this room was thinking with the right body part.

She wore the same blue cloak she'd worn to his chamber afore, but she was not nude underneath as she'd been then. He saw that when she dropped the cloak. She was covered from neck to wrist to ankles by a thin linen bed rail. The shift was plain, but Helga was not. Her blond hair hung loose about her back and shoulders and chest.

Her wide blue eyes took in his state of undress. He saw fear there and in the clenching of her fists at her sides.

In that moment, Vagn forgot his misgivings over his own seeming vulnerabilities. "Helga," was all he could manage to say.

As if given a cue, she flew at him, wrapping her arms around his shoulders and burying her face in the crook of his neck. "I thought this would be easy," she confessed.

So did I. "It will be." *I hope.*

At first, he just held her tightly against him with one arm around her waist and the other hand up under her hair, kneading her nape. He kissed the top of her fragrant head and murmured nothing words to soothe her.

Helga was tall, only a half-head shorter than he. So, with her on tiptoe, they stood breast to bare chest, belly to belly, thigh to thigh, woman-place to manpart. It seemed they fit perfectly together.

In that instant, Vagn realized something important. All his experience in bedsport, all the charm acquired during years of dealing with women—none of it mattered. This joining with Helga was special . . . different. He couldn't say how or why. It just was. In some ways, he would be as much a virgin as Helga. He thought he heard Toste laughing in his head at that outlandish notion.

Helga raised her head finally and looked at him.

He kept one hand on her nape and used the other to cup her cheek. He kissed her then, searching, slow and soft. Seeking the perfect fit.

She kept her hands on his shoulders and followed all his signals with her own mouth. She mimicked his movements, shifting and adjusting. He ran the tip of his tongue along the seam of her mouth; she did the same to his. When he deepened the kiss and filled her mouth with his tongue, she sucked him in welcome.

He hadn't realized that his hands had moved, but they were everywhere, learning the curves and planes of her body. The soft places and the hard. His big palms moved the fabric of her bed rail as he caressed her. Sweeping her shoulders and back. Kneading her buttocks. Testing the smallness of her waist. And all the while, he kept kissing her hungrily.

And, praise the gods, she kissed him back, just as hungrily. And ran her small hands over his shoulders, the flat nipples on his chest, his backside.

"You won't be sorry, dearling," he murmured against her wet lips when he came up for air.

"I know," she said and smiled.

That smile caused his heart to lurch.

He was aroused beyond anything he'd ever imagined, and yet totally in control now. He would go slow. More than anything, he wanted to please Helga as much as himself.

Finally he took hold of Helga's forearm and held her away from him. Maintaining eye contract, he shrugged out of his *braies* and took supreme male pleasure in the way her mouth opened in surprise at the size of his thickening. He was pretty surprised himself. Blue-veined ones were rare and to be prized. Leastways, that's what Toste always said. Then he stepped forward and raised her bedrail up and over her head, leaving them both naked to observe each other.

She was as tall and willowy as a young sapling. Fineboned, with a narrow waist tapering out to small hips. *How does she ever expect to carry a babe there?* Her breasts were so small they would not even fill his hand, but they were capped with big pink nipples that made up for any lack in size of the whole. *Would she nurse a babe? Would her breasts change then? Do not think of that, Vagn. Do not even think it.* Her long, long legs were thin but shapely. *Would her sons be long-legged, too? Dangerous thought, that.* Her woman-fleece matched the blondness of her hair, but was curly. She was different from the women he'd been attracted to in the past. But better. Way better.

He smiled then.

And she did, too.

With a joyous whoop, he took her by the waist and

threw her onto his bed, then landed himself at her side. The bed ropes creaked, but fortunately held.

"You must tell me what to do, Vagn."

"Nothing. For now. Just let me look." He waggled his eyebrows at her. "And explore. If there is one thing we Northmen are good at, it is exploring."

"Comes from a-Viking all these years, no doubt," she teased.

"For a certainty, my saucy maid."

And explore he did. With his eyes, his fingertips. And finally his mouth . . . he had been saving that for last. Well, not last. But he'd been putting off this particular feast. He fingered her nipples, then put his mouth over one of them.

She gasped. "You have no idea how good that feels."

"I know how good it feels to me." He sighed at the sweet taste. "Like succulent raspberries they are." He laved them, and nibbled, and kissed, then suckled and suckled and suckled till it was unclear who was keening in pleasure, him or her.

"I cannot believe that I deprived myself of this bliss for all these years," she said, pulling his head up by his ears. "Why do women hide this news from other women? Oh, I can see why. Fathers would have trouble keeping their daughters virgin if this temptation was waving in front of them."

Vagn did not like this train of thinking. He did not want her to think that just any man could bring her ecstasy. "It is not always this good, sweetling."

"Oh? Is it just you, then, who is so skilled in the bed arts?"

He nipped a nipple with his teeth for her making mock of him. "Yea, just me. And do not forget it."

She probably would have said more, but he had his palm on her belly now, way down, and he could see that he had her attention . . . *there*. He pressed rhythmically several times and watched her face. Her lips parted with wonder, which made him feel . . . well, wonderful.

"Have I ever told you how much I adore your mouth?"

"About a dozen times," she said. Then, "Tell me again."

"I . . . adore . . . your . . . mouth," he said against her mouth.

"What else do you adore about me?" she asked playfully.

"Your breasts."

"Oh, that is such a lie." She tried to sit up in indignation but he forced her back down.

"It is not a lie. You have made me appreciate small breasts. I do not think I will ever be attracted to big-bosomed women again, and that is the truth."

"You ooze charm like sweat, you rogue."

"Flattery will get you everything, m'lady sharp tongue. But enough of this piddling around. 'Tis time to discover some truths about you, Helga."

"Piddling? You call what we've done so far piddling? It does not seem piddling to me. What truths?"

"Like whether you have turned into a raisin down below," he said and dipped his fingers into her damp woman-folds before she could shriek her outrage. Her warm honey welcomed him.

"And have I?" she gasped out.

"What?" Somewhere between her enthusiastic response to their bedsport and the wet signs of her readiness, Vagn had lost his power of reasoning.

"Turned into a raisin?"

He inserted a forefinger into her tight inner folds,

which clasped and unclasped around him. He might have gurgled then, but he was not sure. "Nay," he said, shaking his head. "You are more like a lush, succulent peach."

"Good," she said.

He rolled over on top of her, and she spread her legs wide for him. The ridge of his staff nestled in her woman channel, like a longship coming home. But there was one more thing he had to say. "There is still time to change your mind, Helga," he said. "Once I enter, you can no longer claim virginity. If you choose to wed someday, your husband will be cheated."

"Would you feel cheated if I came to you without a maidenhead?"

"Nay, but surely you know a maidenhead is prized by many."

"I come to you willingly, Vagn." She put a gentle hand on his cheek and let the fingertips trail down his jaw, his neck and the center of his chest. "It is time."

He raised her knees and spread them wider, poising himself at her entrance, his arms braced on either side of her head. With a barely stifled grunt, he drove into her, to the hilt.

She stiffened for a moment, then relaxed.

"Are you all right? Am I hurting you?"

"Just a twinge. Don't move. Let me get accustomed . . . oh. Oh. That is better. Oh, you fill me. And grow. I can feel you growing."

Her voice carried amazement. Bloody hell, he was amazed, too. As her inner folds shifted to accommodate him, his cock had grown even bigger.

"I need to move, Helga. Can I move?"

"I don't know," she choked out with a little laugh. "Can you?"

Turned out he could.

He tried to be gentle. He tried to go slow. But it had been so long. And she was so hot and receptive as she flailed from side to side, crying out for something she did not yet understand. Too soon his long, slow strokes turned short and hard, especially as she bucked her hips reflexively, riding the peak that soon overtook her. With a roar of equal parts satisfaction and frustration, he pulled out of her and spilled his seed into the soft cloth he'd placed under the pillow for just that purpose. Later, he would throw it into the fire.

For now, he lay collapsed over Helga, probably crushing her. But she'd drained him of all energy. By the gods! What would she do to him when she knew how to use her body? He could not imagine. He could not wait.

"What are you smiling about?" Helga asked when he raised his head to look at her.

"I am happy." And that was the truth, which surprised him mightily. Helga had managed to pull him from that pit of depression he'd been wallowing in of late. "And why are you smiling?"

"Because I am happy, too."

"Because you might carry my seed?"

She shook her head. "Because you pleased me, Viking."

Her words reached in and grabbed his heart. For a second, he could not breathe.

"Of course, if I've caught your seed, I will be even more pleased."

But I won't be pleased.

Will I?

Why am I even asking?

"There is one thing I was wondering," she said, twirling one of his chest curls.

"And that would be?" he said, twirling one of her nipples.

"Just how many of those seed catch-cloths do you have?"

He laughed in surprise. "Why?"

"Because it's going to be a long night."

"I hope so, sweetling. I hope so."

I am woman . . . hear me purr . . .

"Well, well, well," Helga murmured to herself four hours and three bouts of lovemaking later.

She gazed down at Vagn, who snored softly in the bed beside her. His arms were thrown over his head in abandon, revealing oddly endearing patches of blond hair in his armpits. His legs were splayed. A small smile lay on his full lips. There was a tooth print on his shoulder, a suck mark on his lower belly and scratches on his back. The man had been knocked on his sweet arse, wrung inside out and flattened.

And Helga had done it. To say that she was supremely satisfied with her hidden talents in the bedsport would be a vast understatement.

Oh, she'd come to Vagn in hopes of catching his male seed, but she would be less than honest if she did not admit how much she'd enjoyed the exercise . . . or how much she looked forward to more of it. But for now, she had to creep back to her own bedchamber before anyone discovered her whereabouts. She feared falling asleep at Vagn's side—though the prospect held appeal—and being discovered in the morn by a chambermaid. Her father would be up here with a sword and a priest in an instant. There would be no sword-point wedding for her. In fact, no wedding at all.

With one last grin of satisfaction, Helga began to slip from the bed. She was almost off when a hand gripped her ankle and pulled her back.

"Where do you think you're going, sweetling?"

He tugged hard and she landed half on and half off the rogue. Not only was he awake but a key part of his body was, too. A part she was growing rather fond of.

"I must get back to my bedchamber afore dawn," she explained.

"'Tis a long time till dawn, and I have much to show you afore then."

He was kneading her buttocks and blowing in her ear the whole time he spoke softly to her, so it was no wonder his words did not immediately register in her brain. "Show me?" she finally squeaked out. "Show me what?"

"The far-famed Viking S-spot, of course."

"Oh? And where might that be?"

"Inside."

Sweet Valkyries! I do not dare ask what he means by that. Instead, she asked something equally lackwitted, "And how would I find it?"

"You wouldn't. I would." By now, Vagn had spread her nether cheeks from behind and was doing wicked things with his long fingers.

"How?" she was fool enough to ask. "With your . . . oh, oh . . . fingers?"

"Nay. With my tongue."

And he did.

No wonder they said Vikings were many-talented men.

No wonder Norse women walked around with smiles on their faces.

No wonder she was falling a little bit in love with Vagn Ivarsson.

* * *

The naked-in-a-crowd nightmare . . .

Helga was in the great hall by mid-morning eating her third bowl of raisin porridge and second piece of man-chet bread slathered with butter, accompanied by a huge wooden cup of ale. She was ravenous, for some reason.

"Helga, what ails you?" her father asked. "I have ne'er seen you eat so much at one sitting."

"Must be the storm and all this inactivity inside." Now, that was an ill-thought-out answer. Everyone knew that just the opposite was true; activity bred appetite. Oh, well.

He stared at her disbelievingly. "Your face is flushed, and your lips are puffy. Are you sure you are not ill?"

Rona made a snorting sound as she passed by just then, and Finn, who sat on her father's other side, said, "She looks like a maid who's been well-tu . . ." His words trailed off, luckily, at the glare of warning from Helga. He grinned pointedly, however, as he sipped his own ale and watched her squirm.

"Nay, I am not ill. Cannot a lady eat to her content without everyone gawking at her?"

Everyone turned away, but she could see from the corner of her eye the frown of confusion on her father's face.

Just then, Vagn swaggered up.

Oh, good gods! Did he have to swagger? Everyone will suspect what went on, if they don't already.

Then she noticed his collarless tunic, which exposed the bite mark on his shoulder near the curve of his neck. She hoped no one would notice, but no such luck! A quick glance found her father, Finn, Rona and several others staring at said mark and grinning.

Her father had not yet connected the mark with her, though, because he remarked to Vagn, "Appears that your celibate life has ended, boy. Good for you! A man must needs release his body humors on occasion, lest he explode."

Vagn grinned and winked before sitting down beside her.

She put her face in her hand and groaned.

"I am starving," Vagn said. "I don't know why, because I ate several hours ago, and a tasty repast it was, too."

She groaned again.

Under the table, she felt Vagn's hand on her thigh and it was creeping upward. Her head shot up and she glowered at him. But did that stop him? Nay. He pretended to be listening to something her father said about a wild boar being seen near the keep the night before. And while her father and some of his guardsmen discussed a hunt planned for later that morn, Vagn ate with one hand and brought her to peak with the other.

Finally her father glanced her way, then glanced again. "Helga! You are definitely looking flushed, and now you are breathless. I insist you go back to your bed and rest. I will be gone for several hours and will check on you later."

"Perhaps you are right," she said, standing on wobbly legs.

As she nodded her farewells to everyone, she started to walk away. That was when she heard Vagn tell her father, "Actually, I think I must pass on the boar hunt today. My wound has been aching all night, and my head is beginning to pound. Methinks I should take to my bed, as well. Do you mind?"

"Nay. Go on, boy. There will be other boars."

After they left, everyone looked at each other at the high table, then burst out laughing. Gorm laughed hardest of all. And the wagers flew hot and high.

CHAPTER ELEVEN

&

Oh, the webs we weave when first we deceive . . .

It was the second sennight of December. Snow and ice storms had made prisoners of them all at Ravenshire, except for Eirik, Tykir and Bolthor, who'd gone off before the weather change to Winchester to address the Witan. And except for Toste, who was, of course, a real prisoner these past five days.

Toste's "disappearance" had raised no alarm bells the day after Esme had tricked him into going to the woodcutter's hut. Everyone assumed that he had gone with Sister Margaret and was off somewhere searching for his brother's killer. Actually, a stableboy had traveled with Sister Margaret, thanks to the release of another of Esme's precious coins.

Esme's plan was not going at all as she'd expected. In fact, she felt as if she'd put her head in the mouth of a tiger, and now she didn't know how to pull it out. As a result, she had taken to biting her fingernails to the quick and wringing her hands in nervousness—gestures which did not escape Eadyth and Alinor, who assumed that Esme was distressed over potentially bad news their husbands might bring back from the king. If they only knew! That was the least of her problems at the moment.

Girding herself with resolve, she entered the hut. She

brushed snowflakes off her cloak, laid it over a chair and her bundle of food on the floor, then stoked the fire to make sure it would adequately heat the small room. Only then did she turn to look at Toste. The gag was in his mouth, as it always was when he was alone, to prevent him from yelling for help, but his eyes shot blue daggers at her. Somehow the fur pelt had slipped off him, and he lay there as nude as any man could be. She tried not to look below his neck.

No one would go near Toste with a razor to shave his face, not even Lars, Bertha's bed companion. So his face was covered with bristles. Instead of looking scruffy, he looked dangerous. Which of course he was.

Walking over, she removed the gag from his mouth. "Would you like a drink of water?"

He refused to answer, just continued to glare at her.

"Is there anything I can do for you?"

"Release me."

"Only if you will agree to stay till I am secure in my place at Evergreen." Really, the man was as stubborn as a mule. She'd thought for sure he would have acquiesced by now.

"Release me," he demanded again, refusing to agree to anything.

"I can't," she said.

"I'm going to kill you, Esme. You give me no choice. Once I am free, I am going to kill you."

He said that often, every time she visited him at the hut. One of the things he objected to most was the fact that Bertha or her aged lover came several times a day to put a pan under his buttocks so he could take care of bodily functions. Bertha also bathed him daily, and took great delight in that chore. Esme knew it all must be demeaning for Toste, but what choice did she have?

Seeing that his death threats were getting him nowhere, Toste said, "If I lie here much longer without exercising my body, I will develop bedsores on my arse."

He was probably correct. Esme had seen Mother Wilfreda treat many such sores on elderly people who were unable to walk about.

"Well, couldn't you contract and release the various muscles in your body? You know, focus on a particular body part. That should bring blood to the surface."

His eyes went wide. "Are you suggesting that I flex my arse cheeks?"

"Coarse clod," she muttered under her breath.

"Better yet, mayhap it is another body part you wish me to flex."

And while she watched, he showed her which body part he meant by making it flex and then grow, without any touching. Even the birthmark on his inner thigh seemed to move. It was probably a talent that men considered awe-inspiring. But to a woman, it was just yawn-inspiring.

"Coarse clod!" she said again, and this time she didn't bother to keep her voice low. With a snarl of disgust, she yanked the fur pelt up to his chest . . . something she should have done when she first entered the hut.

He just laughed.

She unwrapped her bundle and made up a plate of cold slices of roast duck and venison, hard cheese, an apple, a circle of manchet bread still with the hole in the center, and two honey cakes. "Are you hungry?" she asked.

He nodded and she pulled a chair over, next to the bed. She fed him morsel by morsel, alternating with sips of ale from a small jug. While she fed him, she talked, never stopping to see if he would carry on his end of the conversation. He never did.

"The storm is still going strong. I don't know if Eirik and Tykir and Bolthor have been able to leave Winchester yet. I doubt it. The roads are said to be impassable and covered with a sheet of ice.

"Alinor is teaching me to weave. What pretty cloth she makes from her own specially dyed wools. And Eadyth is showing me how to extract honey from the combs to make different grades of honey. I made these honey cakes myself.

"Methinks I will try to raise bees and sheep at Evergreen when I get back. My mother's family only worked the land, but this might be another way to make it prosper.

"Alinor and Tykir have the most beautiful little boys. Four of them! And all of them rascals. Like their father, I imagine.

"Sarah and Sigrud have been swooning over you. All they can talk about is your broad shoulders and devilish eyes. Surely even you would not go after a seventeen-year-old at your advanced age, would you? On the other hand, many people would not raise an eyebrow over a fourteen-year difference in ages, I suppose. Ah, I can see that you consider it none of my business.

"Do you still get those pains in your abdomen—the pain that mimicks your brother's injury? Well, you don't have to answer. I know you do.

"Sometimes I envy you, Toste."

For the first time, she got a reaction from the silent brute. His eyes widened with interest, and he tilted his head to the side on the pillow.

"I know you suffer from your brother's death, but I envy the love that you two shared whilst together. It was special and rare—something to be cherished. I have never experienced that kind of love—any kind really—and suspect I never will. I know, I know," she said with a laugh, "you are thinking that I never will because I will be dead. Well, some things are worth dying for. You are willing to die for your brother's honor. I am willing to die to regain my home.

"Bolthor told the most awful saga afore they left for Winchester. It was about Alinor having a tail and her teasing a Viking named Rurik. I thought Alinor would wring his neck, but the men all laughed uproariously.

"I wager that Bolthor would love to tell some outrageous saga about this event," she said, indicating his bonds and nakedness. "Not that he will ever hear about it, but, Blessed Lord, it would probably have some such atrocious title as 'How the Cock Got His Feathers Plucked,' or 'She Had Her Way With Him.' Ha ha ha.

"Oh, well, if you are not going to talk to me, I might as well return to the keep."

She was about to put his gag back on when he said, "Esme . . ."

"What?" she asked hopefully.

"I am going to kill you."

It seemed like a good idea at the time . . .

The next morning, Esme was in the kitchen with Eadyth, Alinor and the twins, Sarah and Sigrud, making plans for a huge yuletide feast to be held at Ravenshire.

Eadyth and Alinor were in especially high spirits because the streak of bad weather had finally broken, and the sun shone warmly outside, melting the snow and ice. For a certainty, their husbands would return within the next few days.

Which brought Esme even more distress. How much longer could she hold Toste against his will without anyone finding out? And if he didn't agree to her demands, what then?

"Dost think Toste will return in time for the feast?" Sarah asked shyly.

Her sister Sigrud nudged her with an elbow. "We only wondered because he loves to dance and surely there will be dancing at the feast."

Eadyth smiled at the two blushing girls, who were quite attractive with the silver-blond hair and violet eyes of their mother.

"I'm sure he'll be back by then," Alinor interjected. "And, yea, Toste and Vagn were always expert dancers, as I recall."

"Toste is a little old for you girls," Eadyth said gently.

"Moth-er!" the twins exclaimed as one.

After the twins left to search their wardrobes for garments fine enough to wear to the feast, Esme still sat at the table with the two women, who regaled her with stories.

"I cannot believe some of the outrageous things we did as young women," Alinor began. "One time, when Tykir and his men kidnapped me to take me back to King Anlaf's court, I put a potion in his ale. Blessed Lord, he spent two whole days in the garderobe for my misdeed."

"Well, I pretended to be an aged crone for the first few months of my marriage to Eirik. How outrageous is that?"

"I can beat that. There was the time I tied Tykir's hair to a chair so he could not chase after me when I ran away. He was naked at the time, of course." Alinor grinned impishly at the memory.

"I think the most outrageous thing I ever did was planning my own mock death. I put all these animal bones and entrails in a shed, hoping that Eirik would think it was me."

Esme was amazed that these women admitted—nay, took great pleasure in—their outrageous antics. It was probably why she blurted out, "Well, none of that is as outrageous as what I have done."

She immediately slapped a hand over her mouth, but it was too late. Eadyth and Alinor were staring at her with decided interest.

"What have you done, Esme?" Eadyth asked softly.

"Oh, I cannot say. You would think me the most evil woman on earth. You would hate me. You would be so shocked. You would banish me from Ravenshire forthwith."

"Esme, my dear, there is nothing you can say that would shock us. Believe you me, we have seen and done it all." Alinor's freckled hand patted Esme's pale white one in comfort.

Esme was not comforted. "You are wrong. You would be shocked."

"The reason for your nervousness these past few days—it is not because you worry over the Witan's verdict, is it?" Eadyth asked hesitantly.

"I worry over that, of course, but it is not my biggest concern. I am in *such* trouble."

"What have you done?" Alinor demanded to know.

"I kidnapped Toste and have him tied to a bed in the woodcutter's hut, naked," she blurted out all in one breath. Surprisingly, it felt good to finally unburden herself of this secret.

And Alinor had been wrong. They could be shocked, as evidenced by their gaping jaws.

"Now? He's in the woodcutter's hut *now?*" Eadyth finally managed to choke out.

"Naked? Tied to a bed?" Alinor added, also in a choked voice.

Esme nodded. "But I can't release him till he agrees to my proposal."

"A marriage proposal?" Alinor beamed at her.

"Nay, not a marriage proposal. God's bones! Why would I want to marry the lout?"

Alinor and Eadyth grinned at her vehement reply. Then Alinor said, "Tell us everything," and Eadyth concurred with, "Yea, everything."

After she'd explained everything to them, the two women just stared at her with astonishment. At first, Esme didn't know how they felt about her outrageous actions. But then Eadyth whooped and patted her on the back. "I said from the beginning that you and I were going to get on well."

"Yea, you are a woman after my own heart." Alinor gave her a warm hug. "You saw a need in your life and took matters into your own hands. Who can argue with that?"

"Well, Toste, for one. And probably your husbands."

"Men!" Alinor exclaimed as if their opinion was of little importance.

"Show us," Eadyth said then.

"Yea, you must show us Toste so that we can help you," Alinor added.

Esme wasn't sure anyone could help her at this point, but she was happy to have two cohorts. Well, if not exactly cohorts, then confidantes.

Soon the three of them arrived at the woodcutter's hut. Toste turned to look at her when she entered, then went wide-eyed with surprise, and indignation on seeing the two women who followed her. At least his body was covered decently. She'd spared him that indignity. She went to him and removed his gag.

Eadyth and Alinor were trying not to show their

shock or amusement, but Alinor made the mistake of giggling.

"Are you three dimwits here to release me?" he asked icily.

"Well, nay," Eadyth said.

"'Tis Esme's decision," Alinor said.

"Not yet," Esme said.

"Then leave," he ordered. *"Now."*

"I just wanted to say—"

"Begone!" he roared.

Eadyth and Alinor scurried out of the hut, laughing loudly enough for Toste to hear.

As Esme raised the gag, about to put it back on his mouth, he told her, "I am going to kill you, Esme. And I am going to take great joy in the act. But death will be the easy part. It is what will come before that will be long and, let us say, difficult. You would not credit my vast imagination for torture."

Welcome, home, baby . . . boy, have I got news . . .

Eirik, Tykir and Bolthor returned the next day, their voices booming with good cheer. The yuletide season was almost upon them. There would be guests aplenty at Ravenshire within a sennight, it turned out. And though the news from the Witan was not wonderful, it was not bad either.

Tykir took one look at his wife, Alinor, from whom he'd been rarely separated these ten years of their marriage, winked at her, then picked her up with a gleeful laugh and carried her off to their bedchamber for a *real* welcome. Eirik looked at Eadyth, and though normally not as playful as his younger brother, picked her up and did the same. Those left behind in the great hall just shook their heads at the brothers' besotted behavior.

An hour later, Eadyth lay in her husband's arms, both of them naked and sated, listening while he told of the Witan's decision, or lack of a decision.

"Lord Blackthorne and his sons were there as we expected," he told her. "A more scurrilous bunch I have never met. And the lies they told."

"King Edgar . . . and the ealdormen of the Witan . . . did not accept his stories?" Eadyth asked running her fingers through the thick hair on his chest. Almost fifty years old, her husband was still a devastatingly handsome man. And he could still thrill her in the bed furs.

"Keep looking at me like that and I will not be able to answer," he said with a chuckle, not at all displeased. "The king ever was Blackthorne's bosom friend. Well, actually, 'tis Blackthorne's son who is his comrade. But some on the council were swayed by Archbishop Dunstan, who counseled treading carefully. Dunstan is not one to be bullied . . . by anyone."

"Dunstan! He was there?" Everyone knew that Dunstan had been the power behind the throne ever since he'd been called from exile three years earlier. "That wily weasel in monk's garb!"

"That wily weasel in monk's garb will be coming to our yuletide festivities, along with a whole contingent of Saxon nobles. They claim to want a personal audience with Lady Esme, but methinks they just want to lie about swilling your famous mead."

"Here?" Eadyth shrieked. "They are coming here. Oh, Esme will die. And, Toste . . . oh, good Lord, Toste!"

"Interesting that you should mention Toste. I spoke with a priest who came from the minster in Jorvik, and he said Sister Margaret arrived there with one of our stableboys, not Toste. And no one has seen him anywhere."

"Ummm . . . Eirik, there is something I must tell you."

He sat up abruptly, alert to his wife's nuances. "What are you up to now?" He knew her so well.

"It is not me who is up to something. It is Esme."

"Esme?" He shook his head like a shaggy dog. "Why must you always confuse me? Speak plainly."

"Toste. Kidnapped by Esme. Woodcutter's hut. Tied to bed. Naked."

Within seconds, Eirik was pulling on his *braies*, laughing heartily. "I cannot wait to see this. Finally the rogue has met his match."

Laughing his arse off . . .

In another bedchamber several doors away, Alinor was sitting atop her husband's stomach. Naked, the way he liked her.

Tykir was splayed out, arms and legs extended, panting for breath. Sated well and good, the way she liked him.

"Tykir, heartling, there is something I must tell you."

His eyes cracked open a bit. "Uh-oh. I suspect trouble is on the way, especially when you call me heartling whilst sitting on my limp cock."

"Tsk tsk tsk!" she chided him. "'Tis about Toste."

"I already know about Toste. Gone missing, he is." He proceeded to tell her about meeting the priest from the Jorvik minster.

"Not missing, precisely," she told him. "Actually, he is here at Ravenshire. Never left."

"Really?" He frowned. "I did not see him when we arrived."

"Well, he could not come to the hall."

"Because?" he prodded her.

"He is tied to a bed in the woodcutter's hut, naked," she said in a breathy rush.

"Stop talking in riddles. Who did this to him?"

"Esme."

Tykir gaped at her for only a moment, then burst out laughing. He laughed so hard that his manpart jiggled inside her woman-place, which caused her woman-place to clasp and unclasp him, which caused him to make love to her another time, the whole time laughing. Once they were both fully dressed and preparing to leave the bedchamber, Tykir said, "I cannot wait to see this." He was still laughing.

Out in the hallway, he met up with Eirik and Eadyth. Eirik was laughing, too. Downstairs, they told the story to Bolthor, who started laughing, too.

So, it was quite a hilarious entourage that made its way down the still snowy path to the woodcutter's hut. Bolthor was already composing a saga. In fact, he said he expected to get two or three poems out of this happenstance.

Just before they opened the door of the hut, Eirik squeezed his wife's shoulder and said, "Methinks this is going to be the most lively yuletide season we have had at Ravenshire in years."

Sweet revenge . . .

Ten days of captivity and Toste was grinding his teeth once again at Esme's stubborn streak. Despite all manner of threats, she just would not release him. He was running out of torture ideas.

"Stop chewing on your fingernails," he snapped. "There will be none left for me to pluck out. And your whistling is not melodious, believe you me."

She looked up from her chair by the fire, which she'd been gazing at pensively. And continued to gnaw nervously on her thumb. "Eirik and Tykir and Bolthor should be home soon, now that the weather has turned warmer," she commented. Water could be heard dripping steadily from the roof into a rain barrel outside. "Dost think the news will be bad for me?"

"The news will be bad for you no matter what the Witan has decided."

"How so?"

"Even if they rule in your favor, you will have me to contend with."

"I had no choice, Toste."

"Oh, you had a choice, m'lady. I know of no other noble-born woman who would have done what you have."

She shrugged. "If a man had done what I have, people would have said he was justified. Why must women be treated differently?"

"Because women *are* different." He told her explicitly how they were different.

She ignored his crudity and asked of a sudden, "Have you ever been in love . . . with a woman, I mean?"

Nay, only with men. By thunder, she insults me even when she doesn't try to. "Nay. Why do you ask?"

"Methinks that if you ever loved a woman the way you loved your brother, well, that woman would be very fortunate."

"Are you trying to win your way into my favor with compliments? Forget it!"

"Nay. I am just making conversation."

"Are you a virgin?" he asked, figuring she wasn't the only one who could change the subject at will.

Her eyebrows shot up with surprise. "Yea, I am. Why would you think otherwise?"

"A woman who is so doggedly determined to get her home back at any cost might be tempted to use her body as a bargaining chip."

"Like a prostitute? That is what you think of me?"

"Absolutely."

He saw tears well in her eyes at his insult, but he did not care. The woman had unmanned him with her trickery. She was a whore, if not in actuality, then in spirit.

They had no chance to pursue the subject further because there was a commotion outdoors. Then all hell broke loose. His own personal hell, that is.

Eirik, Tykir, Bolthor, Eadyth and Alinor crashed into the small room. The men's heads touched the low ceiling. All of them were bunched close together gaping at the outrageous sight of him tied to a bed with only a fur pelt across his middle to cover his nudity.

All five of them just gawked for a long moment. Then slow smiles crossed all their faces.

Without his usual introduction, Bolthor burst forth:

> *"Once was a maid*
> *who tricked a lad.*
> *Tied him to a bed,*
> *bent him to her will,*
> *with a smile and a wink.*
> *But how did a Viking*
> *get himself in this position?*
> *Methinks he was thinking*
> *not with his head brain,*
> *but with his 'other' brain.*
> *That is the downfall*
> *of many a Viking."*

"Good poem!" Alinor said.

"So, how are things going, Toste?" Eirik asked, sitting at the bottom of the bed. "Anything new happen whilst we've been gone?"

"Dost think we can play this game when we get back to the keep?" Alinor asked Tykir.

"We've already played this game afore," Tykir reminded her.

Alinor didn't even blush as she replied, "Oh, that is right. Now I recall."

"Sarah and Sigrud would like for you to dance with them at the yule feast, Toste. Dost think you will be up by then?" Eadyth inquired sweetly as she batted her lashes at him.

"He is too old for the girls," Eirik told his wife.

"That is what I told them," Eadyth said.

"Does anyone want to hear another saga?" Bolthor asked.

"No!" they all exclaimed.

"Do not dare to go through that door," Toste ordered as he saw Esme edging toward escape. "Bolthor, block her way."

Of Eirik he demanded, "Cut my ties."

When he was standing free, uncaring of his nudity, he ordered all of them, "Out! Except for you, Esme. You will stay."

"Now, Toste, do not be too hard on her—" Eadyth began.

"You will not interfere in this, Eadyth," he told her. "Nor you, Alinor. This is betwixt me and her. Begone!"

Both Eirik and Tykir led their protesting wives away, and Bolthor followed, chuckling and no doubt composing a dozen verse poems, all at Toste's expense.

Within seconds, he was alone with Esme in the hut.

He could have put his *braies* on at this point. He should have put them on. He did not. He wanted to intimidate her with his nudity, or anything else, for that matter.

To give her credit, she did not cower in fright. Instead, she raised her chin defiantly, ready to take whatever punishment he would deliver. She was either very brave or very dumb.

He moved toward her.

She sidled away from the door, closer to the fire.

He leaned back against the door, folded his arms over his chest and crossed his ankles. Then he just stared at her.

She did her best to look back at him, but only above the waist.

What to do with the wench? Well, actually, he had ideas aplenty. The question more accurately was: What to do with her *first?*

"Take off your clothes, Esme," he said so softly that the ice in his voice could barely be discerned.

"What?" she squawked.

"You heard me. Take off your clothes. I would even the battlefield here—for the first time in ten days, I might point out."

"You can kill me with my clothes on," the obstinate witch said. "I do not mind if you bloody my gunna."

"Take . . . off . . . the . . . damn . . . clothes."

"You don't have to yell," she muttered as she began to disrobe.

Yell? The gall of the woman. He would say she had a death wish if she hadn't depleted her lifetime supply of death wishes by her vile treatment of him these past ten days.

She'd already taken off her surcoat and gunna. She stood before him in a chemise thin enough to show her thigh hose underneath. "You're not going to kill me, are you?"

"Not right away," was all he would disclose. Actually,

it was all he knew at this point. He waved a hand for her to continue disrobing.

While she lifted her chemise over her head and bent at the waist to roll down her hose, she remarked, more to herself than to him, "I may as well take my final vows as a nun, since it appears you will not be helping me to regain Evergreen."

The sight of her standing now, nude and absolutely glorious in her beauty, took his breath away. When he was able to speak, he said, "M'lady, there isn't a convent in the world that would take you when I am done with you."

She tilted her head to the side in question. When she understood his words, a flush swept over her face, down her long neck and over her breasts, which were full, rose-tipped and glorious. Her gaze fixed then on that part of him which was especially appreciative of her bodily charms. "You would rape me, then? That is to be your method of punishment?"

"There will be no rape."

She exhaled on a sigh of relief.

"But there will be sex. Lots of it."

Her eyes shot wide. She appeared about to say something nasty to him, then thought better of it. "So be it," she said, lifting her mulish chin. "Let us get it over with so I can get on with the rest of my life . . . whatever that will be."

She walked grimly over to the bed, like a Christian to the lions' den. She should be quivering with fright. She should be begging him for mercy. She should be apologizing till she was blue in the face for what she had done to him. That was what he wanted of her. Wasn't it?

Within minutes, she was spread-eagled on the bed, just as he had been, arms and legs tied to the bedposts. He

would not bother with the gag because no one would defy
his wrath by coming to her aid, even if she screamed . . .
which she did not. Instead, she just stared levelly at him,
awaiting his next step.

Some men might feel guilty for shaming a woman so.
He did not. His wounded pride and thwarted plan to
avenge his brother's death rankled too much.

He dressed himself and pulled a chair near the bed.
Rubbing a hand over his mouth, he studied her. He was
aroused by her nudity, of course. What Viking worth his
salt wouldn't be? But he was in control of his senses and
would not assault her while his temper roiled. In truth,
he would not assault her at all, despite his fury. He would
couple with her at some point, though . . . that he knew
without a doubt.

"Are you not even curious as to the Witan's decision?"
he asked finally.

He saw the shock that overtook her. "Yea. Of course.
Oh, Blessed Mary, how could I have let such an important thing slip my mind?"

"Well, you were distracted," he remarked.

"Go. Find out," she demanded.

He had to laugh at her nerve. Bare-arse naked and
trussed up like a chicken and still she ordered him about.
"I will go when I am ready."

She made a tsk-ing sound of disgust.

"I have been thinking—and, yea, I have had plenty of
time to think—about your situation with Evergreen. I
understand your overpowering drive to regain what is
rightfully yours, but why would your father, a wealthy
man in his own right, care so much for such a small
estate?"

"Greed?"

"Greed goes only so far. There must be something

about this property that makes it valuable to your father. Ponder the question whilst you lie in the bed you have made for yourself."

She curled her upper lip at him.

He soon uncurled it when he reached over and touched one nipple with a forefinger. It immediately peaked, as did the other one. Two obedient soldiers standing to attention . . . his attention.

He pulled his chair closer and examined her breasts in more detail. He should have pinched and prodded her in punishment till she was black and blue, but instead he used gentle fingers and soft sweeps of his palm to fondle her. Against her will, her body betrayed her. It liked what he was doing. He could see that in the widening of her eyes and the flare of her nostrils.

He moved his hand lower then, spending some time on her indented navel and the smooth skin of her flat belly. Finally he allowed himself to touch the silky curls of her woman-fleece and the damp folds hidden within.

She groaned aloud.

He swallowed his own groan.

"Are you going to eat me . . . again?" she asked.

"What?" He whipped his hand back. He could not believe she had asked him *that.* "Uh . . . not right now. Mayhap later. I do not want to give you pleasure. This is supposed to be torture."

A voice in his head asked, *For her or for you?*

He stood abruptly and walked away from the bed. As he was reaching for his cloak on a wall peg, she asked him in a panic, "Where are you going? Are you going to leave me here . . . alone?"

He secured the wolf brooch on his cape and walked back over to her. Taking one last look at her luscious body, he flipped the fur pelt up to cover her from the coolness which would fill the room once the fire died down. "I am going back to the keep. There is much news that I must catch up on."

She nodded.

"But you are not to worry, wench. I will be back to sleep with you."

She said something then that ladies rarely say. But then, she was not a lady. Hadn't he learned that the hard way?

Sometimes laughter is the best medicine . . .

Toste was soaking in a large brass tub in an upper bedchamber of Ravenshire.

He'd eaten a huge meal belowstairs, then come up to his room to shave his bristly face. Finally he'd lowered himself into the hot water. It seemed a year and not ten days since he'd bathed completely.

The relaxing soak also gave him time to think. What to do about Esme? He still did not have all the answers, but one thing she'd accomplished with her outrageous abduction was that he didn't intend to leave right away in pursuit of Vagn's killer. That could wait till he'd resolved some other problems. Like Esme.

His relaxation was soon broken by the entrance of Eirik, Tykir and Bolthor, who'd been in the stables helping a mare with a difficult birth.

"How goes it?" he asked.

"Not so good. The colt did not survive, and the mare probably will not, either," Eirik said.

"Sorry. I know that Sunlight was one of your favorites."

"She was. But she has given us four other colts in the past, and she had a good life."

"Speaking of the good life," Tykir said, pulling over a

low stool and sitting near the foot of the tub. Eirik sat on the bed, and Bolthor leaned back against the wall. "How is yours?"

"Just wonderful."

They all grinned at him, waiting to hear the whole story. Figuring they would not leave him alone till he told them everything, he began with the seductive message he'd received and how he'd wound up tied to the bed. He even told them how he'd originally misheard Esme's name as "Eat me." When he finished, the three of them stared at him as if he'd grown another head.

Eirik was shaking his head from side to side. "You and Vagn always did have a talent for attracting preposterous situations."

"You think I invited this?"

All three men nodded their heads vigorously.

Bolthor, to no one's surprise, gazed off into the distance dreamily as the verse mood overcame him. "Methinks I should call this one 'Men and Their Convenient Ears.'"

"Huh?" the other three said.

"The lady said Ess-me.
The man heard 'Eat me.'
She asked, 'Will you beat me?'
He thought she said, 'Heat me.'
Eat me, heat me,
one and the same,
especially for a Viking man
with a convenient ear."

"How true! How true!" Tykir said.

"What will you do with her?" Eirik asked.

"Damned if I know!" Toste said, then immediately

added, "Whatever I decide, none of you are to interfere, and that includes your meddlesome wives."

"Did you leave her back at the woodcutter's hut?" Eirik asked.

"I did, and there she will stay till I decide otherwise."

"Naked?" Tykir inquired.

Toste did not answer. He didn't have to. The other three men in the room grinned.

"And, really, none of you can condemn me. You have done as much and more. You, Tykir, once locked Alinor in a bedchamber at Dragonstead for days."

"Yea, I did, and some of the best memories of my life took place there. Wouldst like to borrow my collection of feathers? It was given to me years ago by a sultan who used it with his harem slaves."

Three male mouths went slack with disbelief. One never knew when Tykir was teasing or telling the truth.

"No, thank you, Tykir. I can come up with my own methods of torture."

"Might I suggest—" Eirik began.

"Nay! And one more thing. No one . . . I mean, *no one* . . . is to go within shouting distance of that hut. Is that clear?"

"Well, you'd better have this resolved by next week," Eirik said.

"Why is that?"

"Because this castle is going to be overflowing with guests for the yuletide festivities."

Toste put his face in his hands. "I am afraid to ask, but what guests?"

"Archbishop Dunstan, Ealdormen Byrhtnoth of Essex, Aelfhere of Mercia, Aethelwold of East Anglia, Aelfhead of Hampshire and various other notables. I would not be surprised to see the king or one of his closest *thegns* arrive, though they made no promises. And though not invited by any means, Lord Blackthorne may very well show up to claim his daughter."

"Can my life get any worse than this?" Toste asked.

Without asking, Bolthor walked over to the fire and got a bucket of hot water warming there. He dumped it in the tub, figuring that Toste was getting cold, if not wilted.

"Well, actually, life could get worse." Tykir stared at him grimly. "I fear for Esme . . . oh, you are no danger to her . . . but her father and brothers are. They are a scurvy lot. I suspect that her early years at home were not pleasant."

"You know, I had the same feeling," Eirik said. "There are some men who hate women. They marry them, have daughters and sisters and yet, at heart they hate women."

"I love women—always have." Tykir took a long swig from the mug of ale he'd brought with him.

"We know," everyone else said.

"Don't let Alinor hear you say that, though," Eirik told his brother.

"She knows. As long as I keep my hands and my manpart to myself—and her—she does not mind."

"That's what women say, but it is not what they really feel," Bolthor advised. Bolthor giving Tykir advice about women was like a nun giving a harem houri advice on swiving.

Tykir turned his attention back to Toste. "What I was trying to say before I was so rudely interrupted, Toste, is that you must not be too harsh with Esme till you understand from whence she came. And she came from a snake pit."

"Mayhap that means she is a snake, too." Toste refused to make excuses for the deceitful witch.

"Or a mouse who has managed to escape the snakes . . . thus far," Eirik offered.

They discussed the situation further while Toste dried himself off and dressed in clean clothes lent to him by Eirik. They all went down to the great hall then to partake of the evening meal. The subject of Esme was avoided by everyone. It was midnight before Toste made his way down the path again, carrying a bundle of food, soap, linens, a comb and various other items.

He wondered if Esme would be waiting for him, wide-eyed and scared. Would she beg for mercy? Or suffer in silence?

Instead, as he was about to open the door, he heard the oddest thing. Whistling. His captive, who should be shaking-in-her-skin fearful, was bloody hell whistling.

Turnabout is fair play . . . or is that fun play? . . .

Esme was lying flat on her back, naked, whistling. She always whistled when she was nervous. She was *really* nervous now.

"You are a terrible whistler," Toste remarked as he hung his cloak on a wall peg and then threw several logs on the fire.

"The quality of the whistle is not so important as the fact that I whistle at all." *Dumb, dumb, dumb! The man is making me dumb. Next I will be conversing about the quality of breathing.* "Believe you me, whistling has been the only thing to keep me sane on many an occasion in the past."

His eyes shot up at her words. He waited for her to elaborate. Hah! She would not tell him she'd whistled when her father's birch rod whipped her back. She would not tell him she'd whistled when her brothers had locked her in a root cellar for two full days as part of a youthling prank. She would not tell him she'd whistled on many an occasion at the nunnery when her loneliness had become nigh unbearable.

"To be a good whistler, you must wet your whistle first," he told her and sat down on the edge of the mattress.

He must be as dumb as I am . . . continuing a lackwit discussion on the art of whistling when there are more important things to discuss, like my imprisonment. "I don't need to—"

It was too late. He was already leaning down and outlining her lips with the tip of his tongue. She noticed irrelevantly that he must have shaven his face and his skin smelled of soap. Then he dipped his tongue inside her mouth and laved her lips with moisture. Over and over he did this till her lips were more than moist. Then he stuck his tongue inside again, and kissed her long and deep. As much as she disliked the rogue, her body liked his ministrations. *Well!* she thought. *Wellwellwell!*

He pulled back just slightly and said against her wet mouth, "Now whistle."

Apparently, I'm the only one overcome with passion here. "Whistle this!" she said and nipped his lips before he could pull away.

He jerked back, then stood. "Not a smart move, Esme. Now you will have to be punished even more." He rubbed his mouth as if she'd severely wounded him when in fact she hadn't even broken the skin. "But first, are you hungry?"

She nodded.

"Good," he said and took great pleasure in making her eat tiny morsels of manchet bread dripping with honey from his hand, like a pet dog. After each bite, he forced her to lick clean his fingers. She seriously considered, biting one of those appendages, but decided to pick her battles. She suspected that licking his fingers might be the least of the offenses he planned to inflict upon her. When she finished, he gave her a cup of cool water, then asked, "Do you have to relieve yourself, Esme?"

She did, but she would wet the bed afore she let him put a pan under her bottom and watch her empty her bladder.

He just laughed when she raised her chin defiantly. Then he loosened her ties, telling her, "I'm only untying you for a few moments while I go out to gather wood for the fire. You have a very short amount of time to take care of yourself," he said, pointing to the chamber pot in the far corner.

She'd done everything she had to do and was back in the bed, covered to her chin with the fur pelt, when he returned carrying a large load of logs. He went out two more times for other loads, which he piled next to the hearth. He must be planning a long stay in the hut. Or was he building up the fire for her so he could go back to the keep?

She got her answer soon enough when he took off his belt and raised his tunic over his head. Esme already knew the man was stunning in his physical appearance, having seen him naked when he was brought to the nunnery from the battlefield and again here in the woodcutter's hut. He no doubt knew how stunning he was, too. Women fell at his feet like weeds under a soldier's boot. *But not me. I am stronger than that. I hope.*

He sat down to remove his boots, watching her the whole time. She turned on her side away from him, but she assumed he then stepped out of his tight *braies*, too. She was proven right when he slipped under the bed furs behind her and she felt his nakedness against her back . . . *all* of his nakedness. *Is it possible to see a man with one's eyes closed? Well, yea, it must be . . . because I am seeing vivid pictures behind my eyelids.*

"Turn over, Esme, so I can secure your ties."

Does that mean I have to open my eyes? "Why do you need to tie me when your big body blocks my escape?"

"I might fall asleep and you could crawl over me."

Crawl over him? Naked? I . . . do . . . not . . . think . . . so!

He laughed. "You do not like my big body?"

She didn't answer. *Truth to tell, I like your big body too much.*

"Perhaps I will tie you *to me*," he said and took her left hand in his right one, palm to palm, fingers entwined, then tied them together at the wrists. He raised both their arms so they rested on the pillow above her head.

"Relax, Esme, I am not going to tup you tonight. I am too tired. But if you move or squirm about, I will interpret that as meaning you want me now. And I may decide to change my mind."

As a final outrage, he let the fur pelt remain where it was, mid-body, so that her breasts were visible to his eye. And eye them he did. Then he yawned loudly, laid his head next to hers, his mouth against her ear, and proceeded to fall asleep.

Esme couldn't believe what was happening. She had expected the brute to come back and rape her . . . or at least have his way with her. Instead, she was lying naked in a bed, her arm tied above her head, her breasts exposed, while he snored beside her, oblivious.

It was utterly humiliating.

Which, of course, was his point.

CHAPTER TWELVE

❧

planning a road trip . . .

"We are going to Ravenshire for a yuletide celebration," Gorm announced to all those at the high table.

"*What?* That is the first I have heard of this," Helga said with alarm. She and Vagn had been at each other like dogs in heat the past sennight, and the prospect of their being separated, even for a short time, filled her with surprising panic. Once separated, would he forget about her? Find someone else? No longer be interested?

"I have known for some time that Eirik and Eadyth planned a great feast, but did not think we would be able to go because of this winter storm that has beset us. Now that the roads are passable again, it seems a grand idea. All of us will go," Gorm explained, making a sweeping gesture that included Vagn.

Helga breathed a sigh of relief. Not separated, after all.

"Actually, Gorm, I think I will stay here," Vagn said.

Helga's heart constricted. There was no way she could stay behind, too, without her father becoming suspicious . . . if he was not already.

"My side still pains me betimes, and I am not sure I could stand a full day on horseback," Vagn said, reaching low where no one could see his hand to pinch her buttock . . . probably a signal to her to attempt to stay, too . . . which she could not do.

She let out a little yelp of surprise at his pinch.

Her father raised an eyebrow at her.

"Indigestion," she explained.

Her father nodded, being an expert on chest pains. "I can understand your concern about traveling too soon, Vagn. You have been looking peaked of late, and you have dark circles under your eyes from lack of sleep. Nightmares, I imagine. Actually, I have an ulterior motive for wanting to go." He winked slyly at Helga.

"What? What have you done now?"

"I have done naught," he said as if wounded. "But Lord Ravenshire's son John from Hawk's Lair will be there, and methinks 'tis time for you to give him another look."

"For what?"

"Husband."

Helga slanted a surreptitious glance at Vagn and noticed with satisfaction that he looked rather green. He squeaked out, "Marriage?"

"Father! John is too young for me."

"He is twenty and five," her father argued.

"And I am twenty and eight."

"Pfff! Three years! 'Tis nothing."

"It is, when the *woman* is three years older."

"'Twould be like robbing the cradle," Vagn concurred.

She cast him a glowering look.

"On the other hand, I am thirty and one. A good age," Vagn said.

Everyone turned to stare at Vagn. Where had that irrelevant remark come from? It was irrelevant, wasn't it? *A good age for what?*

Then her father threw in more irrelevant remarks. "I understand that John has grown into quite a handsome fellow. On the down side, he's a Saxon through and through . . . grim and way too serious, unlike us Vikings who enjoy a good jest."

"I enjoy a good jest," Vagn said.

Helga sank lower in her seat. Why was he calling attention to himself this way? Did he want people to know of their relationship?

"On the up side," her father continued, "John has his own estate, which is said to be prosperous. What say you, Helga? Will you at least reserve judgment till you've had a chance to look him over?"

Before she had a chance to answer, Vagn told her father, "Actually, I think I will go to Ravenshire with you after all. Eirik is an old comrade of mine, as is his brother Tykir, who lives in the Norselands. There are sure to be other Vikings of my acquaintance there. Yea, 'twill be good to meet up with old friends. We will all have a jolly good time."

"Lackwit!" she mouthed to him in an aside. She'd like to show him a jolly good time.

He just winked at her and pinched her buttock again.

"So, it is settled then." Gorm raised his cup of mulled ale high in a toast. "We will leave for Ravenshire five days hence. Will that be enough time for your sewing ladies to make fine garments for us all, or refurbish the old ones?"

Helga nodded. Sewing duties were the least of her concerns. Somehow, deep down, she knew that her time with Vagn was coming to an end. And she suspected that the end would come at Ravenshire.

Why should it matter? She'd known all along that this

was to be a short-lived affair. In that instant, she realized what was bothering her.

I love him. Oh, my gods! I love him.

And that was the worst thing that could have happened.

Men and their epiphanies! . . .

Oh, my gods, I love her!

Vagn came to this amazing revelation while buried deep inside Helga, trying to fight off his fast-coming peak. He'd stopped his long, slow strokes seconds ago in hopes of slowing himself down before starting the short, hard strokes that would bring them both crashing to ecstasy.

Helga was staring up at him adoringly. All right, she adored the things he did to her body. And he adored the things she did to his body.

But *Oh, my gods, I love her!*

In the midst of this mind-shattering tension, Helga asked him a most irrelevant question. "Vagn, you once mentioned that you have been celibate for a year. Why? I mean, I cannot imagine a man of your skill giving up the delights of the body."

Vagn liked her mentioning his skills and the delights of the body, but, good gods, how could she put together so many words when engaged in the heat of coupling? When he was able to speak above a croak, he said, "We were Jomsvikings. They lead celibate lives whilst at the island fortress. It was a bad idea, believe you me."

"What are Jomsvikings precisely?"

"Helga, my sword is planted in your sheath up to the hilt. Your sheath is quivering around me. Can we not discuss this later?"

She laughed seductively, and he realized she was distracting him with these questions deliberately. The witch! Mayhap she was right. 'Twas best to prolong the peaking as long as possible. In truth, there was sometimes as much ecstasy in the anticipation as the end result. And so he began to blather like an idiot.

"Jomsvikings are an elite group of military men of proven courage, none older than fifty years. They live in a huge circular fortress on the island of Trellenborg on the west coast of Sjaelland . . . the Danish lands. Jomsvikings adhere to strict rules of fellowship. Each must avenge the other as a brother. None must ever speak a word of fear. No man can be absent from the fortress for more than three nights, unless engaged on a military campaign. And, most important, no women are permitted in the castle itself."

"Sounds like foolishness to me."

He pinched her behind for making light of serious men's business and went on. "It is quite an honor to be admitted to this society. A foster brotherhood, some call it. At the initial swearing-in ceremony, a large ring of turf is cut from the ground in such a way that two ends are still held fast and under it is laid a razor-sharp spear. Four men are required to pass beneath it till they draw blood, lots of blood, and their blood mixes with each other's and with the earth beneath. After that, they clasp hands and pledge an oath to the brotherhood."

Her eyes widened with disbelief. "That really is foolishness. Men! What utter nonsense, that they would spill blood just for the sake of making an oath. I tell you, women would never do that!"

He laughed. She was probably right.

"In any case, that is why I was celibate for a year . . . that, and my battle injury."

"Ummmm," she said.

He was not certain if she said "Ummm" as an indication that she understood or as appreciation of the throbbing of his cock inside her tight channel. Talented fellow, his cock was. He continued to hold himself as still as possible inside her, trying to control the game as much as he could.

She stared up at him, waiting.

While he held himself rigid over her, she did not question him. The woman trusted him implicitly. That he would not hurt her. That he would bring her pleasure. That he would keep his word as a man of honor. That he would hide her secrets.

Vagn knew she was ready—nay, anxious—for impending bliss because her inner folds were already clutching at him, but still she *trusted* him to know what was best for them in the bedsport. A heady compliment, that was: trust. It carried responsibility, too. Did he want that responsibility? Did he have a choice?

Apparently, I do, because, Odin help me, I love her.

As if reading his troubled thoughts, Helga reached a hand up and caressed his cheek, trailing her fingers over his parted lips. "Vagn," she murmured huskily.

He began to pound her then, as if in punishment, but in reality to drive home to her what he could not say: *I love you.* To some men that might not be such an amazing revelation, but to Vagn it was mind-shattering. He had never thought love would come to him . . . love of the man-woman kind. And he'd never needed it before, not while he had his brother.

Helga flailed from side to side now, keening with the continuous pleasure he gave her. Her body went from one peak to another as the inner ripples went on and on. He'd never known a woman to have multiple peaks like this, but his Helga did. The anticipation of his own peak went on and on, too, to the point of pain . . . painful yearning, wonderful torture.

I love her. He could not say the words. Not yet. Maybe not ever.

But he showed Helga that he loved her in the best way he could. With a roar of male exhilaration, Vagn shot his seed *inside* Helga's welcoming womb.

And it felt so right.

Making sweet butter, Viking style . . .

Tears welled in Helga's eyes, which she hid from Vagn by pressing her face against his heaving chest. What a miracle lovemaking was! What a miracle lovemaking was when love was involved, as it was on her part!

I love you, Vagn. She wished she could say the words aloud, but she would probably scare him spitless. Not that he would abandon her to her own devices, but it would make their relationship strained. She wanted to relish this peace between them for a while longer.

But there was something more important to consider. Vagn didn't have to say the words for her to know what he had just done. For the first time in what seemed like a hundred bouts of lovemaking, he had stayed inside her body and given her his seed. And it was deliberate, she knew it was.

What does it mean?

And what a joke on him . . . because she was probably already with child. As careful as he had been in spilling himself into a cloth, he had made love to her so many times that the chances of her conceiving accidentally were high. Oh, she did not know for a certainty that she carried his babe, but her monthly flux was late. She would not tell him. Not yet. Not till she was sure. Mayhap not even then . . . nay, that would be dishonorable of her. If she was indeed pregnant, she would let him know. But not yet.

He kissed the top of her head and said, "Helga, you are going to wear me down to a nub."

"Am I too much for you, Viking?" she teased, nipping at one of his flat male nipples.

"Hardly," he boasted. "In truth, dearling, your enthusiasm in the bedsport gives me much pleasure. Thank you." He patted her hand which lay over his heart. "You heal me."

What a touching thing to say! Tears welled again in her eyes, and this time he noticed.

"Tsk tsk tsk! What kind of lover am I to make you weep?"

"The best kind," she said, "but do not let your head get big. I am sure I would be just as pleased with any other man . . . Finn, for example."

"Liar!" he hooted, obviously believing that what existed betwixt them in the bed furs was unique. Smart man!

She nestled herself into a more comfortable position with her face against his chest, one arm across his waist and a leg thrown over his thigh. Sleep was fast approaching. She loved sleeping in Vagn's arms, though she must be sure to awaken before dawn and return to her own bedchamber.

But Vagn brought her fully awake with his question, "Helga, what do you have against marriage?"

She moved her leg off his but still rested her face on his chest and her arm over his waist. "I don't think there was any one happenstance that made me mistrust marriage. My mother died when I was only three. My father did not raise me as a boy, as many sonless men do with their girlings, but he did breed independence in me."

" 'Tis unusual, you must admit that."

She nodded, and breathed deeply of his skin. He had his own unique skin scent, like salt and leather, masculine, and not at all offensive. But she was being distracted from the subject at hand. "I know my father gives the impression of being a crude oaf betimes, but he really is a fair-thinking man. He taught me—and all his people, really—to use their gods-given talents. In my case, that talent lay in a needle and thread." She shrugged.

"How does your plan for a child fit in with all this? Is it yet another notch in your goal to be independent?"

"Of course not. When he taught me independence, my father's only miscalculation was in his yearning for a grandchild . . . something he did not realize till recently. I truly think he does not mind my being husbandless. He knows I could carry on for him when he is gone. I may not be a soldier, but there are soldiers aplenty who would work for me."

"But what about you, Helga? You speak of a child for your father's sake. What about you?"

"I want a child, too. I did not realize that afore. The maternal instinct came late to me, apparently." That was all she would say for now . . . all she could say, as her throat closed with emotion.

"Is it fair to the child not to have a father? Why can't you do both—marry and have a child?"

"Really, Vagn, how many men would allow their wives to have such independence? What man would allow me to continue operating my trading stall in Jorvik? What man would allow me to travel to the trading towns of the Norselands seeking new fabrics and dyes and threads? What man would allow me to be a woman, a mother, and a merchant, too?"

"You are looking at this from the wrong angle."

"How so?"

"The right man would relish your independence. The right man might want to protect you from the dangers of solitary travel or trading in a risky manner, but he would find ways to cooperate with you in your endeavors. Compromise—that is the key to a good husband-and-wife relationship methinks, and thus far you have not considered budging even the slightest bit."

"So it's my fault?"

He laughed. "Just a little."

"You're saying I need the right man to husband me and father my child, and I need to compromise my too-high standards?"

He gave her a one-armed squeeze. "That about sums it up."

Was Vagn saying he could be that man? Was that what this was all about? Oh, she had to admit the prospect filled her with foolish hopes. But she waited a good long time, and he said nothing more. He must be thinking of some other right man for her.

Ah, well, 'twas what she had expected. Time she changed the subject lest she burst into tears, as was her wont of late.

"Well, my wordy Viking, now that you have awakened me from my near-slumber, methinks 'tis time to try another of Rona's tricks."

"I thought you had tried all of Rona's tricks already, numerous times," he said with a chuckle.

"There is one more. 'Tis called the Butter Churn."

He laughed outright.

"You see," she said, swinging her legs so that she

straddled his thighs and taking his hardening penis in her fingers, "the trick is in the grip, like the pole of a butter churn, two hands, up and down. The skin will move thus."

"Holy Thor!" Vagn said within seconds. "I will show you what this pole can do when it does its own churning." And he did.

Unfortunately . . . or fortunately . . . there was no more talk of marriage or babies that night.

And then the other boot drops . . .

Vagn knew that Helga was pregnant, but she did not tell him, and it hurt him deeply.

Obviously, she wanted him to play no part in her life or that of the babe. His heart wrenched at the thought. No wonder he held off telling her of his growing affection for her. She would no doubt interpret it as directed toward his child and not her . . . which was far from the truth, although he did feel almost weepish whenever he thought of a child of his loins. Where these newfound paternal feelings came from, he had no idea—possibly from his love of the mother.

There was only one thing of which Vagn was certain. He would marry Helga, come hell or high water. They would raise this child together, no matter what notions of independence she held close to her heart. His son or daughter would know both parents. That was a fact she would have to accept.

How this would fit in with his plans to search for his brother, he had no idea yet. First of all, he had to make absolutely certain that Toste was really gone to the Other World. Once they returned from Ravenshire, he would settle everything. He could wait that long before making his proposal to Helga, and her father.

In the meantime, Helga could keep her secret if she wanted. And she could churn his butter all she wanted. He didn't mind one bit.

Daddy dearest . . .

"Helga, this has got to stop," her father said sternly.

He was standing in her sewing solar, being fitted for a new tunic. It would be black wool, embroidered with a hem of silver briars in honor of Briarstead. Everyone was getting at least one new garment for the trip to Ravenshire, including Vagn, who wore fine raiment like he was born to it, which he was.

"What has to stop?" she asked distractedly as she let out the seams to make more room for her father's massive girth.

"Your diddling with Vagn."

She gasped. Did her father know about their clandestine lovemaking? Did everyone know?

"You cannot tease a man so and not expect him to want something from you. Like marriage."

She breathed an inner sigh of relief. By "diddling" her father meant teasing, not . . . well, diddling.

"Vagn is not interested in me that way," she said.

"I am not so sure of that."

She stopped fussing with his garment. "What makes you think that?"

"The way his eyes follow you everywhere. The way he refrains from bedding any of the women about the keep. The way he teases you incessantly."

She decided to make light of his warning. "Teasing equals a desire to wed? I think not. Otherwise we would have lots more marriages at Briarstead than we do. Teasing is an innate part of the Viking man's personality. I swear, Viking males must come out of the womb laughing."

Gorm shrugged at her easy dismissal of his views. "Teasing can be the way of lovers. I used to tease your mother."

"You did?"

He smiled dreamily in remembrance. "I teased her and teased till she gave in and—"

"Father!"

"—and agreed to marry me." He widened his eyes at her. "What did you think I meant?"

"Tsk tsk, now you are teasing me."

"Take heed, daughter, Vagn Ivarsson is a man full-grown. A warrior of note. Yea, he has a mirthsome side, but do not delude yourself that you can grasp such a man by the tail."

And a very nice tail he has, too, Helga thought.

"Why are you smiling?"

"Just picturing you teasing my mother."

He nodded, then concluded, "Vagn would not be the worst man for you to choose as husband."

"Do not bring all that up again. I beg you, Father. Do not humiliate me so." She knew what Vagn's answer would be, and it would be a crushing blow to her, for many reasons.

"I will not bring up the subject," he agreed, "but think about what I have said."

She did. Way too much.

Fathers know more than we think they do . . .

Vagn, with sweat pouring off his body and his heart beating as if it would burst, wondered idly, *Am I having fun yet?*

Wearing only *braies* and half-boots, he was engaged in swordplay with Finn Fairhair in the exercise room at Briarstead, as he had been for the past hour. About them, other soldier pairs did the same. He had to give Finn credit. He gave as good as he got in the warrior arts, despite his coxcomb appearance.

Vagn felt a tap-tap-tap on his shoulder. He turned to see Gorm crooking his finger at him. Another soldier stepped into Vagn's place to engage Finn.

Wiping perspiration off his chest and belly with a linen cloth, he watched the old man eye him craftily as they walked to a more secluded spot.

"Well?" Vagn asked.

"Don't you think it's time you did something about my daughter?"

"Huh?" It was the last thing he'd expected from Gorm.

"You know she's pregnant, don't you?"

That was definitely the last thing he'd expected. "What makes you think so?" He would not betray Helga by acknowledging what he already knew.

"Pfff! She weeps at the least provocation. She yawns all the time. She has been ooh-ing and aah-ing over various babes in the village. She has vomited in the morn on occasion and is always munching on dried manchet bread. She is happy as a lark one moment and mean as a boar the next. I would say that spells pregnant."

I would, too. "Mayhap it is just that time of the month. You know how some women get half-demented just afore their monthly flux."

"A father knows."

"Well, whether she is or she isn't, this is something betwixt me and Helga. I assume 'a father knows' when his daughter has been engaged in certain acts, too. So I will not deny my involvement."

"What do you intend to do about it?"

"I intend to marry Helga."

"Have you asked her?

"Nay."

"How can you be sure she will accept?"

"I will wed with her . . . that, I assure you."

"Does she know that you know she is breeding your child?"

"Nay."

"Does she know that she is breeding?"

"I do not know. Probably."

"What a mess!"

"It is not a mess. Everything will work out in the end." *I hope.* "Just . . . do . . . not . . . interfere."

"You dare to say that to me when I have stood back and allowed you to swive my daughter."

Help me, Odin. I am dying here. "Don't you think it's a mite crude to speak so of your daughter?"

"I mean her no disrespect. Just don't you do her any disrespect."

"And how would I do that?"

"By failing to offer for her."

"I told you, I am going to, in my own good time."

"Would ye like some advice, boy?"

"Nay."

"Do not give her a choice. Women claim to want a choice, but they really want a man to take over."

"In a million years, I cannot imagine Helga wanting no choice. She would clout me over the head for daring to take over her life, even if I wanted to, which I do not."

"Our forefathers had the right idea. Toss a wench over your shoulder and carry her off to your lair."

"I have no lair."

"My lair is your lair."

"Aaarrgh!"

Gorm slapped a hand over his burly chest suddenly

and exclaimed, "Oh, Oh! Methinks it is my heart again. Methinks I will not live to see a wedding, let alone my first grandchild. Best you stop dawdling, boy."

Vagn would have felt sorry for the old man if the sly-boots weren't shifting his eyes guiltily. "You fraud! Stop swilling ale and eating fatty sausages, and your chest pains will disappear like that," he said, snapping his fingers.

Gorm changed direction then, after trying to pull a fast one on him. "Mayhap there will be a Christmas wedding yet. You're half Christian, aren't you? Pray."

"I am not going to pray for a Christmas wedding. Not to the Norse gods, or to the Christian One-God."

"You need all the help you can get, boy."

"I do not."

"I will pray for you then." As Gorm swaggered off, well-satisfied with the lackwit advice he had given him, Vagn heard him mutter, "A father's work is never done."

On the road again . . . almost . . .

Carts were piled high with chests and supplies outside in the bailey, awaiting the start of the trip to Ravenshire. Horses were shifting restlessly. Guardsmen muttered amongst themselves, anxious to get on their way.

Still, Helga sat on a chair in her solar, as if all the world could wait for her . . . which it must. There was no way she was getting on anything that moved, whether it be cart or animal, till her stomach settled down.

Vagn walked into the solar and approached her. She could see the concern on his face. "Are you all right?"

She nodded. "My stomach is just a bit queasy. Probably the start of my monthly flux," she lied. Despite all that she and Vagn had shared in bed, she found herself oddly embarrassed to discuss such bodily functions.

He seemed to accept her explanation, but shifted uneasily from foot to foot. "Well, this delay gives me time to say something I have been wanting to say to you for days."

She waited, but he still did the foot-shifting exercise. Tilting her head to the side, she asked, "Are *you* all right?"

It must be his wounds hurting him again and he does not know how to tell me he will stay behind.

Nay, 'tis worse than that. He will go with us to Ravenshire, but he will not be returning to Briarstead with us after the visit. It is over. Oh, my gods and goddesses! It is over.

She really did feel like throwing up then.

But wait. Vagn was doing something that caused her even more concern. He dropped to one knee before her and took one of her hands in both of his. "Helga, there is no smooth way for me to say this, except, Will you marry me?"

"What?"

"Now, now, sit still and hear me out. Do not say me nay till you hear my proposal."

"Vagn, please, you know how I feel—"

He put the fingertips of one hand to her lips. "I wish to take you for my wife. I want to protect you under my shield. I want to stop sneaking about at night. I want to wake beside you in the morning. I want to make love with you whene'er I wish without having to hide. I want to have children with you. I want to grow old with you." He shrugged at his inability to express himself better. "Will you marry me?"

His proposal could easily have charmed Helga into compliance, except for one word which stood out like a sore thumb. *Children.* "You know," she accused him. "You know that I am with child, and now you want to marry me."

"I do know, Helga, but—"

She stood abruptly and shoved his beseeching hands aside.

"Nay, I will not marry you."

"Now, Helga, be reasonable." He stood, too.

"Reasonable?" she practically shrieked, then lowered her voice for fear she would attract attention. "We had an agreement."

"Yea, we did, and part of that agreement said I would ask you to marry me if you conceived," he argued. *The stubborn lout!*

"Why? Why do you want to wed me?" Deep down, Helga knew that if he said three simple words to her, she would capitulate.

Unfortunately . . . or fortunately . . . he did not utter those words. "It is time for me to wed. We do well together. Why not?"

"Ooooh, I would like to clout you a good one."

"Huh?"

"Vagn, if it were not for this child"—she put a hand protectively over her flat belly—"would you be asking me to marry you today?"

He thought for a moment, then answered honestly. "Probably not *today*, but mayhap someday I would have. I like you, Helga, and I think you like me, too."

Like? Like? The dunderhead! "I would ask you one more question, Vagn. If your brother were still alive, would you be asking me to marry you?"

"That is an unfair question. If my brother were alive, I wouldn't even be here."

Her shoulders sank with defeat. She'd given him a

chance, and he'd failed her. "If I were ever going to marry, Vagn—and I am not—I would want more from a marriage than that. I am sorry, but nay." He was about to say more but she put up a hand to halt him. "I will not deny you access to this child, and you may acknowledge it, if you wish."

"Of course I will acknowledge my child, you foolish wench." He wagged a finger in her face menacingly. "Be forewarned, though, I do not accept your rejection. We *will* marry. You can bet your luscious lips on that."

To prove his point, he kissed said luscious lips soundly, then stomped away. Helga loved the way Vagn loved her lips. He didn't love her, but he loved her lips.

In the hall outside the solar, she heard her father ask him, "How did it go?" *Frigg's foot! My father knows, too?*

And Vagn replied succinctly, "Just bloody hell wonderful!"

CHAPTER THIRTEEN

❦

Tiptoeing loudly . . .

It was two days later.

Down the stairs and through the great hall of Ravenshire, Toste carried a brass tub on his head, with a bundle of various supplies slung over his shoulder. And he was whistling.

The whistling was his downfall.

He'd almost made it to the wide double doors that led down the steps and out to the bailey when Bolthor called out, "Is that you whistling, Toste?"

With a sigh of resignation, he turned, still with the tub on his head, and said, "Yea, 'tis me."

Bolthor was sitting at one of the long trestle tables at the far end of the mostly empty hall, whittling a piece of wood. "Dost know you have a tub on your head?"

"Of course I know I have a tub on my head."

"You need not snap at me. I did not cause you to have a tub on your head."

"*Why* do you have a tub on your head," Tykir inquired silkily, having coming up behind him. So surprised was Toste that he almost dropped the tub.

"Because I want to bathe." *Could I say anything more lackwitted than that?*

"Why can't you bathe in the spring house or up in

your bedchamber?" It was Eirik speaking now. He'd come up on his other side. His three friends were surrounding him, all of them grinning.

"Because I like to bathe in private." *They ought to call me Toste the Lackwit.*

"Ah, suddenly modest, are you?" Tykir remarked.
Or lackwitted.

"Well, that is understandable," Eirik said. "I do not like to show off my body parts to one and all either, impressive as they are."

"Pffff!" Toste said, whether in regard to Eirik's observation or his own awkward situation, he was not sure. It was an all-encompassing "Pffff," he supposed.

While he stood there with a tub on his head, Bolthor of course launched into one of his poems, sure to be a jest-arrow directed at him.

"Viking men are very clean,
wasting much time on daily hygiene.
Yea, Norsemen are rarely stinksome,
which is what makes them so winsome.
'Tis why Saxon women think them nice,
unlike their own men infested with lice.
But there are times wenches like a man dirty,
and it's not in a tub with water squirty."

"Is that it?" Toste asked Bolthor.

"For now. Methinks I will add some more verses later, when the ladies are nearby to appreciate my sentiments," Bolthor explained. Eadyth and Alinor were off somewhere preparing for the huge yuletime celebration. Toste hoped to be gone by then.

"Come have a drink with us afore you cart your tub hither and yon," Tykir invited.

If Toste declined, they would just tease him more. So he sat down, placing the tub and bundle on the rushes at his feet. They all waited till a servant poured them fresh mugs of Eadyth's famous mead before speaking.

"So, how is Esme?" Tykir inquired with a waggle of his eyebrows.

"Just fine."

"Really?" Eirik asked. "She does not mind being locked in the woodcutter's hut?"

"She loves it."

"Naked? Is she naked?" Tykir wanted to know.

"And tied to the bed, as you were?" Bolthor added.

He declined to answer, but Tykir answered for him. "Of course she is."

Toste felt his face heat with a blush, which was rare for him.

"Eadyth and Alinor are livid over this, you know," Eirik pointed out.

"Over what?" he asked before he had a chance to bite his tongue.

"The way you are treating a highborn lady," Eirik said.

They were all grinning at him, clearly not sharing their womenfolks' outrage.

"Hah! 'Twas a highborn lady who treated me in the same way. Ah, let me think. Yea, 'twas the *same* highborn lady."

His friends continued to grin.

"She deserves to be punished. Surely you recognize that."

"Toste, Toste, Toste," Eirik said with a sad shake of his head. "Was there ever a punishment intended for a woman that did not backlash onto the man?"

"Whatever the hell that means!"

"It means that men never win in a battle with women," Tykir explained.

"I will handle this in my own way."

"Yea, I agree. Let Toste handle this his way," Bolthor said.

"You just want more fodder for your sagas," Eirik commented with a hoot of laughter.

"There is that, of course," Bolthor admitted, "but in the end, every man must make his own mistakes."

"She is not so bad off," Toste argued. And a feeble attempt it was, too. "When I returned to the hut last night, she was whistling."

Three jaws dropped open, then clicked shut.

"Methinks she likes you," Bolthor said.

I cannot believe I am sitting here listening to this drivel. "I don't think so. She bit me."

"Where?" The smirk on Tykir's face was pure . . . well, Tykir.

"What you need is advice from men more experienced in the art of charming women—like me," Eirik said.

He told Eirik what he could do with his advice. Then, "What I need is to get out of here."

"Anxious to get back to your punishing, eh?" Bolthor inquired.

"I have a whip I can lend you," Tykir said.

"What I meant about getting out of here was something entirely different. Number one, I think I should be gone when your Saxon notables arrive. I may have fought against some of them at Stone Valley. Saxons hate Vikings, 'tis a fact of life. No offense to you or your wife, Eirik."

"This is a rare peaceable time in Britain, Toste," Eirik said. "Yea, I know many died at Stone Valley, but mostly the Saxons and Norsemen are at a truce, if not peace. In truth, much of Northumbria is overridden with the Vikings who have settled here. We are a mixture here now—a melting pot of the two cultures."

"Bloody hell, Toste. I am as Viking as you are," Tykir said. "If you are leaving for that reason, then I should go, too."

"And me, as well," Bolthor said.

"No one should leave Ravenshire for fear of a fight," Eirik insisted. "None of my guests would dare object to your being here . . . any of you."

"I have never walked away from a fight," Toste said.

"Nor I," Tykir and Bolthor said.

"There is something else to consider," Eirik said. "I know it is a long shot, but what if Vagn's killer were amongst the guardsmen accompanying my guests?"

Toste froze at the possibility. He agreed it was remote, but it was worth being on watch. "In any case, you all have a way of diverting a conversation this way and that."

"Us?" they said.

"Yea, you. What I started to say before you all diverted me is that I need to get away from Ravenshire and travel to Evergreen."

"Esme's estate?"

"Yea. As I have told you before, something is not quite right about her situation. Why would a lord as powerful and wealthy as Blackthorne try so desperately for so many years to gain such a piddling little piece of land? Methinks I should take a day or two and ride there. Investigate a bit."

They all nodded.

Eirik stroked his chin pensively. "My stepson John's estate at Hawk's Lair is not far distant from Evergreen. We could go there, see what John knows, then study the estate as well as we can without raising eyebrows."

"That sounds like an excellent idea," Toste said, "except for the *we* part. I go alone."

"Why?" Bolthor asked in a wounded tone. "I thought we were partners, you and me . . . especially now that Vagn is gone."

"We are. We are." He patted Bolthor's arm. The skald was too sensitive by half. "But this is something best done alone, in disguise. What we don't want is four big hulking Norsemen raising eyebrows about the countryside."

Everyone nodded hesitantly in agreement.

"Will you go soon? On the morrow?" Eirik asked.

Toste shook his head, then smiled. "Nay, not till the beginning of next week. I have much more punishing to do." With that, he picked up his tub and swaggered off.

And he was whistling.

The Clueless Viking Hall of Fame . . .

"Eirik, have you seen my large brass tub?" Eadyth asked that night.

"I might have."

"Where?"

"Passing through the great hall."

"You saw my tub going through the castle? By itself?"

"Not exactly. It was on Toste's head."

"Has he lost his mind?"

"Methinks so. Or another body part."

They looked at each other and smiled.

When women get ideas, duck . . .

Tykir was panting for breath in his bedchamber later that night.

Really, sometimes his wife forgot that he was forty-

and-seven years old and that he had trouble keeping up
with her ten-years-younger body. Well, actually, he had
no trouble keeping up, being a lusty Viking and all that,
but she did make him pant more these days.

"I have a wonderful idea," Alinor said, snuggling up
to him and placing a hand lovingly over his limp manpart.

"Uh-oh!" Anytime Alinor mentioned "a wonderful
idea," especially when holding his cock, he knew he was
in for trouble.

"I think Toste should marry Esme."

Where that ludicrous idea had come from, he had no
clue. Women's minds flitted here and there like humming-
birds. Flit, flit, flit. "No matchmaking, Alinor. Toste asked
us not to interfere. Remember?"

"It wouldn't exactly be matchmaking."

"It would be exactly matchmaking if you are involved."

"Toste needs someone to love now that Vagn is gone."

"A man does not need someone to love."

She removed her hand from his nether region and
smacked him on the chest.

"Not *all* men need someone to love," he amended, not
being a total lackwit.

She moved her hand back where it belonged, so she
apparently forgave his loose tongue. *Smart wife!* "Toste
has a hole in his life."

"Which you intend to fill?"

"Mayhap."

"Alinor, do you not have enough to do helping Eadyth
prepare for this grand feast?"

"Everything is arranged. All the plans are made.
Eadyth has more than enough servants to carry through
once the guests arrive. In the meantime . . ."

"How about our sons? Dost know what Thork did today?" Their eleven-year-old son was a handful—a rogue in the true spirit of Viking males. Their other three sons, Starri, nine, Guthrom, six, and Selik, two, showed signs of following the same mischievous path.

Alinor sighed. "What did Thork do today?"

"He pinched a chambermaid on the arse."

She giggled. "Did you reprimand him?"

"Of course I did." *Actually, I couldn't stop laughing, especially when he told me this particular chambermaid had a huge arse which begged to be pinched.*

"Now that you bring up your son's misdeeds . . ." Alinor began.

Why was it that they were his *sons when they did something bad, but* her *sons when they proved angelic?*

". . . Starri and Guthrom had a spitting contest over the parapet, some of which hit a milkmaid passing by, which caused her to lose the contents of her stomach."

Tykir didn't want to tell her, but he was the one who had taught them about spitting contests. On the other hand, she probably already knew that.

"Back to Toste . . ." she said.

Holy Thor! She is like a dog with a bone once she gets started on something. She never lets go.

"Wouldn't it be nice to have a yuletide wedding?" She was moving her hands on him in a most delicious way now.

Tykir placed his hands over his face and said, "I surrender." He meant it in more ways than one.

Rub-a-dub-dub . . .

"Why are you bringing a tub in here?" Esme practically shrieked her question because she had a pretty good idea why.

Toste just smiled and said, "Greetings, Esme. Did you miss me?"

"Miss you, you goat-breath idiot? I . . . don't . . . think . . . so."

He blew dramatically into a palm placed in front of his mouth and nose, then sniffed. "Smells fresh to me."

Why does he always home in on the most irrelevant part of what I say? "How could I miss you? You're here all the time."

He winked at her. "Bolthor thinks you like me."

"Bolthor is a dunderhead."

"I'll tell him you said so."

"Nay. Don't do that," she said, immediately contrite. It wasn't the kindly skald's fault that Toste was behaving like a beast.

Toste had slept with her in the small bed for two nights now and been gone off and on during the daylight hours. Last night he'd tied her wrist to his again, then laid a hand possessively over one of her breasts. Every time she moved he took it as an excuse to fondle her breast. And of course she remained nude and tied to the bedposts every time he left the hut. He hadn't bothered with the gag, since apparently no one would come to her rescue even if she screamed loudly.

He placed a cauldron over the fire and filled it with a bucket of water from the rain barrel outside. Now he was traipsing in and out, filling the tub. Cold air rushed in from the open doorway, which chilled Esme even though she was covered with the fur pelt.

"I am not getting in that tub," she declared.

"Wouldst like to wager on that?"

"A lady deserves her privacy when bathing."

"One, there is no lady here. Two, you gave up any rights to privacy when you deprived me of mine."

Three, you are a loathsome lout. "What do you hope to gain with this vengeance?"

"Vengeance is its own reward. Besides, I find that I like the idea of having my very own sex slave."

"Se-sex slave?" she sputtered.

"Yea. You did not think I was going to be satisfied with a loaf of unleavened bread in my bed forever, did you? I mean, there is a charm in looking at you bare-arse naked, flat on your back, legs spread in invitation, but at some point you must earn your keep."

He was probably teasing her, but she decided not to test him on the issue. Another thought came to her un-bidden. "Did anyone see you bringing that tub here?"

"Hah! *Everyone* saw me."

She groaned, imagining the jests that must have been made.

The man was an infuriating lout. If he was going to torture her or force himself on her sexually, she wished he'd just do it and get it over with. This procrastination was driving her mad. Which, of course, was his goal.

"What scent do you prefer, Esme? Lavender or rose?"

"Huh?"

While her mind had wandered, Toste had filled the tub half full of cold rainwater, warmed up with two caul-drons of boiling water. Another cauldron was on the fire. He held two cloth packets in the air. "Never mind. I think I prefer the rose." With that, he dumped the pow-der in the tub and stirred it about. The scent of roses soon filled the small room. Next, he walked over to the bed and untied her restraints.

"Get in the tub," he ordered, turning his back to her.

She made a face at his back as she sat up, using the fur pelt to cover her front.

He went outside to gather wood, leaving the door

open. When he returned, he gave her a pointed look, acknowledging that she hadn't moved a bit yet and he was losing patience with her.

Esme didn't have a chance to think twice about what she did next. Toste was bent over the fire, his back to her, when she dropped her pelt and flew out the open doorway. She didn't stop to think that she was naked and barefooted and, though the sun was shining brightly, the ground was still covered with a thin layer of snow. Nor did she consider where she was headed. Escape had been her only goal.

She glanced back over her shoulder, fully expecting to see Toste at her heels. Instead, she saw him leaning against the door jamb of the hut, arms folded over his chest. He wasn't even coming after her. And he was smirking. The troll! But then he pushed away from the door frame and began to walk after her. *Walk.* He was so confident of catching her that he didn't even bother to run.

Esme glanced right and left, shivering with cold, as she decided which direction to head. Several cotters standing outside their huts noticed her and were pointing. She decided to run in the opposite direction, away from the castle. There should be some outbuildings in the fields where cows grazed, or farther on where Eadyth's conical beehives rose in the distance.

She had almost reached a three-sided cow byre when Toste tackled her from behind and she landed flat on her face in the mud. Because milch cows came into this area for a period of time every day, the ground was not covered with snow, nor was it frozen. Just muddy. Luckily, there were no cow pies under her. Leastways, she thought she would smell them if there were.

"Esme, Esme, Esme," Toste said against her ear.

"What a foolish wench you are! Dost know how much you are adding to your punishment with this latest misdeed? You truly must have a death wish."

"I care not anymore," she proclaimed. "Get off me, you big overblown lout. You must weigh as much as a . . . cow . . . nay, a bull . . . a randy old bull."

He laughed and rolled off her, standing and pulling her to her feet all in one motion. His eyes went wide as he gazed at her . . . all of her . . . covered with mud, from her face to her breasts and belly and woman place, even her legs and toes. He, on the other hand, had only a small amount of mud on him . . . his hands and his *braies*. But then he seemed to notice something else. Her teeth were chattering and her body was shaking uncontrollably with cold.

"Tsk tsk tsk!" he tutted as he swept her up in his arms and began to carry her swiftly back to the hut. He seemed not to care that the mud on her body rubbed off onto the front of him as he held her close against his chest with her dirty face nestled in the crook of his neck.

As soon as they entered the hut, he placed her in the tub of lukewarm water and carefully poured another cauldron of boiling water in to heat it up more. Washing his hands, he then used palmfuls of water to rinse his neck where her muddy face had been buried. He gave her a quick glance, taking in her still chattering teeth with a frown. Without speaking, he went out to get another bucket of rainwater, which he put into the cauldron to heat up. Next, he poured a cup of mead into a metal tankard and set it among the hot coals. Within moments he handed it to her and ordered, "Drink."

"I'm not thirsty." Now that her body's chill had dissipated, she sank lower into the scented water, wondering what would come next.

"Drink!" he said more forcefully and placed the cup against her lips. She would have to drink or have it running down her chin. Once she'd swallowed half of it, he took pity on her pleading eyes and set the cup aside. The mulled mead had done the job he'd intended, warming her from the inside as the water did from the outside.

Toste knelt down on the floor next to the tub, which made her uncomfortable because the water, though cloudy, was clear enough to give him a view of her naked body. She thought about covering herself with her hands under the surface, but didn't bother. He could see her anytime he wanted . . . and had.

He wiped a finger across her cheek and it came away covered with mud. He did the same to her hair. Same effect. She must look wretched. Before she had a chance to realize what he was about, Toste pushed her head down under the water. She came up sputtering. She glared at him as she combed her fingers through her still muddy hair. Which prompted him to dunk her again. This time she came up spewing foul words an almost-nun shouldn't even know.

"What? You are going to drown me as part of my punishment?"

"Nay, sweetling, I just like my bedmates to be . . . well, sweet. Pigs might like to wallow in mud, but I am not a pig."

"I think you're a pig."

"Do you, now?" He chuckled and began to lather her hair with a handful of soft soap which he scooped out of a small pottery container.

"I can do that myself," she said, reaching for the soap.

He held it out of her reach. "I prefer to do it."

"And I prefer not."

He dunked her under to rinse, then lathered her up

again. This time, he didn't just lather, he used the fingers of both hands to massage the soap into her scalp for a long time . . . way beyond the time necessary to clean her hair. His magic fingers kneaded her scalp in little circles, which caused her body to relax and her senses to heighten.

"Who taught you to do that?" she asked, her eyes closed and her chin on her chest.

"A houri."

"A whore-y. What's that?"

He chuckled. "A harem girl."

"Oh," she said. Then, "*Oh!*"

When her hair was clean, he moved behind her and combed her hair till it lay over her ears and down her back in a wet swath. Then he moved around to the side again, still kneeling, and told her, "Kneel in the tub and face me."

She didn't want to. The water wouldn't even reach her woman-place. "Why?" A feeble question, but she asked it just the same.

"Because you are dirty, and I would wash you."

She stifled a groan. She was no longer dirty, of course.

While she hesitated, he took off his belt and drew his tunic over his head, tossing it somewhere behind him. He was not muddy, except for his *braies*. Why was he removing . . . oh.

He made a peremptory motion of his hands that she should kneel. She did so, but she scrunched her eyes closed tight.

"Open your eyes."

"Why?"

"Stop asking why all the time. Just accept that I know what I'm doing."

She opened her eyes and gave him a look that said it

was questionable, but before she could voice that thought, her tongue froze in her mouth. He was soaping his hands. Both of them. A lot. And she knew just where he planned to place those hands, because that's where he was staring.

When his hands were slick with soap he spread them over her breasts, first in wide circles which got smaller and smaller till he worked her nipples into hard peaks. She wanted to beg him to stop. She wanted to beg him to never stop.

"You have beautiful breasts, Esme."

Am I supposed to react to that? I do not care that he admires my breasts. I do not care that he makes them ache deliciously. I do not care that his fingers weave magic.

"Would you like me to suckle them?"

"Whaaat?" *Where did that question come from?* "Nay, I don't want you to . . . to . . . do that."

He had already moved his hands to her arms, which he soaped, even the armpits, and her shoulders. Then he ladled clean, warm water over her and said, "Now stand."

She was about to ask why, but bit her bottom lip to stop herself. She knew why. "If I asked you to take pity and spare me this indignity, would you?"

"Nay."

Well, that answer was short and to the point. She stood and lifted her chin defiantly. She was Esme, Lady of Evergreen. Let him do what he would with her. He could not take away her pride. Still, she whistled softly.

Actually . . . she soon changed her tune.

With a new dollop of soft soap, he lathered her abdomen and belly, then spent a great amount of time on her woman's fleece and the private folds between her legs.

Even the crease of her buttocks got his attention. The rogue knew what he was about, too, because he touched her in places and in ways that only an expert libertine would know of. If she had not realized it before, she did now . . . she was way beyond her depth with this man.

She licked her suddenly dry lips and glanced at him.

To her satisfaction, she saw him lick his own lips. The Viking was equally affected by this little game of his. She was surprised that he did not grab for her, but she should not have been. He was an experienced man. His moves would be smoother than that.

Handing her a linen cloth, he said, "Dry yourself, Esme. We have a contract to discuss."

"What kind of contract?" she asked as she put the cloth to good use, then stepped out of the tub and used it to shield herself.

He grinned at her sad attempt at modesty after what he'd just seen and done. "Your punishment contract," he said as he pulled the tub toward the door, then dumped the water outside. After that, he brought more wood inside and built up the fire.

Finally he answered her as he began to disrobe himself,

"You kept me captive here for ten days. I figure that turnabout is fair play. Ten for ten. Except that you bit my lip that one time, which brings you up to eleven days, and your attempt at escape certainly counts for at least two more days. So your debt is thirteen days minus the two already spent here for a total of eleven days."

"You should wipe my debt out totally for having forced me to take such drastic measures in the first place."

"What kind of feminine illogic is that?"

"Men just don't recognize that women have brains."

"It's not your brain I'm interested in."

"Have I ever mentioned that you are a loathsome lout?"

"About a hundred times. I consider it a compliment, coming from you."

She reminded herself not to give him that "compliment" again.

He stood then, totally nude, and she couldn't keep herself from staring. The man was magnificent, from his blond hair which lay about his shoulders to his perfectly proportioned body. Actually, one body part seemed a little out of proportion with the rest. How could the Viking speak so calmly to her when he had *that* sticking out from him, like a flag waving its interest?

"Here is the deal I am offering you, Esme. For every time you initiate and make love to me, I will take off one day."

"Define making love."

He laughed. "My cock in one of your hot, wet orifices."

She wasn't exactly sure what he meant by that, but the smirk on his face told her that asking might not be a good idea. "What do you mean by *my* initiating love-play?"

"You start it. You do the work. Unless I agree to take over betimes, which I probably would on occasion, unless you beg me to do something particularly wicked. Mostly, it is in your hands."

"My hands? Hah! I wouldn't have a clue how to make love to a man."

"Learn. Do what comes naturally. Bloody hell, just touch me and I will probably explode. I have not been with a woman for a year, Esme. Believe me, I will not be picky."

There was probably a half-insult in there. "If any woman would suffice, why me?"

He shook his head at her. "I did not say any woman would suffice. I want *you*."

It took all her willpower not to ask "Why?" What she did say was, "You are suggesting that I sell my body."

"I prefer the word barter."

"You would take everything from me, including my pride."

"I would give back as good as I got."

Whatever that meant!

"Besides, you had no care for *my* pride." He stared at her for several long moments, waiting for her decision. When she remained silent, he said, "So be it." With those words, he walked over to the bed and lay down.

"Now what?"

"Now I am going to sleep, and you are going to be in this hut for eleven more days. I hope Eirik's noble guests don't ask to come have a peek at you."

"How would they even know I am here?"

"Hah! Bolthor has been telling one saga after another about this event. Dost think he will suddenly shut his teeth?"

She hadn't considered that. Also, she suspected that Eirik and Tykir teased Toste every time he entered the keep about having been hoodwinked by a female. And Alinor and Eadyth, if they were the good women she knew them to be, probably berated the men at every turn for allowing her imprisonment to go on.

Yea, any guests at Ravenshire would know of her ig-nominious situation.

She decided to try a different approach. "It's still day-light."

"Who says it has to be dark to sleep . . . or swive?"

With that, he pulled the fur pelt up over his body and turned his back to her.

"And what will happen to me when my confinement is over? Will you then help me regain Evergreen?"

He shrugged.

"What does that shrug mean?"

"I am not talking to you anymore. I am sleeping."

"You are not sleeping."

"I'm trying."

"You forgot to lock the door."

"If you run away again, I will add a week to your term of confinement. And I will put a chain around your neck and take you up to the keep like a trained bear."

"You wouldn't dare."

"Try me, Esme. I am not in a good mood."

"You are never in a good mood . . . lately."

He muttered some foreign word that she was fairly certain was foul.

A long period of silence followed in which she pondered all her choices. There weren't many. Finally, with a long sigh, she said, "All right."

At first, she didn't think he'd heard her. He still lay with his back to her, the fur pelt pulled up to his waist. But then he rolled over onto his back.

To his credit, he didn't smirk or snicker or say anything demeaning. He just watched her, waiting for her next move.

Hah! As if I know what move to make next. "A little help would not be amiss," she said snippily.

His only response to her plea for help was to lift the bed fur on one side for her.

She practically dragged her feet as she walked toward the bed.

His hot eyes raked her nude body as she approached.

Her nudity no longer bothered her all that much. She had much bigger problems to cope with. Like how to seduce a Viking. Or what to do with that thick pole standing up midway down his magnificent body.

She slid into the bed beside him and felt his body heat like the blast of a bonfire. He pulled the fur pelt up over them both. Enveloped in that warmth, with his chest against her face and her arm across his waist, she felt an odd lethargy. "Mayhap we could sleep for a while," she suggested.

He laughed, and his mirth rumbled in his chest under her cheek. "Or mayhap not," he said.

She ran a palm over his lightly furred chest and over his flat nipples. She thought he must like that, because she felt his heart rate accelerate noticeably. When her hand skimmed lower over his abdomen and belly, his heart practically jumped against her face. He must *really* like that, she thought, smiling to herself. It was kind of fun discovering she could have an effect on him with just the stroke of a hand. When her hand started to move lower, he grabbed her wrist and growled, "Not yet."

"What do you want?"

"What do *you* want, Esme?"

She thought a moment. "Well, I liked the kissing you did before."

He nodded. "I liked the kissing, too."

Still on her side, she leaned up over him so that her breasts rested on his chest. And wasn't that an amazing sensation . . . her nipples brushing against his chest hairs. She thought she heard Toste groan, but when it wasn't repeated, she figured she'd been mistaken. First she kissed the cleft in his chin . . . she just couldn't resist the temptation. Then she burrowed her fingers in his silky hair to hold him in place—not that he was moving at all—shifted her lips over his and tried to find the right position. At one point, she admitted, "Your breath doesn't really smell like goat."

He smiled against her mouth. "I know." Then, "You smell like roses."

And she said, "I know."

Quite the conversationalists, they were. More like two dunderheads.

Mostly he let her fumble her way through the kissing process till she slid her tongue inside his mouth. He opened wider for her, sucked on her tongue and made low masculine sounds of appreciation in his throat. When he reciprocated with his tongue in her mouth, she did the same. Esme ever was a good pupil. And she made low feminine sounds of appreciation in her throat.

She wasn't sure what to do next, except she realized belatedly that she'd been unconsciously rubbing her breasts back and forth across his chest, abrading the nipples into hard pebbles which ached for . . . something.

He noticed the direction of her gaze and took her by the waist, lifting her so that she lay on top of him, her belly on his abdomen, her thighs spread on either side of his hips, her breasts hanging over his face. "Give it to me," he asked huskily.

At first, she did not understand his meaning, but he looked pointedly at her breasts, and she knew. It was an oddly surrendering thing to do, but Esme lifted her breast from underneath, then lowered herself till the nipple pressed against his mouth. Without warning, he began to suckle her, wet and hard in an unending rhythm. She tried to jerk back at the incredible ripples of torturous pleasure he set off in her body, but he had one hand on the back of her waist and the other on her nape, holding her firmly in position. While he continued to alternately lave and suckle her, he moved the hand at her waist to the other breast, which he fondled unmercifully. Then he switched breasts. There seemed to be a direct erotic thread between the tips of her breasts and her nether region. Without thinking, she began to buck her hips against him, trying instinctively to rub that place between her legs which throbbed and throbbed.

Esme had felt much the same way that time when Toste had put his mouth there. So she knew what her body was yearning for . . . that wonderful, awful peaking business.

Once again, he lifted her by the waist and arranged her body over his . . . this time with her sitting on his belly, her female folds forming a perfect channel for his hard, hard manpart. She glanced up at him in question. He half reclined now, his upper body braced on his elbows, as he looked at the place where their bodies met. His blue eyes were misty with arousal. His full lips were parted as he panted slightly. Esme felt oddly exhilarated that she could bring such pleasure to a man, especially an experienced one like Toste.

"Move," he said in a raw voice.

"How?"

"Any way that feels good to you."

Hmmm. She undulated her hips forward, her slick folds moving with surprising ease.

He groaned.

She smiled.

"Witch," he said.

"Wretch," she said.

This time she undulated back and forth and noticed that the knob at the end of his manpart hit a particular bump in her channel, causing her eyeballs to practically roll back in her head with bliss. She did it more slowly this time, just to experiment. By the saints! What was this marvelous spot?

When she repeated the process twice more, Toste asked her, "Does that feel good?"

"Nay."

"Liar," he laughed.

Then Esme decided to experiment with other moves. Side to side. Bouncing. Circles. But always she came back to the undulations which had her riding the ridge of his staff, then bumping her bud.

"Why am I so wet there?" she asked.

He made a choking sound, then said, "Because your body wants me. It is preparing for my entry."

"Oh."

"Can you guide me into your body, sweetling?"

"I don't know."

"I'll help. Raise yourself up a bit."

He placed himself at her entrance, but she knew . . . she just knew . . . his massive size would never fit in her. She was right. Only the head went in.

She looked at him with dismay.

But Toste, still leaning back on his elbows, was staring with carnal concentration at the place where they were partially joined. Then he reached one hand forth and used his forefinger to strum that bud which was apparently exposed by her widespread thighs.

She saw stars for one brief moment and her inner muscles clasped and unclasped him, pulling him in halfway.

"That's a good girl," he encouraged her. "I don't want to hurt you. Go slow. Just a little more."

She had no idea how to go fast or slow. She was obeying her body's commands at this point.

He tweaked her nipples, and she took more of his manpart.

He spread her thighs wider, and she took a bit more.

He tap-tap-tapped her woman-bud with his thumb, and she screamed as her body began to peak.

With a roar of frustration, Toste flipped her over on her back and thrust himself into her, up to the hilt. She winced at the pinching sensation, but he made soothing sounds in her ear and did not move. Only when her body relaxed did he pull out slowly, almost all the way, then go in again, very slowly.

She sighed.

"Are you all right?" he asked. "Am I hurting you?"

She shook her head. "Am I hurting you?"

He laughed. "Only in the best possible way."

No more talking after that. He took her ankles and pressed them up against her buttocks, then spread her knees wider. For a long, long time then, he stroked her, long and slow. Then he got faster and faster and shorter and shorter, till she was wailing and peaking almost continuously. Was it possible to die of too much pleasure? She loved the friction of his plunging on her inner walls. She loved the way the base of his manpart hit her woman-bud every time he came home. She loved the fullness of him imbedded in her.

When it seemed she could take no more pleasure, and Toste was gasping for breath, he raised himself on straightened arms, his neck thrown back. Like a Norse god he looked. Blond and glorious. Then he thrust himself into her one last time and roared out his triumph. She rippled around him in yet another peaking.

After that, he slumped over her body, completely sated. In truth, he might have fallen asleep for a moment.

When he raised his head finally, he gazed at her in wonder, leaned down and kissed her lightly on the lips, and murmured, "That was good." Then he grinned and remarked, "One down and ten more to go."

Esme glowered up at him, as if he'd given her a painful reminder of their punishment pact, but in truth she did not mind at all. Sometimes, "punishment" was not such a bad thing.

It's hard work, but someone's gotta do it . . .

Toste awakened after midnight with a smile on his face. And not just because he smelled like a bloody rose.

He should get up and put more wood on the fire. The room was cool because the fire had burned down to embers. He did not get up immediately, though. He was too comfortable with Esme curled up on him like honey on a hot rock. He chuckled to himself at that apt description. She made honey like a busy little bee, and he was definitely hot and rock-hard.

Already Esme had chipped three days off her confinement. And though she would never admit it, she had enjoyed the process immensely, as much as he had . . . or more. Holy Thor, his almost-nun had taken to lovemaking like a harem houri. The second time she'd made love to him, she'd ridden him like a horse. And a fine rider she was, too. The third time she'd licked him till he was the one to surrender, even though she'd avoided that most important place of all.

His nose was starting to get cold. So finally he eased himself off the bed and went to the far side of the room, where he relieved himself in a chamber pot. Hunkering down before the fire, he quietly laid several logs on the grate and blew the embers aflame. Soon he had a roaring fire once again.

He dusted off his hands and turned to go back to the

bed. Only then did he notice Esme lying on her side, watching him.

"You are awake," he said unnecessarily.

She nodded, and from the way she stared at him he knew what she had in mind. A part of his body knew, too, and reacted accordingly.

Esme grinned with satisfaction.

He shook his head at her as he slid back under the fur pelts. "You are not going to wipe out your entire punishment in one night, Esme. So forget about it."

"What? You could not rise to the occasion eleven times in one night?"

Rise to the occasion? She certainly had a way with words. He looked at her to see if she was serious.

She was.

I am good, but I am not that good. "Nay, I cannot do it eleven times in one night."

"I could."

"I doubt it." *What kind of wanton have I created here?*

"What is this mark here?" she asked, tracing the cloverleaf imprint on his inner thigh, up high.

"A birthmark."

She continued to trace the outline with her forefinger. He could even feel her breath there, which he liked immensely. His staff liked that tracing and breathing business, too, and began to thicken.

She giggled. "Does . . . did . . . your twin brother have the same mark?"

His chest constricted and he realized that he hadn't thought of his dead brother in days . . . or leastways he hadn't been dwelling on his absence the way he had since the battle. Esme was responsible for that.

Bored with the birthmark, she curled up against him once again, like a pet cat. In fact, she might have even purred. "Toste, you said that you have been celibate for a year. Why is that? I mean, I cannot imagine a man of your appetites depriving yourself of such . . . uh, pleasures."

Toste felt great satisfaction in her mentioning the pleasures he'd gotten from their bedsport, because her words also revealed that she'd gained those same pleasures. "My appetites?" He hooted with laughter. "Well, actually, I was not celibate by choice. Vagn talked me into joining up with the Jomsvikings, and they are celibate whilst living on their island fortress."

She nodded. "Poor fellow. Must be you need a woman's touch to satisfy hungers."

"Yea, I do," he said with mock seriousness. "In fact, Esme, there is something special I would do for you, in return for your . . . uh, ministrations this day to my . . . uh, hungers." *By thunder, what a great idea I have just thought of. Will she go for it?*

She narrowed her eyes at him, not at all fooled by his sad demeanor. "Something you would do *for me?*"

"Yea, it is a particular sexual position that women adore and men . . . well, we abide it, though it is not our favorite." *Vagn would get such delight out of this ploy of mine. Will Esme?*

"Really?" She was still skeptical, but interested.

That's it, Esme, girl. Let your curiosity take over.

"And this thing you would do for me—would it count toward my decreasing days . . . you know, since you initiated it, not me?"

Esme, you are way too smart for a woman. "I suppose I could bend the rules a bit. I am a kindhearted fellow."

She slanted her eyes at him and said, "I don't know. Explain this particular sexual position that women adore."

"Have you ever seen dogs engaged in coupling?"

"Yea," she said and curled her upper lip with distaste.

All right, so mentioning dogs was not the best mind-picture to give her. But, bulls and cows or stallions and mares probably wouldn't have gone over any better. "Well, this position is called dog-swiving."

"It sounds awful."

Time for a little damage control. I do not want to scare her off. "Well, like I said, it is not a man's favorite, but they do it betimes to please their women." *I am so good, I amaze myself.*

"Well," she said. "Is it as good as that other trick you taught me? The Viking S-spot?"

"Nothing is as good as that, dearling. But close." He sensed that she was softening. Time to go in for the kill, but first he must sweeten the pot. "Methinks I could even take two days off your tally if you agree to this. Trust me, Esme, you will not be sorry." *Said the wolf to the lamb.*

"All right," she said.

With those words, Toste whipped the fur pelt off the bed and began to spread it out afore the fire. Esme sat up and watched him carefully. She was not fooled by the rogue, not one whit. The Viking was up to no good, but two days off her tally? She couldn't resist that.

Any more than she could resist him. The things he had taught her about her body and sex play were amazing. She would have to go to confession first chance she got, of course, and would be doing penance for years, but it might very well be worth it. On the other hand, she might be dead.

But now, the rogue stood unabashedly naked and aroused, beckoning her toward him with the fingers of both hands. She stood and walked toward him, not so unabashed about her nakedness but getting better at it.

"Down on all fours," Toste instructed, pointing to the fur pelt.

"Like a dog?" she inquired, arching an eyebrow at him.

"Like a very pretty dog," he said, smiling in such a winsome way that she probably would have stood on her head if he'd asked.

He came up over her from behind, placing one hand over her breast which hung embarrassingly loose and his other hand over her woman-fleece. "See, isn't this nice?"

"It seems crude." She felt way too open to his wicked fingers this way. In addition, she had no control in this position with her hands and legs out of commission.

"Sometimes crude is good," he said. Already he was proving his point by nipping at her shoulder with his teeth. He'd pulled her hair back above her ear to give him greater access. At the same time, he was alternately twirling the nipples of both breasts between his thumb and forefingers. "Do you like it yet?"

"I'm not sure." But she rubbed her rump back and forth against his manpart and heard him groan against her ear. "Now I'm liking it."

He bit at her earlobe and stuck the tip of his tongue inside, which caused her whole body to tense up with a fierce spasm of pleasure. "Let me do that again when my finger is inside you," he said.

And he did.

And she went absolutely rigid, fighting the erotic ripples that passed over her entire body.

"Relax, sweetling."

"Hah! As if that's possible. Let me up. I want to go back to the bed where I can see you."

"Not yet, sweetling. Not quite yet."

His fingers were doing incredible things between her legs, and his hips were bucking against her from behind.

"Put your face on the furs and fold your arms above your head," he directed.

Which would place her buttocks in the air. "I . . . don't . . . think . . . so."

"Please."

Oh, that is just wonderful. Now he pulls the please ploy. Now I will never be able to resist him. She put her face down, though she was still on her knees, and even let him spread her legs wider. She was about to protest this horribly vulnerable position, and she was beginning to doubt that it was a favorite of women when Toste entered her woman's channel from behind. She might have screamed—she wasn't sure—at the shock of his filling her and going in even farther than he had before—not to mention the shock of her peaking suddenly with hard, clasping grasps on his staff. It was wonderful and humiliating at the same time.

"By the saints, what are you doing to me?" she whimpered.

"Making love."

And then he began to thrust in and out of her, while at the same time strumming the bud which seemed to be the center of a woman's pleasure. She peaked again.

And he stopped, imbedded in her. Even farther than before. Even wider.

"Don't you dare stop now," she gasped out.

"Shhh," he said and began massaging her breasts with wide-sweeping, kneading motions till the nipples felt like points against his palms.

"You are torturing me," she wailed.

"Good torture or bad torture?"

"I do not know," she cried, then bucked her bottom upward to try to get him to resume his thrusts.

He did, so long and slow she wanted to scream in frustration. Mayhap she did. Her mind was roiling with emotion. She was beyond knowing what she was doing.

He put one hand on the back of her neck to hold her down, and plunged wildly into her now, so hard and fast that it was hard for her to distinguish pain from pleasure. Nay, it was pleasure . . . hard pleasure. And he was mimicking his thrusts with a matching flick-flick-flick of his fingertips against her woman-bud.

She peaked and peaked and peaked then as he plunged into her one last time, hard and deep. Her convulsing woman's channel and throbbing woman-bud brought her the most intense, unending pleasure. Almost too much pleasure to bear.

She collapsed on the floor, and he fell on top of her. For several long moments, neither of them spoke. They couldn't.

When she finally rolled over on her back and gazed up at Toste, she saw the stunned look on his face. So this thing that happened between them was not a common occurrence.

Without saying a word, he carried her to the bed and lay down with her. He tucked her into his embrace with her face on his chest and pulled another fur pelt over them.

In that moment, Esme realized something awful. She had fallen in love with her captor.

A crazy little thing called love . . .

Toste stayed awake, shocked to the core by a realization that had struck him of a sudden. He had fallen in love with his captive.

Heart, soul, everything.

How had it happened? When? Why?

He shrugged. It did not matter. It just had.

After their monumental sex event in front of the fire, Toste had made love to Esme again. Slowly. With adoration. He hoped she understood what he was trying to say with his body. Or did she need the words?

Well, before he could declare himself, he had other things that must be done first. He slid carefully off the bed and covered Esme's sleeping form more completely. She was snoring slightly. He smiled, realizing he'd worn her out. Well, she'd worn him out, too.

He dressed and returned to the castle, having no trouble making his way along the path by the light of the full moon. He went upstairs and got the items he required. When he came back down, he noticed Bolthor sitting alone before the fire. All around him, soldiers and servants slept in alcoves and on floor pallets.

"Bolthor, what are you doing up?"

"I could not sleep," he said. "My leg wound bothers me betimes."

Toste nodded, understanding fully. He still got megrims on occasion from his head wound.

"You smell like roses."

Toste sniffed his own arm and grinned.

"So, how is the punishing going?" Bolthor asked with an answering grin.

"Wonderful," he said, grinning back. They were a couple of grinning fools.

"I can see that," Bolthor said. "You look different."

"Happy?"

"Mayhap," he replied. "Methinks I should compose a special rhyming poem for you. Methinks a good title would be 'Rhyme and Punishment.' Do you like that?"

"I do. I like it."

Bolthor noticed the saddlebag slung over Toste's shoulder then and said, "So, you are off. To Evergreen?"

He nodded.

"Are you sure you want to go alone?"

"It is something I must do alone. Take care of my Esme for me."

Bolthor's eyes widened at his words, but then he nodded and said, "Be safe."

When Toste returned to the hut, he placed all the items he'd gathered at the keep on a chair. Walking to the bed, he looked down at Esme's still sleeping form. Should he awaken her? Or not? In the end, he chose to let her sleep. But he leaned down and kissed her lightly on the lips.

I love you, Esme.

Wait for me.

Gone . . . gone . . . gone . . .

Esme awakened just after dawn with a smile on her face.

Toste was absent, but that didn't concern her. He'd probably gone up to the castle to get them some food . . . and clean bed linens.

Replete from last night's bedsport, she fell back to sleep and did not awaken till mid-morning. Almost immediately, she realized that Toste had not returned. And the fire was out.

Rising warily, she looked across the room and saw arranged on a chair, her gown, shoes, hose and a cloak. She did not have to check the door to know that it was unlocked. It was clear that Toste had left the clothing so that she could return to the Ravenshire keep.

And it was equally clear that he would not be there

when she did. He was gone. He'd had his fill of her, even before her "punishment" was completed, and this was his way of releasing her from their pact.

She sank to her knees on the floor and sobbed out her pain. It seemed that once again, her dreams were not to be fulfilled. She snuffled and wiped a hand across her dripping nose. Standing, she began to don her clothes. She would return to the castle; she would fight for Evergreen.

But she would never be the same again.

CHAPTER FOURTEEN

⊕

L *ove hurts . . .*
   By early afternoon, Esme was back at the castle.
Although her eyes were probably red and her nose
puffy from crying all morning, she had no more tears to
shed. And, surprisingly, no one at Ravenshire made any
mention of the activities of the past sennight and more—
not of her taking Toste captive, then his taking her captive, not even of Toste's current abandonment of her. It
was as if the past thirteen days had not even happened.
She suspected that everyone had agreed ahead of time
not to discuss those things to spare her embarrassment.
   Ravenshire itself had changed dramatically in her
short absence. Mistletoe and holly were arranged everywhere, even hanging in swags from the rafters. Esme
was not surprised to see mistletoe amongst the other
greens in this partly Norse household. The custom of
kissing under a piece of mistletoe was often associated
with Balder, a beloved Viking god similar to the Christian Jesus Christ. Balder had been killed by a mistletoe
arrow and restored to life by a sprig of mistletoe. There-
after, Vikings considered the sight of it a signal that the
kiss of peace and love should be given.
   Fragrant candles burned in practically every corner.
Delicious odors of foods being prepared for the upcoming

feast wafted through the castle—roasted boar, red deer, chicken and duck; salted cod, pickled kidneys, creamed eels and the loathsome *lutefisk*; honey cakes, dried apple tarts and sweet raisin custards; hard and soft cheeses, including the Viking *skyr*; mountains of breads, especially the loaves of circular manchet bread with the hole in the center which were arranged on long broom handles in the scullery. And of course Lady Eadyth's famous mead, supplemented by a batch of Margaret's Mead which had been left behind.

Many of the guests would arrive tomorrow, but already the castle overflowed with extended family and friends, all with children running hither and yon. Of course, there were Eirik and Eadyth's twin seventeen-year-old daughters, Sarah and Sigrud, but two other daughters had also come home, twenty-four-year-old Emma who worked in an orphanage in Jorvik, and Larise, the twenty-six-year-old widow of a Northumbrian merchant, not to mention the darkly brooding son John of Hawk's Lair, who was much too somber for his twenty-five years.

Also still in residence for the holiday season were Tykir and Alinor and their four wild sons. The boys had been teaching Abdul some yuletide ditties, some of which were rather naughty. Between the bird's squawking and the children's squawking, it was hard to think . . . which was a good thing in Esme's case.

Among the early guests were Adam from Hawkshire with his wife, Tyra, along with their baby Edward, who was crawling everywhere, an Arab servant named Rashid and a clumsy twelve-year-old boy, Alrek, who tripped over everything in sight. Adam was a noted healer; beautiful Tyra, a giant of a woman, was a soldier. Amazing people!

The guests that worried Esme most, though, were the

ones who would begin arriving tomorrow, some of them members of the Witan, possibly even Archbishop Dunstan, who would represent the king. Despite all that she had done to Toste, she'd never thought he would abandon her to face these notables alone. Her life . . . her future . . . was at stake, and he had just ridden off.

She found Bolthor sitting at the far end of the great hall before a small hearth, sipping a cup of mead. Apparently, he had needed to escape the din and chaos, as well. Perhaps he felt abandoned by Toste, too.

She put a hand on his sleeve and sat down on a bench beside him. "I cannot believe the noise," she said.

He nodded. "'Tis always this way when Vikings get together. And Eirik and Eadyth, though they can claim only one-fourth Norse blood betwixt the two of them, are more Viking than some pure-blooded ones. Comes from Eirik being raised mostly in Viking households, I suppose."

"Do you . . . or Toste . . . have any blood connection to them?"

He shook his head. "No direct or close kinship, but we have been comrades for years in battle and at Norse althings. I fought beside Tykir at the Battle of Brunanburh where I lost my eye."

"And Toste—do you not feel abandoned by him now? Like me?"

He raised his eyebrows. "Abandoned? Why would I feel abandoned? Why would you? He should be back tonight or on the morrow at the latest, methinks."

Esme shook her head to clear it of the fuzziness caused, no doubt, by so much weeping. "What mean you?" Suddenly, a question occurred to her. "Did he not go looking for his brother's killer?"

"Nay."

"Where did he go?"

"He did not tell you?"

"Tell me what?"

"Where he was going."

"Nay, he did not." Esme felt like shaking the giant skald . . . as if she could! "Where did Toste go?"

"To Evergreen," he said. "I thought you knew."

Shock rippled over her. It was the last answer she would have expected. Softly she informed him, "No one told me."

He shrugged. "No doubt everyone thought you knew."

Now she felt like shaking Toste. But he had gone to Evergreen. For her? "Why did he go?"

"To help you."

Tears, which she'd thought dried up, welled immediately in her eyes and her heart seemed to constrict in her chest. "For me?"

"Yea, we talked—Toste, Eirik, Tykir and me—and we have concluded that there is something odd going on at Evergreen . . . something unusual. Else why would your father covet such a small estate? Toste went to investigate. He hopes to return with information that can be used in your petition afore the Witan."

She bit her bottom lip with worry. "It could be dangerous."

"Mayhap, but Toste is dangerous, too. Do not worry. He will return. He specifically asked me to keep you safe till he does."

Esme brightened and slapped a hand over her racing heart. Toste must care for her. He must.

With that, she went off to find Eadyth and Alinor. Suddenly her life seemed hopeful. Toste had not abandoned her, after all.

Eadyth and Alinor were in a storage room on an upper level, sorting through silver knives, wooden platters, spoons and goblets, and pretty cloths to put on the tables for the feast. They looked up and said, "Greetings, Esme."

"Greetings," she said. "Can I help?"

"Yea," Eadyth answered. "Help us set aside anything that can be used by all our extra guests."

"We will need more bed linens, too," Alinor reminded Eadyth.

While they worked, Esme asked, "Why did you not tell me that Toste had gone to Evergreen?"

"You did not know?" Eadyth seemed genuinely surprised.

"The lackwit did not tell you," Alinor remarked, more as a statement than a question. "How like a man."

"Alinor is right in her assessment. Men do not think words are necessary. They think we can see into their thick heads."

"Have you fallen in love?" Alinor inquired of a sudden, then immediately put up a halting hand. "Nay, you do not have to answer that, Esme. It was impertinent of me."

But she answered just the same. "I am sore angry with the lout for some of the things he has done, but, yea, I suspect that I have fallen in love with him. More the fool am I."

"Oh, I don't know about that. Does Toste love you?" Leave it to Alinor to get right to the heart of the matter.

Esme threw her hands in the air. "If he did not tell me he was going on a chivalrous errand on my behalf, dost think he would inform me of his inner feelings?"

"Betimes a woman can sense these things," Alinor said.

"Well, his lovemaking was spectacular," Esme revealed with a flaming face.

"Do tell," both women said with avid interest, placing the objects they'd been sorting back on a table and giving her their full attention.

"I couldn't speak of *that*, except to say that he did that thing for me that men don't like but which women adore."

"And that would be?" Alinor asked, a suspicious tone in her voice.

"You know—the woman's favorite position in bedsport."

Eadyth grinned at Alinor and said, "I cannot wait to hear this." They both looked at Esme.

There was no escape now. So Esme said bluntly, "Like a dog."

Eadyth looked at Alinor, and Alinor looked at Eadyth. Then they both burst out laughing. And they continued to laugh till tears rolled down their faces. Esme just gaped at them in puzzlement.

Woof, woof, woof . . .

'Twas said that, in many bedchambers at Ravenshire that night, dog-sex took place. Bolthor swore he would write a saga about it.

Next day, male voices were heard to make barking noises in jest as they elbowed each other. Many a woman walked about weak-kneed, with a perpetual blush on her face.

And they all had Toste to thank.

The road trip from hell . . .

"Stop touching me," Helga said, slapping at Vagn's hand which had once again crept up to the side of her breast.

"Stop jiggling your arse. You're tempting me."

"I was not jiggling . . . oh, forget it. Just put me down."

Helga was riding in front of Vagn on Clod. They were on their way to Ravenshire, and everyone was getting tired of having to stop so often so that she could rest her churning stomach. It seemed that the bouncing rhythm of the cart had made her sick. Riding on the horse with Vagn made her feel better, but *he* made her sick.

"How is your stomach?"

"Just fine."

"Do you have to piss?"

"Do you have to be so crude? Nay, I do not have to relieve myself."

"Do your breasts hurt?"

"Vaaaagn!"

"Well, I was just concerned about your well-being. I would be willing to massage them, if need be."

She exhaled with a whoosh of exasperation.

"Has the baby moved yet?" he asked, placing a hand on her flat belly.

"I am less than one month pregnant, Vagn. Babes do not move in the womb this early."

"How was I to know? This is the first time I have been pregnant . . . I mean, . . . well, you know what I mean. When precisely will it be moving?"

"I have no idea."

"Will you let me know when it moves?"

"Yea, if you are around."

"I will be around." There was a brief period of silence and then he said, "Marry me, Helga."

It was only the hundredth time that he'd urged her to marry him. She had to admit she liked to hear him plead, but she was no more convinced now than she had been the first time around. "Give me one good reason why I should."

"Because it is the right thing to do."

"Wrong answer."

"What do you want me to say, Helga?"

"Nothing," she said wearily. "Nothing at all." Soon she was nodding off to sleep, rocked by the soothing motion of the horse and the warm comfort of Vagn's cloak wrapped around them both.

Through a haze of near-sleep, she heard Finn Fine-hair ride up and inquire too sweetly, "Have you won her over yet?"

"Nay, but methinks she is softening."

"I could give you tips," Finn offered magnanimously.

Vagn told him, "Go pluck some arse hairs." Whatever that meant. Finn just laughed.

Her father rode up then. "Did you ask her again?"

"I did," Vagn said.

"I presume she did not agree."

"Nay, but methinks she is softening."

"Best you soften her quick. Ravenshire draws near, and there will be little time for softening once we arrive."

Dolts; all the men in my life are dolts, Helga thought, yawning loudly.

An hour or more later, she was awakened from a sound sleep by cheers around her. She opened her eyes and turned to look up at Vagn in question.

"That is Ravenshire up ahead," he said.

She turned to look forward. It was a magnificent timber and stone castle which had been added to over the years as the Ericsson family of Ravenshire grew. She had been here many times in the past. Eadyth, who was so clever about marketing the products of her beekeeping, had been a model to Helga from an early age. She'd given her much advice on starting her own embroidery business.

As they got closer, they became aware of fellow

guests traveling toward Ravenshire from other direc-
tions. There were at least three other noble parties coming from what must be Jorvik and the eastern shires.
And in the distance, a lone horseman on a hilltop also
approached the vast estate.

They advanced to the drawbridge, which was down
today with the wolf banner favored by the lords of Ravenshire floating on the wind to show that the lord was in
residence. That was when Helga felt Vagn stiffen behind
her and murmur, "By the gods, can it be?"

"What?" she asked, turning halfway to see his face,
which was white with shock.

"Bolthor . . . that giant Norseman standing in the
courtyard . . . I swear it is Bolthor the Skald."

"I thought he died at Stone Valley."

"So did I."

Vagn felt an odd prickling at the back of his neck. A
warning. Something was not as it should be. In addition,
he sensed the presence of his brother Toste, more strongly
than he had since the battle. He could swear he actually
heard Toste whistling in his head. The sense of Toste's
nearness was overpowering. It must be the presence of
Bolthor that brought this on. Obviously, Bolthor, like Clod,
had survived the battle.

Bolthor stepped forth with a puzzled frown on his
face, and Vagn slid off his horse, handing the reins to a
stable boy. Why was Bolthor not as shocked as he to
recognize a survivor of the battle?

"Bolthor," he said, rushing forth to hug the huge man
warmly, then hold him at arm's length to take in his good
friend's healthy countenance. "I thought you died at Stone
Valley."

"Huh?" Bolthor said. The poet nodded then at Gorm and
Finn, who were alighting from their horses, and remarked

slowly, as if sorely confused, "I thought you went to Evergreen. What are you doing with Gorm and his party? Briarstead is in the opposite direction."

"What?" Even as he shook his head to clear it, Vagn noticed a beautiful black-haired woman staring at him, then at Helga. She appeared stricken by their appearance here together, though Vagn could swear he'd never seen her afore. But wait—this was the wench he'd seen in his dreams . . . dreams of Toste. Before he had a chance to comprehend what she was about, she stomped up with tears streaming from her eyes, slapped him across the face and said, "You cad! Did you have dog-sex with her, too?" Then she stomped away.

Dog-sex?

Everyone appeared confused . . . most of all Vagn.

But then he saw Eirik, Eadyth, Tykir and Alinor up on the steps, staring wide-eyed and gape-mouthed at something beyond the moat. Alinor and Eadyth started squealing and hugging each other and sobbing happily. Eirik and Tykir whooped with glee and began grinning from ear to ear. Bolthor hugged Vagn then, a big, bone-crushing bear hug that lifted him off the ground. Against his ear, he whispered, " 'Tis a miracle."

Everyone must be going barmy.

But then Bolthor set him down, turned him about and said, "Look! Can't you see?"

Vagn did look then. He saw a lone rider coming over the drawbridge. The rider, stopped midway across and was staring . . . *at him.* Suddenly the man jumped off his horse and came running toward him yelling, "Vagn! Thank the gods. Is it really you?"

At the same time, Vagn rushed forward as recognition hit him. He could barely see for the tears burning his eyes, nor could he speak over the lump in his throat.

It was his brother Toste, come back from the dead. Nay, he must have survived the battle, too. Somehow. No matter. His brother was here.

They held each other's faces in their hands. They ran fingertips over each other's hair and lips. They embraced over and over, then held on to each other as if fearful they might be separated again. They even kissed each other soundly on the cheek. Finally they stood back and smiled.

Words were not necessary. They spoke to each other in the silent method they'd perfected over the years.

I have missed you sorely, brother, Vagn thought.

Likewise. That is some wound you got, Vagn. I have been suffering your pain.

Hah! I still get your headuches. What have you been doing all this time?

I have been in a nunnery. Toste waggled his eyebrows mischievously. *How about you?*

Ah, so that explains the black crows. Me, I have been recuperating at Briarstead—Gorm's estate. I have something important to tell you, Vagn began.

Do not tell me, Toste said, *I can sense your joy, and not just about our reunion. It is . . . can it be? You are going to be a father? Congratulations! Oh, I am going to be the best uncle in the world.*

The two brothers walked toward the keep then, arms looped over each other's shoulders, beaming at one and all. Suddenly Toste stopped in his tracks, which caused Vagn to stop, too. With a hoot of laughter, Toste said, "Holy Frigg! Look who's over there. It's Helga the Homely."

Vagn glanced toward Helga, who was standing next to Clod, watching somberly as he was reunited with his brother. He saw the stricken expression on her face at Toste's words. Vagn knew Toste was just teasing. Anyone looking at Helga would know she was not homely . . . not anymore. But she did not know that.

With a deep sigh, Vagn pulled away from his brother and did the only thing he could do. He punched him in the nose. Toste swayed on his feet and almost fell backward. Instead of fighting back, as would be the normal practice, Toste put a hand to his bleeding nose and cocked his head in question. "Up till a few moments ago, you thought I was dead. Now you punch me?"

Vagn shrugged and said, "You insulted the mother of my child. What else could I do?"

He reached out an apologetic hand, and Toste grasped it without question. Then Toste walked over to Helga, lifted her in the air and twirled her about. "My apologies, beautiful lady. Welcome to our family."

"Put me down! Put me down, you lout," Helga said, punching Toste about the ears. Some of those punches were probably retaliation for his long-ago youthling taunt.

And Vagn told his brother, "Uh, Toste, she is not my wife . . . yet."

"What? You are losing your touch. Good thing I have come back from the dead to help you, brother. I was ever the more charming brother," he told Helga, kissing her soundly on the mouth before setting her on the ground.

Just then, Toste seemed to notice the red-faced lady standing at the back end of the crowd that filled the courtyard. "Esme, why are you hiding back there?" he called out. "Come here. I would have you meet my brother."

She dragged her feet forward till she stood before them.

"Ah, it is the wench who slapped my face?" Vagn said with a grin, rubbing his cheek as if it still hurt.

"You did?" Toste asked the woman. "Why?"

"Because I thought he was you, and he was with that woman, and . . . well, I think you are both loathsome louts."

Everyone around them laughed.

As they all started up the steps to enter the great hall where a great celebration would now surely take place, Vagn said to Toste, "There is one thing I would ask you, brother."

"Anything."

"What is dog-sex?"

Off the wall . . .

It was hours before Toste could get away and talk to Esme alone. The problem was finding her.

After much searching, he entered an upper bedchamber where she slept along with Eirik and Eadyth's four daughters. Leastways, the others were sleeping on pallets spread about the room whilst Esme sat nervously in a low chair afore the fire. He could tell she was nervous because she whistled softly.

"Toste!" she exclaimed in a loud whisper when he crept into the room without knocking. "You should not be here. 'Tis not proper." She indicated the young women sleeping.

"Since when am I proper?" he asked, also in a loud whisper, coming up to hunker down next to her.

"Go away," she said.

"Come with me to the woodcutter's hut. I need to talk with you."

"Hah! I know what you want, and it is not talk."

He grinned at her and tweaked a ribbon on the voluminous night rail she wore. "That, too. But, really, I must tell you what I discovered at Evergreen." Esme looked glorious to him, with her black curls furling out about her shoulders and down her back. Her blue eyes appeared red-rimmed, though. Had she been crying?

"Well, tell me here, or out in the corridor. I am not going to that hut again . . . ever."

"Esme," he said in a wounded voice. "I have fond memories of that hut." But almost immediately he pulled her to her feet and offered, "A compromise then. Get your cloak and we will go out on the parapet to talk."

She did, and as they walked toward the doorway leading to the ramparts, she said, "I am angry with you, Toste."

"For going to Evergreen?"

"Nay, for going to Evergreen without informing me first."

"Ah. Well, I am angry with you, too. Did you have to tell everyone about the dog-sex?"

She gasped. "I only told Eadyth and Alinor. I did not tell everyone."

"Same thing."

He took her hand as they climbed the steps, and he found himself smiling for no reason at all. He liked Esme. A lot. And he had missed her. "Did you miss me, sweetling?"

"Nay."

"Good. I missed you, too."

"Do you hear only what is convenient for your ears?"

"Yea. 'Tis the best way."

"You are impossible."

"I know. 'Tis one of my best assets."

"I do not want to know what the others are."

"You already know most of them," he said, waggling his eyebrows at her.

There was a full moon out, but it was chilly up on the

parapet. He nodded to a passing guardsman and pulled
Esme back into an alcove where there would be some
protection from the wind.

"You must be ecstatic to have found your brother
alive."

He nodded, still too overcome with emotion to discuss
his joy at being reunited with Vagn. They had talked and
talked for hours on end, bringing each other up to date,
once they were able to remove themselves from all their
well-meaning friends. Right now, Vagn was off somewhere trying to convince Helga to marry him. Who ever
would have thought that his brother would end up with
Helga the . . . nay, he must stop thinking of her that way.
Helga the Handsome? Yea, that was how he would think
of her now.

"Did you discover anything at Evergreen?"

"Yea, I did," he said, brightening. "It is all about
water, Esme."

"Water? You mean water, as in wells, underground."

"Nay, I mean water as in river, as in water rights."

She frowned with confusion. "Are you speaking of
Evergreen River which passes along the northern border
of the estate?" The holding was a fairly small and narrow one, rectangular in shape, with the river going along
its northern, longer length.

"'Twould seem that your father recognized some fifteen years ago that the neighboring estates had need of
that waterway to feed their cattle and for passage of peat
boats from the western shire to eastern towns. He has
been charging exorbitantly for that privilege these many
years."

"I don't understand. My mother's family always permitted neighbors to use that water, which is abundant. It
is an unspoken agreement."

"Can I assume you have seen none of these toll monies?"

She shook her head.

"As I thought. In addition, your one brother owns a peat works and the other owns the boats that carry the products to market. Your father is a shrewd businessman."

"My father is an evil businessman. I suspect that all that peat is contaminating the water for livestock."

Toste shrugged, knowing nothing about that. "In any case, that explains why the property is so important to your father."

"He was willing to end my life so he could continue to amass his wealth."

"Some men are like that. You are not to worry, though. This information will help us with your plea to the Witan. You may very well have your answer within the next few days if enough of them are here."

"Thank you, Toste. You are a lout in many ways, but thank you for doing this for me."

"Ah, I do so love backhanded compliments," he said. "I wonder how you are going to thank your knight for this latest chivalry." He pressed her back against the wall.

"A silken scarf?" she offered.

"I have way too many silken scarves already," he said, nuzzling her neck. "By the by, Esme, why did you leave the woodcutter's hut? Your 'punishment' was not yet over."

She tilted her head at him in question. "You left all my clothing on the chair. I assumed that was your silent message that I was free to leave."

"I was giving you a choice, dearling. I thought . . . I hoped . . . that you would wait for me there."

She slapped his shoulder. "You rogue! You did no such thing. As far as I knew, you were never coming back."

That surprised him. "You thought I had abandoned you?"

"Of course I did."

"Heartling," he said—and he could see that she liked that endearment ever so much and made a note to himself to use it again—"I would never abandon you." That was as much as he intended to say at this time. Later, he hoped he would be in a position to say more.

"What are you doing?" she squealed as he lifted her gown by the hem up to her waist and began to undo the laces on his *braies*.

"It is not a question of what I am doing, but what *you* are doing," he said against her mouth. He kissed her deeply, till she was slack with surrender, then explained, "*You* are welcoming me home."

With that, he lifted her off the ground by the buttocks, arranged her legs around his hips and entered her moist folds with an exultant, "Yea!" And she did welcome him then with hot, rhythmic embraces of his hard staff. It was the best kind of welcome, in Toste's opinion.

A short time later, when they leaned against each other, panting out their mutual release, she eyed him suspiciously and asked, "Is that another one of women's favorite sexual positions?"

"Yea. Wall-sex," he said. Then quickly added, "But do not tell anyone about it."

"You are such a scamp."

He looped his arm over her shoulder and kissed the top of her hair as they walked back toward her bedchamber. "That is another of my best assets."

"You have many of those assets, do you?"

"Hundreds."

She laughed, then asked, "Will you and Vagn both be coming back to Evergreen with me, to head my troops . . . assuming we get the right answer from the Witan?"

"Nay. Vagn has other irons in the fire."

She arched her brows at him.

"A babe."

"Really? How wonderful! I mean, I assume it is wonderful." Her face clouded over then. "You and your brother have never been separated . . . except in death. Will you be going with him?"

He shook his head.

"Will you come to Evergreen with me, then, to be my castellan?"

"I am sorry, but I want more from life than that. Vagn's 'death' taught me much about what is important in life. I will not be your hired soldier, Esme." Toste was about to add, *but I will be your husband.*

Before he could get those last words out, however, Esme's face suffused with the red of outrage and she shoved him away from her. "Once a lout, always a lout!" she proclaimed as she stormed away from him.

He thought about going after her and making a formal declaration of his intentions. But he wanted everything to be just right before he asked her to wed with him. One more day . . . two at the most . . . and he would make everything right.

And after she accepted his proposal, he was planning on suggesting a different type of sex to her—a favorite of most women, hahaha. It was called cock-in-mouth sex.

Lights out at ten, candles out at eleven . . .

Vagn came to Helga's tiny bedchamber carrying candles.

Her room was right next to the garderobe—not the most desirable location, but he suspected she found it a welcome spot, what with her often uneasy stomach and her frequent need to relieve herself.

"What are you doing here, you bothersome oaf?" were her first words of welcome. Her second were, "Those candles had better not be for what I think you intend."

"Tsk tsk, Helga, get your mind out of the midden. I knew you were in a small room and would welcome some light when we talked."

She was under a bed fur, naked he hoped, but not asleep, though the room was dark. Her long blond hair hung in a single braid down over her shoulder. "I do not welcome the light."

Too bad. He'd already lit four of Eadyth's precious beeswax candles and placed them about the chamber, which was so small there was scarce room for him to turn around.

He smiled cheerfully at her.

She stuck out her tongue at him.

He took that as a good sign.

He got down on one knee beside the bed and took her hand in his. "Helga, will you marry me?"

"Do you have a moat betwixt your ears, Vagn? Nay, nay, nay! How many times do I have to say that?" She tried to pull her hand out of his grasp while clutching her bed fur with the other. The fur had slid down to her breasts. She was indeed naked underneath.

Thank you, gods. "Till the answer becomes yes."

"You have your brother now, Vagn. You have no need of me."

"Well, yea, I do have a need of you," he said, staring pointedly at her breast area.

"Not that kind of need, you libertine."

"You say libertine in the most affectionate way, Helga. Didst know that?"

"Aaarrgh!"

"It is cold in this room without a hearth, Helga. I'd better slide under that bed fur with you . . . to warm you up."

"Don't you dare."

He was already daring. He removed his half-boots and pushed her against the wall with his hip. The bed was barely big enough for one person, let alone two. *Good!* Then he turned on his side to stare at her.

He put a hand on her bare belly and asked, "Has the babe moved yet?"

She slapped his hand away. "I told you, babes don't move this early."

"Let's have sex." *There are times when directness is the best policy.*

"Let's not."

And sometimes not. "Are your nipples more sensitive now, sweetling? I have heard that pregnant women have exceedingly sensitive breasts."

Before she had a chance to slap him away or clout him on the side of the head, he placed a cool hand on her warm breast and fondled the large nipple.

She groaned. He could tell that she did not want to groan, but that his brief ministration had been more pleasurable than she could resist. Like any good soldier who knew to take advantage when given an opening, he flipped the bed fur downward and placed his mouth over one of her breasts and at the same time fondled the other. Wet and hot, he laved and flicked at her till the only words out of her mouth were, "Oh, Vagn." And somehow—*more thanks to the gods*—her hands were at the back of his head holding him in place.

He moved his face lower then. There was something he'd been wanting to do for days now. He placed his mouth against her belly and whispered, "Hello, babe. Here I am. Your father. Are you a handsome fellow like your father? Or a pretty girling like your mother? I cannot wait to see you. I will be here when you come, that I promise, little one."

When he moved over her then, belly to belly, chest to breasts, he noticed that she was weeping silently. "What?" he asked, wiping away some of the moisture with a thumb.

"You do wear a lady down, Vagn. I swear, you could charm the fleece off a lamb."

He took that as his cue to do some more charming. He unlaced his *braies*, then spread her thighs with his own, resting himself on the cradle of her hips. He would be a fool to risk getting off the bed and removing his clothing, giving her a chance to have second thoughts. With no forewarning, he slid into her welcome sheath and remained still for a moment. "I think I felt the babe move," he murmured with awe.

"You dolt!" she said. "That was me."

"Even better."

He made slow, adoring love to her then. No words were exchanged. They seemed unnecessary. He showed her with his body how very much he had missed her. When they both reached their peaks, he asked again, "Helga, will you marry me?"

And she asked that infernal question of hers, "Why?"

It occurred to him that there might be some magic answer that he could give which would unlock the door to her acceptance, but for the life of him, he couldn't figure out what it was.

"I would be a good husband to you and father to our

child. I would take over your father's estates when he is gone, *if* that is what you want. I would not take any authority from you if you did not want me to. I would help you with your merchant business." He looked expectantly at her.

"And?"

"We could have a good life together. Partners, that is what we would be. Husband and wife, but partners."

"Nay," she said with a deep sigh of disappointment. "I will not wed with you."

CHAPTER FIFTEEN

❧

A medieval Ann Landers . . .

The next morning, Alinor found Toste and Vagn out in the stables, sitting in an empty stall, swilling down mead.

She did not blame them for trying to escape the crowded keep. More guests kept arriving, and the din of talk and laughter was overpowering.

"Why the long faces, you two?" she asked, dropping down to the clean straw next to them. Vagn handed her the jug and she took a long swallow, then wiped the back of her hand over her mouth.

"Neither of us is having much woman-luck," Vagn revealed.

"Hard to believe, is it not?" Toste added.

Yea, 'twas hard to believe that these two accomplished womanizers had met their own personal stumbling blocks.

"Helga will not marry me, even though she carries my babe," Vagn said.

"Esme has forgiven me for the captive business. In truth, methinks she liked it, though she would not admit such . . . yet. But she wants me only as her castellan at Evergreen."

Alinor stared at the two brothers, so very identical in appearance, so bone-meltingly handsome. "Do you love her?" she asked, looking pointedly at each of them in turn.

They both turned red-faced at her blunt question.

"Well, yea, I suppose I do," Toste said finally.

"Of course I do," Vagn said more forcefully.

"Have you told her?" Again she looked at each of them separately.

"Not in words," Toste said.

"You thick-headed fool. In what? Signs from the heavens?"

"There is no need to be sarcastic," Toste snapped back.

"I must have told Helga that I love her." Vagn was rubbing his chin thoughtfully. "I mean, I think I did. Didn't I? Surely, even if I didn't, she knows." He looked up and inquired of Alinor, "Doesn't she?"

"Words should not be necessary," Toste argued.

"Believe me, words are necessary."

"I can't believe I didn't say it. I felt it. Why didn't Helga feel it?"

"Vagn, three words. I . . . love . . . you. That is what she needs to hear. Enough with this feeling the sentiment."

Alinor rose to return to the keep, her mission accomplished . . . she hoped. One never knew with thick-headed Vikings. "And, by the by, Bolthor is in the great hall regaling one and all, with a saga entitled 'Dog and Candle Sex and Vikings.'"

Toste and Vagn bolted to their feet and rushed ahead of her back to the castle, both of them muttering something about adding skald soup to the yuletide menu.

Alinor whisked her hands together and grinned with satisfaction. A meddling woman's work was never done.

When a man loves a woman . . .

Vagn was wasting no time.

He entered the great hall, which was overflowing with people though it was not yet midday. At first, he was disoriented by the dimness after the bright sunlight outside and by the amount of mead he'd already drunk on an empty stomach. But then he spotted Helga at one of the upper tables sitting with her father and some of the Briarstead soldiers, including Finn Finehair. *Is that coxcomb everywhere?*

Slowly he moved through the aisle created by the trestle tables. He knew the moment that she saw him. She smiled reflexively, then immediately wiped the mirth from her face, not wanting to give him any encouragement, no doubt.

When he arrived at the table, breathless—whether from excitement, or fear, or too much mead, he did not know—he told her right off, "Stand up, Helga."

"What?" she squawked.

He loved it when she squawked. It meant he'd done something particularly outrageous. Everyone in the surrounding area was staring at him. He probably looked wild . . . or something. Mayhap there was straw sticking out of his ears. He saw Toste on the far side of the hall give him the victory sign that only they understood. And in his head, his brother said, *You can do it, Vagn. Sweep her off her feet.*

Without ado, he shoved a cloth-wrapped parcel in front of her. "This is for you." Betimes Vagn forgot to be smooth.

She stared at the package, then slowly unwrapped it. Inside was the silk fabric with the heart embroidery which he'd purchased from her. He'd had it made into a fine gown—he hoped a wedding gown.

He could see that Helga was touched. She ran her fingertips over it slowly, and her eyes clouded over. But then she stood and said, "Have you lost your mind, Vagn?"

"Yea, I have. Over you."

"You are embarrassing me."

You haven't seen anything yet. He licked his lips and took both her hands in his. "Helga, I love you."

People all around them heard and smiled at him. Helga, on the other hand, lowered her head and murmured, "Don't do this to me, Vagn. I cannot take this kind of jest."

"I love you. Why is that a jest?"

"You do not love me."

"Yea, I do."

"You are just saying this because you want me to accept you as husband so that you can be a legitimate father to our child." He could tell that her long-winded reply was hurtful for her to make in front of all these people. He would have spared her this if he'd thought ahead of time. But he hadn't.

"I love you, I love you, I love you."

"If that is true, why have you never said it afore?" She met his eyes now.

And gods help him, he saw hope there. He must tread carefully now. "A wise woman . . . rather, a meddling woman . . . pointed out to me that women need to hear those words. In truth, I must have forgotten that fact. Well, actually I have never loved any other woman afore, so the subject wouldn't have even come up. Have I never said the words to you? I thought I had, but then I wondered if I'd just shown you in a thousand ways but never . . ." He let his words trail off as he realized that he was rambling.

"Oh, Vagn." There were tears in her eyes, but then, there were tears in her eyes all the time lately due to the pregnancy.

"I did not mean to make you weep."

"You love me?"

"I do."

"Will you marry me?" she asked then.

"I thought you would never ask, heartling." With a whoop of delight, he swept her up in his arms and carried her out of the great hall, to the cheers of the crowd, especially his brother, who cheered loudest of all.

Vagn noticed something odd then. There were tears in his own eyes. *Must be the pregnancy*, he decided with a shrug.

Pleading his case . . . all right, just pleading . . .

Toste did not have such good luck in talking to Esme.

He was in the Ravenshire business solar off the great hall with her later that afternoon, but at least two dozen other people were there, as well. Unlike his brother, he was averse to baring his soul in public.

Besides, Esme was casting dagger stares his way. But she also whistled under her breath, so nervous was she over the proceedings about to take place. It did not help matters that her father and two brothers sat in the front row, having shown up uninvited an hour ago.

An unscheduled meeting of the Witan was being held for the benefit of Esme's petition to regain Evergreen. It was not an official meeting, only seven members being present, including Archbishop Dunstan—and what an imposingly grim cleric he was!—along with five ealdormen.

The Witan had already heard Toste's evidence, Esme's

recital of past sins against her by her family, and her father's lying testimony of "only wanting what is best for my daughter." Dunstan, to give him credit, ran a tight proceeding, not fooled a bit by any of them, least of all Blackthorne's accounting of all the funds from ten years of water tolls. It turned out that the Crown had no objection to the practice, but it wanted its fair share in taxes. In other words, Blackthorne had not only been cheating his daughter, he had been cheating his king, as well. Not a wise political move!

Dunstan stood finally and said, "Lady Esme, I believe you have just right to Evergreen. And I am impressed by your ten years spent in a convent, and the letter of commendation I have received from Mother Wilfreda concerning your conduct there." Everyone knew that Dunstan considered women instruments of the devil, and his attitude was evident in his condescending tone. "However, I am not convinced that a woman . . . even a woman with your skills . . . can run an estate on her own. You need the guardianship of your father till that time when you wed."

"Nay!" Esme blurted out. She knew as they all did what this would mean. Either she would be forced to wed a puppet husband of her father's choice, or she would be dead. Neither was a palatable choice.

Dunstan's nostrils flared with outrage that a mere woman would question his decision.

"Your Grace," Toste said, standing. "I believe I have a solution." He glanced over at Esme beseechingly. This was not the way he would have chosen to bring up this subject.

"Ivarsson," the archbishop acknowledged reluctantly.

Toste recognized that the priest considered the decision already made and did not appreciate any last-minute interference. But he could not refuse to listen. Too many eyes were watching . . . some of them politically powerful.

The archbishop nodded for him to go on. The curl of Dunstan's upper lip seemed to indicate that he included Vikings in the same lowly class as women.

"I would take Esme for my bride. I would protect her and Evergreen. Though Viking by blood, I would swear allegiance to your Saxon overlord, if it would help Esme in her petition."

Shock rippled around the room, especially from Blackthorne and his sons.

"Nay!"

"This is outrageous!"

"He's a bloody Norseman. You can't trust a one of them."

These statements did not sit well with Dunstan, nor the Viking nobles who sat about the room, including Tykir, Eirik, Gorm and others.

"And what of you, Esme?" Dunstan inquired, as if he cared. "Wouldst accept Toste Ivarsson as your husband?"

Before she had a chance to answer, Toste interjected, "Your Grace, Ealdorman, could I have one moment to speak to Esme alone?"

"Speak fast, brother," Vagn said to him from his side where he'd been sitting. "And remember Alinor's advice."

Toste did not wait for the Witan's approval but rushed over to Esme, who appeared stunned, grabbed her hand and pulled her out into the corridor.

"I love you, Esme," he said right off. No one could accuse him of being a total lackwit. He could tell that his declaration was not what she'd expected.

"You do not need to say that, Toste. I appreciate your offer of marriage, but I would not have you sacrifice your freedom for me. You have done enough."

"Not nearly enough. I should have told you earlier . . . I thought you knew, or leastways suspected. Did you suspect?"

"Suspect what?"

"That I love you."

"Stop saying that."

"Why?"

"Because 'tis not true."

"Yea, 'tis."

"When did you make this amazing discovery?"

"Just afore I left the woodcutter's hut for Evergreen."

She punched him in the stomach, which barely hurt, but he winced just the same. "What was that for?"

"For not telling me."

"About going to Evergreen? I already apologized for that."

"About loving me. You are a dunderhead."

"Yea, I am. Does that mean you believe me?"

"I do not know. Say it again."

"I love you."

She smiled.

"Do you perchance love me, Esme?"

"Mayhap." She was still smiling.

"Will you marry me?"

"Of course. There was never any question of that."

Some women liked to torture men. He kissed her deeply, then whispered in her ear, "Did I ever tell you about this sexual position that is a favorite of betrothed women?"

She laughed and said, "Is it just you, or are all Viking men so irresistible?"

"We are all irresistible," he said. And that was the truth.

EPILOGUE

Rock-a-bye . . . Vikings . . .

It was summertime at Briarstead, and Vagn Ivarsson's first child had been born two hours ago.

Maeva had taken a terrifying day and a half coming into this world. Terrifying to Vagn and Gorm, that is. The midwife and Helga had taken it all in stride.

Helga finally slept, thanks to a sleeping potion. Gorm had gone down to the great hall to drink himself dotty in celebration. He and Toste planned to join him soon.

"I hate to tell you this, Vagn," his brother said, looking over his shoulder at the bald-headed, shrivel-faced babe in Vagn's arms, "but your babe is a mite homely."

"She is not!" Vagn declared adamantly. "Maeva is beautiful." And she was. To him.

He saw Toste's grin and knew he was teasing him, as usual.

Toste and Esme had come from Evergreen a sennight ago so they could be present for the birth. Esme was down in the scullery preparing a fortifying beef marrow broth for Helga when she awakened.

Toste and Vagn had married their lady loves at Ravenshire in a double wedding ceremony performed by Archbishop Dunstan. Everyone had agreed that it was the best yuletide celebration they'd ever attended. Later,

they'd had wild Viking ceremonies at their own estates.

"We've been given a gift," Vagn said dreamily.

"Dost mean you and Helga and the babe?"

He shook his head. "Nay. You and me. We met the
Raven of Death and escaped her clutches. It really was a
miracle, our surviving the battle, then being reunited. A
miracle."

Toste nodded.

Vagn laughed then, looking down at his precious
girling who was sleeping peacefully, her tiny thumb
stuck in her mouth. "Finally I have done something first.
Right from the beginning, you came from the womb first,
and you have always been one step ahead of me thereaf-
ter. But I . . . *I* had the first child."

"That you did, Vagn," Toste conceded, "but I will of
course outdo you once again. Esme is breeding, and"—he
paused dramatically—"the midwife predicts twins."

Outdone! Again! Well, not really. "Congratulations!
Another miracle!"

Both brothers laughed heartily then, cherishing the
miracle that was a Viking's life . . . *their* life.

It was appropriate that Bolthor came into the room
then and said, "Methinks this occasion merits a special
saga."

"For a certainty," both brothers concurred, for once
welcoming a praise-poem from the world's worst skald.

"A good title for this one would be 'A Tale of Two
Vikings.'"

"Lost they were in the sea of life,
Two brothers who faced much strife.
Twins they were, bonded from birth,
In everything they always found mirth,

Till one day the Raven called them home,
And that is the subject of this poem.
Because death met its match
When it tried these twins to snatch.
In the end, they were brought to their knees,
By two women, if you please.
The moral of this saga, my friend?
Love conquers all in the end."

READER LETTER

Dear Reader:

Well, I gave you not one but two Vikings this time with *A Tale of Two Vikings*. What did you think of Toste and Vagn?

And, by the way, remind me never again to give my Vikings unpronounceable names. My critique partners berate me about this all the time. In fact, the first time I heard my friend pronounce Toste's name as Toasty, I almost died. The truth is, I never intended these twins to be heroes, else I would have thought this through better. No one knows for sure how these names were pronounced a thousand years ago, but this is how I say them. Toss-tee. Vay-gan.

I learned something about myself in writing this book. What I like most to do . . . in fact, what I instinctively do . . . is provide a hero's journey. Yes, the heroines are important in my novels, but writing the man's point of view is essential. At one time books were written from one point of view only, and in the case of women's fiction, it was the heroine's journey. How far we have come! Interesting, isn't it, that we women understand ourselves better when we see ourselves through men's eyes . . . especially gorgeous Vikings with a sense of humor.

One more thing. It has long been my contention that in the best romance novels, the writer causes the reader to smile as well as cry. I hope you at least sighed at this tale of two very close brothers who thought they'd been separated by death. And I hope you laughed out loud at their separate journeys through separate love connections, until they made their way back to each other.

Please check out my website on occasion for news. Contests are held just before every new book release. And if you sign up for my email list, you will get two, possibly three, newsletters per year.

As always, thank you so much for your continued support. I cannot tell you how much you are appreciated.

Sandra Hill
PO Box 604
State College, PA 16804
Shill733@aol.com
www.sandrahill.net

GLOSSARY

Althing—an assembly of free people that makes laws and settles disputes. It is like a Thing but much larger, involving delegates from various parts of a country, not just a single region.

Asgard—home of the gods.

Berserker—an ancient Norse warrior who fought in a frenzied rage during battle.

Bladder window—a scraped animal skin used in place of glass in ancient times, almost transparent when treated and scraped properly.

Braies—slim pants worn by men, breeches.

Castellan—one who oversees a castle in the absence of the castle's lord.

Drukkinn (various spellings)—drunk, in Old Norse.

Ealdorman—a royal official who presided over shire courts and carried out royal commands within his domain. Comparable to later earls.

Ell—a measure, usually of cloth, equaling 45 inches.

Gunna—a long-sleeved, ankle-length gown for women, often worn under a tunic or surocat or long, open-sided apron.

Halberd—a weapon consisting of a long shaft with a double edged axe blade on one end and a spearhead on the other.

Hectares (of land)—equal to about two-and-a-half acres.

Hersir—a military commander.

Hide—a primitive measure of land, equaling the normal holding that would support a peasant and his family, roughly 120 arable acres.

Hird—permanent troops, war band.

Hnefatafl—a Viking board game.

Houri—an alluring woman, often associated with eastern harems.

Housecarls—troops assigned to a king's or lord's household on a longtime, sometimes permanent basis.

Jarl—a high-ranking Norseman, similar to an English earl, could be a chieftain or minor king.

Jomsvikings—an elite group of Viking mercenaries.

Jorvik—Viking-Age York, known by the Saxons as Eoforic.

Manchet—a type of flat bread, usually baked into a circle with a hole in the center so it could be stored, stacked on a pole.

Mancus/es (of gold)—a weight of gold of about 70 grains, or equal to six shillings or thirty pennies/pence (one shilling = five pennies).

Minster—a church, often connected with a monastic establishment.

Niflheim—a place of eternal cold, darkness, and fog, ruled over by Hel: abode of those who die of illness or old age.

Nithing—one of the greatest Norse insults, indicating a man is less than nothing.

Norsemandy—tenth-century name for Normandy.

Northumbria—one of the Anglo-Saxon kingdoms, bordered by the English kingdoms to the south and in the north and northwest by the Scots, Cumbrians, and Strathclyde Welsh.

Paternoster—the Lord's Prayer.

Seneschal—an agent or steward.

Sennight—one week.

Shert—a shirt.

Shield wall—a battle formation.

Skald—a poet.

Skyr—a soft Norse cheese similar to yogurt or cottage cheese.

Steward—a man responsible for day-to-day running of the castle or keep.

Straw death—an odious form of death for a Viking, to die on his bed (straw mattress) rather than in battle.

Svinfylkja—swine wedge battle formation.

Sword dew—blood.

Thegn—a member of the aristocratic class of men ranking between earls and ordinary freemen, and granted lands by the king or by lords for military service.

Thrall—a slave.

Valhalla—Viking heaven.

Valkyries—Odin's female warriors, who led valiant fighting men after their death in battle to Valhalla, the hall of the slain.

Wergild (or wergeld)—a man's worth.

Witan, or witenagemot—the king's council of advisors, precursor to the English Parliament.

Can't get enough of *USA Today* and *New York Times* bestselling author Sandra Hill?
Turn the page for glimpses of her amazing books. From cowboys to Vikings, Navy SEALs to Southern bad boys, every one of Sandra's books has her unique blend of passion, creativity, and unparalled wit.

Welcome to the World of Sandra Hill!

The Viking Takes a Knight

⟡

*F*or John of Hawk's Lair, the unexpected appearance of a beautiful woman at his door is always welcome. Yet the arrival of this alluring Viking woman, Ingrith Sigrundottir—with her enchanting smile and inviting curves—is different . . . for she comes accompanied by a herd of unruly orphans. And Ingrith needs more than the legendary knight's hospitality; she needs protection. For among her charges is a small boy with a claim to the throne—a dangerous distinction when murderous King Edgar is out hunting for Viking blood.

A man of passion, John will keep them safe— but in exchange, he wants something very dear indeed: Ingrith's heart, to be taken with the very first meeting of their lips . . .

Viking in Love

❧

*C*aedmon *of Larkspur was the most loathsome lout* Breanne had ever encountered. When she arrived at his castle with her sisters, they were greeted by an estate gone wild, while Caedmon laid abed after a night of ale. But Breanne must endure, as they are desperately in need of protection . . . and he is quite handsome.

After nine long months in the king's service, all Caedmon wanted was peace, not five Viking princesses running about his keep. And the fiery redhead who burst into his chamber was the worst of them all. He should kick her out, but he has a far better plan for Breanne of Stoneheim—one that will leave her a Viking in lust.

The Reluctant Viking

*T*he self-motivation tape was supposed to help Ruby Jordan solve her problems, not create new ones. Instead, she was lulled into an era of hard-bodied warriors and fair maidens. But the world ten centuries in the past didn't prove to be all mead and mirth. Even as Ruby tried to update medieval times, she had to deal with a Norseman whose view of women was stuck in the Dark Ages. And what was worse, brawny Thork had her husband's face, habits, and desire to avoid Ruby. Determined not to lose the same man twice, Ruby planned a bold seduction that would conquer the reluctant Viking—and make him an eager captive of her love.

The Outlaw Viking

❧

As tall and striking as the Valkyries of legend, Dr. Rain Jordan was proud of her Norse ancestors despite their warlike ways. But she can't believe it when she finds herself on a nightmarish battle-field, forced to save the barbarian of her dreams.

He was a wild-eyed warrior whose deadly sword could slay a dozen Saxons with a single swing, yet Selik couldn't control the saucy wench from the future. If Selik wasn't careful, the stunning siren was sure to capture his heart and make a warrior of love out of **The Outlaw Viking**.

The Tarnished Lady

☙

*B*anished from polite society, Lady Eadyth of Hawk's Lair spent her days hidden under a voluminous veil, tending her bees. But when her lands are threatened, Lady Eadyth sought a husband to offer her the protection of his name.

Notorious for loving—and leaving—the most beautiful damsels in the land, Eirik of Ravenshire was England's most virile bachelor. Yet when the mysterious lady offered him a vow of chaste matrimony in exchange for revenge against his most hated enemy, Eirik couldn't refuse. But the lusty knight's plans went awry when he succumbed to the sweet sting of the tarnished lady's love.

The Bewitched Viking

✧

Even fierce Norse warriors have bad days. 'Twas enough to drive a sane Viking mad, the things Tykir Thorksson was forced to do—capturing a red-headed virago, putting up with the flock of sheep that follows her everywhere, chasing off her bumbling brothers. But what could a man expect from the sorceress who had put a kink in the King of Norway's most precious body part? If that wasn't bad enough, Tykir was beginning to realize he wasn't at all immune to the enchantment of brash red hair and freckles. Perhaps he could reverse the spell and hold her captive, not with his mighty sword, but with a Viking man's greatest magic: a wink and smile.

The Blue Viking

✧

*F*or Rurik the Viking, life has not been worth living since he left Maire of the Moors. Oh, it's not that he misses her fiery red tresses or kissable lips. Nay, it's the embarrassing blue zigzag tattoo she put on his face after their one wild night of loving. For a fierce warrior who prides himself on his immense height, his expertise in bedsport, and his well-toned muscles, this blue streak is the last straw. In the end, he'll bring the witch to heel, or die trying. Mayhap he'll even beg her to wed . . . so long as she can promise he'll no longer be . . . **The Blue Viking**.

The Viking's Captive

(originally titled MY FAIR VIKING)

Tyra, Warrior Princess. She is too tall, too loud, too fierce to be a good catch. But her ailing father has decreed that her four younger sisters—delicate, mild-mannered, and beautiful—cannot be wed 'til Tyra consents to take a husband. And then a journey to save her father's life brings Tyra face to face with Adam the Healer. A god in human form, he's tall, muscled, perfectly proportioned. Too bad Adam refuses to fall in with her plans—so what's a lady to do but truss him up, toss him over her shoulder, and sail off into the sunset to live happily ever after.

A Tale of Two Vikings

❧

oste and Vagn Ivarsson are identical Viking twins, about to face Valhalla together, following a tragic battle, or maybe something even more tragic: being separated for the first time in their thirty and one years. Alas, even the bravest Viking must eventually leave his best buddy behind and do battle with that most fearsome of all opponents—the love of his life. And what if that love was Helga the Homely, or Lady Esme, the world's oldest novice nun?

A Tale of Two Vikings will give you twice the tears, twice the sizzle, and twice the laughter . . . and make you wish for your very own Viking.

The Last Viking

⊕

He was six feet, four inches of pure, unadulterated male. He wore nothing but a leather tunic, and he was standing in Professor Meredith Foster's living room. The medieval historian told herself he was part of a practical joke, but with his wide gold belt, ancient language, and callused hands, the brawny stranger seemed so . . . authentic. And as he helped her fulfill her grandfather's dream of re-creating a Viking ship, he awakened her to dreams of her own. Until she wondered if the hand of fate had thrust her into the loving arms of . . . **The Last Viking**.

Truly, Madly Viking

❧

A *Viking named Joe? Jorund Ericsson is a tenth-* century Viking warrior who lands in a modern mental hospital. Maggie McBride is the lucky psychologist who gets to "treat" the gorgeous Norseman, whom she mistakenly calls Joe.

You've heard of *One Flew Over the Cuckoo's Nest*. But how about *A Viking Flew Over the Cuckoo's Nest*? The question is: Who's the cuckoo in this nest? And why is everyone laughing?

The Very Virile Viking

*M*agnus Ericsson *is a simple man. He loves the* smell of fresh-turned dirt after springtime plowing. He loves the feel of a soft woman under him in the bed furs. He loves the heft of a good sword in his fighting arm.

But, Holy Thor, what he does not relish is the bothersome brood of children he's been saddled with. Or the mysterious happenstance that strands him in a strange new land—the kingdom of *Holly Wood*. Here is a place where the folks think he is an *act-whore* (whatever that is), and the woman of his dreams—a winemaker of all things—fails to accept that he is her soul mate . . . a man of exceptional talents, not to mention . . . **A Very Virile Viking.**

Wet & Wild

❧

*W*hat do you get when you cross a Viking with a Navy SEAL? A warrior with the fierce instincts of the past and the rigorous training of America's most elite fighting corps? A totally buff hero-in-the-making who hasn't had a woman in roughly a thousand years? A dyed-in-the-wool romantic with a hopeless crush? Whatever you get, women everywhere can't wait to meet him, and his story is guaranteed to be . . . **Wet & Wild**.

Hot & Heavy

☙

*I*n and out, that's the goal as Lt. Ian MacLean prepares for his special ops mission. He leads a team of highly trained Navy SEALs, the toughest, buffest fighting men in the world and he has nothing to lose. Madrene comes from a time a thousand years before he was born, and she has no idea she's landed in the future. After tying him up, the beautiful shrew gives him a tongue-lashing that makes a drill sergeant sound like a kindergarten teacher. Then she lets him know she has her own special way of dealing with over-confident males, and things get . . . **Hot & Heavy**.

Frankly, My Dear . . .

*L*ost in the Bayou . . . *Selene had three great passions:* men, food, and *Gone with the Wind*. But the glamorous model always found herself starving— for both nourishment and affection. Weary of the petty world of high fashion, she headed to New Orleans for one last job before she began a new life. Little did she know that her new life would include a brand-new time—about 150 years ago! Selene can't get her fill of the food—or an alarmingly handsome man. Dark and brooding, James Baptiste was the only lover she gave a damn about. And with God as her witness, she vowed never to go without the man she loved again.

Sweeter Savage Love

The stroke of surprisingly gentle hands, the flash of fathomless blue eyes, the scorch of white-hot kisses . . . Once again, Dr. Harriet Ginoza was swept away into rapturous fantasy. The modern psychologist knew the object of her desire was all she should despise, yet time after time, she lost herself in visions of a dangerously handsome rogue straight out of a historical romance. Harriet never believed that her dream lover would cause her any trouble, but then a twist of fate cast her back to the Old South and she met him in the flesh. To her disappointment, Etienne Baptiste refused to fulfill any of her secret wishes. If Harriet had any hope of making her amorous dreams become passionate reality, she'd have to seduce this charmer with a sweeter savage love than she'd imagined possible . . . and savor every minute of it.

The Love Potion

ame and fortune are surely only a swallow away when Dr. Sylvie Fontaine discovers a chemical formula guaranteed to attract the opposite sex. Though her own love life is purely hypothetical, the shy chemist's professional future is assured . . . as soon as she can find a human guinea pig. But bad boy Lucien LeDeux—best known as the Swamp Lawyer—is more than she can handle even before he accidentally swallowed a love potion disguised in a jelly bean. When the dust settles, Luc and Sylvie have the answers to some burning questions—can a man die of testosterone overload? Can a straight-laced female lose every single one of her inhibitions?—and they learn that old-fashioned romance is still the best catalyst for love.

Love Me Tender

☙

*O*nce upon a time, in a magic kingdom, there lived a handsome prince. Prince Charming, he was called by one and all. And to this land came a gentle princess. You could say she was Cinderella . . . Wall Street Cinderella. Okay, if you're going to be a stickler for accuracy, in this fairy tale the kingdom is Manhattan. But there's magic in the Big Apple, isn't there? And maybe he can be Prince Not-So-Charming at times, and "gentle" isn't the first word that comes to mind when thinking of this princess. But they're looking for happily ever after just the same—and they're going to get it.

Desperado

☘

Mistaken for a notorious bandit and his infamously scandalous mistress, L.A. lawyer Rafe Santiago and Major Helen Prescott found themselves on the wrong side of the law. In a time and place where rules had no meaning, Helen found Rafe's hard, bronzed body strangely comforting, and his piercing blue eyes left her all too willing to share his bedroll. His teasing remarks made her feel all woman, and she was ready to throw caution to the wind if she could spend every night in the arms of her very own . . . **Desperado**.

At Avon Books, we know your passion for romance—once you finish one of our novels, you find yourself wanting more.

May we tempt you with . . .

- **Excerpts** from our upcoming releases.

- Entertaining **extras**, including authors' personal photo albums and book lists.

- Behind-the-scenes **scoop** on your favorite characters and series.

- **Sweepstakes** for the chance to win free books, romantic getaways, and other fun prizes.

- Writing **tips** from our authors and editors.

- **Blog** with our authors and find out why they love to write romance.

- **Exclusive content** that's not contained within the pages of our novels.

Join us at
www.avonbooks.com

AVON
An Imprint of HarperCollins*Publishers*
www.avonromance.com

Ava ⸺ -331-3761 to order.

3 1901 04939 5272